"What did my fa

Sarah rose and picke~~d~~ doesn't matter."

"If he's upset you—"

"Logan, I'm not upset." It was true. She was pretty much over Max and his issues with her as a potential bride for his oldest son.

She *wasn't* a potential bride—not for Logan or anyone. And Max had done her no harm.

In fact, their little chat had been a good thing. It had served to remind her that she was single and planned on staying that way. She liked Logan— maybe too much. He was kind and so generous. He made her laugh and she loved being with him. And whenever he kissed her, she wanted him to kiss her again, to keep kissing her and touching her and doing all those wonderful things to her that made her feel desired and satisfied in all the best ways.

But he wouldn't break her heart. She wouldn't let him. What they had together was no lifetime commitment. She wasn't counting on anything. They were both having a wonderful time for as long as it lasted.

And, she promised herself, she was perfectly happy with that.

RESISTING THE RANCHER

New York Times Bestselling Author

CHRISTINE RIMMER

& MELISSA SENATE

2 Heartfelt Stories

Her Favorite Maverick
and *Rust Creek Falls Cinderella*

Special thanks and acknowledgment are given to
Christine Rimmer and Melissa Senate for their contribution
to the Montana Mavericks: Six Brides for Six Brothers continuity.

HARLEQUIN®

ISBN-13: 978-1-335-42734-2

Recycling programs
for this product may
not exist in your area.

Resisting the Rancher

Copyright © 2022 by Harlequin Enterprises ULC

Her Favorite Maverick
First published in 2019. This edition published in 2022.
Copyright © 2019 by Harlequin Enterprises ULC

Rust Creek Falls Cinderella
First published in 2019. This edition published in 2022.
Copyright © 2019 by Harlequin Enterprises ULC

For questions and comments about the quality of this book, please contact us
at CustomerService@Harlequin.com.

Harlequin Enterprises ULC
22 Adelaide St. West, 41st Floor
Toronto, Ontario M5H 4E3, Canada
www.Harlequin.com

Printed in U.S.A.

CONTENTS

Christine Rimmer came to her profession the long way around. She tried everything from acting to teaching to telephone sales. Now she's finally found work that suits her perfectly. She insists she never had a problem keeping a job—she was merely gaining "life experience" for her future as a novelist. Christine lives with her family in Oregon. Visit her at christinerimmer.com.

Books by Christine Rimmer

Harlequin Special Edition

The Bravos of Valentine Bay

Almost a Bravo
Same Time, Next Christmas
Switched at Birth
A Husband She Couldn't Forget
The Right Reason to Marry
Their Secret Summer Family
Home for the Baby's Sake
A Temporary Christmas Arrangement
The Last One Home

Montana Mavericks: What Happened to Beatrix?

In Search of the Long-Lost Maverick

Montana Mavericks: Six Brides for Six Brothers

Her Favorite Maverick

Visit the Author Profile page
at Harlequin.com for more titles.

HER FAVORITE MAVERICK

Christine Rimmer

Thanks to the brilliant and beautiful Kimberly Fletcher, who named the sweet white kitten in this story. Kimberly suggested I call the kitten Opal—and I did. I love that name so much! As a thank-you, I offered to dedicate this book to Kimberly. She asked instead that I give her a different kind of dedication...

Her Favorite Maverick is dedicated to Wildflower and Miss Clack and to everyone who has survived cancer. Kimberly would also like to dedicate this story to those who live with a cancer survivor and to anyone who has suffered the loss of a loved one to cancer.

Cancer touches all of us in one way or another. Fight hard, reach out to those you love and know that you are not alone.

Chapter 1

As Sarah Turner emerged from the tiny back-room office of the former train depot, Vivienne Shuster Dalton glanced up from a worktable covered in fabric swatches, to-do lists, project folders and open sample books.

"There you are," said Viv.

"Just giving it all one more look." Sarah tried for a light tone, but going over the books yet another time hadn't changed a thing. The news was not good.

"Please tell us you've found a solution to our problem."

If only.

Viv's business partner, Caroline Ruth Clifton, stood across the worktable from her. Caroline turned her big dark eyes on Sarah and asked hopefully, "We can swing it, right?"

The answer was no.

And for Sarah, whether she was trying to claw her way up the food chain at the biggest accounting firm in Chicago or working in her dad's little office right here in Rust Creek Falls, Montana, her least favorite part of the job remained the same. She hated telling clients that they were in trouble—especially clients she liked and admired.

Viv and Caroline were a couple of dynamos. They'd even opened a second location down in Thunder Canyon, Montana. Caroline spent most of her time there.

And here in Rust Creek Falls, all the brides flocked to the old train depot to get Viv to create their perfect wedding.

Unfortunately, both the rustic train depot and Viv's primary local wedding venue—the brick freight house nearby—needed new roofs. All new. They couldn't just slap a fresh layer of shingles on. Both buildings required tear-outs and rebuilds. Plus, there were structural issues that would have to be addressed. Viv had collected bids. She knew what the work would cost.

It was a lot.

And the wedding planners had already stretched every penny to the limit.

Gently, Sarah laid it out. "I'm sorry. I've been over and over the numbers you gave me. The money just isn't there. You need a loan or an investor."

"A loan against what?" Viv was shaking her head. "The buildings and the land belong to Cole's family." Her husband, Cole Dalton, was a local rancher. Cole and his large extended family owned a lot of the land in the Rust Creek Falls Valley. "I can't take a loan against my in-laws' property. We're doing great, but,

Sarah, you already know it's all on a shoestring—and frankly, I struck out on my own so that I could do this *my* way." Viv's big green eyes shone with sheer determination. "An investor is going to want a say in how we run things."

"Not necessarily. Some investors just want a percentage of—"

The little bell over the front door cut Sarah off midsentence.

"Good morning, ladies," boomed a deep male voice. The imposing figure in the open doorway swept off his black Stetson to reveal a thick head of silver hair. "Maximilian Crawford, at your service." The man plunked his big hat to his heart. Tall and powerfully built, with a handsome, lived-in face and a neatly trimmed goatee and mustache, the guy almost didn't seem real. He reminded Sarah of a character from one of those old-time TV Westerns. "I'm looking for Vivienne Dalton, the wedding planner," he announced.

"I'm Viv." Viv started to step out from behind the worktable.

But Maximilian was faster. In five giant strides, he was at her side. He took Viv's hand and kissed it. "Such a pleasure to meet you. I've heard great things." He turned to Caroline, kissed her hand and then took Sarah's and brushed his mustache across the back of it, too.

Viv, who'd looked slightly stunned when the older man bowed over her hand, recovered quickly and made introductions. "Maximilian, this is Caroline, my partner, and Sarah Turner, with Falls Mountain Accounting."

"So happy to meet you, all three of you—and please

call me Max. My sons and I have bought the Ambling A Ranch east of here. We're newly arrived from the Dallas area, but we have Crawford relatives here in Rust Creek Falls. We're putting down roots in your fine community."

"Welcome to town, Max." Viv cut to the point. "How can we help you?"

"I have an important job that needs doing. And, Vivienne, I know you are the one to tackle it."

"Well, if it's a wedding you're after, you've come to the right place. I take it you're the groom?"

Max threw back his silver head and let out a booming laugh. "Sorry, Viv. Not me. I've had enough of wedded bliss to last me three lifetimes. But my boys are another story. I've got six, each one better lookin' than the one before. Goodhearted, my boys, if a bit skittish on the subject of love and marriage. As we speak, all six are single." He shook a finger. "You ask me, that goes against the laws of God and man. It's about time my boys settled down."

Caroline wore a puzzled frown. "So, then, what you're saying is that all six of your sons are engaged?"

Max let out a low, rueful chuckle. "No, pretty lady. What I'm saying is that my boys need brides. And, Viv, that's where you come in. I want you and the lovely Caroline here to find each of my boys the perfect woman to marry—for a price, of course. A very nice price."

A silence followed. A long one. Sarah, who'd moved back from the worktable to let the wedding planners do their stuff, couldn't help wondering if maybe Max Crawford was a few bucking broncs short of a rodeo.

And judging by their carefully neutral expressions, Viv and Caroline also had their doubts.

However, the train depot roofs weren't going to replace themselves. Viv needed a large infusion of cash, stat. And if Max *was* for real, cash was exactly what he offered—too bad he was ordering up services Caroline and Viv didn't provide.

"But, Max," Viv said patiently, "we *plan* weddings. We aren't matchmakers."

"And why not? Matchmaking is an honest, time-honored practice. A lucrative one, too—at least it will be for you, with me as your client."

Viv slowly shook her head. "I'm so sorry. But we just don't—"

"A million," Max cut in, bringing a trio of stunned gasps from Viv, Caroline and Sarah, too. Max nodded at Viv. "You heard me right. A million dollars. You find my boys wives and the money is yours."

"Max." Viv let out a weak laugh. "That's just crazy."

"That's where you're wrong. I've made my fortune thinking outside the box. And that makes me living, breathing proof that anything can be achieved if you're willing to make your own rules."

Sarah took another step back from the worktable. She couldn't have disagreed more. Rules mattered. And as much as she would like for Max to be the solution to Viv's money troubles, fast-talking men were dangerous. Sarah had learned that sad lesson the hard way.

Viv wasn't going for it, either. "Are you asking us to set up six arranged marriages? No. Definitely not. Caroline and I could never do that."

"Arranged?" Max huffed out a breath. "No way.

My boys would never go for that. They'll choose their own brides. All I'm asking is that you find the perfect woman for each of them."

"Right," Viv scoffed. "Easy peasy."

"Love isn't something you can force." Caroline added her quiet voice to Viv's mocking one. "It really does have to develop naturally and—"

"Caroline, darlin'." Max patted her shoulder. "I couldn't agree with you more. We're on the same page. You won't be *arranging* anything. You won't need to. I've heard all about Rust Creek Falls. Love is everywhere you turn around here and the percentage of pretty women is satisfyingly high. You set my boys up and they are bound to fall."

Sarah took another step back. How could they believe a word the guy said? He talked too fast and he'd openly admitted that he made his own rules.

As if he'd sensed her retreat, the big man shifted his glance to Sarah. "So how 'bout you, darlin'?"

Sarah straightened her shoulders and hitched up her chin. "What about me?"

"Are you looking for the right guy to marry?"

She was looking for anything but. "Excuse me? You want to marry me off to one of your sons?"

"Sweet, sweet Sarah, just say yes." Max actually winked at her. "You won't regret it."

"Sorry, but I'm not on the, um, market."

"Got a sweetheart already, then?"

"No. I'm simply not interested."

Max heaved a big sigh. "That's a crying shame, and I mean that sincerely. You're a beautiful woman with a sharp brain, I can tell. You'd be just perfect for—"

"Dad. What are you up to now?" At the sound of another commanding male voice, Sarah whirled toward the open door.

"Patience, Logan," Max replied. "Just give your old man a few minutes more."

"They plan weddings here, Dad. You don't have a fiancée, so you don't need a wedding. Xander and I are getting tired of waiting in the truck."

Sarah tried not to stare. But really, who could blame her? The cowboy in the doorway was hot—tall and lean, with thick brown hair and a mouth that would have just about any girl thinking of long, scorching kisses.

At the moment, though, that gorgeous mouth was scowling at Max. "What's going on here?"

As he spoke, another fine-looking cowboy entered behind him. The second guy said, "Whatever you think you're pulling, Dad—don't."

Max only laughed. "Come on over here, boys. Let me introduce you to Viv, Caroline and Sarah." His big white teeth gleamed as his smile stretched wide again. "What did I tell you, ladies? Meet my oldest son, Logan, and third-born, Xander."

The first cowboy, Logan, flicked a glance in Sarah's direction—and froze. Now he was staring right at her. "Hello, Sarah," he said low. Intimately. As though they were the only two people in the room.

And then he was on the move again, coming straight for her. He stopped a foot away, right up in her space. The breath fled her lungs. The guy was even hotter up close. It should be illegal to have eyes so blue.

With a little shiver of unwelcome delight, she took

his offered hand. His big, warm fingers engulfed hers. More shivers skittered up her arm.

Absurd. Sarah Turner had no time for the shivers. Not anymore. No way was she letting a pair of bedroom eyes lead her astray again.

But Logan wasn't making it easy for her. He stared at her like she was the most beautiful creature he'd ever seen.

Why? She so didn't get it. She was not at her best and hadn't been for way too long now. A year and a half ago, she'd been hot...ish.

Now, though? She wore her hair in a ponytail to keep it out of the way and didn't bother with makeup beyond a swipe of mascara and maybe some lip gloss. On a good day, she made it all the way to dinnertime without getting spit-up on her shirt.

Max just kept talking. "Boys, Viv and Caroline here not only plan weddings, they also serve as the Rust Creek Falls dating service." Such a liar, that Max. He wouldn't know the truth if it bit him on the butt. "And Sarah is not only gorgeous—she's got a mind for figures, works as an accountant right in town. Falls Mountain Accounting, I believe. Have I got that right, Sarah?"

Logan still held her hand. She really ought to pull away. But she didn't. "I'm a CPA, yes," she said as she continued to stare into Logan's blue eyes.

"I think I need an accountant," said the killer-handsome cowboy in that deep, smooth voice of his, never once letting go of her gaze—or her hand. "And a dating service works for me. Sign me up. I'll take you, Sarah. To dinner. Tonight."

"Uh, yeah. Right." She laughed, playing it off, as her traitorous heart flipped cartwheels inside her chest.

Ridiculous. Impossible. She had no time for dates. If she had any extra time, she would spend it sleeping. And never again would she believe the lies of a handsome, smooth-talking man.

Max was still talking. "Sarah, Logan here is a self-made man. He grew up on our ranch in Texas, but he couldn't wait to get out on his own. Earned his fortune in Seattle, in real estate."

Logan chuckled. "Shut up, Dad."

Max didn't miss a beat. "Son, why don't you and Sarah go on into town? Take her to the donut shop. You can firm up your dinner plans over bear claws and coffee."

Sarah opened her mouth to give both father and son a firm no when a baby's cry from the back room did it for her.

"Huh?" Max blinked in surprise. "That sounds like a—"

"Excuse me." Sarah pulled her hand free of Logan's warm grip and managed a breezy smile. "My little girl wants her mother." Turning neatly on her heel, she headed for the back room.

Was she disappointed that a certain dreamboat of a man was bound to lose interest fast when faced with a crying baby?

A little, maybe. But not *that* disappointed.

Really, it was for the best.

Logan Crawford watched Sarah's bouncing ponytail as she trotted away from him. What was it about her?

Those big golden-brown eyes, all that shining bronze hair? That smile she had that was shy and devilish simultaneously? Damned if that smile didn't dare him to kiss her.

He would take that dare at the first opportunity.

Was she married?

He hadn't seen a ring—and yeah, the baby kind of gave him pause.

But not that much of a pause. He could work around the baby. As long as she was single, well, why shouldn't the two of them have a little fun? Nothing lasted forever and he liked it that way.

It was chemistry, pure and simple. Sexual attraction. And damn, it felt good.

His dad was still talking to the other two women, while Xander just stood there looking midway between vaguely intrigued and slightly annoyed by what they were saying.

Logan, on the other hand, felt downright invigorated. He hadn't felt like this in years. Maybe never. Lately, he'd been kind of off his game when it came to women. He just had no drive to hook up and hadn't been with anyone in months.

But everything had changed the minute he set eyes on Sarah.

Just let her be single. That was all he asked.

She emerged from the back room with a backpack-style diaper bag hanging off one shoulder, a giant leather tote dangling from one hand and a pouty-faced infant in a baby carrier on the other arm. "Sorry, everyone. We'll just be going."

Uh-uh. Not yet. In four strides, Logan reached her.

"Here. Let me help you." The baby stuck a fist in her mouth and stared up at him, wide-eyed.

"No, really." Sarah seemed flustered. Her cheeks had turned the sweetest shade of pink. "There's no need. I'm good."

He ignored her objections and eased the diaper bag off her shoulder. "What's her name?" He took hold of the tote. For a moment, she held on like she wouldn't let him take it.

But then she let go. "Sophia," she said. "Her name is Sophia."

"Pretty name. How old is she?" He wiggled his eyebrows at the baby, who had a pink cloth flower tied around her mostly bald head.

"Five months," said Sarah.

The baby took her slobbery hand out of her mouth long enough to announce, "Ah-da!" and stuck it right back in.

Behind him, his dad started flapping his jaws again, apologizing for trying to set them up. "I'm so sorry, Sarah. I didn't see a ring on your finger and I assumed—"

"You assumed right," Sarah responded coolly. "I'm not married."

Excellent. "But are you engaged?" Logan rattled off the pertinent questions. "Living with someone? Dating exclusively?"

"None of the above," she replied. "It's just me and Sophia." As if on cue, the little girl let out a goofy giggle around the fist in her mouth. Sarah added, delectably defiant, "Just us. And we like it that way."

So she's free. It was all Logan needed to know.

Unfortunately—and for no reason Logan could understand—Max moved in next to him. "Son, Sarah has to go. Give her back her things."

Not happening. Not yet. "Give us a minute, would you, Dad?" He turned his back on his father and moved in closer to Sarah and little Sophia. That caused Sarah to retreat a step. Logan closed the distance. The process repeated—Sarah retreating, Logan eliminating the space she'd created—until they reached the door.

A glance over his shoulder revealed that Max had started talking to the wedding planners again. His dad and the blonde wedding planner shook hands. Logan made a mental note to find out what that was about as he turned his attention back to the irresistible brown-eyed girl.

She said, "I really do have to go."

Logan held on to her tote and diaper bag and started talking, pulling out all the stops, flirting shamelessly with both the woman and her baby. He made silly faces at Sophia as he coaxed information from Sarah, learning that she'd moved back to Rust Creek Falls a month before and had a cottage in town.

"Truly, Logan." Sarah's pretty white teeth nibbled nervously at her plump lower lip, driving him just a little bit crazy. He wanted to nibble on that lip himself. "I'm not interested in dating. I'm way too busy for anything like that."

He nodded. "I understand. Let me help you out to your car."

"No, that's not necessary."

"Yeah, it is. You've got too much to carry and I've got a couple of perfectly good free hands."

Her sweet mouth twisted with indecision—and then she gave up. "Well, um, okay. Thank you."

He walked her out to her white CR-V and waited while she strapped the baby's carrier in the back seat, handing her the giant bag and backpack when she was ready for them. She set them on the floor, shut the door and went around to the driver's door. Admiring the view, Logan followed after her.

"Well," she said with an overly bright smile as he held open the door for her. "Good luck, then—with the ranch and all."

"'Preciate that," he replied. She jumped in behind the wheel, her denim skirt riding up a little, giving him a perfect glimpse of one smooth, shapely thigh. "Drive safe," he said and shut the door.

She waved as she pulled out. He stood in the warm June sunlight, watching her drive away, thinking that he would be good for her, that she needed to get out and have some fun.

Sarah Turner deserved a little romance in her life and Logan Crawford was just the man to give her what she deserved.

Chapter 2

"Logan, it's a bad idea," his father said. "You need to forget about Sarah Turner."

It was past six that evening. Logan, his dad and Xander were out on the porch of the ranch house at the Ambling A enjoying a beer after spending a few hours plowing through the stacks of boxes that weren't going to unpack themselves. At some point, one of them needed to go inside and hustle up a meal. But for now, it was nice out and the beer was ice-cold and refreshing.

Logan stared off toward the snow-tipped mountains. The sky was cloudless, perfectly blue. "I like her, Dad. And it's not your call." He didn't point out that he was a grown-ass man and would do what he damn well wanted to do. Max ought to know that by now. "I'm curious, though. She's single, smart and pretty. She works for a living. She's got it all going on as far as I can see. What have you got against her?"

"Nothing," Max answered gruffly. "You're right. She seems like a fine person."

Xander rocked back in his chair and hoisted his boots up onto the porch rail. "So what's the problem then, Dad? I was standing right there when you struck that crazy deal with the wedding planners to find us all brides for a cool million bucks. To me, that means you want us all to get married. Whether that's ever gonna happen is another question entirely. But the way I see it, if Logan's found a girl already, you should count your blessings."

A million dollars to marry them off? Logan hadn't heard that part. Sometimes his dad came up with the wildest ideas. Logan had no plans to marry anybody. But that wasn't the point. He followed Xander's lead. "Yeah, Dad. You were eager enough to hook Sarah and me up until the baby started crying."

Max sipped his beer. "I do want you boys married. It's about damn time. But when kids are involved, well, things get too complicated." He pointed his longneck at Logan. "Take my word for it, son. You don't need that kind of trouble. Viv will find you someone perfect—someone sweet and pretty without a baby hanging off her hip."

"I'll say it again, Dad. *I* like Sarah and I'm going to move on that."

"I don't want you—"

"Stop. Listen. There is no problem here. You don't want me marrying Sarah Turner? Great. I'm not going to marry her—or anyone. The last thing I want right now is a wife, with or without a baby in the bargain, so you can save that million bucks. When my time comes to tie the knot—if it ever does—I'll find my own bride. I don't need anyone setting me up."

Xander recrossed his boots on the railing. "That's too bad. Because Dad's got that wedding planner setting us *all* up."

Logan leveled a warning look on his dad. "Are you listening? Because you ought to know your own sons better than that. I think I can speak for all six of us when I say that we're not letting anyone choose brides for us—not you, Dad, and not those two wedding planners back at the train depot."

"Nobody's choosing for you," Max insisted. "Viv and Caroline are just going to be introducing you to some lovely young single ladies. You should thank me for making it so easy for you to develop social connections in our new hometown."

Xander grunted. "Social connections? You're kind of scaring me now, Dad."

"I just don't get it," Logan said to Max. "For years, you've been going on about how marriage is a trap—and now suddenly you're shelling out a million bucks to make sure we've each got a wife?"

"Yeah." Xander scowled. "Seriously, Dad. You need to cut that crap out."

"Don't get on me, boys." Max assumed a wounded expression, but he didn't say he would give up his matchmaking scheme.

Not that Logan really expected him to. Unfortunately, once Maximilian Crawford got an idea in his head, telling him to cut it out wouldn't stop him.

They would have to warn their brothers that Max had brokered a marriage deal for all of them and they shouldn't be surprised to find a lot of "lovely single ladies" popping up every time they turned around.

Just then, a quad cab rolled into the yard. A tall, solidly built cowboy got out.

Max stood from his chair. "Nate Crawford. Thanks for coming."

The guy did have that Crawford look about him—strong and square-jawed. He joined them on the porch. Max offered him a beer. They made small talk for a few minutes.

Nate, Logan learned, was a mover and shaker in Rust Creek Falls. He owned controlling interest in the upscale hotel just south of town called Maverick Manor. Logan thought Nate seemed a little reserved. He couldn't tell for sure whether that was because Nate was just one of those self-contained types—or because Max's reputation had preceded him.

Logan loved his dad, but Max was no white knight. The man was a world-class manipulator and more than a bit of a scamp. Yeah, he'd made himself a fortune over the years—but there was no doubt he'd done more than one shady deal.

Yet people were drawn to him. Take Logan and his brothers. They were always complaining about Max's crazy schemes. Yet somehow Max had convinced each one of them to make this move to Montana.

For Logan, it was partly a matter of timing. He'd been between projects in Seattle and ready for a change. When Max had offered a stake in a Montana cattle ranch, Logan had packed his bags and headed for Big Sky Country.

If nothing else, he'd thought it would be good for him to get some time with his brothers. And yeah, he couldn't help wondering what wild scheme his dad might be cooking up now.

Never in a thousand years would Logan have guessed that Max had decided to marry them all off.

Max clapped Nate on the shoulder. "I really do appreciate your dropping by. Wanted to touch base, you know? Family does matter, after all. And now that me and the boys are settling in the area, we'd like to get to know you and everyone else in the family here."

"How about this?" Nate offered. "Saturday night. Dinner at Maverick Manor. The Rust Creek Falls Crawfords will all be there."

"That'll work," said Max. "My other four boys will be up from Texas with the breeding stock by then. Expect all seven of us."

"Looking forward to it." Nate raised his beer and Max tapped it with his.

The next morning at nine sharp, Logan paid a visit to Falls Mountain Accounting.

The door was unlocked, so he walked right in.

Inside, he found a deserted waiting room presided over by an empty front desk with a plaque on it that read, Florence Turner, Office Manager. The door with Sarah's name on it was wide open. No sign of his favorite accountant, though.

The door next to Sarah's was shut. The nameplate on that one read Mack Turner, Accountant. Something was going on inside that office. Faintly, Logan heard muffled moans and sighs.

A woman's voice cried softly, "Oh, yes. Yes, my darling. Yes, my love. Yes, yes, yes!"

Logan debated whether to turn and run—or stick around just to see who emerged from behind that door.

Wait a minute. What if it was Sarah carrying on in there?

It had damn well better not be.

He dropped into one of the waiting room chairs—and then couldn't sit still. Rising again, he tossed his hat on the chair and paced the room.

What was this he was feeling—like his skin was too tight and he wanted to punch someone?

Jealousy?

Not happening. Logan Crawford had never been the jealous type.

He was…curious, that's all, he reassured himself as he marched back to his chair, scooped up his hat and sat down again.

The sounds from behind the shut door reached a muted crescendo and finally stopped.

A few minutes later, a flushed, dewy-eyed older woman who looked quite a bit like Sarah emerged from Mack Turner's office. Her brown hair needed combing and her silky shirt was half-untucked.

"Oh!" Her blush deepened as she spotted Logan. "I, um…" She tugged in her shirt and patted at her hair. "I'm so sorry. Just, um, going over the calendar for the day. I'm Florence Turner."

Hiding his grin, he rose again. She marched straight for him, arm outstretched.

"Logan Crawford," he said as they shook.

"Please just call me Flo. I manage the office. We're a family business, just my husband, our daughter, Sarah, and me." Flo put extra heavy emphasis on the word *husband*. Apparently, she wanted to make it perfectly clear that whatever he'd heard going on behind Mack Turner's door was sanctioned by marriage. "Are you here to see Mack?"

"I'm waiting for Sarah."

"Oh! Did you have an appointment?"

"Not exactly." He tried a rueful smile.

"Well, I apologize for the mix-up, but Sarah has meetings with clients—all day, I think she said."

"Really? That's inconvenient." He patted his pockets. "I seem to have lost my phone." He'd left it in the truck, but Flo didn't need to know that.

"Oh, I'm so sorry," Sarah's mom said.

"Unfortunately, that means now I don't have Sarah's cell number…" Okay, yeah. He'd never had a cell number for her. But it was only a *little* lie.

And it worked like a charm. Flo whipped out Sarah's business card. It had her office, home and cell numbers on it.

"You're a lifesaver. Thank you."

"Any time, Logan—and you're more than welcome to use the phone on my desk."

"Uh, no. I need a coffee. I'll use the pay phone at the donut shop up the street."

That was another lie. He called her from his truck as soon as he was out of sight of Falls Mountain Accounting.

* * *

Sarah was with a client when the call came in from an unknown number. She let it go straight to voice mail. The day was a busy one, appointments stacked up one after the other.

When she finally checked messages in the late afternoon, she found one from Logan.

"Hello, Sarah. It's Logan Crawford. Call me back when you get a minute."

She played it through twice, sitting in her white CR-V with Sophia snoozing in the back seat. His voice, so calm and commanding, made her feel strangely breathless.

The truth was, she hadn't been able to stop thinking of him, of the way he'd looked at her, like she was the only person in the room, of the way he'd kept hold of her hand when there was no excuse for him to be holding it beyond the fact that he wanted to. She'd loved how he'd been so sweet to Sophia and that he'd insisted on carrying her diaper bag and tote out to the car.

Plus, well, he was way too good-looking and she hadn't been with a man in over a year.

The plan was to give up men, after all. At least for a decade or so—maybe longer.

And really, hadn't she made her unavailability perfectly clear to him?

Annoyed and flustered and oddly gleeful all at the same time, she called him back.

"Hello, Sarah."

"Hi, Logan. How did you get my number?"

"I stopped by your office. Your mom gave me your card." Dear Lord in heaven, his voice. It was so smooth, like raw honey. She pictured it pouring from a mason jar, all sweet and thick and slow. And then he added, "Your mom and dad are obviously very happy together."

Sarah felt her face go hot. Stifling an embarrassed groan, she answered drily, "Yeah. I try to be out of the office as much as possible." Then she changed the subject. "Logan, I'm flattered you went to all that trouble just to get my number, but really, I meant what I said. I hardly have time to wash my hair lately. I'm not dating anyone, not even you."

"I get it. I called on business."

"Oh." Did she sound disappointed? Well, she wasn't. Not at all.

He said, "We're just getting moved in at the Ambling A and frankly, the accounts are a mess. We need a professional to get the books on track. We want to hire local. And that means Falls Mountain Accounting."

Her heart rate had accelerated at just the idea of being near him as she gathered the information to whip those books of his into order—but no. She needed to keep her distance from him, which meant he would have to work with her dad. "Did you meet with my dad yet? He's the best. I know you'll be happy you hired him."

"Sarah." He made her name into a gentle reproach. "Your dad seems to have his hands full—with your mom."

She did groan then. "I do not believe you said that." He didn't immediately respond and she suddenly had a burning need to speak, fill the silence between them. Bad idea. But she did it anyway. "They never used to be like that, I swear. I don't know what happened. I haven't asked. I doubt I ever will."

"I understand."

"Yeah," she grumbled. "Sure, you do." He made a soft, amused sort of sound. "Did you just chuckle, Logan? I swear to God I heard you chuckle."

His answer was actually more of a demand. "*You*, Sarah. I intend to hire *you*." He was just so...commanding. She'd never liked bossy men, but she found herself longing to make an exception in his case. In a strictly professional sense, of course.

And she might as well be honest—at least with herself. It was a definite ego boost to have this hot rancher so interested in her, even if she would never let it go anywhere.

Plus, well, he'd insisted he wanted to work with her. If she said no, he would go elsewhere. It wasn't good for business to turn away work.

"All right, Logan. Have it your way."

"I love it when you say yes. How about I meet you at your office?"

Her office, where there was no telling what her parents might be up to? "Er, no. I'll come out to the Ambling A."

"That's even better. I feel I should warn you, though, it's kind of a mess, old records all over the place. Some are on floppy disks, believe it or not. There are even some dusty, leather-bound ledgers that go back to the fifties."

"It will be fine, don't worry. Mostly, I need the current stuff."

"Well, I've got that, too."

She quoted her hourly rate.

"That works. Today?"

"Logan, it's almost five. I need to go home, feed my baby, maybe even stretch out on the sofa and veg out to the new season of *GLOW*."

"You're tired." He actually sounded as though he cared. "Tomorrow, then."

"All right. I have a nine o'clock that should go for an hour, two tops. After that, I'm flexible. Is it all right if I call you when I'm ready to head over to the Ambling A?"

"Works for me. Call me on this number."

She said goodbye and then sat behind the wheel for a moment, thinking how she would have to watch herself tomorrow, make sure she kept things strictly business. In the back seat, Sophia made a soft, happy sound in her sleep, and that had Sarah thinking how good Logan was with the baby.

Too good, really. The last thing she needed was him being charming and wonderful with Sophia. That could weaken her already shaky defenses.

Sarah bent her head over her phone again and texted her dearest friend since childhood, Lily Hunt.

Hey. You on the job at the Manor tomorrow?

Lily was an amazing cook and worked at Maverick Manor as a part-time chef.

Not tomorrow. Why?

Now, that was a long story. One she didn't really want to get into via text—or in a phone call *or* face-to-face. Because what was there to say, really? Nothing had happened between her and Logan and nothing was *going* to happen.

I have to go visit a new client, Logan Crawford. He and his dad and five brothers have bought the Ambling A. I think things will go more smoothly if I'm not trying to take care of Sophia while I'm setting up their accounts. So how 'bout a cushy babysitting gig at my house?

There. That sounded simple and reasonable without giving away too much. She hit Send.

And Lily took it at face value: You're on. Tell Sophia that Aunt Lily can't wait. When to when?

Be at my place at 8:30. I should be back by two or three.

I'll be there. But I want something from you in return.

What? You think I won't pay you?

Sarah, I know you'll pay me. You always do. If I didn't take the money, you would chase me up Pine Street waving a handful of bills.

Very funny.

These are my terms. Saturday at 6. Dinner at the Manor. You and me, my treat. A girls' night out. We deserve it. Get your mom to take Sophia. That's what grandmas do. Come on, it will be fun.

It did sound kind of fun. Sarah hadn't been out to dinner in so long, she couldn't remember the last time. And Lily didn't get out enough either, really.

Sarah, I meant it. Ask your mom.

Grinning, Sarah replied, Okay. I'll ask her.

Yes! See you tomorrow morning, 8:30 sharp. And don't put it off, call your mom now.

Sarah did call her mom. Flo answered on the first ring. "Honey, I'm so glad you called. Here you are back in town and we're all working together—and yet, somehow, we hardly see you. How's my sweet grandbaby?"

"Asleep at the moment."

"She is an angel—oh, and by the way," her mom began much too coyly, "a handsome cowboy showed up at the office this morning looking for you."

Who are you and what have you done with my real mother? Sarah thought but didn't ask. Florence Turner used to be quiet and unassuming. A nice person, but a grim one. Not anymore. When she wasn't disappearing into her husband's office for a quickie, Flo bounced around Falls Mountain Accounting full of energy and big smiles. It had been that way since Sarah moved home from Chicago a month ago. Who knew when it had started?

Sarah was afraid to ask.

Her mom prompted, "Did he call you?"

"Logan Crawford, you mean?"

"That's him."

"Yes, he called me."

"Honey, that is one fine-looking hunk of a man, a complete hottie, I don't mind telling you."

"Yeah, I've seen him. Thanks, Mom."

"You should snap that one up."

"Mom. He wants me to straighten out his accounts, that's all."

"Oh, I think he's hoping to have you *straighten out* a lot more than his accounts."

"Mom!"

"Sweetheart, don't be a prude. Life is beautiful and so are you. You deserve the best of everything—including a tall, hot cowboy with gorgeous blue eyes."

"Yes, well. I didn't call to talk about Logan. I was wondering if you would watch Sophia Saturday night. Lily and I want to get together for dinner."

"Honey, at last!"

"What do you mean by that?"

"You've been home for weeks and this is the first time you've asked me to take Sophia for you."

"Oh, well, I…" Sarah didn't know what to say. Her mom had offered, but it had never really been necessary.

"It's all right," Flo reassured her. "I'm just glad you've finally asked me—and yes, I would love to."

"Perfect." Sarah thanked her and ended the call before her mother could say another word about Logan Crawford and his hotness.

Armed with her laptop, her business tote and the steely determination not to be seduced by a sweet-talking cowboy, Sarah arrived at the Ambling A at eleven the next morning.

Logan was waiting for her on the long front porch of the giant log-style house. He wore faded jeans that fit his strong legs much too perfectly and a dark blue shirt that clung to his lean chest and arms and brought out the color of his eyes. He dropped his hat on one of the porch chairs and came down the steps to open her car door for her.

"Where's Sophia?" he asked. She'd just picked up her laptop from the passenger seat. He reached in and took it from her, tucking it under his arm as he offered his hand to help her from her car.

She hardly required assistance to get out from behind the wheel and she really was trying not to let him get too close. But to refuse him just seemed rude.

"The baby?" he asked again as his warm, slightly rough fingers closed around hers. His touch felt way too good. She grabbed her giant leather tote with her free hand and hooked it over her shoulder.

"Sophia's at home today." She emerged from the car into the late-morning sunlight. "My friend Lily was free and agreed to babysit." They stared at each other.

His fine mouth twitched at one corner as he quelled a smile. "I'm disappointed. I was looking forward to another lively game of peekaboo."

Just like the other day at the train depot, she had to remind herself to ease her hand from his.

He led her inside, where there were moving boxes stacked in the front hall.

"It's a great house," she said, staring at the wide, rustic staircase that led up to a gallery-style landing on the second floor. "I vaguely remember the Abernathy family. They owned the place first and built the house, but they left a long time ago."

"We got a hell of a deal on the place from the last owners, I'll say that much." He put his hand on the fat newel post. "The house needs work, but we'll get around to that eventually. Right now, we're just trying to get everything unpacked—my dad and Xander and me. My other brothers will be showing up in the next couple of days. Then we'll be focused on buying more stock. The barn and stables need repair. Lot of ditches to burn and fences to mend. Fixing up the house is low on the list of priorities."

She should move things along, tell him she needed to get going on the work he had for her. But she was curious about him. "So, you're from Texas, I think your dad said?"

He nodded. "We had a ranch near Dallas. Me and my brothers grew up there."

"You *had* a ranch?"

"We put it on the market when we decided on the move here."

"So, you've always been a rancher, huh?"

He shook his head. "I went to college for a business degree and then moved to Seattle. Been there ever since."

"Seattle." She remembered then. "That's right. Your dad said you were in real estate."

"Property development, to be specific. I got there just in time for the boom years, and I did well. But then my dad got this wild hair to move to Montana, get us all together working a new spread. The timing was right for me. I'd been thinking that I was ready to try something different." He was looking at her so steadily. She liked having his gaze focused on her. She liked it way too much.

Then he asked, "How 'bout you? Where did you go to college? Have you always lived in Rust Creek Falls?"

His questions were perfectly reasonable.

Her response took her completely by surprise.

All of a sudden, her throat was too tight and there was pressure behind her eyes.

Really, what was the matter with her? Out of nowhere, she hovered on the verge of bursting into tears, right here in the front hall of the Ambling A ranch house with this too-handsome, charming man looking on.

Crying? Seriously? She wasn't a cryer. Crying was pointless and completely uncalled-for in this situation.

And yet still, she wanted to put her head in her hands and bawl like a baby over all the ways her life hadn't turned out as she'd planned, just stand here sobbing right in front of this superhot guy. A guy who seemed hell-bent on seducing an overworked, constantly exhausted single mom who wanted nothing more to do with the male of the species, thank you very much.

She gulped the ludicrous tears down and managed an answer. "I went to Northwestern and then I worked in Chicago for a while."

Now he was frowning at her, a worried sort of frown. Those eyes of his seemed to see way too much. "Sarah, are you okay?"

"I'm fine." She pasted on a wobbly smile. "Really. And don't you have a mountain of records and receipts to show me?"

He gave her a long look, a look both considering and

concerned, as though he was trying to decide whether to push her to confess what was bothering her or back off. She breathed a sigh of relief when he said, "Right this way."

They went down a central hallway, past a big living room and a kitchen that could use a redo to an office at the back of the house.

By then, she'd pulled herself together. "You weren't kidding." She gave a low laugh as she approached the big mahogany desk that dominated the room, its surface piled with old ledgers, dusty CDs and floppies.

"Most of this is probably meaningless to us, I realize," he said, setting her laptop on a side chair.

She put her tote down beside it. "Yeah, it's doubtful I'll need any of the records generated by the former owners."

"If you don't need them, we can just toss them out."

"I *might* need them. I can't say until I look through all the current records. And *you* might want to look through it all later. You might find out you own something you didn't even know you bought."

"Even the floppies? They would need converting just to read them, wouldn't they?"

She shrugged. "Doesn't hurt to keep them for a while. If you decide at some point you want to go through them, we have a guy in Kalispell who will convert them for you."

"That sounds really exciting." He put on a dazed expression, even crossing his eyes. His playfulness made her grin and caused a flare of warmth in her belly. The man was way too appealing. But at least she was no longer about to cry and he'd stopped looking worried that she might have a meltdown right in front of him.

She said, "What I'll need to set you up are your current records, including whatever you've got up till now of the Ambling A's inventory, income and expenses."

"Income?" He chuckled. "Not hardly. Not yet."

"Well, okay then. Just your expenses and whatever inventory you have of machinery, equipment and livestock—including your best judgment of their value. I'll need the documents you received from the title company when you closed the sale. I'll put it all together using a basic accounting program that should be easy to keep current. That will be a few days to a week of work for me here at the ranch, if that's all right?"

"Sounds good to me." He had that look, like he was talking about a lot more than bookkeeping.

She pretended not to notice what a shameless flirt he was. "I'll be in and out because I need to keep up with my other clients, too. But if I do the work here, I can come right to you with any questions I have about the records you've given me. We can clear up any issues on the spot."

"Works for me." He said it in a low rumble that stirred a bunch of butterflies to life in her belly.

She tried valiantly to keep a professional tone as she rattled off more suggestions. "After you're all set up, you'll need someone to post transactions regularly. I have a couple of local people who can do that. Or you can just put in the time every week or so and do it yourself. I suggest you reconcile the bank balance and the general ledger at least once a month."

"Sure. And I'll hire whoever you suggest. What about tax time?" he asked.

"I'll be happy to do your taxes."

"Good." He arched an eyebrow and teased, "How 'bout an audit?"

She laughed. "Very funny. You know I can't audit my own work."

"Damn. Busted." He tipped his head to the side, his gaze lazy and warm. It felt so good just to have him looking at her, to be staring right back at him, thinking all kinds of naughty thoughts as she went through her stock suggestions for keeping accounts in order.

Really, this was getting out of control. They were more or less having sex with their eyes. If she didn't watch out, she would do something crazy, like throw herself into his arms and beg him to kiss her.

Uh-uh. It needed to stop.

"I should get to work," she said.

"Right." He pointed at the piled-high desk. "I think everything you need is there, including that big manila folder jammed with receipts, the inventory lists and the packet from the title company. You can tell the current stuff by the lack of dust."

"Okay, then." She moved behind the desk and pushed the records she would be using to one side. That left the piles of ledgers and old disks.

He got the message. "You need space to work."

"Do you have another desk you want me to use? A table works fine, too."

"The desk is yours for as long as you need it. I'll box up the old records, get them out of your way."

There were empty boxes waiting against one wall.

Together, they started putting the ledgers in one box and piling the old disks in another.

She'd straightened from the boxes and was turning to the desk to grab another handful of disks when she spotted Max leaning in the open doorway to the back hall. He looked like some old-time gunslinger in black jeans, black boots, a white shirt and a black Western-cut jacket.

"The lovely Sarah," the older man said. "What a surprise." Something in his tone made her uneasy, some faint edge of...what? Mistrust? Disapproval?

But why?

"Hi, Max." She gave him a big smile.

He didn't smile back or even give her a nod, but turned to Logan as though she wasn't even there. "Give me a few minutes?"

"Can't it wait? Sarah and I were just—"

"Go." Sarah faked an offhand tone. She felt completely dismissed by Max and that had her emotions seesawing again the way they had in the front all. There was absolutely no reason she should care if Logan's dad didn't like her. But she did care. There was a clutch in her throat and a burning behind her eyes as her totally inappropriate tears threatened to rise again. She waved Logan off. "Talk to your dad. I'll finish clearing the desk and get to work."

Impatient to return to his favorite accountant, Logan reluctantly followed Max out to the back porch.

The old man leaned on one of the posts that framed the steps down to the yard. He stared out at the ragged clumps of wild bunchgrass that extended to the back fence. Like too many fences on the property, it needed repair.

Logan braced a shoulder against the other post. "Okay, Dad. What's so important we have to deal with it right this second?"

Max's gaze remained on the backyard. He took a long count of ten to answer. "I can see now why you suddenly decided we needed to get the books in order."

Why deny it? "You know I like Sarah. It shouldn't be a surprise—and we do need someone to set up a system to keep track of everything."

"You've got a fancy business degree. You can do all that yourself."

"Dad, I didn't come to Montana to take up book-keeping. Sarah is equipped to do it fast and efficiently."

Max slanted him a narrow look. "Maybe you don't trust your old dad. You think you need a professional to tell you that everything's on the up-and-up."

Logan snorted out a dry laugh. "Oh, come on. I wouldn't have signed on for this if I thought you were up to something you shouldn't be. Still, it never hurts to have a professional putting a good system in place, keeping everyone honest."

"So you're telling me she's only here for her book-keeping skills? You've got absolutely no interest in those big amber eyes and that pretty smile?"

This conversation was a complete waste of time— time he could be spending with the woman he couldn't stop thinking about. "I'm thirty-three years old," Logan said flatly, "long past the age I have to run my personal choices by you. I'll date who I want to date." *At least, I will if I can somehow convince Sarah to give me a shot.*

"A woman with a child, Logan. It's a bad idea. If it doesn't work out, the kids are always the ones who suffer."

Logan had had about enough. He straightened from the porch post and turned to face his father directly. "What is it with you all of a sudden? Are you talking about Sheila?" Sheila was his mother. She'd left them when Logan was seven. It had taken him several years to accept that she was no mother to him in any way that mattered. Even saying her name made a bitter taste in his mouth. Max shot him a bleak glance, but then, without a word, he turned and stared off toward the fence again.

"You dragged me out here," Logan prodded. "Talk. I'm listening."

But Max only waved a dismissive hand and continued to stare at nothing. Fed up with him, Logan went back in the house.

When he entered the office, Sarah glanced up sharply from behind the desk. He didn't like the look on her face, a tense look, kind of teary-eyed, a look a lot like the one she'd had in the front hall earlier.

He pushed the door shut behind him. If Max had more to say, he could damn well knock. "What's wrong?"

She had her laptop open and the big packet of sale documents spread out in front of her. Shutting the laptop, she rose. "You know what? I should go." She swiftly lined up the stack of papers and closed the packet. "I know of a perfectly good bookkeeper in Kalispell. I'll text you his number."

"Sarah."

She didn't answer, just scooped up her laptop and took a step out from behind the desk. Logan stopped her by blocking her path, causing her to clutch the laptop to her chest and stare up at him defiantly. "Excuse me, please."

"Sarah."

She hitched up her pretty chin. "You are in my way."

"What's the matter?" It took everything he had not to touch her, not to grab her good and tight in his arms. "Talk to me."

Her soft lips trembled. "It's, um, quite obvious that your dad doesn't want me here."

"It's not about you, not really."

"Of course you would say that."

"Look. Sometimes I don't think *he* knows what he wants. He gets these wild ideas, that's all. You can't take him seriously. Bottom line, we need the accounts in order and that means we need *you*."

"But I just don't understand. It's like he thinks I'm after you or something, trying to trap you into—I don't know, putting a ring on my finger, I guess. And I'm not. I swear I'm not. I've got no interest in marriage. I don't want to trap anyone." She stared up at him through eyes swimming in barely held-back tears, so earnest, so very sincere. "Especially not, um, you."

He tried to tease her. "You know, if you keep talking that way, you're bound to hurt my feelings. I'm a very sensitive guy." And he did dare to touch her then. Clasping her shoulders, he held her gaze.

"I...oh, Logan." She looked absolutely miserable and he should probably just let her go. But he held on.

What *was* it that she did to him? He didn't get it.

He felt like ten kinds of selfish jerk to be putting her through this. But still, he just stood there, hands holding her slim shoulders, keeping her in place.

Finally, she spoke again. "See, the thing is, it hasn't worked out for me, to get involved with a man. So I promised myself I wouldn't. Not for years. Maybe never. And then you show up and, well, frankly, Logan, you really tempt me."

This was *bad* news? "Excellent."

"No. No, it's not. It's not excellent in the least. All it does is confuse me to feel this way about you. I don't need it, all this confusion. I'm already overworked and exhausted. The last thing I need is a sexy cowboy in the mix."

"Hold on," he said tenderly. "So then, what you're saying is you think I'm tempting and sexy?"

She huffed out a frustrated breath. "That is so not the point."

"Maybe not. But you can't blame me for being pleased to hear how you feel." He wanted to kiss her, just pull her close and put his mouth on hers. But he wasn't sure how she would react to that. She seemed really upset and he didn't want to make her any more so.

"It's all too much, don't you get it?" she cried. "I'm just plain on overload." And then, as if to illustrate her point, a single tear got away from her. It slipped over the dam of her lower eyelid and traced a gleaming trail down her cheek.

"Sarah. Damn it." He let her go, but only so he could get his hands on the laptop she clutched so tightly. When he tried to take it, she resisted. "It's okay," he coaxed. "Come on, now. Let go." And she did. When she gave in and released it, he plunked it down on the desk and took her shoulders again. "Sarah, don't cry."

Another tear escaped. And another after that. "Too late," she said in a tiny voice.

"Aw, Sarah..." He pulled her close and she let him, collapsing against him, her soft arms sliding around his waist.

For a too-short span of perfect seconds, she clung to him. He breathed in the clean scent of her silky hair, wondered what she'd done to him, hoped that whatever it was, she would never stop.

But then she looked up again, her eyes wet and so sad, a tear dripping off the end of her pretty nose.

"Here," he said. "Sit down." He pushed her gently back into the old leather desk chair and looked around for a tissue. There weren't any.

She sniffled. "Give me my tote, please." He went around the desk to grab it from the chair where she'd left it and handed it to her. She pulled out a travel pack of tissues, took one and wiped the tears from her cheeks. "I'm a mess," she said.

"No." A hank of her hair had escaped from her ponytail. Gently, he guided it back behind the shell of her ear. Retreating, but only a little, he hitched a leg up on the corner of the desk. "You're tired and overworked. And completely gorgeous."

She gave a little snort-sniffle at that. "Yeah, right."

He put up a hand, like a witness about to swear to tell the truth and nothing but the truth. "You're gorgeous," he said again. "And I mean that sincerely."

She started to smile, but couldn't quite manage it. Her shoulders slumped. "I'm just so tired, you know?

Tired of working nonstop and trying to be a decent mom to Sophia and really not doing either all that well. I don't get it, I really don't. How did everything go so wrong?"

He leaned closer. "What went wrong? Sarah, come on. Tell me. I need to know everything that's bothering you."

She scoffed. "Why?"

"So I can try to make it better." He actually meant that, he realized as he said it. He wanted to be with her—for as long as it lasted. And during that time, he wanted to be good for her. When they parted, he wanted her to remember him as a good guy who had treated her well.

She shook her head slowly. "If you keep pushing, I'm just going to go ahead and unload it all on you. My whole life story, all the ways I messed up. It will be a lot. It will be a really bad case of extreme oversharing and you will wish you'd never asked."

"No, I won't."

She scoffed. "Yes, you will. Believe me. Let's talk about something else."

"Uh-uh. For you to talk to me about what made you cry is exactly what I want." And he did want it. He really did. "Tell me. Tell me everything."

She stared at him, considering. "You're sure?"

"I am. Talk to me, please."

"Logan, I—"

He stopped her with a shake of his head. "Tell me."

For a long moment, she just stared at him. And then, at last, she let it all out.

Chapter 3

"My parents used to be so different," Sarah began.

Logan thought of Flo Turner the day before, coming out of her husband's office with her shirt untucked, her hair sticking out on one side and a smile of complete satisfaction on her flushed face. "How so?"

"When I was growing up, they were both so gloomy, always bleak and determined."

"You're not serious."

"As an IRS audit," she sneered. "They got married because they 'had to.'" She air-quoted that. "Because I was on the way. And they stayed married out of a sense of duty—they actually used to say that, how they stayed together because it was their duty. They were so noble. I couldn't wait to get out of that house, to live my own life, make things happen, get out in the big world and have everything. Success. True love. A great marriage.

Kids. And a whole lot of fun. But somehow, once I was on my own, there just wasn't enough time for fun, you know?"

"Why not?"

"I'm really not sure. I guess, because the way they raised me did rub off on me at least a little. I was driven, a straight-A student. I got a scholarship to Northwestern and my parents covered everything the scholarship didn't. I had a full ride and was driven to get through college fast and get on with my life." She'd studied like crazy, she said, and spent all her free time building her résumé.

To get a head start on her accounting career, she began interning in her sophomore year. She'd crammed six years of college and work experience into four and passed the CPA exam at the very young age of twenty-two. By then, she was already working at Chicago's top accounting firm.

And up until then, she'd never had a serious boyfriend.

"I met Tuck Evans not long after I got my CPA license. He was so charming. He also had a good job and claimed to be crazy for me. He was my first and only love—or so I thought." They'd moved in together.

But two years later, Tuck was perfectly happy with the status quo. "He said he saw no reason for us to get married. He said that we had it all without the ring. To teach him a lesson, I moved out and waited for him to come crawling back to me." She fell silent.

He prompted, "And?"

"Didn't happen. Finally, I called him. He was sweet and good-natured as ever, saying how right I was to end it. Really, he said, it wasn't working out and we both knew it." She glared up at Logan defiantly. "I was such an idiot."

"No, you weren't. Tuck wasn't good enough for you. He did you a favor."

Sarah glared harder. Logan could see her sharp brain working, trying to find something objectionable about what he'd just said. She wanted a fight.

He wasn't going to give her one. "Go on," he said gently.

She blew out a breath—and continued. "The day after I called Tuck and he said how glad he was that he and I were over, I headed off for a big conference in Denver. When a handsome bachelor came on to me at the conference, I decided a rebound fling was just what I needed."

"This handsome bachelor got a name?"

"Mercer Smalls. Does it matter?"

"No," he said honestly. "You're right. His name doesn't matter." Except that Mercer Smalls was a ridiculous name for a man. But whatever the guy's name had been, Logan would have disliked him on principle. Not that he was actually in any position to judge. He'd enjoyed more than one fling himself. Way more. And a lot of one-night hookups, too.

"I spent the three nights of the conference with Mercer," she said. "When we parted, he promised to call, but he didn't."

"Good riddance." Logan kept his tone mild, but he had to grit his teeth to do it.

Sarah sighed. "I was philosophical about it. Those three nights with Mercer helped me realize that flings just aren't for me. I knew I wouldn't be doing that again." She fell silent.

He realized that he was maybe a little like her first boyfriend, Tuck. And like the guy at the conference, too. Out for a good time, not looking for anything too serious. She was making it painfully clear that having a fling with a guy wasn't for her—that right now, she didn't want a guy at all.

He should back off, walk away.

But the thing was, she really got to him. And he *would* do right by her, damn it. She needed fun—all the fun she'd never had yet. She needed a man who knew how to treat a woman like a queen. It might not be forever, but when it ended, she would be glad for what they'd shared. He could make certain of that, at least.

And the silence between them had stretched out too long.

He guessed. "Mercer Smalls is Sophia's father?"

She nodded. "I couldn't believe it when I found out I was pregnant. It wasn't like we hadn't used protection. We had. But the stick turned blue anyway."

"Does Mercer know?"

"Of course. I knew the city he lived in and the name of his firm, so I reached out to him. I didn't imagine he would go down on one knee or even that he might be the guy for me, but a man has a right to know when he's going to be a father."

"He absolutely does," Logan agreed. A man deserved to know about his child, to be a part of his kid's life— even if the man was a player named Mercer Smalls who'd said he would call and never did.

"But as it turned out," she said, "Mercer wasn't a

bachelor, after all. He was married with children and wanted nothing to do with me or the baby I was going to have. I couldn't believe it," she muttered, her eyes full of shadows, her gaze far away. "My rebound fling was a cheating husband who denied his unborn child outright. He just wanted to sign off all responsibility for the baby and be left alone."

He thought of Sophia, with her goofy little grin and her baby sounds that seemed like real words to him. Mercer Smalls was ten kinds of douchebucket. And a damn fool, to boot. "You gave him what he asked for?"

"You bet I did. His loss, the schmuck."

"I'm guessing this is the part where you swore off men forever?"

"How did you know?" She troweled on the irony. "I decided I would forget men and love and all that. I would be a successful single mom—and, Logan, I tried. I really did."

But fighting her way up the corporate ladder in the big city wasn't compatible with tackling motherhood solo on a tight budget. "The cost of day care for an infant was through the roof and I just couldn't keep up the pace at work."

In the end, she'd accepted the inevitable and moved home to Rust Creek Falls. "It's great, it really is—or it should be." She swiped another tear away. "I've got this cute, cozy cottage my parents own and a job in the family business. I can take Sophia with me to work whenever I need to. I mean, things could be so much worse. My baby is the light of my life and my parents are here to help and support me. Right?"

He nodded on cue and then prompted, "But?"

"Well, you've heard about Homer Gilmore, haven't you?" At his puzzled frown, she grinned through her tears. "Nobody's told you about Homer?"

When he shook his head, she launched into this story about a local eccentric who made moonshine that had everyone doing crazy stuff. A few years ago, at a wedding on the Fourth of July, Homer had spiked the wedding punch. People had danced in fountains, gotten in a whole bunch of crazy fights—and had sex. A lot of sex. So much sex that nine months after that wedding, Rust Creek Falls had actually experienced a baby boom.

"My point being," she said, "that sometimes I wonder if my mom and dad have somehow drunk the Homer Gilmore moonshine. I mean, you've been to the office. You've witnessed firsthand how they are now. Their marriage of grim duty has turned into something completely different. My mother and father have fallen in love."

And if Flo and Mack weren't doing it in the office, she said, they were suddenly heading out the door, going who-knew-where together.

"Not to visit clients, that's for sure," she grumbled. "So yeah. I'm back in my old hometown, still trying to be a good mom while putting in killer hours doing my best to catch up with the workload my parents are currently too busy *schtupping* to shoulder."

He looked at her sideways. "Did you just say *schtupping*?"

"*I did. And* I have no idea where that came from. I've never used that word before in my life." Her sweet mouth was trembling—and not with tears this time. She laughed out loud, tipping back in the chair, the sound free and open and so good to hear.

He just wanted to hold her, though he doubted she'd allow it.

Still, he had to try. Rising, he offered his hand. She put hers in it. He pulled her up and into his arms, guiding her head to rest on his shoulder.

They laughed together, holding on to each other, until he tugged on the end of her ponytail.

She looked up at him. "What?"

"Is that it? Is that everything?"

"Pretty much, yeah. I'm working nonstop and still somehow barely keeping up. I adore my baby, but I hate being constantly frazzled and frumpy."

He put a finger to her lips. They were so soft, those lips. He ached to kiss them. "You're not frumpy. Not in the least. You're beautiful and you're doing a great job and it's all going to work out."

She actually smiled at him. "I shouldn't believe a word you say. But you know what? I kind of love it. Because all this flattery and praise, well, I can use a little flattery at this point. I really, really can."

"Sarah." He touched her silky cheek. And she didn't even try to stop him.

She didn't stop him when he traced the perfect shape of her ear, either. Or when he put his finger under her pretty chin and lifted it a fraction higher. She smelled so good, like flowers and baby lotion and something else, some delicate spice.

And then she whispered his name so softly and just a little bit hesitantly, lifting her chin even higher, offering up those plump, tempting lips to him.

He took what she offered. Carefully, at first, not wanting to push her, he brushed his mouth back and forth across hers until she opened to him, her lips parting on a soft, hungry cry.

It was all the invitation he needed.

He went for it, settling his mouth more firmly on hers, smiling a little when she made a sweet humming sound.

Her body was pliant in his arms. Every inch of her felt just right, giving and womanly, soft where he was hard. He could kiss her forever.

But too soon, with a tiny moan, she lowered her chin and broke the perfect kiss. Suddenly shy, she pressed her face into the crook of his shoulder.

He kissed her temple, her hair, even gave a quick nip to her earlobe. That brought a giggle. She lifted her gaze to him again. They regarded each other. Her eyes were almost pure gold right now.

"Let me take you out," he said. "Friday night. There's this great little Italian place in Kalispell I discovered a week or so ago when I got tired of eating Xander's cooking."

"Really, Logan. Didn't you hear a word I said?"

"I heard *every* word. Let me take you out."

"I just can't."

He touched her chin again, ran his thumb back and forth across those perfect, kissable lips of hers. "*Can't* has got nothing to do with it. You know you *can*. All you have to do is say yes."

"You are the sweetest man."

Sweet? Had any woman ever called him that? Doubtful. And he wasn't sure he liked it all that much. But he'd take it if it got him what he wanted. What they *both* wanted. Because she was drawn to him as much as he was to her. If he'd had any doubts on that score, the kiss they'd just shared had ended them. "So that's a yes, right?"

Her head went from side to side, that ponytail swaying slowly. "I've got no time for fancy restaurants."

"The restaurant I'm thinking of is a great place, but not that fancy, I promise you."

She sighed. "Logan, I shouldn't have kissed you and nothing is going to happen between us."

What was it about this woman? He'd never worked so hard to get a girl to say yes—and not even a yes to spending the night in his bed. Uh-uh. So far, he couldn't even convince her to let him buy her dinner.

He should give up.

But she had those golden eyes and she smelled so good and, well, something about her had him willing to do whatever he had to do just to get the raw beginnings of a chance with her. "How 'bout a quiet evening at your house, just you and me and little Sophia? I'll bring takeout."

"Really, I—"

"Yes." He said it firmly. "That's the word you're looking for. Three little letters. Just say it. Say it now."

"Oh, but I—"

"Yes. Come on, you can do it."

"Logan, you—"

"Yes."

"I—"

"Yes."

She bit her lower lip, adorably torn.

"Yes," he whispered yet again, holding her gaze nice and steady, keeping his tone gentle but firm.

And finally, she gave in and gave him what they both wanted. "Oh, all right. Friday night, takeout at my house. Yes."

The next day, Thursday, Logan's other four brothers arrived from Texas bringing a caravan of stock trailers full of horses and cattle. Sarah drove up not long after they all pulled in and Logan made the introductions.

Once she'd greeted them all, Sarah retreated to the office and got to work. That day and the next were busy ones at the ranch, what with getting the stock and the rest of the family settled in. Logan didn't have a lot of free time.

But for Sarah, he *made* time. He really liked the simple fact of her being there at the Ambling A, of knowing that he could see her whenever he had a spare minute or two. All he had to do was visit the office at the back of the house.

Both days, she brought Sophia with her. The baby slept in her carrier on the edge of the desk or rolled around in the collapsible play yard on the floor at Sarah's feet, making her cute little noises, staring up at a mobile of butterflies, birds and airplanes, happily gumming a series of rattles and rubber toys.

Logan checked in every two or three hours in case Sarah had questions. If Sophia was awake, he would spend a few minutes bent over the carrier or the play yard. The little girl made her goo-goo sounds at him and he answered each one with, "You're right" or "I agree completely" or "Yes, your mama is looking even more beautiful than usual today."

Sarah pretended to ignore him whenever he kidded around with Sophia. She focused on her laptop, her slim fingers working the mouse, swiftly tapping the keys. But Logan didn't miss the slight flush to her cheeks or the smiles she tried so hard to hide.

If Sophia was fussy, he would pick her up and walk her around the office a little until she quieted. The first time that happened, Sarah said, "You don't have to hold her. She's fine, really. I usually wait a few minutes before I rush to calm her. Half the time, she settles down by herself."

He stroked the baby's wispy hair and kept walking back and forth. "Are you saying you don't *want* me to pick her up?"

"Of course not. You're sweet to do it. Hey, knock yourself out."

"Thanks." He grinned at the baby and she grinned right back. "Because Sophia and I, we have a good thing going on."

Sarah kept right on typing. "She has you wrapped around her teeny-tiny finger is what you mean."

"Exactly," he answered proudly. "And Sophia and I, we like it that way."

Once he'd had a little quality time with Sophia, Logan would answer any questions that Sarah had for him and then leave her to her work. It wasn't easy, keeping his visits to the office at a minimum and his hands to himself. Every time he went in there, he longed to move in behind her, bend close, breathe in the scent of her, maybe turn her chair around and steal a steamy kiss. But he needed to show her that he was capable of respecting her workspace.

By Friday afternoon, though, he was anticipating the coming evening like crazy.

He hoped that she was, too.

There was a white van parked at the curb in front of her Pine Street cottage when Sarah answered the door at seven Friday evening with Sophia in her arms.

"Cute house," said Logan, looking way too hot in dress jeans, a snow-white shirt and a leather jacket that probably cost more than a Ford Fiesta.

She saw over his shoulder that his fancy crew cab pickup was right behind the van—the van that had "Giordano's Catering for All Occasions" printed in flowing red script across the side. He was having dinner catered? That wasn't the deal. She was about to question him when Sophia seemed to recognize him.

The baby pulled her fist from her mouth and giggled out a nonsense word, "Adaduh," as her face lit up in a giant, toothless smile. Before Sarah could stop her, she swayed toward him, fat arms outstretched.

"Whoa," he said. "Okay." And he caught her neatly on one arm. "I've got you."

"Gack!" She patted his face with her little hand.

"She'll get drool on your jacket," Sarah warned.

"I don't care." He made a silly face at Sophia, who giggled in delight and patted his cheek some more.

A dark-haired woman emerged from the passenger side of the van and bustled up the front walk as the driver got out, went around and opened the van's rear doors.

"This is a lot more than takeout," Sarah chided.

"It'th better than takeout," he said with a lisp because he was gumming Sophia's fingers. He caught the baby's hand and kissed her tiny fingertips. Sophia chortled as he suggested, "Wait and see."

Really, the guy was impossible.

The caterer introduced herself. "I'm Mia." The burly driver came up the steps behind her. "This is Dan." She asked where Sarah wanted them to set up.

Sarah led Mia and Dan into the dining alcove. "How can I help?" she asked.

Logan took her arm and pulled her over next to him. "Step back and let them work."

Mia and Dan swiftly set the table with white linen, fancy china, real silver and shining glassware. There were candles—tall, white ones in silver candlesticks. It was really beautiful.

Logan still held Sophia. The baby waved her arms and jabbered away as Mia and her assistant took the food into the kitchen. They put the salads and dessert in the fridge and set the rest out on the counter in chafing dishes to keep it warm.

"We'll serve ourselves," Logan said when the caterers were finished setting up.

Mia explained that she would be by around eleven the next morning to collect the dishes and everything else. "Just leave it all on the porch if you're not going to be here or if you plan to sleep late." She and her helper headed out the door. Sarah followed, thanked them again, and stood there in the doorway as the van started up and drove away.

She turned back to the man and the baby. He'd given

Sophia the rubber frog Sarah had left on the coffee table. Sophia chewed on it contentedly, resting her head against his broad chest.

"You shouldn't have," said Sarah flatly.

"You love it," he replied.

And yeah, she kind of did.

Logan was getting downright attached to Sophia. She seemed to really like him, too. Yeah, she got drool on his jacket, but so what? She chewed on her rubber frog and occasionally glanced up at him. "Ack," she would say, or "Bah," like she was telling him something really important.

She was wearing pajamas, white ones with pink sheep printed on them, all ready for bed. Sarah said no way was she sitting down to that beautiful dinner while the baby was still awake.

When Sophia started to get fussy, Sarah took her. "You can hang your jacket on that rack by the door," she said, as she knelt to put the baby on a play mat on the living room floor, setting a mobile over her with little forest animals hanging from it. Sophia didn't even try to turn over as she often did when Sarah had her in the play yard at the ranch. She just gummed her frog and stared up at the slowly rotating bears and squirrels.

Logan caught Sarah's hand as she rose from the floor. He turned her around so they were facing each other. Back at the ranch earlier that day, she'd been wearing dress jeans and a pale green button-up. Now, she wore a silky bronze-colored shirt with a nice low neckline that clung to the rounded curves of her breasts. "I like this shirt." He liked her snug jeans, too, which were a little darker brown than the shirt. On her feet she wore flats in a leopard print.

"Thank you." She smiled at him. Slowly. All he wanted was to kiss her.

Somehow, he controlled himself. "You should give me a tour."

She pointed at the short hall a few feet away. "Two bedrooms and a bath through there." And she gestured past the dining area. "Kitchen through that arch there. It's small, but it's home." She gave a wry grin, a grin that enticed him because everything about her enticed him.

And he couldn't resist a moment longer. He reeled her in, caught her face between his hands and kissed her. She tasted so good and she kissed him back, shyly at first and then more deeply.

The feel of her against him was temptation personified. He wanted to take it further. But now was hardly the moment, with their dinner still uneaten and her baby staring up at them from the floor.

Reluctantly, he broke the kiss and pressed his forehead to hers. "I could get used to this."

She pulled back. He caught her fingers before she could fully escape him. They stood in the middle of her small living room, holding hands, regarding each other. "You're a very determined guy, Logan."

"You noticed, huh?"

She did that thing, catching her lower lip between her teeth. He loved when she did that. It also drove him just a little bit wild. He ached to bite that lip for her.

"You're here in my house," she said. "My baby has a crush on you. I don't believe this is happening. This is everything I promised myself I wasn't going to do again."

"It's just dinner," he reminded her—though it was a whole lot more than that. And both of them knew it.

But he would tell whatever little white lies he had to tell to get closer to her.

She glanced down at Sophia. He followed her gaze. The baby lay, her arms above her head, rubber frog abandoned, sound asleep, as the mobile of forest animals continued to turn slowly over her head.

"I'll just put her in her crib," Sarah whispered, easing her fingers from his grip and kneeling to gather the little girl into her arms. Sophia's tiny mouth stretched wide in a yawn, but she didn't open her eyes.

Sarah carried the baby down the short hall and Logan followed. She entered the room on the right. He remained in the open doorway as she laid Sophia in her crib and settled a light blanket over her.

When she turned and saw him standing there, he felt a little guilty for trailing after her. He was constantly pushing the boundaries with her and he knew he had to be careful not to go too far. Sarah just might send him packing.

But apparently, the sight of him in the doorway to her baby's bedroom didn't bother her. Those golden eyes were soft and accepting of his presence there.

She came to him. "Let's have dinner," she whispered. "I'm starving."

Sarah dished up the food as Logan lit the candles and opened the bottle of Chianti he'd ordered to go with the meal.

They sat down to eat. It was heaven, Sarah thought, even if it was exactly the kind of intimate evening she should never have let happen.

But still…

A beautiful meal and a nice glass of wine, a gorgeous man across the table from her. It really was a special treat. She hadn't had a single sip of anything with alcohol in it since the day the home pregnancy test came out positive. Not only was drinking bad for the baby, who had time for it? Not Sarah.

However, she'd stopped nursing two months ago. The stress in Chicago had been killing her and it was just too much, all that pumping to get enough milk for when Sophia was at day care. Sarah had given up the fight and switched to formula. It wasn't as good for her baby—or her wallet—but at least Sophia seemed to be doing fine on a bottle. She was even starting to eat pureed foods.

And if Sarah had a glass of wine or two tonight, her baby wouldn't suffer for it.

"Hey," said the killer-handsome guy across the table. "Hmm?"

"You're frowning. Something wrong with the wine?"

"No way." She raised her glass to him. "It's delicious. And the veal is amazing."

He seemed pleased. "Told you so."

The conversation flowed easily. They talked about her progress on the Ambling A accounts. Logan reported that his second-born brother, Hunter, and his six-year-old daughter, Wren, had moved into one of the three cottages on the property. Knox, fifth in the birth order, had claimed a second cottage. Finn and Wilder had taken rooms in the main house with Max, Logan and Xander.

"Six of you boys and Max, too," Sarah teased. "That's a lot of testosterone."

"We get along," he said. "Mostly. Dad can drive us all kind of crazy, but his heart's in the right place."

Was it? She didn't know what to think about Max. "If you say so. How did your brothers react to the news that Max has offered Viv and Caroline a million bucks to find you guys brides?"

He laughed. "They're used to his wild ideas and schemes. Mostly, we all told him to knock it off, that we could find our own brides when we were damn good and ready. But Dad won't give up. He's relentless when he's got a plan and more often than not, he makes his plans come together, no matter how out-there they might seem at first."

What was he telling her, exactly? She shouldn't even let herself try to figure out what he meant. But she did wonder.

Would he be going out with the women Viv and Caroline introduced him to? Did he actually expect he would end up married to one of them? He certainly couldn't mean *her*. She wasn't marrying anyone, thank you very much. And Max had made it more than clear that he didn't want Logan getting too close with the single mom from Falls Mountain Accounting.

Not that Logan seemed like the kind of guy who did things his father's way. And the simple fact that he was here, sitting across from her over this perfect meal he'd arranged, well, that said something, didn't it? He really did seem to like her and her little girl, too.

And what about those amazing kisses they'd shared—the ones she probably shouldn't have let happen? Was he going to go from kissing her so thrillingly to taking some other girl out next Friday night?

He gazed across the table at her, those superfine blue eyes full of humor—and other things, sexy things she also wasn't going to think about.

She held out her wineglass and he filled it again. "So, tell me about your life in Seattle."

He said he'd gone to the University of Washington and teamed up with college friends to start investing in real estate. The business had grown. He'd scored big with some large commercial properties. "I loved it," he said. "There's always something going on in Seattle. The nightlife is great and the work kept me interested. But I missed the wide-open spaces, I guess you could say."

"Any serious relationships?" she asked. Because why not? She wanted to know. And after her TMI crying jag at the ranch the other day, she figured she deserved to hear at least a little about his past loves.

"None," he said.

She laughed. "Did you really have to go into so much detail?"

He lifted one hard shoulder in a half shrug. "Okay, I've dated exclusively a few times. But I've never been married or engaged, never even lived with a woman."

She turned her wineglass slowly by the stem. "So, you're a player?"

"Smile when you say that."

She raised the wine to her lips and savored its rich taste of earth and dark cherries. "Looks like Viv and

Caroline will have their work cut out for them with you."

He gazed at her way too steadily. The look in his eyes caused a warm shiver to slide over her skin. "There's only one girl I'm interested in and I think you know that. I want to be with *you*, Sarah, and I'm hoping that you'll realize you like being with me, too."

She did realize it. She realized the hell out of it and that didn't ease her mind one bit—and what was she doing right now?

Exactly what she *shouldn't* be doing, staring at his mouth. Staring at those lips of his and remembering the delicious pleasure of his kiss.

Blinking, she refocused. Somehow, this meal seemed to be turning into a seduction. She couldn't allow that.

But the food was so good and the man across from her so very charming. Plus, as usual, she was exhausted. The delicious wine seemed to be going straight to her head, making her body feel loose and easy, giving everything a sort of hazy glow.

He asked her about the brushstrokes of different-colored paint on the wall next to the dining-room hutch and in the kitchen and the hallway and the baby's room, too.

She explained that she had plans to paint the cottage, to make it bright and cheery and really hers. "Unfortunately," she admitted with a resigned sigh, "painting my new place is low priority right now. Too many other things come first."

"Like?"

"Making a living and taking care of my baby. I've got a million things to do if I ever get a free minute. Starting with sleeping. That would be a thrill."

When their plates were empty, Logan granted her a slow smile full of sexy devilment. "Ready for dessert?"

He insisted on serving her. It was chocolate semi-freddo, essentially a frozen mousse. And it was amazing. She ate it slowly, savoring every bite, trying to keep her moans of sheer delight to a minimum.

When she was done, Logan pushed back his chair. "I'll clean up and put everything out on the porch, all ready for Mia and Dan to pick up in the morning." He came to her side of the table and held out a hand to her.

She stared at that offered hand, a shiver of awareness warming her skin to have him so close. "Oh, no," she said.

"Oh, no what?"

She shifted her gaze up, into his waiting eyes. Really, she felt so good, easy and lazy with the wine and the wonderful food—and what was it she'd been about to say? She blinked and remembered. "You sit back down. I'll do it."

"Give me your hand." When she hesitated, he took it anyway and pulled her to her feet.

"Logan, seriously," she protested. "You provided this amazing dinner. The least I can do is clear the table."

"Uh-uh." He took her by the shoulders and turned her around. "Start walking."

"No, really, I—"

"Straight ahead." He guided her to the living room sofa, turned her around a second time and then gently pushed her down. "Relax. I've got this." He seemed determined.

And she *was* relaxed—more than relaxed. She felt

downright lazy. "Go ahead." She waved him away. "Do all the work."

He bent close and pressed his lips to her forehead. "I will."

She watched him stride back to the table, admiring the width of his shoulders and his truly stellar behind. Really, did he have to be so good-looking both coming and going?

"Not fair," she muttered as her eyelids kept trying to droop shut and her body sagged against the armrest. She grabbed the throw pillow and stuck it under her head.

What could it hurt to shut her eyes? Not for long, of course. Just for a minute…

Chapter 4

Twenty minutes later, Logan had the table cleared, the leftovers transferred to plastic containers and stored in the fridge and everything else stacked and waiting on the front porch, ready for pickup the next day.

By then, Sarah was completely conked out on the sofa, looking so cute, with her head on a pillow, her lips softly parted, her feet still on the floor.

She stirred when he knelt to slide off her shoes. "Wha…? Logan?"

"Shh," he soothed her. "It's okay," he whispered. "Close your eyes."

"Hmm…" And she drifted back to dreamland again. He eased her feet up onto the cushions, settled the sofa blanket over her and placed a chaste kiss at her temple.

Should he grab his jacket and let himself quietly out the door?

Probably.

But what fun was that?

He took the easy chair across from the sofa, hooked one booted foot across the other knee and settled in to watch her sleeping.

What was it about her? he asked himself for the umpteenth time. He liked her. Too much? Maybe. But she had grit. He admired that. She was beautiful and smart with a wry sense of humor. And every time he kissed her, he wanted more.

More of the taste of those sweet lips of hers. More of her laughter and more of her sighs. More of all of her.

It surprised him, his own patience in this never-quite-happening seduction of her that he'd been knocking himself out to orchestrate—so far to minimal success.

There was just something about her. She gave him… *feelings*, which was emo and weird for him. But good. Somehow, it didn't bother him at all, having feelings for Sarah. She was so independent and determined, but so womanly, too. She tried to be tough, but she had a tender heart. He could sit here across from her in the easy chair all night, watching her sleep, wanting to sketch her.

Logan had always been good at drawing things. Give him a tablet full of paper and a pen or a pencil and he could spend hours doodling pictures of trees, houses, horses—you name it.

Early on, he'd discovered that women loved a cowboy with a little artistic talent. In high school and later, at UW, he would carry a sketchpad wherever he went. If he saw a woman he admired, he would draw a picture of her, which would get her attention and also bring other women flocking around him. If guys ribbed him about being an artsy-fartsy type, he would just shrug and say it worked great with the girls.

Nobody needed to know it went deeper. Drawing pictures of the things and the people around him focused him somehow, brought him a sense of peace within himself.

And he'd just happened to notice that Sarah had a small desk tucked into a corner of her kitchen. Would she be pissed at him if he looked in there for some paper and a pencil?

He got up to check and found just what he was looking for: a large spiral-bound notebook of unlined white paper. She also had several #2 pencils in the pen drawer, all of them sharpened to perfect points. No surprise there. He could have guessed that Sarah was a woman who kept her pencils sharp. He took two, just in case he broke the lead on one.

Back in the easy chair, he got down to it, quickly sketching his favorite accountant as she snoozed on the couch. He finished a first attempt of her, head-to-toe, her hands tucked under her chin on the pillow, the bottom half of her covered in the brown-and-white couch blanket that looked good with her hair and that silky shirt she was wearing. He could almost wish he had colored pencils or pastels to capture the colors of her, too.

He'd just started on a close-up of her face when whiny sounds erupted from the baby monitor on the hutch in the dining alcove.

"Ahduh. Unh. Ga?" Sophia was awake and if he didn't do something, Sarah would be, too.

Pencil and notebook still in hand, he scooped up the monitor as he passed it.

The door to the baby's room was shut. He pushed it open. Enough light bled in from the living room for him to see that she'd kicked off her blanket and grabbed hold of her own toes.

"Maaa?" She'd turned her head to look at him through the slats of her crib.

Laughing a little at the sight of her with her little hands clutching her feet, he switched on the table lamp and shut the door to mute the noises she was making.

"Duh," she said. "Uh?"

He dropped the pencil and notebook by the lamp, turned off the monitor and put it down on top of the pad.

Sophia let go of her feet and fisted her hands. She made a sound that was more of a cry than a nonsense word.

He went to her and scooped her up. "Hey. Hey, it's okay."

Her lower lip was quivering. And then she did start to cry. She smelled like a dirty diaper, which was probably the problem. It couldn't be that complicated to clean her up, could it?

The dresser a few feet from the crib had a pad on top and shelves above with stacks of diapers and wipes.

He could do this.

Sophia chewed on her hand and looked at him through big, blue tear-wet eyes.

"It's okay. We got this," he promised her as he laid her down on the pad with its soft cotton cover printed with ladybugs and smiling green caterpillars.

Actually, it wasn't that difficult. Everything he needed was right there within reach. Sophia whimpered softly up at him as he worked, watching his every move as though she couldn't quite trust him to know what he was doing.

He couldn't blame her for having her doubts. His experience with babies was nil. When Hunter's little girl, Wren, was born, Logan had been busy making his mark in Seattle real estate. Yeah, he'd gone home to Texas maybe twice while his niece was still a baby. He'd done the classic uncle things—shaking a rattle over her crib, holding her while someone snapped a picture. That was it. Diaper changing never once came into play.

But he managed it with Sophia well enough. By the time he got her back into her pajamas, she'd stopped fussing.

He took her in his arms. "What'd I tell you? Stick with me, kid. Ready to go back to bed now?"

"Unh." Her lip started quivering all over again.

Sixty seconds later, she was making soft bleating sounds—not a full-out cry, but he had zero doubt she would get there if he didn't figure out what she needed very soon. He paced the small room, patting her back, trying to soothe her.

Maybe she was hungry.

He hated to open the door. Her cries were bound to wake Sarah—which would be good, wouldn't it?

Hell, yeah. Sarah would know what to do.

But she'd been sleeping so peacefully when he left her. And she really could use a little rest. He didn't want to disturb her unless there was no other choice.

Advice from an expert. That was what he needed. Wren's mom had died shortly after her birth, leaving Hunter to raise his daughter on his own. Hunter had been a hands-on kind of dad.

As Logan paced the floor and did his best to soothe the baby, he dug his phone from his pocket and attempted to text his brother, which turned out to be a losing game with Sophia squirming in his arms.

He gave in and punched the call button.

Hunter answered on the first ring. "Logan. What?" By then, Sophia was steadily fussing. "Is that a baby? What are you doing with a baby?"

Logan continued to pace the floor and pat the baby as he briefly explained that Sarah was sleeping and he didn't want Sophia to wake her.

"Sarah. Sarah Turner, you mean? The woman you hired to set up the ranch accounts?"

"Right."

"You've got a thing going on with the accountant? Fast work, big brother."

"Hunter, focus. I need some help here. I changed Sophia's diaper, but she's still not settling down."

"You, of all people. Falling for the bean-counting single mom." Hunter chuckled.

"Think you're pretty funny, huh? The baby's crying and I need some help here."

Hunter got serious. "She could be sleepy."

"She *was* sleeping. She woke up."

"Uh, right. How old is she, exactly?"

"Who? Sarah?"

"The baby."

"Five months?"

"What? You're not sure?"

"I'm sure enough. Five months."

"Okay, so I see three options to start. Is she flushed and feverish?"

Sophia's cheeks were pink, but that could be from fussing. He felt her little forehead. "I don't think she has a fever."

"She's probably hungry, then. Or maybe teething." He said Logan should look in the freezer for a cold teething toy. As for something to eat, he should look for formula and follow the instructions on the packaging. "Or wait. Is Sarah nursing? I know zip about that. Wren was on formula from the first."

Was Sarah nursing? Logan didn't know, and that really bugged him. A guy should know if the woman he couldn't stop thinking about was nursing. Shouldn't he? "I've never seen her nurse the baby. But bottles. I've seen her feed Sophia with those."

"Are you in the kitchen? If there's formula, follow the directions on the packaging." Hunter added, almost to himself, "Or then again..."

Logan kept pacing, the phone tucked under his chin so he could use the hand that wasn't supporting the baby to stroke her back and hold her steady as she squirmed. He really didn't get what his brother was trying to tell him. "You're saying that I shouldn't look for formula, after all?"

"No. I was just thinking you could look for baby food, too. Sarah might be introducing her to solids at this point."

Sophia gave a loud cry that faded into a pained whine. She flopped her head down on Logan's shoulder with a sad little sigh.

"Logan? You okay?"

"Not exactly. If I go in the kitchen, Sarah will probably hear her fussing and wake up. The whole point is for Sarah *not* to wake up."

"Then put the baby in her crib and go to the kitchen without her."

"She's upset. I don't want to leave her alone."

"Yeah, I know. It's hard when they can't tell you what's bothering them. But I don't know what more to suggest. You've already changed her diaper and she doesn't have a fever. Your best bets are that she's hungry or teething."

"Gotcha. Gotta go."

Hunter was wishing him luck as Logan ended the call. He dropped the phone on top of the notebook next to the baby monitor. Then he carried Sophia back to her crib.

"I'm going to put you in your bed," he explained, as if she could understand actual words. "And then I will run and see what I can find to make you feel better. I'll be right back." He peeled her off his shoulder and gently laid her in the crib.

She let out a sharp cry and then a longer one, her little face scrunching up, her arms reaching for him.

"Right back. Promise." Before he could relent and pick her up again, he got out of there, shutting the door on Sophia's unhappy cries.

As he raced by the living room, he noted that at least Sarah was still dead to the world. He really hoped he wouldn't end up having to wake her.

In the kitchen, he found powdered formula and some jars of pureed baby food in the cupboard. There were also a couple of plastic baby toys in the freezer. He decided to try the frozen toy pretzel first. Grabbing it, he rushed back to the baby's room, where Sophia was miserable, wailing now, her face scrunched up, beet red. He slid in and quickly shut the door behind him.

She continued to cry and he felt terrible. If the teething toy didn't work, he would have to get Sarah.

"It's okay. I'm here." Her crying stopped when he picked her up, but then started in again. "Come on. Try this." He touched the pretzel to her lips and a miracle happened. She took it in her mouth and even grabbed hold of it with her little hand.

A relieved sigh escaped her as she worked her gums on the frozen toy. She chewed the toy and regarded him so seriously, a last tear shining on her fat cheek, reminding him of her mother the other day, so sad over all the ways her life hadn't turned out as she'd planned.

He gently rubbed the tear away. "Feel better?"

"Unh."

"I'm going to take that as a yes."

He carried her over to the rocker in the corner and sat down. She gummed her pretzel and drooled on his shirt as he rocked her gently.

Eventually, she let go of the pretzel. It fell to his lap. That was when he realized she'd gone back to sleep.

He just sat there rocking her for a while longer because really, she was just the cutest thing, smacking her lips now and then as she slept, yawning once or twice. When he finally got up and tucked her back in her crib, she didn't even stir.

Before he turned off the lamp, he grabbed the spiral-bound notebook he'd stolen from the kitchen desk and dashed off a few sketches of her all cozy and peaceful, looking like a little angel as she slept.

* * *

Sarah came awake slowly.

She was lying on the sofa with a blanket over her. The lamp in the corner, turned down low, cast a soft glow over the living room. Across the coffee table, in the easy chair, Logan snored softly, his drooping head braced on a hand. She sat up and squinted at the little clock on the side table.

It was after two in the morning. The baby monitor that had been on the hutch was now on the coffee table next to a plastic teething pretzel that she remembered putting in the freezer the afternoon before. The only reason she could think of for Logan to remove the toy from her freezer was to soothe Sophia's teething pain.

Also on the coffee table were a full-size notebook and two pencils, most likely from her desk in the kitchen. The open pad was turned away from her, the top pages turned back. He'd been drawing something, though from this angle, she couldn't see what.

Quietly, so as not to disturb him, she picked up the notebook and flipped through the pages.

There were eight drawings total, five of her and three of Sophia. Logan had been sketching pictures of her and her daughter as they slept. They were beautiful, those sketches. Who knew the guy had that sort of talent? She'd had no clue.

It felt a little strange to think of him watching her, drawing her without her knowledge. But it didn't bother her, not really. And that was strange in itself, that she didn't mind he'd done the sketches without her knowledge. She wasn't really that trusting of a person, especially when it came to Sophia. She had a hard time counting on anyone but herself. Yet she'd dropped right off to sleep last night and left him to take care of Sophia. She did trust him, at least a little. And she loved the drawings.

She wanted them—especially the ones of her little girl. Maybe if she asked him nicely, he would give them to her.

And maybe she was growing kind of attached to him already. *Fond* of him, even. On top of being so strongly attracted to him.

Not good. Not wise at all.

But right now, she was too tired to ponder where this thing between her and the gorgeous, surprisingly artistic, baby-soothing man sleeping in her easy chair might be going. She got up, covered him with the blanket, grabbed the baby monitor, switched off the lamp and headed for her bed.

Sarah woke to daylight, feeling more rested than she had in months.

She blinked in surprise when she saw the time. Past eight. Sophia often slept through the night lately, but never as late as eight in the morning.

The monitor by the bed was silent, the screen dark. She touched it and it lit up with an image of Sophia's empty crib.

Sarah's heart started racing with the beginnings of alarm—until she remembered the baby-soothing rancher she'd left sleeping in her easy chair last night.

As soon as she opened her bedroom door, she heard Logan's low laughter and her baby's happy cooing. She followed the sounds into the kitchen where he sat at the two-seater table with Sophia on his lap. He fed her baby cereal as she waved her arms and babbled out nonsense syllables.

A messy business, feeding Sophia.

Sarah leaned in the arch to the dining alcove. "I would bet you that more cereal has ended up on you and the baby than in her mouth."

With the back of his hand, he wiped a dab of the stuff off his beard-scruffy cheek. "I never take a bet I know I'll lose." And then his gaze wandered over her, down the length of her body and back to meet her waiting eyes again.

Her hair was a mess. She wore her old robe over sleep shorts and a T-shirt with a frayed neckline. And yet somehow, that lingering glance of his made her feel like the prettiest girl in Rust Creek Falls.

"Sleep well?" His voice was low and deliciously rough.

"I did, yeah." She must have gotten a good ten hours total. Because of him. "Thank you."

"Anytime." And he smiled at her.

She felt that smile of his as an explosion of warmth in the center of her chest.

Oh, this guy was dangerous. She could so easily get in over her head with him.

"Bacon and eggs?" she asked.

"I would love some."

A half hour later, he reluctantly headed for the door. She thanked him again for the beautiful evening and the priceless hours of glorious sleep.

"I'll call you," he promised as she ushered him out.

She made a noncommittal noise in response and quickly shut the door.

In the living room, the pictures he'd drawn were still there on the coffee table. Apparently, he didn't want them. Which was great. Because she did. She would find frames for the ones of Sophia. And the ones of her, well, she would keep them as a reminder of him. Because he was a great guy and last night had been lovely.

But it was just too risky to go there. Her life now at least had a certain equilibrium. She couldn't afford to take chances with her heart.

He texted her that afternoon. I had a long talk with Sophia last night. She finally opened up to me and admitted that she wants us to spend more together.

Even feeling edgy and sad that she had to call a halt with him, she couldn't help smiling. Right. Sophia's a big talker. Too bad she doesn't use actual words yet.

I understand her. We communicate, Sophia and I. How about tonight? I'm supposed to go to this family thing. Come with me. Or if you want to go somewhere just the two of us, that's even better. I know a steak house in Kalispell. You're going to love it.

Her hopeless heart filled with longing—to spend another great evening with him. But that had to stop. Lucky for her, she already had a date with Lily for tonight. Sorry, I can't. It's a girls' night. Just my friend Lily and me.

Damn. Sunday? Come out to the ranch? Or maybe a picnic in Rust Creek Falls Park? Sophia would love it.

No, really. I can't. I'll see you Monday at the ranch. I still have a couple more days' work getting everything set up.

He didn't respond right away. But then, an hour later, her phone rang. She saw it was him and tried to hold strong, to let it go to voice mail. They could talk about it Monday. She could explain that it wasn't going to work, that she couldn't go out with him anymore.

But having it out with him Monday wouldn't be right, would it? She was going to the Ambling A to work. She needed to keep personal discussions out of the work environment.

Really, it had to be done now. She answered on the third ring. "Hi."

"What's going on, Sarah?" His voice was so careful. Flat. Controlled.

She needed to just do it. Get it over with. Move on. "I really can't do this, Logan. I can't go out with you again—I mean, I *won't* go out with you again. You're a wonderful man and I really like you, but it's not going to happen between us."

Dead silence from his end.

"Logan? Are you still there?"

"Yeah. And all right. I hear you. I'll see you Monday—and don't worry. You want it strictly business, so I'll give you what you want."

Chapter 5

Sarah's mom arrived right on time that night. She took Sophia into her arms and followed Sarah into the kitchen and then the baby's room as Sarah explained what to feed her, when to put her to bed and how the baby monitor worked.

"Amazing," declared her mother, thoroughly impressed. "Nowadays a baby monitor is a mini-security system. And the picture is so clear, honey."

Sarah still had trouble reconciling this pretty, confident, enthusiastic woman with the quiet, dutiful mouse of a mother who had raised her. "Yeah, well. As you can see, it's pretty simple. You shouldn't have any trouble with it."

Flo blew a gentle raspberry against Sophia's cheek and the baby giggled. Sarah watched them. Never in her life had she expected to see her mom blow a raspberry. It was all too strange and hard to believe.

"How's my girl?" Flo asked the baby.

Sophia giggled again and added, "Bah. Ga."

Sarah kind of tuned them out. She kept thinking about Logan, feeling heartsick about cutting things off with him.

She knew it was for the best.

But why did it have to hurt so much?

She'd only had the one evening with him. How could she have gotten so attached so fast?

"You seem kind of down, sweetheart. What's bothering you?" Flo asked as Sophia chortled in glee and bounced up and down in her grandma's arms. "Could this have anything to do with the fancy pickup that was parked in front of your house overnight last night?"

"Who told you that?"

"Honey, this isn't Chicago—it's Rust Creek Falls," her mom said as if that explained everything. And really, it kind of did.

In Rust Creek Falls, everybody pretty much knew everything about everyone else. They shared what they knew because they cared about their neighbors and also because it was a form of local entertainment to speculate about who was doing what—and with whom.

Sarah's mom regarded her with understanding, inviting her to share. And she really *wanted* to share…

But no. Uh-uh. Not happening. Bad idea.

It was over with Logan. Over without ever having really gotten started. There was nothing to talk about.

"Burdens are lighter when you share them," Flo advised with a radiant smile.

Say something. Anything. Just not about Logan.

"Actually, I, um, have noticed how well you and Dad seem to be getting along lately." Talk about an understatement. Sheesh. "And I've been kind of wondering what's happened between you two?"

She had been wondering, though she'd never planned to actually go there. Right now, though, even hearing about her parents' sex life would be preferable to discussing the man who'd become way too important to her way too fast.

"Oh, honey," said Flo. "I was beginning to think you'd never ask."

Beaming with pleasure, Sarah's mom told all. It had started with a routine visit to her new gynecologist and a pelvic exam that had led to a simple procedure that had changed everything for Flo and Mack.

"You see," said Flo, "as it turns out, I didn't heal properly after your birth, but I never realized that was the problem. It was just so painful to be intimate. And your father and I were hardly experienced. There was just that one time. Prom night. We got a little carried away. It was the first time for both of us.

"After that, we swore to wait. And then we learned you were coming and we got married earlier than we'd planned. We were just a couple of kids. What did we know? You arrived and your father went off to college. The next time we tried, well, it was awful for me. And no fun for him. We gave up, stopped trying—for years and years. Looking back, I can't believe we didn't at least try to figure out what might be wrong. But that's all changed now and I can't even describe how wonderful it is…"

There was more. Lots more. Stuff Sarah so didn't need to hear. Some of it was kind of nice, though, about how her mom and dad had gotten counseling to increase their intimacy emotionally, too.

Eventually, when she'd heard way more than enough, she put up a hand. "So what you're saying is that you're happy together now, you and Dad?"

"Oh, sweetheart. Words cannot express."

"I'm glad, Mom." And she *was* happy for her parents. Plus, she'd managed to keep her mouth shut about Logan. "And look at the time! I really should get going."

"Have fun, darling. Say hi to Lily for me."

"Thanks, Mom. I will." Sarah kissed her baby and got out of there.

Maverick Manor had been built back in the eighties as a private home. Perched on a rise of land back from the highway, it was a giant log structure, one that had been enlarged even more when it became a hotel. Surrounded by manicured grounds, the place was rustic and luxurious at once. In the lobby with its vaulted, beamed ceiling, a giant mural depicted the early history of Rust Creek Falls and the pioneer families who had founded it.

When the hostess ushered Sarah into the dining room, Lily Hunt was waiting at a quiet corner table. They ordered their meal and a glass of house wine each.

Wine two nights in a row, Sarah thought. She was living the wild life, no doubt about it.

She studied her friend across the small table. Lily had striking red hair and gorgeous green eyes, yet most people in town considered her plain. She rarely wore makeup and kept her beautiful hair pulled smoothly back and anchored low at her nape. Some called her shy, but she wasn't, not really. Not with Sarah, anyway.

Once the waitress had served them their food, Lily said, "You mentioned the other day that you were working out at the Ambling A, setting up the books for Max Crawford and his sons…"

Sarah guessed where her friend was going. "You heard about the deal Max made with Viv and Caroline to find brides for Max's sons, didn't you?"

"Yep." Lily's smile bloomed slowly. "Me and everybody else in town."

"Why am I not the least surprised?"

Lily buttered her bread. "I also heard that Logan Crawford is completely smitten with a certain brilliant accountant, a beautiful single mom with an adorable little girl."

"Brilliant *and* beautiful, huh? You're flattering me. Why?"

"I only speak the truth." Lily was all innocence.

Sarah savored a bite of her petite filet and said nothing.

Lily leaned closer. "Tell me everything." Her green eyes gleamed with eager interest. "Hold nothing back."

After all that had happened since Lily babysat for her last Wednesday, Sarah could no longer pretend that nothing was going on between her and Logan.

She laid it all out. From her powerful attraction to Logan to Max's opposition to her as a possible match for his oldest son, to Logan's unflagging pursuit of her and their first "date" the night before.

"Logan's been nothing but wonderful," Sarah reported glumly. She explained that she'd ended it with him when he called that afternoon.

"I don't get it." Lily frowned. "Logan Crawford provides a sit-down catered dinner with all the trimmings, thrills you when he kisses you, takes care of Sophia both night and morning so you can get what you need the most—a good night's sleep. The man draws beautiful pictures of you and your baby. He doesn't leave you hanging but instead calls the next day to ask you out again. And yet you've decided it can't possibly work?"

Sarah loved Lily. But sometimes her friend was just way too logical. "I told you I've had it up to here with men and all the trouble they cause."

"So stay away from the jerks and troublemakers. But, Sarah, when a good one comes along you need to give the guy a chance."

"He's in his thirties. He's never been married. Yes, he's a great guy. But he's not interested in anything long-lasting."

"He *told* you that?"

"No. I just know it. I, well, I *sense* it."

Lily tipped her head to the side, frowning. "Suddenly, you're psychic?"

"Of course not. It's just that he told me he's never even lived with anyone. I seriously doubt he's suddenly decided he wants to try marriage, that's all."

"Where to even start with you? So he's in his thirties? It's a prime age for a guy to finally find the right woman. He's mature enough to know what he really wants—and anyway, what about you? Do *you* want to get married?"

"Did I say that? No, Lily. I don't want to get mar-

ried. I'm not looking for a serious relationship. I honestly don't even want a date. I'm through with all that. I
have Sophia and a job I'm good at and a cute little cottage that will be even cuter if I ever find the time and
energy to fix it up a little."

"So then, be flexible."

Sarah slanted her friend a suspicious glance. "What,
exactly, are you getting at?"

"Have a wonderful time with a terrific man for as
long as it lasts. Because if you don't, Viv Dalton's dating service will be finding him someone who will."

Sarah sat up straighter. "That's okay with me."

"You don't mean that."

"Yes, I do." She tried really hard to tell herself that
it wouldn't bother her in the least if Logan started seeing some other woman in town.

A murmur of voices rose from the far side of the big
dining room.

Lily leaned in. "And speaking of the Crawford family…"

Sarah followed the direction of her friend's gaze and
saw that the hostess was ushering in several new arriv-
als. They included Nate Crawford and his wife, Callie,
a nurse at the local clinic. Nate's parents came in, too,
as well as his pretty sister Natalie and his brothers and
their wives.

And behind the local Crawfords came Max and six
big men who looked a lot like him—including the tall,
blue-eyed cowboy who made Sarah's heart beat faster
and her cheeks feel much too warm. The Crawford clan
took seats around a long table in the center of the room.

Lily whispered, "Max Crawford and sons, am I right?"

"How did you guess?" Sarah asked wryly.

"Everyone says they're all really good-looking." Her friend sipped more wine. "Everyone is right."

"Now that I think about it, Logan mentioned that there was some kind of family get-together tonight."

"A Crawford family reunion," said Lily. "Who's the cute little girl?" She gave a slight nod toward the blonde sprite who'd entered with Logan and his family.

"That would be Wren," said Sarah. "Her dad is Hunter Crawford. He's sitting to her left. Logan told me that Wren's mom died shortly after she was born."

"How sad." Lily was silent for a moment, kind of taking it all in. "Hmm…"

Sarah focused on her friend and tried really hard not to let her gaze stray to Logan. "Hmm, what?"

Lily tipped her head toward a table on the far side of the dining room. Viv and Caroline sat there, along with three other women who lived in town—single women, Sarah was reasonably sure. As Sarah watched, Viv turned in her chair and spoke to a woman at the next table over. Interestingly enough, that table was women-only, too.

Lily said, "Looks to me like Viv and Caroline's dating service is very much open for business."

Logan sat down at the table full of Crawfords, ordered a glass of eighteen-year-old Scotch and tried not to think about Sarah.

He noticed the wedding planners right away, as well as the pretty women at the table with them *and* at the next table over. Apparently, the wedding planners were already on the job providing potential brides for him and his brothers.

And his father, who had somehow ended up sitting next to him, was looking right at him. When Logan met Max's eyes, his dad winked at him. Logan gave his dad a flat stare—and then turned to face the other way.

Viv came over just to say hi. Max introduced her to Knox, Finn, Wilder and Hunter. She exchanged a few words with each of them, said hello to the local Crawfords and then rejoined the women.

Logan sat back and sipped his drink slowly as Nate Crawford explained how he and a few other movers and shakers in town had created Maverick Manor so that Rust Creek Falls would finally have a resort-style hotel.

When Nate finished his story, Finn, who was twenty-nine, fourth-born after Xander, got up and went over to where all the women sat. Viv introduced him to each of the women. He nodded and chatted them up a little before eventually wandering back to his seat. Wilder, last-born, rose a little later and strolled over to introduce himself, too. No way was Wilder ever going to let himself get tied down to one woman. But all the pretty ladies would have to find that out for themselves.

Logan's dad just couldn't leave it alone. As Wilder took his chair at the table again, Max leaned close and pitched his voice low for Logan's ears alone. "Yep. Lots of fine-looking women in this town. Take your pick, son. Viv will introduce you."

Logan didn't bother to answer. He just turned his head slowly and gave the old man another flat, bored stare.

Max got the message. He started yakking with Nate's dad, who was seated on his other side.

Logan was about to signal for a second Scotch when he spotted Sarah and a red-haired woman sitting in a small, tucked-away corner of the dining room. He wasn't sure what made him turn halfway around in his chair and glance over there, but when he did, his eyes collided with hers.

She quickly looked away.

He should look away, too. But he didn't. Man, he had it bad. It hurt just to see her. And he was feeling sorry enough for himself at that moment to go ahead and indulge his pain by turning in his chair and staring.

Yeah, it was rude. But he didn't care.

Sarah wore a cream-colored sleeveless dress and her hair was down, soft and smooth on her shoulders. As he watched, the waitress appeared and set a check tray on the table between Sarah and her friend. The redhead whipped out her credit card. Sarah tried to argue, but it appeared that the redhead won. The waitress left to run the card. A few minutes later, she dropped off the tray again on her way to take an order at another table. The redhead signed the receipt and put her card away.

Any minute now, Sarah and her friend would get up and leave.

Today, she'd made it more than clear that she refused to get anything going with him. He needed to take a hint, order that second Scotch and let her go. He turned away.

And something inside him rebelled at the sheer wrongness of the two of them, so acutely aware of each other and trying so hard to pretend that they weren't.

Forget that noise. He couldn't let her go without at least saying hi.

Logan shoved back his chair.

Ignoring his dad's muttered, "Logan. Let it be," he pushed in his chair and turned for her table.

In three long strides, he was standing above her.

She put on a fake smile. "Logan, hi. This is my friend, Lily Hunt."

The redhead said, "Happy to meet you," and actually seemed to mean it. She got up. "I think it's time for me to go."

"Lily," Sarah protested. "Don't—"

Lily didn't let her finish. "Gotta go. Call me," she said and then she walked away.

Logan claimed the empty chair before Sarah could leap up and disappear.

"This is pointless," Sarah said—softly, in a tender, hopeful voice that belied her words. She had her hands folded together on the table.

When he put his palm over them, she didn't pull away.

In fact, she looked up at him, finally meeting his eyes.

Their gazes held.

The packed dining room and all the other people in it faded into the background. There was no one but the woman in the cream-colored dress sitting across the table from him, the connection he felt to her, the cool, smooth silk of her skin under his hand.

"How's Sophia?" he asked as he slipped his thumb in between her tightly clasped fingers.

A smile tried to pull at the corner of that tempting mouth. "Same as this morning. My mom's watching her."

"Does she miss me?"

A chuckle escaped her and a sweet flush stained her cheeks. "Stop…"

"You need to say that with more conviction—or not say it at all." He pretended to think about it. "Yeah. Say something like, 'Logan, I'm so glad you're here and I've changed my mind and would love to go out with you any time you say.'"

"I…"

"You…?" He succeeded in separating her hands and claimed one for himself, weaving their fingers together. They stared at each other across the table. Her fingers felt just right twined with his, and her cheeks had a beautiful, warm blush on them. He never wanted to let her go.

"Logan, I do like you. So much."

"Which is why you need to spend more time with me. And I don't mean as my accountant. I mean quality time. Personal time."

She drew in a slow, unsteady breath.

He knew then with absolute certainty that she was going to change her mind, tell him yes. Finally. At last.

Except that she was easing her hand free of his. "No. It can't go anywhere." She rose. "I meant what I said this afternoon. I would really appreciate it if you would please keep it business-only while I'm working for you at the ranch. And right now, I really do need to go."

Logan knew when he was beaten. She wasn't giving an inch and he needed to accept that. "All right. I'm through. See you Monday, Sarah. You can finish setting up the books. And that will be that."

With a tiny nod, she turned and walked away.

He rose and went back to join the family. The waitress brought him that second Scotch. He sipped it slowly and considered his options, of which there really was only one.

It was time to wise up, quit playing the fool. Sarah was never giving him a damn break and he needed to stop following her around like a lovesick calf.

A pretty blonde sitting with the other women at Viv Dalton's table gave him a friendly smile. He raised his glass to her and her smile got wider. She had dimples and big blue eyes.

What was that old song? *If you can't have the girl you want—want the girl you're with.*

Or something like that.

Chapter 6

The following Wednesday night, Logan took the blonde, whose name was Louise, out to that steak house he liked in Kalispell. Louise was a nice woman. As it turned out, she worked in Kalispell, teaching high school English. But she had her own little house in Rust Creek Falls inherited from a beloved aunt. She loved dancing, she said, especially line dancing.

Logan sat across from her and listened to her talk and wondered what it was about her.

Or more correctly, what it *wasn't* about her. She was pretty and friendly, intelligent and sweet. There was nothing *not* to like.

Except, well, he just didn't feel it. *Want the one you're with*, huh? Maybe. In some cases.

For him and Louise, though? Not so much.

Still, he nodded and smiled at her and tried to make

all the right noises while his mind was filled with thoughts of Sarah.

She'd finished up at the ranch just that day. He wouldn't be seeing her again until tax time—except for now and then, the way people did in a small town. They would end up waving at each other as they passed on the street or maybe dropping by Buffalo Bart's Wings To Go at the same time.

"You're awfully quiet." Louise sent him another sweet, dimpled smile and sipped her white wine.

He was being a really bad date and he knew it. Sitting up a little straighter in his chair, he ordered his errant thoughts back to the here and now.

Later, when he took her home, Louise asked shyly, "Would you like to come in?"

He thanked her, said he had to be up before dawn and got the heck out of there.

Viv called him the next day. She said she'd talked to Louise, who'd reported that she really liked Logan but she just didn't feel that the "chemistry" was there. Logan had to agree.

He'd meant to tell Viv that he didn't need another date. But somehow, before he hung up, Viv had talked him into spending an evening with a girl named Genevieve Lawrence.

He and Genevieve met up on Friday night—in Kalispell again, at a cowboy bar she knew of. They danced and joked around. Genevieve knew ranch life and horses. She was a farrier by profession. They got along great, him and Genevieve.

But right away, Logan had that feeling, like she was his sister or something. He could be best buds with

Genevieve. But tangled sheets and hot nights with her to help him forget a certain amber-eyed accountant?

Never going to happen.

Plus, more than once between dances, Genevieve teased that he seemed like he was a million miles away.

And he kind of was. He was thinking of Sarah, and ordering himself to *stop* thinking of her. And then thinking of her anyway. Because dating other people didn't make him forget the woman he wanted. It just made him want her all the more.

At the end of that evening, Genevieve gave him a hug and whispered, "Whoever she is, don't be an idiot. Work it out with her."

It was great advice. Or it would have been, if only Sarah wanted to work it out with *him*.

When Viv called the next day, he explained that he really wasn't in the mood for dating. "So I won't be needing your, er, services anymore, thanks."

But evidently, Vivienne Dalton was downright determined to earn her million-dollar payout. Before he hung up, she'd convinced him to try a coffee date at Daisy's Donut Shop. "It's a half hour out of your life," promised Viv. "You get a coffee and a maple bar and if it goes nowhere, you're done."

Monday afternoon when Sarah dropped in at Falls Mountain Accounting, her mom was actually *not* behaving inappropriately behind the shut door of her father's office. Flo sat at her desk, her hair neatly combed, her shirt on straight. She was smiling, as she always did nowadays, typing away. The waiting area was empty.

"Hey, Mom."

Flo looked up from her desktop monitor with a welcoming smile. "Honey."

Sarah went on through to her own office and put the baby carrier, her backpack and laptop on her desk. In the carrier, Sophia was sleeping peacefully. Leaving the door open a crack so she would hear if the baby woke, Sarah returned to the main room, where her mom was now on the phone.

She picked up the stack of mail from the corner of Flo's desk and went through it, finding three envelopes addressed to her and setting the rest back down.

"Dad?" she asked as her mom hung up the phone.

Flo tipped her head toward Mack's shut door. "He's with a client."

"Okay, I'll be in my office if you—"

"Sweetheart." Her mom took off her black-framed reading glasses and dropped them on the desk. "I'm just going to ask."

Sarah had no idea what her mother could be getting at now. "Uh, sure. Ask."

"What went wrong between you and Logan Crawford?"

Just hearing his name hurt. Like a hard jab straight to the solar plexus.

"That face." Her mother made a circular gesture with her right hand, fingers spread wide. "That is not your happy face. Are you ever going to open up and talk to me?"

"I don't…" Her silly throat clutched and she hard-swallowed. "I really don't want to talk about Logan."

"Oh, yes, you do. You're stubborn, that's all. You always have been. But here's what I know. A week ago last Friday, Logan's pickup was parked in front of your house all night. Since then, well, *something* has gone wrong. The light has gone out of your eyes—don't argue. Your eyes are sad. They're full of woe. Then an hour ago, I drop by Daisy's for a cruller and a coffee and I see Logan sitting in the corner having donuts with some elegant-looking brunette. What *happened*, honey?"

"He was out with an elegant brunette?" God. That hurt so much—even though she knew very well she had no right at all to feel brokenhearted that he might be seeing someone else.

"Yes." Flo's tone had gentled. She gazed at Sarah with understanding now. "And yes, it was only coffee and a donut. I can't say beyond a shadow of a doubt that it absolutely was a date. But, well, sometimes a woman can just tell. You know?"

"No, Mom. I don't know."

"It's just that, the two of them together, well, there was a definite 'datish' feel about it."

"*Datish?* What does that even mean?"

"You *know* what I mean."

"I just said I didn't."

Flo waved her hand some more. "In any case, seeing your guy with another girl—"

"Mom, he is not my—"

"Yes, he is. If he wasn't your guy, you wouldn't be so crushed to learn that he had coffee with someone else." The phone rang.

"Aren't you going to get that?"

"Voice mail will get it. This is more important." They stared at each other through two more rings. As soon as the phone fell silent, Flo went right on. "Honey, I do understand your fears. You were always so sure of where you were going and how it would be for you. All your growing-up years, while your dad and I were stuck on a treadmill of unhappiness and emotional isolation, I just knew that for you, things would be different."

"You did?" Sarah felt misty-eyed that her mom had actually paid attention, had believed that Sarah would make a success of her life.

Flo nodded. "You had a plan and you were going to have it all—a high-powered job you loved, the right man at your side. And eventually, children to love and to cherish."

"Well, I do have Sophia, right? Things could be worse."

"But they could also be better, now, couldn't they? You haven't shared specific details with me, but here you are back at home, single with Sophia. It's patently obvious that things didn't work out according to your plan. You've been disappointed. Deeply so. But you can't just shut yourself off from your heart's desire because you've been let down a time or two. If you do that, you'll end up nothing short of dead inside. Take it from your mother who was dead inside herself for far too many years. Honey, you need to give that man a shot. If you don't, some other lucky girl is going to snap him right up."

That afternoon and through way too many hours of the night that followed, Sarah couldn't stop thinking about the things her mom had said.

In the morning, she had a nine o'clock appointment

with a client out in the valley not all that far from the Ambling A. The meeting took a little over an hour.

When she finished, she secured Sophia's seat in the back of her car, got in behind the wheel—and called Logan before she could think of all the reasons she shouldn't.

It rang twice. She was madly trying to decide whether to leave a message or just hang up when he answered. "Sarah?"

All he said was her name, but it was everything. Just to hear the slightly frantic edge to his always-smooth voice. As if he'd missed her. As if he was afraid she'd already hung up.

"Hey." Her mind went blank and her heart beat so fast she felt a little dizzy.

"Sarah." He said her name like it mattered. A whole lot.

And that gave her the courage to suggest a meeting. "I'm maybe five miles from the Ambling A and I was wondering if—"

"Yes. Meet me at the house. Come straight here."

She sucked in a deep breath and ordered her heart to slow the heck down. "Yeah?"

"I'll be waiting on the front porch."

Hope flaring in his chest and sweat running down his face, Logan stuck his phone back in his pocket. Luckily, he was within sprinting distance of the house.

"Gotta go." He jammed his pitchfork into the ground.

"What's up?" demanded Xander.

"Everything okay?" asked Hunter.

"Everything is great. Got a meeting with my favorite accountant," he called over his shoulder as he took off at a run, leaving Xander and Hunter staring after him, on their own to finish burning out the stopped-up ditch behind the main barn.

Entering the house through the back door, he hooked his hat on a peg, toed off his dirty boots and then headed for the utility room, where he stripped off his shirt and used the deep sink there to wash away the smoke and grime.

Clean from the belt up, he raced upstairs to grab a fresh shirt and a pair of boots free of mud and cow dung. He was just stepping out the door, tucking his shirt in as he went, when Sarah's white Honda pulled up in front.

She got out before he could get there to open her door for her. God, she looked good in snug jeans, boots tooled with twining flowers and a white shirt, her thick hair swept up in the usual bouncing ponytail.

He skidded to a stop a foot away as she pulled open the back door and bent to unhook Sophia's seat.

"Here. Let me take her."

"Ga! Ba!" The baby waved both fat fists and smiled that gorgeous toothless smile at him as Sarah passed him the carrier.

"It's really good to see you, too," he said to Sophia.

"Pffffft," the little girl replied and then laughed that adorable baby laugh of hers.

Sarah anchored her baby pack on one shoulder. "I was wondering if we could talk?"

He almost had a heart attack from sheer gladness right then and there. "Absolutely. Let's go to the office."

* * *

In the office, Logan put Sophia's carrier on the desk.

Sarah dropped her pack beside the carrier, opened the front flap and pulled out a teething toy to keep the baby busy for a little while. She offered the toy and Sophia took it.

Pulse racing and a nervous knot in her stomach, hardly knowing what she was going to say, Sarah turned to face the man she hadn't been able to stop thinking about.

How could such a hot guy just keep getting hotter? Surely that wasn't possible. Still, his eyes were bluer, even, than she remembered, his sexy mouth more tempting. His hair was wet, his shirt sticking to him a little, like he'd washed up quickly and hadn't really had time to dry himself off.

No doubt about it. He was, hands down, the best-looking man she'd ever seen. She wanted him so much. And she was so afraid it wouldn't work out.

But then he said, "Sarah," sweet and low and full of yearning.

The very same yearning she felt all through every part of her body.

And then he was reaching out. And she was reaching out.

She landed against his warm, hard chest with a tiny, hungry cry. His arms came around her and she tipped up her mouth to him.

His lips crashed down to meet hers. She sighed at that, at the perfection of being held by him, of having his mouth on hers. He smelled of soap and hay and something kind of smoky—and man. All man. So good. So right. So exactly what she needed.

She moaned low in her throat, her hands reaching, seeking, sliding over the hard, muscled planes of his chest and up to link around his neck.

He lifted his head, but only to slant that wonderful mouth the other way. His big hands roamed her back, pulling her closer, as though he could meld their two separate bodies into one.

And then from the doorway, a gravelly voice said, "Ahem. Hope I'm not interrupting."

With a gasp, Sarah broke the kiss.

She would have jumped back from Logan's embrace, except he didn't allow that. He cradled her close to him and said to his father, "Well, you *are* interrupting. Go away and close the door behind you."

"Aw, now." Max glanced down at his black boots and then up again with a rueful half smile. "I just need a minute or two."

"Whatever it is, it can wait."

"No, it can't. Come on, son. This won't take long."

Sarah felt awful and awkward and very unwelcome. It was disorienting—one minute swept away by the glory of a kiss and the next feeling somehow like an interloper in the Crawford house. "I should go."

Logan only held her tighter. "No way."

She couldn't stand this. Max in the doorway, refusing to leave them alone, Logan holding her too tightly, glaring at his dad.

"Really, Logan. Please. Let me go." She pushed more strongly at his chest and he finally released her.

Grabbing the baby carrier, she hitched the pack over her shoulder and turned for the door. Max stepped back. She swept past him and fled.

* * *

Max blocked the doorway again as soon as Sarah darted through it.

Logan barely held himself back from punching his own father right in the face. "Get out of my way, Dad."

Max didn't budge. "Now, son. You need to just let her go. She's not the one for you. She has a child and no man, which tells me things went bad with whoever that baby's daddy is. That's not a good sign. And beyond that, you never know. The father could show up any day now."

"You don't know what you're talking about. The father is out of the picture. Period. End of story."

"Well, whatever happened with the guy before you, I don't think I'm out of line in assuming it didn't end well. That means Sarah's been hurt and it won't be that easy to win her trust. I just don't get it. Why choose a woman with all that baggage? You're just asking for heartbreak."

Faintly, Logan heard the front door shut. "I don't know where you think you get off with this crap, but it's got to stop."

Max looked at him pleadingly. "Just give someone else a shot, that's all I'm saying."

"Pay attention, old man. Shut your mouth, open your eyes and use your ears for once. I've done it, let that wedding planner of yours set me up, gone out with the women she found for me. And you know what that's done for me? Not a thing—except to make me more certain that if there ever could be the one for me, Sarah's it."

"Now, that's not true."

"You're still not listening, Dad. It's a problem you have. Sarah is the one that I want. All your plotting and scheming isn't going to change that." Outside, he heard a car start up. He needed to go after her. "Move aside."

Max only braced his legs wide and folded his arms across his chest.

Fast losing patience, Logan made one more attempt to reason with the stubborn fool. "Okay. I get that whatever's eating you about Sarah is somehow related to what happened with Sheila way back when. You want to talk about that, fine, you talk about it. Just cut all the mystery and say right out what you're getting at. Because frankly, you're making no sense to me *or* to my brothers. For years, you've warned us off getting seriously involved with a woman. 'Have fun, boys,' you always said, 'but don't tie yourselves down.' And 'Marriage is like a walk in the park—Jurassic Park.'"

Max had the nerve to chuckle. "You have to admit, that was a good one."

"Not laughing." Logan glared at his father until Max's grin vanished. "What I want to know is why, out of the blue, you want all six of us married—just not with any woman who already has a child?"

"Think about it. It's not good for that baby, Logan. To get all attached to you and then to lose you. That's bad."

"Who says anyone's losing me?"

"You don't know what can happen."

"Nobody does. That's life. What I do know is that the way you just behaved with Sarah was rude. Unacceptable. Sarah's done nothing wrong and she's nothing like Sheila. Sarah would never turn her back on her own child the way Sheila did to us."

Max got the strangest look on his face. His straight shoulders slumped. All of a sudden, he looked every year of his age. "Maybe *I* did a few things wrong, too, you know? Maybe you and the other boys don't know the whole story of what happened with your mother."

"Maybe?" Logan got right up in his face over that one. "Dad, you are so far out of line, I don't know where to start with you."

"Son, I—"

"I'm not finished. If you haven't told us the whole story about Sheila, remedy that. Tell it. Do it now."

Max put up both hands and mumbled, "I'm only saying, if you really care about Sarah and her baby, you should do the right thing and walk away now."

"You're saying nothing and we both know it. And I am finished with listening to you tell me nothing. You keep that wedding planner off my back. You tell her I'm not going on any more dates with the women she's constantly calling to set me up with. I'm done dating women I don't want. I want Sarah. And right now, I'm going to do my level best to convince her to give me a real shot. Out of my way."

That time, Max didn't argue. He fell back and Logan headed for the door.

Outside, Logan found that Sarah's white CR-V was already long gone. At least he'd left his crew cab in front. He jumped in. Skidding and stirring up a mini-tornado's worth of dust, he headed for the highway.

He drove fast and recklessly all the way to town, not even knowing for sure if that was where she'd gone. It just seemed his best bet. If he didn't catch up with her, he would have to call her and he had a bad feeling that when he did, she wouldn't answer.

Damn the old man. This was all his fault. One minute, Logan had Sarah in his arms again and she was kissing him like she'd finally realized that she needed to give him a real, honest shot with her—and the next minute, his dad was there, acting like an ass, hinting of dark secrets, messing everything up.

If Max had ruined things for good with Sarah, there was going to be big trouble as soon as Logan got back to the ranch.

He rolled into Rust Creek Falls on Sawmill Street and slowed down a little—after all, this was his town now. He didn't want to run any of his neighbors down. Plus, it would be hard reaching out to Sarah if the sheriff locked him up in jail. He rolled along at a sedate pace and then had to choose his first destination—her house on Pine or Falls Mountain Accounting on North Broomtail.

He slowed down at Pine—but he just had a feeling she'd gone to her office, so he rolled on by that turn, taking North Broomtail instead.

And he scored.

She was parked in front of her office, the back door open, bending to get Sophia's carrier out when he pulled his pickup in next to her.

Glancing back over her shoulder, she spotted him. Rising to her height, she turned. He jumped out and they faced off over the open car door.

"Sarah, I'm so sorry about my dad. You can't listen to—"

She put a finger to her lips and spoke softly. "Sophia's asleep."

He lowered the volume. "We need to talk. You know we do."

"Oh, Logan. I really don't—"

"*You* called *me*. You know you want to talk this through. Give me a break here. Don't change your mind. I missed you so damn much. Admit you missed me, too."

Her soft mouth hardened. "Yeah. Right. You missed me so much you were going out with someone else."

"Sarah…"

"Shh." She glanced up the street as a couple of older ladies came toward them on the sidewalk. They smiled and waved. He watched as Sarah forced her lips into an upward curve and waved back. Logan waved, too.

The ladies strolled on by, bending their heads close to speak in low voices, glancing more than once at Sarah and Logan.

Finally, the ladies moved on down the street and Sarah said, "Really, I don't—"

"I don't want anyone else," he vowed before she could finish telling him no all over again. "I only went out with those other women because you dumped me."

She scowled. "Dumped you? We had one date. You can't dump a person after just one date."

"Okay, so *dump* is the wrong word. You didn't dump me. You only said you didn't want to be with me and you wouldn't go out with me again. Fair enough?"

"I…" Her sleek brows drew together. "Wait a minute. Other *women*? There was more than just one?"

She hadn't known there were three dates?

He could punch his own face about now—trying so hard to explain himself and just making it worse. "Look. I was miserable. Viv Dalton kept calling. After the first one, I knew I wasn't interested and I told Viv I wasn't. But that woman is really determined and I was just sad, missing you, wanting you and trying to forget you. Those three dates did nothing for me. They didn't help me forget you. How could they when all I did was think about you?"

She was softening. He could see it in those golden-brown eyes, in the way she looked at him. Intense. Reluctant—but expectant, too. "You, um, thought about me?"

"Only you. And I'm done. Finished with trying to forget you by wasting the time of nice women I'm not the least interested in."

"You are?"

"I am. I swear it to you—and I also promise that I'm not rushing you. I'm only hoping that maybe we could try again, take it slower, if you need it slower. Be… I don't know, be *friends*." He tried not to wince when he offered the friend zone. Being her friend wasn't going to satisfy him, no way. "Whatever you want. As long as we can see each other, be together, find out where this thing between us might go. That's all I want from you. It's all I'm asking."

Over the top of the open car door, Sarah stared at his impossibly handsome face.

Really, she didn't need any more convincing. He'd said he missed her, that he couldn't forget her. And she'd missed him, too. So very much.

No, she still didn't see him as the kind of guy who would sign on for forever with a single mom and her baby girl.

But the barriers between them were at least partly because of her. She was afraid to trust him. She'd had a little too much of men she couldn't count on and she was holding back, keeping him at a distance in order not to get hurt again.

But Logan was turning out to be so patient. He really did seem to want to be with her. He was kind and generous and he was crazy about Sophia.

Why not just go with it, for however long it lasted? So what if it didn't go on forever? Why shouldn't she just enjoy every minute she could have with him?

Sarah stepped back. His face fell in disappointment.

But then she pushed the door shut—not all the way. She left it open enough that she would hear if Sophia started fussing.

About then, Logan must have seen her decision in her eyes. "Sarah." He said her name low, with relief. And something bordering on joy.

She moved in close. He opened his arms. And she stepped right into them, laying her hands on his broad chest, feeling his heat and the beating of his strong heart under her palms. "I'm just…scared, you know?"

His eyes turned tender, soft as the summer sky. "I know. And that's okay. Just give me a chance, anyway. Give *us* a chance."

There was a giant lump in her throat. She swallowed it down. "Okay."

One corner of that fine mouth of his hitched up. "Okay…what?"

"Okay, let's give this thing between us a fighting chance."

"You mean it?"

"Yeah. Let's do this. Let's try."

"Sarah…"

For the longest, sweetest moment, they just stared at each other.

And then, at last, he gathered her close and he kissed her, a deep, dizzying, beautiful kiss. She let her hands glide up to encircle his neck and kissed him right back.

Someone was clapping behind her. Someone else whistled. Logan lifted his head and said, "Get lost, you kids."

She glanced over her shoulder in time to see a couple of local boys run off down the street in the same direction the two older ladies had gone.

"All right," he said, putting a finger under her chin and guiding her face back around so she met those fine blue eyes of his. "Where were we?"

She grinned up at him. "Tonight?" she asked.

"Where and when?"

"My house. Six o'clock."

Chapter 7

Sarah turned from Sophia's crib.

Logan was waiting in the open doorway.

He held out his hand. She went to him and he wrapped his arms loosely around her. "Well?" he whispered.

She put two fingers against his lips and mouthed, "Sound asleep."

He caught her hand. "Come on."

She turned off the light and silently shut the door behind them.

After one step, he stopped in the middle of her tiny hallway. "Wait."

She gazed up at him, confused. "What?"

"This." Pulling her close, he lowered his mouth to hers.

She giggled a little against his warm lips. And then

she sighed in dizzy pleasure as he kissed her more deeply. It felt so fine, so absolutely right, to be held in those lean, strong arms of his, to have his lips moving on hers, his tongue exploring her mouth in the most delicious way.

When he lifted his head and gazed down at her, she saw his desire in his eyes. Her bedroom was two steps away. And all at once, what would happen between them tonight was breathtakingly, scarily real. Her heart rate kicked up a notch. She could feel her pulse beating in her neck. He regarded her without wavering, his eyes full of promises, his mouth a little swollen from that beautiful, lingering kiss they'd just shared.

"I haven't, um, been with anyone," she said, every nerve in her body hyperactive, quivering. "Not since that conference in Denver when I got pregnant with Sophia."

He put his hands on her shoulders, so gently, in re-assurance. "You're not sure."

"I didn't say that."

He stroked his palms down her arms in a soothing caress. "How about we make popcorn, stream a movie or something?"

She stared up at him, studying him, memorizing him—the fine lines around his eyes, his square jaw, that mouth she couldn't wait to kiss again. His cheeks were smooth tonight, free of the usual sexy layer of scruff. It pleased her to picture him shaving, a towel wrapped around his lean waist, getting ready for his evening with her.

And her nerves? They were easing, settling. "Not a

chance." She offered a hand and he took it, weaving his fingers together with hers. "This way," she said.

In her bedroom, she turned the lamp on low. The baby monitor was already waiting in there, the screen dark until sound or movement activated it.

"So will it be that gray-blue or the bluish-green color?" He was staring at the paint colors she'd stroked on the white wall.

She stepped in close to him and got to work unbuttoning his dove-gray shirt. "I have to tell you, at this moment, paint colors don't interest me in the least."

Now he was looking directly at her again and it felt like just maybe he could see into her heart, see her tender, never-quite-realized hopes, her slightly tarnished dreams. "Gotcha." And he kissed her, another slow, deep one.

She sighed and melted into him, surrendering to the moment, letting him take the lead.

He claimed control so smoothly, easing her into the glory of right now, his lips moving against hers, his big hands skating over her, stroking her, quieting every worry. Banishing every fear.

She let him undress her. He did it slowly, with care, taking time to kiss her and touch her as he peeled away each separate item of clothing. Time kind of faded away, along with the last of her nervous fears. He laid her down on her bed and she gazed up at him, wondering at the perfection of this moment, the hazy, sweet beauty of it.

He took his phone from one pocket, a short chain of condoms from another and set them all on the night table by the lamp. After that, he took off his own clothes swiftly, revealing his body, so lean and sharply cut. Such a fine-looking man. Everywhere. In every way.

"Is this really happening?" she asked him when he came down to her.

"You'd better believe it." He pulled her close, skin to skin. "At last."

And he kissed her some more, kisses that managed both to soothe and excite her. He kissed her all over, whispering naughty things, his lips skimming down the side of her throat, pausing to press a deeper kiss in the curve where her neck met her shoulder, sucking at her skin in that tender spot, bringing the blood to the surface.

But not stopping there. Oh, no.

He went lower, lingering first at her breasts, making her moan for him, making her cry out his name.

Swept up in sensation, she forgot all about the ways her body had changed with pregnancy, the new softness at her belly, the white striations where her skin had made room for the baby within her—until he kissed them, brushing his lips over them, so sweet and slow. She lifted her head when he did that, blinking down at him, not really believing that any man would linger over stretch marks.

He glanced up and met her eyes. And he winked at her.

She laughed and let her head fall back against the pillow.

He continued his journey, dropping kisses on the crests of her hipbones, nibbling across her lower abdomen, eventually lifting her left thigh onto his shoulder so that he could slide underneath it and settle between her legs.

Intimate, arousing, perfect kisses followed. The man knew what he was doing. He invaded her most secret places.

And she let him. She welcomed him, opening her legs wider, reaching down to spear her fingers in his thick, short hair, urging him on, begging for more, losing herself to the sheer pleasure of his mouth, of the things that he did with those big, knowing hands of his.

She went over the edge, losing herself completely, crying out his name.

And he? Well, he just went on kissing her, touching her, stroking her, luring her right to the edge again…

And on over for the second time.

By then, she was vanquished in the best way possible, limp and so satisfied. She simply lay there, sighing, as he eased out from between her open thighs, rose to his knees above her and reached for a condom.

"Hey." His voice was low, a little raspy, teasing and coaxing.

"Hmm?" She managed a lazy smile.

"You okay?"

"Oh, Logan. Yes, I am. No, wait. On second thought, 'okay' doesn't even come close. I'm much better than okay. I'm excellent. Satisfied. Perfectly content. And ready for more." She lifted a lazy arm and reached out to him.

He took her fingers, bent closer and pressed those wonderful lips of his to the back of her hand. "That's what I wanted to hear." He let go of her to suit up, the beautiful muscles of his arms and chest flexing and bunching as he did so.

Then he braced his hands on the mattress on either side of her and lowered himself down to her, taking care not to put all his weight on her at once.

But she wanted that—all of him, pressing her down.

"Come here. Come closer." She took those broad, hard shoulders and pulled him down.

He gave in to her urging, settling on her carefully, taking her mouth again, kissing her slowly, tasting her own arousal, reminding her sharply of how much she wanted him, of his skill as a lover, which was absolutely stunning in the best sort of way.

She felt him, large and hard and ready. And she wanted him. All of him, with nothing held back.

Did she believe that her dreams would come true with him?

No.

Something had broken in her, after Tuck and then the disappointment of Mercer. It wasn't the men, really—how could it be? She hadn't understood Tuck at all. And Mercer, well, she hardly knew the guy.

No. It wasn't the men. It was about her, about her absolute belief in her plan for her future. She'd been so very sure she had it all figured out, that she wouldn't be like her parents, settling for a colorless, nothing life in her hometown. She would have everything—great success, true love and beautiful children in the big, exciting city, because she knew what she wanted and how to get it.

But what *had* she known, really?

Nothing, that's what. She'd gone forth in arrogance,

ready to conquer the world. And nothing had worked out the way she'd intended.

So no. She wasn't thinking she would get forever with Logan. She wasn't counting on anything.

For her, it was all about right now, here in her bed, with this beautiful man. Having him in her arms, wanting her, holding her.

This moment was what mattered. It was way more than enough.

He was right there, pressing, hot and insistent, where she wanted him so very much. She eased her thighs wider, wrapped her legs around him.

He groaned her name as he filled her.

"Yes," she answered. "Oh, Logan, yes…"

And then they were moving, rocking together and her mind was a white-hot blank of pure pleasure. He made it last for the longest, sweetest time. She clung to him, feeling her body rise again. When she hit the crest, she cried out at the sheer joy of it.

He followed soon after, holding her so tight.

For a while, they just lay there, arms and legs entangled, whispering together, reveling in afterglow.

As for what would happen next, what the future might bring, none of that mattered. For now, for tonight, she belonged to Logan.

And he was hers.

Thursday was the Fourth of July.

They had breakfast together at the cottage—Sarah, Sophia and Logan. He filled more pages of her notebook with sketches of Sarah at the stove flipping pancakes and then of Sophia in her bouncy seat, laughing and waving her little arms.

In the late afternoon, Sarah dressed her baby in red, white and blue, and the three of them joined their neighbors in Rust Creek Falls Park for a community barbecue. Sarah's parents were there and Lily was, too. They all sat together on a big blanket Sarah had brought. When it came time to eat, they shared a picnic table. Everybody wanted to hold the baby. Sophia loved the attention. She hardly fussed at all, even dropping off to sleep in her baby seat when she got tired.

Laura Crawford, Nate Crawford's mom, who was a fixture behind the counter at Crawford's General Store, stopped by to chat with Sarah's mom and dad. Sophia was awake again by then and Mrs. Crawford asked to hold her.

"She's such a good baby," the older woman said as Sophia grabbed her finger and tried to use it as a teething toy. Laura Crawford glanced at Logan. "And she has your eyes."

For a second, Sarah's skin felt too hot and her pulse started racing. She felt thoroughly dissed. Surely everyone in town knew that she was a single mom and that Logan Crawford—a relative of Laura's, after all—was not her baby daddy.

But Laura wasn't a mean person. Most likely, she just meant it in a teasing way, because Logan and Sophia both had blue eyes and Sarah and Logan were making no secret of their current coupled-up status.

And what did it matter what Laura Crawford actually thought? Sarah intended to enjoy every minute of her time with Logan. A random remark by Nate Crawford's mom wasn't going to make her feel bad about herself or her choices.

Clearly, Logan wasn't bothered in the least. He grinned at Laura. "You noticed," he said, at which point Sophia decided she wanted him to hold her.

"Ah, da!" the baby crowed, reaching out her arms to Logan, falling toward him.

Logan jumped up to catch her as Mrs. Crawford reluctantly let her go. Once he had Sophia safely in his arms, she patted his cheek and babbled out more happy nonsense.

A little later, Flo and Mack said they were going on home. Flo volunteered to take Sophia. "Stay for the dancing," she told Sarah. "You can pick the baby up on your way home. Or if it gets too late, she can just stay with us. Come get her first thing in the morning."

"Thanks, Mom." Really, it was nice. To have her mom and dad close by—especially her mom and dad the way they were now, happy and kind of easygoing, fun to be around. Sarah was even starting to get used to her mother's new frankness about sex and relationships. If Flo and Mack would just quit exploring their new sexual freedom at the office, Sarah would have zero complaints when it came to her parents.

She handed over all the baby paraphernalia and promised to come pick Sophia up by ten thirty that night.

"Or in the morning," her mom offered again. "That's fine, too."

As the band started tuning up, Sarah, Logan and Lily sat and chatted. Logan's brothers Xander and Wilder joined them. They all joked about Max and his scheme to get his boys married off.

Xander said to Logan, "At least Dad seems to be making progress with you."

Sarah sighed. Xander so didn't get it. Max wanted Logan married, yeah—just not to her. She looked away and reminded herself that she had no business feeling hurt.

So what if Max didn't consider her a good match for Logan? It wasn't like she was picking out china patterns and dreaming of monogramming her towels with a capital *C*. She and Logan were going to take it day by day and she was perfectly happy about that.

"Hey." Logan leaned in close.

She turned to him. "Hmm?"

And he kissed her, right there under the darkening sky in front of everyone on the Fourth of July in Rust Creek Falls Park. It was a quick kiss, but tender. And so very sweet.

Whatever happened, however it ended, she would remember this moment, sitting on the red, white and blue quilt her grandmother had made years and years ago, Logan's warm lips brushing hers in affection and reassurance.

"Hey, guys. What's up?" Genevieve Lawrence, in a yellow dress and cowboy boots, dropped down on the blanket next to Xander. She gave Logan's brother a radiant smile and then turned to Logan. "So, I see you took my advice."

Sarah didn't know Genevieve well, but she knew that the pretty, outgoing blonde was a true craftswoman, a farrier who trimmed and shod horses' hooves for a living. "What advice?"

Logan leaned close again. "Date number two," he whispered.

"Ah." She asked again, "What advice?"

Genevieve pretended to smooth her flared skirt. "It's all good, I promise." She wiggled her eyebrows at Sarah. "Make him tell you when you're alone."

Right then, the band launched into Lady Antebellum's "American Honey."

Genevieve turned to Xander. "How 'bout a dance?"

Xander jumped up, offered his hand and led the energetic blonde to the portable dance floor set up under the trees just as the party lights strung from branch to branch came on over their heads.

A moment later, another girl wandered over. Sarah vaguely recognized her, but couldn't recall her name.

Not that it mattered. The girl asked Wilder to dance and off they went.

Lily watched them go, a wistful look on her face.

Sarah slid a glance at Logan. Their eyes met and it was as though he'd read her mind.

"Want to dance, Lily?"

Lily smoothed her pulled-back hair. "You should dance with Sarah."

He only gazed at Lily steadily and asked again, "Dance with me?"

Sarah said, "Looks like he's not takin' no for an answer, Lil."

"Oh, you two." Lily waved her hand in front of her face.

But when Logan got up and held down his hand, she took it.

* * *

As they danced, Logan asked Sarah's friend about her job at Maverick Manor.

Lily said she loved to cook and she really wished she could get more hours. "But as of now, I'm part-time. Hey. At least it's something."

Cole and Viv Dalton danced by. Viv smiled at Logan.

He nodded in response and glanced down at Sarah's friend again. "So, have you joined Viv Dalton's dating service yet?"

Lily scoffed. "Yeah. Like that's gonna happen."

"Why not? I can personally vouch for each of my brothers. They can be troublesome and maybe a little rough around the edges, but they're all good at heart, not to mention good-looking. One of them could be the guy for you."

"Seems to me they've got plenty of women to choose from already."

"Give it a chance, Lily. What have you got to lose? If nothing else, you might have a good time."

She frowned up at him, but her eyes gleamed with wry humor. "Logan Crawford, you are much too persuasive."

"Just think about it."

She shrugged. "Sure. I'll do that."

Did he believe her? Not really. And that created the strangest urge in him to keep pushing her—because he liked her and she mattered to Sarah and he really did think it would be good for her, to get out there and mix it up a little.

On the other hand, it was none of his damn business whether Lily Hunt went out with one of his brothers or not. He'd said more than enough about the wedding planner's dating pool.

When the dance ended, he and Lily rejoined Sarah on the blanket. Hunter and Wren wandered over and sat down with them. Max stopped by. Logan prepared to get tough on his dad if he gave Sarah any grief. But Max was on his best behavior, greeting both Sarah and Lily in an easy, friendly way, going on about how great it was to spend Independence Day with the good citizens of his new hometown.

The band started playing another slow one. Logan leaned close to Sarah and breathed in her delicate scent. "Let's dance."

"Yes." Her eyes shone so bright and he was the happiest man in Montana, just to be spending his Fourth of July at her side.

She gave him her hand. They rose together.

Max got up, too. "I think I'll go check in with Viv and Cole. Great to meet you, Lily." He aimed a too-wide smile at Logan. "We need you out at the Ambling A good and early tomorrow."

"I'll be there."

"Fences to mend, cattle to tend," Max added in a jovial tone that set Logan's teeth on edge.

He always did his share of the work and Max knew it, too. Ignoring the temptation to mutter something sarcastic, Logan led Sarah to the dance floor, where he wrapped his arms around her and didn't let go through that song and the next and the next after that.

A little later, they rolled up her grandmother's quilt and wandered over to Rust Creek, which meandered through the center of town. The local merchants association had arranged for a fireworks display right there at creekside. Everyone sat around on the grass and watched the bright explosions light up the night sky.

It was after eleven when the fireworks show ended. Logan and Sarah strolled by her parents' house on the way to Sarah's place, just on the off-chance that her mom and dad might still be up. All the lights were off.

Sarah said it was fine. She would pick up Sophia in the morning. Holding hands, they strolled on to her cottage, where she hesitated before leading him up the front walk.

"I know you have to be up and working early," she said.

He had the quilt under one arm, but he pulled her close with the other hand. "Are you trying to get rid of me?"

She gazed up at him, her mouth so tempting, the moon reflected in her eyes. "No way."

"Good, then. I'll get up before dawn and sneak out. I promise not to wake you." He wrapped his free arm around her and claimed a quick, hard kiss.

Laughing softly, she led him up the walk.

Sarah woke at six fifteen the next morning.

Logan's side of the bed was empty. She slid her hand over there. The sheet was cool.

Longing warmed her belly and made her throat tight. Last night had been every bit as beautiful and fulfilling as the night before. He'd made love to her twice and she'd dropped off to sleep with a smile on her face.

Already, she was getting so attached to him. She

should probably claim a little space between them, let a few days go by at least, before seeing him again.

But then she got up and went into the kitchen and found a drawing of a weathered fence, a barn in the background and a sign hooked to the fence that read, *See you tonight. 6 o'clock. I'll bring takeout.*

And her plans to get some distance? Gone like morning mist at sunrise.

Grinning to herself, she grabbed her phone and texted him.

There had better not be candles or fine china involved in your takeout plans this time. She paused without sending and frowned at the text box before adding, You know what? Forget takeout. I'll fix us something. She hit Send, figuring it would be a while before he had a chance to check his phone.

Not so.

He came right back with, I'll stop at Daisy's and get dessert.

That evening, he arrived right on time carrying a bakery box full of red velvet cupcakes with cream cheese frosting. Then he kept Sophia busy while Sarah got the dinner on. When they sat down to eat, he held Sophia in his lap. With one hand, he helped her keep hold of her bottle. With the other, he ate his chicken and oven-roasted potatoes.

Once Sophia was in bed, he led Sarah straight to her bedroom. He removed her clothes and his, too, in record time and then did a series of truly wonderful things to her body.

Later, after she'd turned off the lamp, as she drifted toward sleep, feeling so safe and satisfied and peaceful, her head on his chest and those hard arms around her, he said, "You need to choose your paint colors. I talked to the guy at the paint store in Kalispell. I can order the paint and he'll send it over with a couple of professional painters. They'll get the job done the way you want it."

She didn't know whether she felt bulldozed or taken care of. "Logan, I don't want to spend my money on professional painters."

He smoothed a hand down her hair and pressed a kiss on the top of her head. "That's okay. I'm going to pay for the paint *and* the guys to do the painting."

She wiggled out of his grip, sat up and turned on the lamp. "No, you're not."

"Sarah," he chided gently. "Yes, it's true that now I spend my working days moving cattle and repairing farm equipment, but that's by choice."

"Back to the land and all that, huh?"

"Essentially, yeah. What I'm saying is I've got money to burn."

"Good for you, Mr. Moneybags. I don't."

"Exactly. So let me do this for you. Don't make a big issue of it."

"But it *is* an issue, Logan."

"It doesn't have to be."

She sat there and glared at him, more annoyed by the second. "How can you possibly be so wonderful and so pigheaded simultaneously?"

He pretended to give that some thought. "I'm getting the feeling the question is rhetorical."

"Let me make this achingly clear—no. You are not paying for the paint *or* the painters."

He studied her, his blue eyes narrowed. "You need

it done. I want to do it for you. This shouldn't be a problem."

"Listen carefully. Thank you for the offer, but I will do this my way."

He didn't answer immediately, which gave her hope that he had finally let it go. And then he reached out, slid his big, rough hand up under her hair and hooked it around the back of her neck. A gentle tug and she was pressed up against him.

She glanced up to meet his eyes. And his mouth came down on hers. He kissed her slowly. By the time he lifted his head again she was feeling all fluttery inside.

"So what's the compromise?" he asked. "How about a painting party?"

She reached over and turned off the light. They settled back down, her head on his chest. She traced a heart on his shoulder. "Hmm. A painting party…"

"You like that?" He sounded way too pleased with himself. "We could at least get a room or two painted, depending on how many people we could get and how long we all worked."

"When would this painting party occur?"

"A week from tomorrow—or sooner, depending on when everyone can come? We could make a list of victims—I mean, volunteers. We'll paint and then feed everybody. I'm thinking pizza and Wings To Go, soft drinks, beer and wine."

"I'll buy my own paint and supplies."

"Hey, you're the boss."

"Yes, I am and you shouldn't forget it."

"I'll bring the food and drinks," he said. She would

have argued, but he added, "Shh. Let me do that, at least."

"All right." She lifted up and kissed him. "Thank you."

The next day was Saturday. Well before dawn, she woke to an empty bed. But then a floorboard creaked and she saw him through the shadows. He was pulling on his jeans.

She sat up, flicked on the lamp and yawned. "Don't you take Saturday off?"

One shoulder lifted in a half shrug. "There's always work that needs doing around the Ambling A."

"You can't possibly be getting enough sleep."

He zipped his fly. A little thrill shivered through her when he looked up and met her eyes. Whatever this was between them, however long it lasted, it sure did feel good. "I set my own hours. Today, I'll only work until around three," he said, "and then I'll get a nap. I'm fine, believe me. I'll be back at six tonight."

She just sat there with the covers pulled up over her bare breasts, thinking he was the best-looking guy she'd ever seen. "I'll do something with the leftover chicken. I mean it, Logan. Don't bring anything. There are still some cupcakes left for dessert."

He'd picked up his shirt, but then he dropped it again and stalked to the bed. Spearing his fingers in her scrambled hair, he hauled her close and kissed her, a deep, slow kiss, morning breath be damned.

When he let her go, she laughed. She couldn't help it—really, she laughed a lot when he was around. "Did you hear what I said?"

"Every word."

Maybe. But that didn't mean he would do as she asked. "You are impossible."

"And you mean that in the *best* possible way, am I right?"

"Yeah, right." She admired the gorgeous musculature of his back as he returned to the chair and scooped up his shirt again. Then she frowned. "Hold on a minute."

He turned as he was slipping his arms in the sleeves and she was presented with that amazing sculpted chest and corrugated belly. "Yeah?"

"I just remembered. I usually try not to schedule appointments on the weekends, but I have a quarterly report to go over with a shoe store owner in Kalispell. We were supposed to meet yesterday, but he asked if I could move our meeting to today. It could go as late as six or six thirty."

"No problem. I'll wait."

"What? Like on the front porch?" That didn't seem right.

He dropped to the chair and pulled on a sock. "Sarah, it's not a big deal." He put on the other sock and reached for a boot.

"No. Really. There's an extra house key in that little green bowl on the entry table. Take it. Let yourself in if I'm not here when you arrive."

"That works." He pulled on the other boot and stood to button his shirt and tuck it in. Then he came to her again, tipped up her chin and gave her another sweet kiss. "Lie down. Go back to sleep." He waited for her to stretch out under the covers and then tucked them in around her.

"Drive carefully," she whispered.

"I will." He turned off the light.

She listened to his quiet footfalls as he left the room. A minute later, she heard the soft click of the lock as he went out the front door and then, very faintly, his crew cab starting up and driving away.

For a while, she lay awake, staring into the shadows, thinking how she didn't want to start depending on him, couldn't afford to get overly involved with him. She wasn't ready to go risking her heart again.

And yet, she'd gone and given him a key to her house.

Chapter 8

Logan worked alone that day setting posts to fence a pasture several miles from the ranch house. It was good, being out on his own. He got a lot done when there was no one else around to distract him with idle talk and suggestions about how this or that task should be done.

Being on his own also gave him time to think—about Sarah, about this thing they had going on between them.

When it came to Sarah, he didn't really know what exactly was happening to him.

There was just something about her. From the first moment he'd set eyes on her that day at the old train depot, he'd only wanted to get closer to her, get to know her better.

It wasn't like him. He adored women, but he'd always been careful not to get attached to any of them, not to let them worm their way into his heart.

There had been some hard lessons in his childhood and those lessons had stuck.

Logan was seven years old when his mom abandoned her family to run off with her lover. Max had said really cruel things about her then, called her rotten names. He'd told Logan and his brothers to get used to her being gone because she'd deserted them without a backward glance and she was never coming home. He'd said that a man couldn't trust any woman, and it was better for all his boys that they were learning that lesson early.

At the time, Logan refused to believe that he would never see his mom again. How could he believe it? Until she vanished from their lives without a hint of warning, Sheila had been a good mom, gentle and understanding, always there when he or his brothers needed her. For years, into his middle teens, he refused to lose faith in her basic goodness, in the devotion he just knew she felt to him and to his brothers. No matter what his dad said, he was waiting for her to return.

But she never did. She never so much as reached out. Not a letter or a phone call. Nothing. Radio silence. Year after year after year.

On his fifteenth birthday, when once again she didn't call or even send a card, he finally got it. He accepted the hard truth. Max was right. Sheila was gone for good and he needed to stop waiting for her to change her mind and return to her family.

That day—the day he turned fifteen—he finally accepted the lesson Max had tried so hard to teach him.

A guy needed to protect himself, because if you let her, a woman would rip your heart out and leave you with nothing, dead and empty inside.

By then, it didn't matter that logically he knew it was beyond wrong to blame all women because his mother had deserted her family. Logic didn't even figure into it. The lesson of self-protection had hardwired itself into his brain, wrapped itself like barbwire around his heart.

Of course, he knew that there had to be lots of women in the world who kept their promises and took care of their own above all. He just didn't see any reason to go looking for one of them. He liked life on his own.

And in the years that followed, Logan never allowed himself to get too close to anyone. He was more of an overnight meaningful relationship kind of guy, a guy who treated any woman he was with like a queen for as long as it lasted—which was never very long. He always made it clear to any woman who caught his eye that he wasn't a man she should pin her hopes on.

But with Sarah…

It was different with her from the first moment he saw her that day at the train depot. To him, there had seemed to be a glow around her. As though she had a light inside her, a beacon that drew him inexorably closer.

Part of her attraction at first was her very wariness with him. No need to protect himself when she was doing such a bang-up job of pushing him away.

She made it so clear that she didn't want anything from him, wouldn't accept anything from him and would never let him get too close to her. That deep reserve in her just made him want her more.

Because honestly, what man wouldn't want Sarah—with that slow-blooming smile of hers, those golden-brown eyes, that long, thick hair streaked with bronze, her softly rounded curves and her scent of flowers and elusive spice?

He'd been miserable when she ended it before it ever really got started. And then, when she admitted she wanted to try again, he'd been over the damn moon.

And now, this morning, she'd given him a key.

A key, damn it. That should have been enough to have him backing out the door with his hands up, shaking his head, apologizing for giving her the wrong idea. That should have had him drawing the line, saying no, absolutely not. He wasn't a man who ever took a woman's key.

Which reminded him. He'd never had "the talk" with her, never said that he really liked her but she needed to know he wasn't looking for anything serious.

He'd never had the talk and he wasn't going to have the talk. If he did that, he knew exactly what she would say—goodbye. The last thing Sarah needed was reminding that what they had wasn't permanent. She already knew that.

Better than he did.

No, with Sarah, goodbye didn't work for him. He wasn't anywhere near ready to walk away from her.

Did he expect it to last with her?

He kept telling himself he didn't.

But all that day as he set posts for new fences, he couldn't stop thinking about her, about that smile she had that lit up her whole face, about the way she cared for Sophia, always putting the baby first, taking her everywhere, managing to run a business with Sophia in tow. Maybe that was what made Sophia such a happy, trusting little thing. Maybe even a baby knew when she could count on her mother absolutely.

And what about the way Sarah didn't want him to give her things or do things for her?

Well, that only made him want to do more, to give her more. He was having a great time just coming up with new ways to make her life a little easier, to bring a smile to that pretty face of hers, to make her laugh, make her sigh. He had this weird dedication to Sarah *and* to Sophia, to their well-being, their happiness.

Was he in too deep?

Definitely.

Would she mess him over?

God, he hoped not.

Because somehow, with Sarah, he seemed to have misplaced his hard-earned instinct for self-preservation.

Sarah didn't get home that night until ten minutes of seven. Logan's pickup was already there, parked at the curb. She turned into her narrow driveway and got out to open the door of the cottage's detached garage. But before she could do that, Logan emerged from the house.

"I'll get it," he called and jogged across her small plot of lawn to open the door for her.

She got back in behind the wheel and parked in the dim little space. Logan went around and got Sophia in her carrier out of the back seat as Sarah grabbed the diaper bag and tote and got out, too. He shut the garage door and they walked across the lawn and up the front steps together.

At the front door, he reached out and put his hand on her arm. "Before we go in…"

Warmth filled her, just from that simple touch. She slanted him a sideways look as Sophia let out a joyful crow of baby laughter, followed by a gleeful, "Ah, da, na!"

He glanced down at her and grinned. "I'm happy to see you, too, Soph. It's been hours."

The man was a menace—to her heart and her emotional equilibrium. Really, she needed to talk to him, tell him to be a little less wonderful, please. "Before we go in, what?" she asked. His blue gaze lifted to meet hers. Now he looked…guilty, maybe? Or at least marginally apprehensive. "What did you do, Logan?"

He made a throat-clearing sound and took his free hand from her arm to rub the back of his neck. "Well, it's like this…"

She tried really hard not to grin. Because she *shouldn't* be grinning. He'd done something he knew he probably shouldn't do, something that she would have vetoed if only he'd asked her first.

How did she know that? She had no idea. Just, sometimes, she could read him simply by looking at his face.

She forced a stern expression. "I'd better not find my house painted when I go inside."

Another happy giggle from Sophia. And from Logan, "Whoa." Now he looked hurt. "I wouldn't do that. We already agreed about that."

"Okay…" She spoke the word on a rising inflection and waited for him to explain himself.

"Well, see, it was like this. As I'm on my way back to town this afternoon, I see this kid by the side of the road, a little towheaded kid in busted out jeans and a straw hat. He's sitting in a folding chair with this big cardboard box beside him and a sign that says, Kittens Free to Good Home."

She knew what he'd done then. "Logan, tell me you didn't."

He put up his free hand and patted the air with it. "Look, if you don't like her, I'll take her to the ranch, okay?"

"It's a female kitten is what you're saying and it is in my house right now."

"See, Wren might want her. Or I'll keep her for myself if I have to."

"All these options you have for where you might have taken her. And yet, you brought her here."

"Yeah. But first, I stopped at the vet. I got lucky and they were still open. I bought everything she'll need. Food and bowls, litter, a litter box, a scooper thing, a scratching post, a few toys and a bed. The kid who gave her to me said she's ten weeks old and hasn't had any shots. So I had the vet give them to her—along with a checkup. She's a healthy little girl, no sign of fleas. And she'll need her next shots in three to four weeks."

"Thought of everything, did you?"

"Sarah." He'd adopted his most reasonable, placating tone. "Don't be mad, okay? I meant what I said. I don't expect you to keep her."

For some reason, she wanted to burst out laughing.

He looked so worried and she was having way too much fun giving him a hard time about this.

And as for the kitten, the last thing she needed was another baby to care for. However...

"When I was a kid, I always wanted a cat," she heard herself saying.

His eyes went soft as the midsummer sky. "You did?"

"My parents didn't allow pets. As I mentioned that first day in the office at the Ambling A, my parents were different back then. But I'm not saying I'll keep her."

He put his hand to his heart. "What did I tell you? If you don't want her, I'll take her with me tomorrow when I go."

So then, he was staying overnight again? She had no urge to argue about that. In fact, she was glad. Probably gladder than she should let herself be. "Does this kitten have a name?"

"Not yet. I figured you would want to name her yourself—I mean, if you decide to keep her."

"How thoughtful of you."

Now he grinned. "Knock it off with the sarcasm. You just admitted you like cats. And I'm telling you, you're not going to be able to resist this one." And with that, he pushed open the door and signaled her in ahead of him.

She saw the tiny kitten immediately. All white, with a perfect pink nose and ears, and the prettiest, blue-opal eyes, she sat beneath the dining area table. "Oh, my God," Sarah heard herself whisper. "She's adorable."

Those gorgeous, wide eyes regarded her from that perfect little face.

Setting her laptop on the coffee table and letting the diaper bag slide to the carpet, Sarah dropped to a crouch. "Hey there." She held out her hand. "Come here, you little angel. Come on…"

The kitten dipped her head to the side, considering. "Reow?" she said as though asking a question, but she didn't budge.

"Such a pretty girl." She coaxed, "Come on, come here…"

That did it. The kitten stood. Delicately, she stretched her front legs and widened her paws. White whiskers twitching, she yawned. And then finally, after a few extra seconds of ladylike hesitation, she strutted out from under the table. White tail high, she paraded across the dining room and straight for Sarah, stopping when she reached her to delicately sniff her outstretched fingers.

Sarah waited until the kitten dropped to her butt again before daring to reach out. The kitten was already purring. Sarah pulled her close. Cradling the little snowball against her heart, she stood.

From behind her, Logan chuckled. "So then, what's her name?"

"Opal," she said without turning, bending her head to nuzzle the kitten's wonderfully soft fur. "Opal, for those eyes."

"Thank you for Opal," Sarah said. It was a little past eleven that night. They were tucked up in bed together and had been for a couple of beautiful hours. Earlier, after sharing dinner, they'd made the calls to set up the painting party for next week. Sophia had been asleep since eight or so. With any luck, she wouldn't wake up until daylight.

As for the kitten in question, Opal was sleeping in her new bed in the laundry room with the litter box close by. Sarah had wanted to bring her to bed with them, but the vet had advised Logan that she should sleep in her own bed with easy access to her litter box until she got a little older.

Logan chuckled. The sound was a lovely rumble beneath Sarah's left ear because she was using his warm, hard chest for a pillow. "I knew you would want her." He eased his fingers into her hair and idly combed it outward over her shoulders and down her back. "And I've been thinking…"

She stacked her hands on his chest and rested her chin on them. "Uh-oh. What now?"

"You need an electric garage-door opener."

She lifted up enough to plant a kiss on his square, beard-scruffy jaw. "No, I do not."

"Yeah, you really do. And when winter comes, you know you'll thank me. You don't need to be staggering around on your icy driveway trying to get the garage door up."

"There will be staggering whether I have an electric opener or not. I still have to make it from the garage to the house."

"Right." He was frowning. "And you'll be carrying Sophia and a laptop in that giant bag of yours—and that diaper bag, too. It's too dangerous."

"Logan, let it be."

"A side door to the garage and an enclosed breeze-way leading around to the back door would fix the problem. No matter how bad the weather gets, you and Sophia would be safe and protected."

"That's a major project, Logan."

"Just let me deal with it. It's not that big a thing."

It *was* a big thing. Really, he was relentless—and in the most wonderful way. "Stop. I mean it. Let it go."

He guided a lock of hair back over her shoulder with a slow, gentle touch. "Think about it."

She needed to change the subject, fast. And she knew exactly how to do it. They'd already made love twice.

Time to go for number three.

Lifting up again, she pressed her lips to his. He let out a low growl of pleasure as he opened for her. She eased her tongue in, sliding it slowly against his.

His arms banded around her, so hot and hard. "You're trying to distract me," he grumbled.

She caught his lower lip between her teeth and worried it a little. "Yes, I am. Is it working?"

"I still want you to have that garage-door opener." His voice was rough now, his breathing just a tad ragged.

She slid her hand down between them and encircled his hard length. He groaned aloud and she asked in a teasing purr, "Do I have your attention, Logan?"

He released a hard breath. "Sarah…" A harsh word escaped him.

"No. Garage. Door. Opener," she instructed, low and firmly, making each word a sentence. "Got that?"

"I do, yeah." Another groan escaped him. "I definitely do."

"Good, then." She captured his mouth as she stroked him, holding on tight, increasing the pressure, working her hand up and down on him—until he turned the tables, wrapping an arm around her and deftly flipping her over so that she was beneath him. He levered up and reached for a condom.

A moment later, she held him within her, all the way. She stared up into his blue, blue eyes, feeling cherished. Happy. And so very aroused.

When he started to move, she forgot everything but the pleasure of the moment.

Who knew what would happen as the days went by? She didn't know and she really didn't care.

It didn't work to count on a man, not for her. She'd learned that the hard way.

So she wasn't counting on him. She was simply enjoying herself, having the best time, just being with him, being Sarah and Logan, together, for right now.

Sunday, Sarah had no appointments and Logan decided to take a day off.

He stayed for breakfast. Then he herded her and Sophia to his crew cab and drove them to Kalispell, where the paint store he'd chosen opened at ten.

They bought paint and painting supplies. He convinced her to go ahead and buy the paint for all the rooms, even though they would only be tackling Sophia's room and the kitchen during the painting party next week. The bill for all that was pretty steep, but she really did want to get it done.

Of course, he had to offer, "Change your mind. Let me take care of it." She just shook her head and handed the paint store guy her credit card.

Logan wanted to take them out to lunch, but Sophia was a little fussy and Sarah kind of wanted to get back and see how Opal was doing. They bought takeout from a Chinese place they both liked and returned to Rust Creek Falls. After lunch, while Sophia was napping, he suggested they paint one of the rooms.

She cast an anxious eye at the cans of paint and supplies taking up most of the space in her dining room. "I know nothing about painting and the more I think about it, the more I kind of have a bad feeling about this."

He reacted with an easy shrug. "Well, great. I'll call in the professionals."

"Don't even go there." She sent him her sternest frown. "We've been through that more than once and it's not happening."

"So, then, we paint."

"Ugh. You are way too upbeat about this."

He hooked an arm around her and gave her an encouraging squeeze. "Piece of cake, I promise you."

"Oh, like you're some kind of expert?"

"Well, I worked for a house painter part-time during college to earn extra cash and when I first got to Seattle, I flipped houses. To save money, I painted the interiors myself."

She gaped up at him. "It's kind of not fair how much you know about a bunch of random things."

"I'm a Renaissance man, no doubt about it." He kissed the tip of her nose. "Look. You said you don't need to do the ceilings or the trim, right?"

"Yeah. The white ceilings are fine. And the cream-colored trim still looks fresh. I think my mom said they had the place painted a couple of years back."

"So, it's going to be easy." He gave her a thoroughly self-confident smirk.

"You say that with such conviction."

"Because it's true. The trim takes the longest and we're not doing the trim."

"I'm kind of worried we don't have enough tape."

"No problem. We won't need to tape."

"That's crazy. We'll get paint on the trim."

"No, we won't. You can do the rolling and I'll use a brush to cut in—meaning frame everything out, do all the parts that are too tight for a roller..."

"But—"

"Shh. No buts. I've done a lot of cutting-in and I won't get paint on your trim."

He seemed so confident, she agreed to do it his way.

Lily showed up just after they'd finished pushing the living and dining room furniture away from the walls and covering everything with plastic drop cloths.

"I'm going to help," Lily declared. "I'll just run home and change." In no time, she was back wearing worn jeans and a frayed T-shirt. Logan gave her a quick lesson in how to use a roller and she went to work.

Then Sarah's mom showed up with a plastic container full of sugar cookies. They took a cookie break. Sophia woke up and started fussing, so Flo went and got her, fed her and changed her—and then stuck around to watch her and to keep Opal out of the paint trays.

At some point, Flo called a couple of her friends and

Sarah's dad, too. They all came over to pitch in. As it turned out, Sarah's dad and one of Flo's friends both had painting experience. They joined Logan to do the detail work. The rest of them used the rollers.

By seven that night, they'd finished the living room, the dining room, Sarah's room, the hallway and the bath—everything but the two rooms slated for next Saturday's painting party. They even cleaned up, washing rollers and brushes, removing drop cloths and putting all the furniture back where it belonged.

Sarah's mom invited everyone to her house for slow-cooker pot roast. As a group, they walked over to Flo and Mack's house, with Flo pushing Sophia in her stroller.

On arrival, Flo served them all pot roast, with home-made ice cream for dessert. Sarah found it weirdly disorienting, eating dinner in her mother's dining room, everybody chattering and laughing, having a great time. It was so unlike the way things used to be when she was growing up.

That night, after Sophia was in bed, Sarah and Logan streamed a Western on her laptop. Opal joined them on the sofa, snuggling in close to Sarah. The room, now a soothing gray-green, looked amazing. Sarah spent more time staring around her in wonderment than she did watching the movie.

"I think you like the new paint," Logan said as the credits started rolling. She leaned forward to shut down the laptop on the coffee table in front of them. When she sat back, Logan wrapped his arm around her.

"I loved everything about today," she said with a sigh. Opal was curled up next to her in a fluffy white ball, sound asleep. Sarah scratched her head gently, simply to hear her purr. "It was so nice how everybody just showed up—and then stayed to help get the job done. It was really so sweet of them."

"That's the deal around here, right? Everyone pitching in, helping out."

"Yeah. I love that about Rust Creek Falls—but it was strange at my parents' today."

His arm around her tightened as he pulled her a little closer. "Why strange?"

"Well, it's just that when I was growing up, we hardly ever had people over. And the house was always deadly quiet. I felt so lonely. But now, today, everyone was talking over each other, laughing, having a great old time. My mom and dad looked so happy. Sometimes now, when I'm around them, I feel like I've dropped into an alternate universe. They aren't the Flo and Mack I used to know."

"But it's a good thing, isn't it, the way they've changed?"

She took his hand and laced their fingers together. "Yeah. It's definitely a good thing. I could really get used to this, to the way they are now. I feel...kind of close to them. And I love how they have my back now. I believe I can count on them now. Plus, I'm starting to look forward to being here for them as they're growing older." She leaned her head on his shoulder. "I mean, I dreaded coming home partly because I felt that I never had any real relationship with my parents. It was depressing just being around them, trying to do simple things like have an actual conversation with them. They were so closed-off and set in their ways.

But since I've been back—well, you saw how they are with each other now."

He chuckled. "Yeah, no intimacy issues between Flo and Mack."

"Not anymore, that's for sure. It took some getting used to. But now, well, that's who they are and they're happy together. And I'm starting to be really glad about that."

He tugged on a lock of her hair. "So it's all working out."

"A lot better than I expected, yeah."

"Now, all you need is a decent TV."

She groaned and elbowed him in the side. "Don't even go there."

But he just kept on. "I'm thinking at least fifty inches. Flat screens are a steal lately. I can get one for practically nothing."

The guy was incorrigible. She leaned into him and kissed his cheek. "No. That is not happening."

He held her gaze. "I'm here all the time and I like being here."

"I like having you here."

"I also like big screens." He said it longingly.

She shouldn't let herself weaken. He did way too much for her already. But he was looking at her so wistfully, like Opal when she wanted her Fancy Feast. "It's a small living room," she said and then wanted to clap her hand over her mouth the minute she added, "Fifty inches is just too big."

One of his eyebrows inched toward his hairline. She'd just opened the door to a negotiation and he knew it, too. She could tell by that gleeful gleam in his eye.

"Forty-three inches, then. That's thirty-seven and a half inches wide and just over twenty-one inches high."

She tried her best stern look—not that it ever did a bit of good with him. "I see you have all the stats on the fancy TVs."

"You know I do, baby. We can put it in that corner." He pointed at the arch to the dining area, on the right side nearest the hallway to the bedrooms. "It won't overwhelm the space, I promise you."

She was weakening. Because, really, why shouldn't he buy a nice TV? He said that money was no problem for him and she believed him. And if things didn't last between them, she could just insist that he take it back, keep it for himself.

If things didn't last...

She probably shouldn't let herself think that way. They had something special together and she was so happy.

But you just never knew in life. The whole point with her and Logan was to enjoy each other, take it one day at a time together.

He caught her chin and turned her face so that she met his eyes again. "Okay. What happened?"

"Nothing. Really."

"I was about to convince you we need to *compromise* and get a forty-three-inch TV and you suddenly got sad on me."

The man was way too perceptive. As a rule, she loved that about him. Except when he picked up on stuff there was no point in getting into.

She leaned in and kissed him, quick and hard. "I mean it. It's nothing—and okay."

His eyebrow rose again. "Okay, what?"

"Forty-three inches and not a fraction more."

He leaned even closer. His rough cheek touched her smooth one and his warm breath teased her ear. "Now, that's what I wanted to hear. Let's put Opal to bed."

"And then what?"

"I'm thinking that first we need a long, relaxing bath…"

They shared the bathtub and helped each other scrub off all the random dried paint spatters. Then they did other things. Sexy things.

By the time they were through in the tub, there was water all over the bathroom floor. They used their bath towels to mop it up.

And then they went to bed—and right to sleep for the first time since he started spending his nights at her place. He wrapped himself around her, his front to her back. She smiled in contentment and closed her eyes…

And when she woke in the morning, he was already gone.

In the kitchen she found more sketches and a note.

I'll be back by three. I'll bring dinner—don't argue. Just takeout, I promise. And don't try to tell me it's too far to go for takeout. I'm going to Kalispell anyway. Hint: it's 43 inches and it has your name on it.

That night he set up the new TV. He'd even bought surround-sound speakers. She accused him of being extravagant.

"You're going to love it." He grabbed her hand,

pulled her down into his lap and nuzzled her neck. "Now, how 'bout some popcorn?"

She popped up a big bowl of it and they watched a heist movie.

Later, in bed, he was playful, tender and demanding. Really, it was so good with him. Everything. All of it. The sex, definitely. But all the other stuff, too.

He was always looking for ways to please her, to help her, to make her life better somehow. And she liked just being with him, talking about nothing in particular. Or not even talking at all.

And Opal. That he'd given her Opal, well, that meant so much to her. The kitten was healthy, smart, affectionate and just too cute. It was as if he'd found that special something she hadn't even known she longed for, a childhood wish never realized and destined to remain unfulfilled.

Until now. Because of him.

He was so good with Sophia. Her daughter adored him.

That could be difficult if they broke up. Or was Sophia too young to miss him?

Yet again, she reminded herself not to think that way. No way was Logan considering breaking up with her any time soon. He was always saying how happy he was with her, how crazy he was for Sophia. And he proved the truth of his words in action every day. No, it probably wouldn't last forever, what Sarah had with him. But nothing ever did.

Life in Rust Creek Falls was turning out to be pretty good for her and her baby. And she needed to keep looking on the bright side of things.

The bright side most definitely included her relationship with Logan Crawford. She promised herself she would keep that firmly in mind, not let the hard lessons she'd learned from past disappointments ruin a really good thing.

For as long as it lasted, she would love every minute.

Chapter 9

That Wednesday, Logan asked her to come on out to the ranch for a picnic dinner. Her last appointment ended early, so she arrived sooner than she'd said she would, at a little after five.

With Sophia asleep in her carrier on one arm and the always-present diaper bag slung on her other shoulder, she went up the front steps.

The door opened before she reached it.

"The lovely Sarah," said Max. "And her cute little baby." He stepped back and ushered her in.

"Where's Logan?" Sarah asked as Max shut the door behind her.

"He'll be down in a minute. Here, let me help you with that." He took the diaper bag off her shoulder and hung it on the coatrack, then he swept out a hand toward the arch that led to the living room. "Come on in. Have a seat."

She didn't trust him. But she couldn't run for cover every time Logan's dad glanced her way.

Head high, expression serene, Sarah went into the living room and took a seat on the leather sofa. She set the carrier on the cushion beside her.

Max took the big easy chair across from her. "I'm glad to have a moment with you, a little time to talk." He smiled that charming smile of his, but his eyes were cool. Calculating.

She sat up a little straighter. "Look, Max, I don't know what you're leading up to here, but—"

He cut her off with a wave of his hand. "It's simple, really. I just want to, er, touch base."

"Let me be blunt. You and I have nothing to talk about. But if you insist, I think it would better if we included Logan in whatever you're about to discuss with me."

"Now, Sarah, this is not a discussion. I only want to remind you that Logan is thirty-three and has never had a serious relationship. He's a bad bet. And for you, with a baby to think of, well, you have to see that it's unwise for you to get involved with him."

Okay, it was just possible that, given her own not-so-stellar experience with men and romance, she actually kind of agreed with Logan's dad—she'd even said as much to Lily that night at Maverick Manor. But her doubts about Logan were for her to deal with in her own mind and heart. She and Logan had an understanding. They wanted to be together for right now and that was working out beautifully for them. Max Crawford had no right to try to make her choices for her.

True, in the past, it had hurt her that Logan's dad seemed to view her as unsuitable for his oldest son simply because she had a baby. Up till now, she'd just wanted to escape, run away like a hurt child, when he treated her unkindly.

But this was becoming ridiculous. It was time she stood up to him.

Drawing her shoulders back, she folded her hands in her lap and said pleasantly, "So you're saying that Logan is a bad bet for me, but *not* for those other women you had Viv set him up with?"

Max blinked in surprise. Apparently, he hadn't expected a rational argument from her. "Ahem. You don't understand, Sarah."

"That's because you really aren't making any sense, Max."

"It's, um, for your own good and the good of your child. You should at least know the statistics on the situation."

He had statistics to convince her to walk away from Logan? Really? She asked politely, "What statistics?"

"Well, just that if a man of Logan's age hasn't been married or in a serious, committed relationship, his chances of ever getting married are very low—and if he does get married, it's not all that likely to be a marriage that lasts."

Did she believe him? Not one bit. "I have to tell you, Max. I think you just made up those 'statistics' to fit your weak argument. I mean, if Logan were over forty, yeah, I might agree. When a guy gets past forty and he's happily single, any woman could find herself wondering if he simply prefers the single life. That might make him a bad marriage bet. But a lot of men wait till their thirties to settle down, so in Logan's case, your argument doesn't apply—not that I'm hoping to settle down with Logan."

Max's eyes widened. "Er...you're not?"

"We enjoy each other's company and we're having a good time."

"I didn't, er, well..." Max was actually at a loss for words. It was a rare moment and Sarah let herself enjoy it.

"And also," she added, "if you really believe what you're telling me, that he's such a bad marriage bet, why set him up with some other poor girl when, according to your reasoning, he'll only break *her* heart in the end?"

Max hemmed and hawed. "Well, now, Sarah, I'm only trying to help you realize that—"

"What do you think you're doing, Dad?" Logan stood in the open arch to the entry hall. His hair was wet and his lean cheeks freshly shaved. The sight of him made Sarah's heart ache in the sweetest sort of way—and that ache scared her more than all of Max's disapproving glances, dire warnings and fake statistics.

Max jumped up. "Sarah and I were just having a little chat, that's all."

Logan came straight for her, stopping at the other end of the sofa. He gazed down at her with concern. "Whatever he said, don't believe a word of it."

Sophia spotted him then, gave a happy giggle and waved her hands. "Hey there, beautiful." He dropped to the sofa on the other side of the carrier and scooped her up against his broad chest.

"Ga, dah," she said and grabbed for his nose.

"Well." Max stared at the man and the baby. Sarah couldn't tell if he looked bemused—or crestfallen. "I'll leave you alone. Wonderful to see you, Sarah."

She forced a nod and a smile. "See you later, Max."

Logan shook his head as Max disappeared through the dining room and out the door to the kitchen. "What did he say?"

Sarah rose and picked up the empty carrier. "It doesn't matter."

"If he's upset you—"

"Logan, I'm not upset." It was true. She was pretty much over Max and his issues with her as a potential bride for his oldest son.

She *wasn't* a potential bride—not for Logan or anyone. And Max had done her no harm.

In fact, their little chat had been a good thing. It had served to remind her that she was single and planned on staying that way. She liked Logan—maybe too much. He was kind and so generous. He made her laugh and she loved being with him. And whenever he kissed her, she wanted him to kiss her again, to keep kissing her and touching her and doing all those wonderful things to her that made her feel desired and satisfied in all the best ways.

But he wouldn't break her heart. She wouldn't let him. What they had together was no lifetime commitment. She wasn't counting on anything. They were both having a wonderful time for as long as it lasted.

And, she promised herself, she was perfectly happy with that.

* * *

Logan kind of had a bad feeling about whatever had gone down between his dad and Sarah while he was in the shower.

But Sarah insisted it was nothing, so he didn't pressure her to share the gory details. Max wasn't going to change and if she'd come to grips with that and decided not to let the old man bother her, that was all to the good. He had plans for the afternoon and he felt relieved that his dad hadn't ruined Sarah's mood.

Logan had packed a simple picnic, with sandwiches, chips and dip, a bottle of wine and cookies from Daisy's for dessert. It was gorgeous out, with the temperature in the high seventies, not too much wind and the sky a pure, cloudless blue.

Sarah carried the basket of food. He took the baby, the diaper bag and the picnic blanket. They strolled along the dirt road past the barn and the horse pasture to a spot he'd chosen under the dappled shade of an old bur oak.

"It's pretty here," she remarked approvingly. They spread the blanket. He put Sophia down on it and Sarah gave her a toy to chew on. The baby made her happy nonsense sounds and stared up through the branches. She even managed to roll over and push up on her hands a couple of times.

He poured them wine in paper cups and they ate. When Sophia got fussy, Sarah gave her a bottle and they took turns helping her hold it. Sophia was getting better at controlling her own bottle every day, it seemed to him. She also had two teeth coming in on the bottom in front. He could see the white rims peeking out of her gums whenever she gave him one of her giant smiles.

Kids. Logan had never seen himself as a guy who wanted children—no more than he'd ever thought he might get married.

But now he'd met Sophia. And lately, kids seemed like a pretty good idea to him.

And marriage? Well, he was kind of changing his opinion on that, too. The more time he spent with Sarah, the more he started thinking that he wouldn't mind being married at all.

He even *wanted* to be married.

As long as he could claim Sarah as his bride.

He had that urge to go for it—right then and there. The urge to pop the question now, as they sat beneath the old oak eating their cookies, watching Sophia hold her own bottle. He wanted to grab Sarah's hand and tell her exactly how he felt about her, what he wanted with her. To say how good forever sounded as long as he could share it with her.

But then he tried to remember that she'd had a rough time of it, and she wasn't all that trusting when it came to the male species. He felt that he *knew* her, that he understood her in all the ways that really mattered. Sometimes, in the past few days, he kind of forgot that he hadn't known her all his life.

He had to keep reminding himself that they hadn't been together for any length of time at all— just a week and a day. No way that was long enough for her to come to trust him. Any sudden moves involving emotional intimacy could scare her right off.

He didn't blame her for being commitment-shy.

That guy she'd lived with, Tuck Evans, was just a stone idiot. Logan wouldn't mind meeting that fool out behind the local cowboy bar, the Ace in the Hole, and going a few rounds with him. Then he'd thank him for blowing it royally and giving Logan a chance to have Sarah for his own.

As for that Mercer dude, Logan wouldn't mind doing a lot worse than beating him up. That guy had cheated on his wife *and* turned his back on Sophia. There were no words bad enough for someone like that.

Their loss, my gain, Logan reminded himself.

"Got a little surprise for Sophia," he said, as they were packing up the remains of their picnic.

Sarah gave him the side-eye. "I get nervous when you talk like that."

He leaned toward her, pulling her close and claiming her sweet lips in a slow, lazy kiss. Sophia, on the blanket between them, giggled up at them and crowed, "Ah, da, ga!"

Logan ran the backs of his fingers down Sarah's velvety cheek. *This is happiness. Who knew?* "Come on. You're going to love it." He kissed her again, because once was never enough.

She picked up the baby. He pulled his phone from his pocket and zipped off a quick text to Xander.

Bring Petunia. Now.

"What was that about?" Sarah watched him suspiciously as he put on his hat, tossed the blanket over his shoulder and grabbed the empty carrier, the basket and the diaper bag.

"I told you. It's a surprise." He started back toward the house.

She straightened Sophia's little sun hat and fell in step beside him. "Okay, I know you're up to something and I know that it's something I'm not going to like."

He chuckled. "Now, what kind of attitude is that?"

"The attitude of a woman who's seen the way you operate, Logan Crawford."

"You've got it all wrong."

"You're trying to tell me you're *not* up to something?" She was just too cute.

He would have thrown an arm around her if he didn't have his hands full of all the stuff they'd carried out there. "No."

She frowned. "So you're admitting that you are up to something?"

"That's right, I am—and like I said, you're gonna love it."

Right then, Xander appeared from behind the barn leading a palomino pony.

Sarah could not believe her eyes. "Oh, you didn't."

Logan beamed. "He's a rescue. A Shetland. Just ten hands high, about eight years old with a really sweet disposition. I can't wait to see her ride him."

Sarah stopped in her tracks. "Her? You mean Sophia? Logan, she'll be six months old next week. That's way too young to be riding a pony."

He stopped, too. At least he had the grace to look a little sheepish now. "Okay. I know she's too young. What I meant to say was, I can't wait to see her ride him *when* she's old enough."

When she's old enough...

Those words just made it all worse somehow.

Sophia wouldn't be old enough to ride that pony for years.

Years.

Sarah couldn't take on the cost and commitment of caring for a pony in the hopes that someday her little girl might want to ride him. And she couldn't accept the pony as a gift for Sophia and expect Logan to keep him here at the Ambling A for her.

She and Logan, well, they didn't *have* years. That had been brought sharply home to her not two hours ago, thanks to Logan's own father. The point was to enjoy every moment, live completely in the now and not expect anything. Not to start making starry-eyed plans for some lovely, coupled-up future.

Sarah had spent her whole life looking ahead. She'd planned and schemed and set goals and kept her eyes on the prize of a great career, a successful marriage—kids eventually, after she made partner and could afford really good childcare.

And what had she gotten for all her "looking ahead"?

Nothing she'd planned on, that was for certain.

"Sarah." Logan dropped everything right there at his feet in the road. He stepped over the picnic basket and moved in close, pulling her and Sophia toward him, wrapping his strong arms around both of them.

With a long sigh, she let her body sway against him.

Oh, it felt good, so very good, to lean on him.

But she really couldn't afford to lean on a man, to get her hopes up that she could trust him, that she could count on him—and take the chance of having those hopes crushed to bits. She'd had her hopes crushed way more than enough already, thank you.

"Hey," he whispered. "It's okay. I promise. If you don't want her to ride Petunia, she won't ride Petunia." Snuggled in between the two of them, Sophia cooed in contentment. Logan tipped Sarah's chin up. "I get it. I do. I didn't mean to scare you. Petunia needed a home and so I took him and I couldn't help thinking that someday he might be just right for Sophia. But that's all. It was just a thought and it doesn't have to mean anything, I promise. It's nothing on you. *I* took the pony and I am responsible for him."

She sucked in a deep breath and her racing heart slowed down a little. Out of the corner of her eye, she saw Xander about twenty yards away. He'd stopped in his tracks. Smart man. The pony waited right behind him, patiently nibbling the weeds that grew in the center of the dirt road.

Logan pressed his forehead to hers. "You all right?"

"Yeah. I, um, overreacted. Somewhat. I guess."

He pulled back enough that their eyes could meet. "Somewhat?" One corner of that beautiful mouth lifted in a half smile that coaxed her to smile, too. "You freaked."

And then she did smile. "Yeah. I kind of did."

"But you're over that? You're okay?"

"I am, yeah." She thought how amazing he was. She wished she was someone else, someone still capable of really going for it, opening her heart, trusting that everything would work out all right in the end.

But she was just Sarah, strong enough to go on, yet cautious to a fault when it came to trusting a man again.

Even a wonderful man who seemed to want to give her the world.

"And I have to ask…"

"What?"

"Petunia?" she taunted. "Seriously?"

"Hey. He was already named. I didn't want him to suffer an identity crisis on top of everything else."

She knew she shouldn't ask. "So… Petunia has had a difficult past?"

"He had mud fever and cracked heels from being left out in the open in bad weather. The vet's receptionist found him wandering around in the park. No owner ever showed up to claim him."

"How did they know his name was Petunia?"

"He was wearing a frayed bridle with Petunia tooled into the cheekpiece."

"Poor guy."

"Yeah. Dr. Smith treated him. When no owner appeared to take him home, he was offered for sale."

"And you took him."

"I like a survivor. Petunia is my kind of guy." He skated a finger down the bridge of her nose as Sophia let out another of her happy sounds. "How about I introduce you?"

"Sure."

He let her go. She resisted the urge to huddle close a little longer, make him hold her and her baby some more. Xander started forward again, the stocky little pony following right along behind him.

When Xander reached them, Sarah passed Sophia to Logan and petted the pony. Petunia stood placidly as she stroked his nose. When she smoothed his thick mane, he gave a friendly nicker. He really did seem like an amiable creature.

Logan teased, "I think he's going to be so happy living in the backyard at your place."

She groaned. "Don't even kid about it."

"Your loss. Wren's already in love with him."

"Good. I'm sure she'll take wonderful care of him."

The pony was so gentle and easy-natured that Sarah gave in and let Logan set Sophia on his back just for a moment. Logan held the baby steady and Xander moved in close to the animal, taking the lead right up under Petunia's chin with one hand, soothing him with the other.

Sophia waved her fists and bounced in Logan's hold, trusting completely the strong hands that supported her. Sarah might have choked up just a little at the sight. She bent and dug her phone out of the front pocket of the diaper bag and snapped a couple of pictures. What proud mama wouldn't?

Leaning close as he handed Sophia back to her, Logan whispered, "What'd I tell you? Sophia loves her new pony."

Her heart just melted. She gazed up at him adoringly and let herself imagine that they would stay together, that one of her baby's first words would be *Dada*, and when Sophia said it, she would be reaching for Logan.

For a brief and beautiful moment, Sarah knew it would happen.

But really, who was she kidding? Life was a challenge and things didn't always work out as a woman hoped they might.

She wouldn't start counting on anything. Expecting a magical happily-ever-after just wasn't wise.

* * *

Saturday was the painting party.

Logan and Sarah welcomed the same crew as the week before, and also two of Logan's brothers, Knox and Hunter. Hunter brought Wren, who was a sweet girly-girl. She carried Opal around with her and spent a lot of time with Sophia, handing her teething toys, thrilled to get a chance to give her a bottle.

With only two rooms to paint, they were finished in the early afternoon. After cleanup, everyone hung around to eat the wings and pizza Logan had ordered and wandered out to sit on the front porch or to gather under the big tree in the back.

Logan loved watching Sarah play hostess. She was so conscientious. She made sure to visit with everyone, to thank them for coming, to tell them how much she appreciated the help.

Once all the guests had left, he and Sarah straightened up the place and put the dishes in the dishwasher. Sophia was already asleep in her freshly painted room, which had been tackled first so it would have plenty of time to dry before her bedtime.

He and Sarah went to bed early and made slow, tender love.

Later, he held her as she slept and thought about all the things he wanted to say to her. He wanted to talk with her about the future—*their* future.

About where they might go, as a couple, from here.

No, they hadn't been together for that long. And she was skittish about making any real plans with him. He had a feeling his best move was *no* move, that he should just let her be for a while, enjoy this time with her, give her the space to come to fully trust him on her own.

But damn it, life was too short. Why waste a moment being cautious and careful when he knew what he wanted, when he was certain that, deep in her heart, she wanted the same thing?

Yeah, all right. She'd been disappointed more than once. He got that. But he hadn't disappointed her so far, now had he? And he *wouldn't* disappoint her. He would be there for her and for Sophia. Whatever happened, she could depend on him, through the good times and the bad. He aimed to prove that to her.

Yeah, it was a little crazy, how gone he was on her. But he knew what he had with her. He didn't question it. He knew it was real. After all the years of never letting himself get too close to anyone, he finally wanted it all. With Sarah.

It kind of scared him how important she'd become to him—both her and Sophia—and so swiftly, too. But being scared didn't bother him. He found fear exhilarating. He would bust right through it, overcome it to claim what he wanted.

Sarah, though, held back. She guarded her heart. She just couldn't let herself trust him, not in the deepest way.

And he wanted everything with her. He wanted it now, wanted to break through the barriers she put up to protect herself, and show her she didn't need protection—not against him.

She stirred in his embrace.

He smoothed her tangled hair, wrapped his arms a little closer around her. She settled.

And he started thinking that hanging back, waiting

for her to decide it was okay to trust him, was no solution. Action was called for.

He needed to make a real move. The move had to make a clear statement of his intent, of his purpose, of what he held for her in his heart. He needed to prove to her that he wasn't going anywhere. To show her that she was his and he was hers, and she didn't need to be afraid anymore.

He pulled the covers a little closer around them and closed his eyes. As sleep crept up on him, he smiled to himself.

It was really so simple. He knew what to do.

Chapter 10

"Sarah?" her mom called as she came in the door of Falls Mountain Accounting early Monday morning.

"Be right there." She glanced down at Sophia, who was sound asleep in the carrier. The baby didn't stir. Sarah hurried into her office, put the carrier on the desk, set her laptop beside it and then let the diaper bag slide to the floor.

She went on to her dad's office, where her father leaned back in his leather swivel chair, looking happy and relaxed in a way he never had while she was growing up. Her mom, in a silky blouse, high heels and a pencil skirt, had hitched a leg up on the corner of his desk. Flo Turner looked downright sexy, kind of lounging there, eyes twinkling, grinning like the cat that got two bowls of cream.

Mack gave a low, gravelly chuckle. Flo leaned close

to him and whispered something in his ear before turning her glowing smile on Sarah. "Come in and sit down, honey. We need to talk, the three of us, before we open for the day."

For no logical reason, Sarah felt a prickle of unease tighten the muscles at the back of her neck. But her parents seemed happy and totally in love as usual, so what was there to be anxious about?

She entered the room and took one of the guest chairs. "Everything okay?"

Her mom and dad exchanged another way-too-intimate glance, after which her dad said, "We have some big news and we felt it was time to share it with you."

Big news?

The craziest thought occurred to her: Could her mom be pregnant? Growing up, she'd longed for a little brother or sister.

Her mom was only forty-four. Sarah had read somewhere that there were women who didn't reach menopause until their sixties. Was her mom one of those?

If so, well…

A new brother or sister…?

Given the way her parents carried on lately, a new baby Turner didn't seem completely out of the realm of possibility.

The more she considered it, the more she liked the idea—loved it, even.

It would be great. Sophia's new aunt or uncle would be a year or so younger. They would grow up together, do all those things that siblings do. Fight and make up, keep each other's secrets and have each other's backs.

Life. It never ceased to amaze.

Her dad said, "Your mother and I are planning a big change."

"A move," Flo added, excited and so pleased as Sarah felt her big smile fading. "A move to the Gulf. We want to mix it up in a big way. Go where it's warm, live near the ocean."

What?

Wait.

Her mom and dad were moving, going miles and miles away?

No...

It couldn't be. Not now.

Not when she'd just come to realize how happy she was to have them nearby, to know she could turn to them whenever things got rocky. She'd let herself picture them helping her raise Sophia. She'd imagined how she would be there to support them as they grew old.

Yes, all right. There had been that initial shock of coming home to find her dried-up, depressing parents had fallen in love with each other and couldn't stop going at it right here in the office.

But in the past couple of weeks, she'd grown used to the way they were now, even come to like how open and loving they'd become with each other. She enjoyed being around them.

And now they were *leaving*?

They seemed oblivious to her distress. They grinned at each other, so pleased with their big plans. Mack said, "Fishing charters. That's what we're thinking. But first, we'll find a nice little place, get settled in, take it easy, you know, just your mother and me."

Flo leaned toward Mack again. She touched his face,

a tender caress. "Your dad never wanted to be an accountant. Did you know that, sweetheart? This was your grandfather's office and it was always just assumed that Mack would enter the family business."

"I had hopes I would maybe try something different," Sarah's dad said gruffly. "I wanted a job where I could work outdoors."

"But then I got pregnant with you," said her mother. "We had to be responsible. And we were."

"So responsible," her dad echoed sadly, the lines in his face etching deeper as the corners of his mouth turned down.

"And I know, I know, we've spoken of all of this, of the bleak years." Her mom looked sad, too, for a moment. But then she brightened right up again. "What matters is that those days are behind us. You turned out amazing—our baby, all grown up now, with a baby of your own, so capable and smart, taking care of yourself and doing a great job of it. Your father and I feel it's okay now for us to move on, to make a change."

Mack caught Flo's hand and pressed his lips to it. "We're going to live the life we've both been longing for."

"At last." Her mom turned to beam at her again. "Honey, the office will be yours."

"And there's plenty of money," said her dad.

Flo laughed. "My parents and your Turner grandparents were big savers. We inherited a lot. And the business has done well. All these years, we never spent a penny we didn't have to spend."

"And we've invested wisely," added Mack.

"We have a hefty retirement," Flo said, "so we're

all set. The cottage, our house, the business and a nice chunk of cash will all be yours. You'll have no problem hiring an office manager—and another accountant, if you think that's the way to go. And I know you've been resisting day care, but Just Us Kids is right here in town and it's excellent. They take babies. And you can definitely afford it, so just consider that, won't you?" Before Sarah could speak, she continued right on. "Of course, we plan to return often to be with you and our darling Sophia."

"However…" Mack sat forward in his chair and braced his forearms on the desk. "We *have* been thinking about Chicago."

"Yes," Flo chimed in. "We mustn't forget Chicago."

Sarah had no idea what they were talking about now. "Uh. We mustn't?"

Her mom plunked her hand over her heart. "Honey, when you decided to come home to live, we did offer to pitch in so that you could keep your high-powered job and your life in the city. You refused to take our money."

"Mom. You'd already put me through college. You paid for everything my scholarship didn't cover. I've got a degree from Northwestern and I have no loans to repay. It was enough. More than enough."

Her mom made a tutting sound. "Having Sophia was just such a challenge, we understood that. What I'm saying is, we probably should have pushed you harder to take what we offered and keep on with your original plans—and since then, it has occurred to us that maybe what you really want is to return to your life in Chicago. But you insisted on coming home and, well, of course we do love that you're here."

"We should have questioned you further as to what course you really wanted." Mack frowned regretfully. "But we didn't. And that's why we're offering again now. If you want that big-city life you always yearned for when you were growing up, we want you to have it. There should be more than enough money, especially if you sell the properties and the business, for you to make that happen comfortably, without all the stress and pressure you were under before."

"Whatever your dream is, you will be living it," said Flo. "I admit, it has seemed to me that you're making a good life for yourself here. And things do appear to be going so well with you and Logan…"

"But we realize," Mack jumped in, "that we might only be hoping you're happy here because Rust Creek Falls is our hometown and of course we would love to return here whenever the mood strikes and have you and our granddaughter right here waiting for us."

"That's simply not fair," said her mom. "We can just as well come and visit you and Sophia in Chicago. So we want you to know that however you choose to go forward, we will support you one hundred percent."

"Absolutely," Mack agreed. "Whatever you want to do next, we will help make it happen."

Both of them stared at her expectantly.

Sarah realized they were waiting for her to say something.

Well, she had plenty to say. Yeah, okay. They were being sweet and understanding and so very generous.

But it didn't matter.

She wanted to yell at them that their plans were utterly foolish, wildly irresponsible, to argue that they had no right to go pulling up stakes and running off to the Gulf, because…fishing charters? Seriously?

She wanted to beg them to change their minds and stay.

But none of those reactions would be right or fair or kind of her.

In all those unhappy years while she was growing up, she wasn't the only one who'd suffered. Her parents had suffered, too, locked into what they saw as their duty, every day gray and uninspired, a challenge to get through.

And now they'd changed everything. They'd found their happiness. And they had a dream they longed to pursue. She got that, about having dreams—even if her own dreams hadn't turned out the way she'd planned.

Their dreams were all new and shiny. And she wanted them to have those dreams. She wanted them to have it all.

"Honey?" Her mom was starting to look worried now.

"Just tell us," said her dad, "if there's something we're missing. If you have objections, we want to know."

"No." She gave them her brightest smile. "No objections."

"You're sure?" asked her mother.

"I am positive." Surprisingly, she sounded convincing even to her own ears. "And I'm happy for you two. I really am." Well, at least that was true. She was so glad for them, for what they'd found together after all these years. If only she and Logan might…

No. Really, she was fine on her own. *Better* on her

own. It just didn't work for her, to go counting on a man, to start hoping for what wasn't meant to be.

Sometimes she worried that she might be getting too attached to him, that she shouldn't let him spend so much time with Sophia, who might suffer when the relationship ended. Really, though, he was so good with her.

And why would Sophia suffer if Logan left? She was just a baby, after all. Sophia required a steady, loving presence in her life, someone to count on now and all through her growing-up years. Other people—Sophia's father, her grandparents, Sarah's boyfriend, neighbors, babysitters—everyone else might come and go. But Sarah would be there for Sophia, always.

As for herself and her own relationship with Logan, well, maybe she was getting in too deep. Maybe she needed to think about having a talk with him, reminding them both that they shouldn't get serious, that this was just for now and it was absolutely perfect and not everything had to turn into a lifetime of love.

But oh, it did *feel* serious. And, well, she loved how serious it felt. She didn't really know what to do about that. Maybe they actually could have forever together.

Or maybe, once again, she was making plans for a future that would never come true.

What she needed was *not* to get all tied up in knots over her own current happiness with Logan. He was a good man and she would enjoy every moment they had together, with no expectations as to what might happen next.

"And Chicago?" asked her dad.

She shook herself and focused on the subject at hand.

"No. I don't want to go back, I really don't. I'm staying here."

"Sweetheart…" Her mom jumped off the desk and held out her arms.

Sarah rose. Her dad got up and joined them in a family hug. It was so bizarre, group-hugging with her parents, of all people. It made her feel loved and cherished—and lonely already that they would be leaving.

"When will you go?" she asked as they stepped apart.

"It's a process," said Mack.

"We're eager to get started." Her mom looked downright starry-eyed. "We want to get moving on it right away."

"I completely understand."

"We're going to sign over the business and the properties and give you the money we talked about," Flo announced. "We were hoping we could all three go together to see Ben as soon as possible." Ben Dalton was the family's attorney. He had an office right in town. "We want to get everything in your name so you can start the transition—hire your office manager, whom I will be happy to train, and get you ready to run the business on your own. And then we're buying a motor home."

"We're flexible," her dad insisted. "We'll be here for you for as long as you need us."

Her mom practically glowed in her excitement—to be on the way south, to start living their great adventure. "However long it takes to get everything worked out, that's fine with us. The truth is you're carrying most of the workload here already. Falls Mountain Accounting *should* be yours, anyway."

"You're ten times the accountant I ever was," her dad said wryly. "You've been here a couple of months and you've already enlarged our client list, streamlined the office procedures and bolstered the bottom line."

"There will be our house to deal with, packing stuff up, clearing it out a little," her mom chattered on. "You might want to move to the bigger place and sell the cottage. Or rent it. Or sell the house and—"

"Flo." Mack wrapped an arm around her. When she glanced up at him, he brushed a kiss on her forehead. "None of that has to be decided today."

Her mom gazed at him adoringly. "Of course, darling. You're right." She gave Sarah a rueful glance. "Sorry, honey. I got carried away."

"No problem." Except for how much she would miss them and how sad and lost she felt at the prospect of them living so far away. "I promise to consider all the options carefully."

"We know you will, sweetheart. And as for your father and me, if possible, we're hoping to be on our way south sometime in August."

Quietly, Logan shut the door to Sophia's room.

In two steps, he reached the arch that led into the dining room. At the sight of Sarah, he hung back to enjoy the view. She sat on the sofa with Opal in her lap. Even all the way across the room, he could hear that kitten purring.

Sarah scratched Opal's chin and the purring got louder. "What are you looking at?" she asked without glancing up.

"A pretty woman and a dinky white motorboat of a cat."

That got him a grin. "She's a happy baby."

He wanted to linger there, leaning on the door frame, just looking at her. And he also had the urge to go and get the spiral notebook from the kitchen. He wanted to capture the way her slim, pretty hands stroked Opal's soft, white fur.

Most of all, he wanted to go to her, sit beside her, put his arm around her and steal a kiss.

The prospect of getting close won out. He crossed the room, sat down next to her and drew her nice and snug against his side.

When she glanced up, he took her mouth.

It never got old, kissing Sarah. She smelled like heaven and she tasted even better. He nipped at her upper lip. She let out a sigh and he deepened the kiss—for a moment.

Not too long. If he kept kissing her, he would want more than kisses.

But a little later for that.

He lifted away and gazed down at her. "Something on your mind?"

A tiny frown marred the smooth skin of her forehead. She confessed, "Got some big news from the parents today. They're leaving everything—this house, their house, the business—to me and moving to the Gulf of Mexico."

"Wow."

A chuckle escaped her. It wasn't a very happy sound. "No kidding."

"When?"

"As soon as possible. A month or so."

He ran a finger down the side of her throat and then couldn't resist bending close again, sticking out his tongue, tasting her there. She tasted so good, like everything he wanted, like hope and forever. "You don't want them to go." He breathed the words against her silky, fragrant skin.

She caught his face between her hands and pushed away enough that she could look in his eyes. "How did you know that?"

"Easy. You didn't tell me they were leaving until I asked. If you weren't conflicted about them going, you would have said something earlier."

She searched his face. "You're way too observant."

"I get a big thrill out of observing you." He moved in close again and kissed her soft cheek. "Did you ask them to consider staying here in town?"

"No. And I'm not going to, either." She idly stroked the hair at his temple with the tips of her fingers. He loved the feel of her hands on him. "They can't wait to be on their way. And I want them to have what they want. They did everything they were supposed to do for years. It's time they got their chance to be free."

"But what about you?"

"I'll get over myself, believe me. Sophia and I will be fine."

Sophia and I. He wasn't included. She and Sophia were a family of two.

He wanted his chance to hear her say that the *three* of them would be fine, to consider them a unit. A family. Together. And he intended to *make* his chance. The sooner the better. "Let's go out."

She shook her head, laughing. "Sophia's already in bed in case you didn't notice when you put her there."

"I mean tomorrow night or the next one. I'll bet Lily would watch her, or your mom."

She skated a finger along the line of his jaw and he realized he was happy in the best kind of way, all easy and comfortable inside his own skin, just to be sitting here on the sofa with Sarah, Opal purring away on her lap.

"I'll try my mom first," she said. "She loves looking after Sophia and she mentioned today that she hoped to get more time with her before she and my dad ride off into the sunset in the fancy new Winnebago they're planning on buying."

"So that's a yes?"

"Mmm-hmm. I'll check with her, find out which evening's best."

"It's not even eight. There's still time to call. Do it now so I can make the reservation."

"Let me guess." Those golden-brown eyes twinkled at him. "You know this great little restaurant in Kalispell…"

"That's right." He leaned in close again to nip his way up the side of her neck and then nibble her earlobe for good measure. "Dinner at Giordano's because it's *our* place, our Italian restaurant."

"'Our place' that we've never been to together," she teased.

"A mere oversight which we are about to remedy. And we'll go dancing afterward, though I'll admit I'm not sure where to go for dancing around here."

"Well, I know where to go. The Ace in the Hole."

He scoffed at that. "From what I've heard, the Ace is a cowboy bar with peanut shells on the floor and country-western on the jukebox."

"That's right," she said. "When I was a little girl, I always wanted to go to the Ace. You know, have a burger, beg quarters from my parents and play the jukebox. But my parents never went out anywhere—not even for a burger at the Ace."

"You were deprived of an important cultural experience. Is that what you're telling me?"

"That's it exactly. And for some reason I still don't really understand, as I got a little older, I didn't just go there myself or drag Lily there. I was like that as a kid, serious and quiet. I had trouble getting out there and doing the things I longed to do. I kind of lived in the future, planning for college and my life in the big city where I would make everything come together, make all of my dreams finally come true." She looked so sad then. But before he could figure out what to do about that, she brightened. "But then it happened. I did get my chance."

"For a burger at the Ace?"

"That's right." She laughed, a low, husky sound, and her eyes turned more golden than brown as she explained, "I was seventeen, in my senior year of high school and one of the Dalton boys invited me to go."

He wasn't sure he liked that faraway look she had. "Should I be jealous? Which Dalton boy?"

"No, you shouldn't. And which one doesn't matter. He never asked me out again."

"Good," he said gruffly, followed up with a muttered, "What an idiot."

"My point, Logan, is that I loved it. Loved the Ace. It was noisy and there was lots of laughter. Music was playing and everyone was talking too loud. A couple of drunk cowboys even got in a fight, so there was excitement, too. There was everything I never had at home. I remember sitting there across from the Dalton boy whose first name you don't need to know and thinking that the Ace was the best and I wanted to come back every chance I got."

"And did you?"

She shook her head. "It just never happened. And then I left for Illinois in the fall."

"You haven't been there since that one date when you were seventeen, you mean?"

"That's right."

He captured her hand and kissed the tips of her fingers. "I'll take you."

She put her lips to his ear and whispered, "It can be *our* honky-tonk saloon where we make all our most precious romantic memories as we're two-stepping to country standards, peanut shells crunching underfoot. I take it you haven't been there even once yet?"

"Nope."

"Well, then, we're going to remedy that oversight after dinner at Giordano's."

"You're on." He tugged on her ponytail. "Are all accountants as romantic as you?"

"Nope." She kissed him, a quick press of her soft lips to his. "I'm special."

"Oh, yes, you are." He pulled her close and claimed a deeper, longer kiss, gathering her so tightly to him that Opal let out a tiny meow of annoyance at being jostled. The kitten jumped to the floor. When he lifted his head, Sarah's golden eyes were low and lazy, full of promise and desire. "Call your mom," he ordered gruffly. "Do it now."

Logan made the Giordano's reservation for seven Wednesday night. They got a quiet corner table, as he'd requested. He ordered a bottle of wine to go with the meal and the food was amazing as always. Even on a Wednesday night, most of the tables were full.

He hardly noticed the other customers, though. All his attention was on the beautiful bean counter across from him.

She wore a sleeveless turquoise dress, the sexy kind, with spaghetti straps. The dress clung to her curves on top. It had a flirty layered skirt that was going to swing out like the petals of a blooming flower later at the Ace when they danced together. Her gold-streaked brown hair was loose and wavy on her shapely bare shoulders.

He wanted to sketch her in that dress. And he would later, back at her cottage, when they were alone. If he got too eager to get her out of that dress, well, he would sketch it from memory as soon as he had the chance.

More than once during dinner, he almost made his move. But the moment just never seemed quite right. They joked about which Rust Creek Falls bachelorette Viv Dalton had most recently set up with which of his brothers. They spoke of the new office manager she and her mom had just hired. Flo had started training the new employee that morning. They laughed about how the work out at the Ambling A seemed downright endless. The barn needed more repairs and the fence-building went on and on.

For dessert, they had the chocolate semifreddo again, same as that first night when he'd had their meal catered at her house. She joked that it was "their dessert" and now he could never have it with anyone else but her.

He raised his coffee cup to her. "You. Me. Semi-freddo. Forever."

She gazed at him across the small table, her eyes so soft, her skin like cream, her lush mouth begging for his kiss.

It was the exact right moment.

But he decided to wait.

Was he maybe a little freaked out about how to do what he planned—and when? Was he putting way too much emphasis on finding just the right moment?

Maybe.

But he wanted it to be perfect. In future years, he wanted her to remember the moment with joy and admiration for how he'd picked just the right time.

It was almost nine when they left Giordano's. They got in his crew cab and he leaned across the console for a kiss.

And wouldn't you know? One kiss was never enough.

They ended up canoodling like a couple of sex-starved kids for the next half hour or so, steaming up the windows, hands all over each other. Like they didn't have a comfortable bed to go to in the privacy of her cottage.

She'd unbuttoned his shirt and he'd pulled the top of that pretty dress down and bared her gorgeous breasts before they stopped—and that was only because he whacked his elbow on the steering wheel and they both started laughing at the craziness of them going at it right there in his truck at the curb in front of Giordano's. Anybody might see what they were up to.

Probably some innocent passerby *had* seen.

He buttoned and tucked in his shirt and she pulled her dress back up, after which she flipped down the visor and combed her hair in the mirror on the back. She looked so tempting, tipping her head this way and that, smoothing the unruly strands. He couldn't stop himself from reaching for her again.

She allowed him one long, hot kiss—and then she put her hands on his chest and pushed enough to break the connection. "The Ace," she instructed sternly. And then a giggle escaped her, which kind of ruined the effect. "We need to get going. Now."

The Ace in the Hole was a rambling wooden structure on Sawmill Street with a big dirt parking lot behind it and a wide front porch where cowboys gathered to drink their beer away from the music, to talk about horses and spot the pretty women as they came up the steps to go in.

Beyond the double doors, there was the long bar, a row of booths, a stage and a dance floor surrounded by smaller tables.

Sarah gazed out across the dance floor. "So romantic." She leaned close and brushed a kiss against his cheek. "Thanks for bringing me." The way she looked at him right then, her big eyes gleaming, mouth soft with a tender smile—made him feel about ten feet tall.

He got them each a beer and they took a booth. Tonight, a local band had the stage. They played cover versions of familiar country songs.

"Let's dance," she said, smiling, a little flushed, her eyes full of stars to be here at this cowboy bar where she hadn't been since she was seventeen.

They danced every song—fast ones and slow ones, never once returning to the booth.

The whole time, he was waiting as he'd been waiting all evening—for just the right moment. He might have done it there, on the dance floor of the cowboy bar she'd found so thrilling when she was a kid.

But no.

Private was better, he decided at last. He would wait until they got back to the cottage.

Around eleven, as they swayed together, their arms around each other, to Brad Paisley's "We Danced," she lifted her head from his shoulder and let out a giggle. She seemed thoroughly pleased with herself.

"What?" he demanded.

"Nothing—except it's official. I've danced at the Ace with the hottest guy in town. I never thought it would happen, but look at me now."

"You are so beautiful." Words did not do her justice. He dipped his head and kissed her, one of those kisses that starts out gentle and worshipful, but then kind of spins out of control.

She was the one who pulled away. "I'm thinking we probably ought to go soon," she whispered, sweetly breathless.

"I'm thinking you're right."

They left when the song ended.

At the cottage, Flo reported that Sophia had been an

angel. "She had her bottle and ate her mashed peas and then some applesauce and went down at eight thirty. I haven't heard a peep from her since." They thanked her for babysitting.

Flo kissed Sarah's cheek. "Anytime," she said as she went out the door.

And finally, it was just Logan and Sarah, with the baby sound asleep. She scooped the snoozing Opal off the sofa and put her in her bed in the laundry room.

When she came back, he did what came naturally, pulling her into his arms and lowering his mouth to hers, walking her backward slowly as he kissed her.

In the bedroom, he almost guided her down to the bed.

But no. It was time.

Past time—to make his move. Say his piece. Ask her the most important question of all.

She gazed up at him, kind of bemused. Wondering. "What is it? There's something on your mind."

He took the ring from his pocket. She gasped. He was smiling as he dropped to one knee. "Sarah," he said.

And that was as far as he got.

Because she covered her mouth with her hands and cried, "No!"

Chapter 11

Logan felt as though she'd walloped him a good one—just drawn back her little fist and sent it flying in a roundhouse punch. He reeled. "What? Wait..."

"Logan. Get up. Don't do this, okay?" She actually offered him her hand, like he needed help to get up off the floor.

He rose without touching her and put the ring back in his pocket. He had no idea where this was going—except it was nowhere good, that was for sure.

She backed up until her knees touched the bed and then she kind of crumpled onto the edge of the mattress. He watched her hard-swallow. She didn't look well—her face was dead white with two spots of hectic color, one high on each cheek.

"Uh, sit down," she said and nervously patted the space beside her.

He shook his head. "I think I'll stand."

She stared up at him, begging him with her eyes—but for what? "I'm so sorry." She spoke in a ragged voice. "This isn't—I mean, I just can't, Logan. You're the most incredible man and I'm wild for you, you know I am. But I couldn't say yes to marriage. I just couldn't. Please try to understand. This thing with us, it's just for now and we both know that. We have to remember that."

"No." He shut his eyes, drew in a slow, careful breath. "No, I don't know that. I'm not going anywhere. Never. I want to be right here, with you."

"But it's not going to last. We're just, I mean, well, living in the moment, having fun, enjoying the ride. And it's beautiful, what we have together. Why ruin it with expectations that will break my heart and could hurt my daughter when they don't pan out?"

How could she think that? "You're wrong."

"No. I'm not wrong. I'm realistic. Nothing ever really does last, you know?"

"No, Sarah. I don't know." He also didn't know what to do next, how to reach her, how to recover from this. But then it came to him that he had to go all the way now, to say it out loud, to give her his truth. It was all that he had. "I love you, Sarah Turner. I want to marry you."

She let out another cry and clapped her hands to her ears this time. Her eyes glittered with moisture. A tear got away from her and carved a shining trail down her cheek.

He tried reassurance. "You don't have to be afraid. I'm not going to stop loving you. Not ever. This is for real. I swear it to you."

"You say that now—"

"Because it's true. Because what we have, what I feel for you, I've never felt before. I trust what we have. I love you. I love Sophia. I want to take care of you, of both of you. I want to be here when Sophia says her first real word, when she takes her first step. I want to be here for all the days we're given, you and me. This is where I'm happy. This is where it all makes sense. With you, with Sophia. The three of us. A family."

"I can't," she said again. "I just can't. I can't do that. It's one thing for us to take it a day at a time. To enjoy what we have while it lasts. But marriage? Logan, that's not what this is about."

"Yeah, it is."

"No. It's not." She said it so firmly, her shoulders drawn back now, her expression bleak, closed down.

He kept trying to reach her. "It's so simple. It's just you and me doing what people do when they love each other, starting to build a life together. Making it work."

"Your father hates me."

Really? She was going to go there? Patiently, he answered her, "No, he does not hate you. My mother broke his heart and ran off with her lover, abandoning him and me and my brothers. We never heard from her again."

She gasped. He saw sympathy in her eyes. "That's horrible."

"Yeah. It was pretty bad for all of us. And that's why he is the way he is. He's a lonely old man with some weird ideas about love and marriage. You're too smart to let Max Crawford chase you away."

"It's not only your dad. It's, well…" She blew out a

breath, folded her hands and then twisted them in her lap. "Love just never works out for me."

"That's faulty reasoning, Sarah. You know it is. There was what? That idiot Tuck who didn't know the best thing that ever happened to him when he had it? Good riddance. And that Mercer guy? That wasn't love anyway, was it?"

Her eyes reproached him. "You're making fun of me."

"No, I'm not. I'm just saying that whatever you're really scared of, I don't think it's anything you've brought up so far."

"I, well, it's only… Logan, what if a year goes by and you realize you made a mistake?"

"That's not going to happen. I know what's in my heart. You're the one for me. That's never going to change."

"But, Logan, what if your feelings did change? What if we, you and me, didn't work out after a year or two or three? Think back. Try to remember how it was for you when your mother deserted you."

"I know exactly how it was, which is all the more reason I will never desert you."

She just couldn't believe him. "In a couple of years, Sophia will be old enough to suffer when you leave us."

"You're not listening. If you say yes to me, I will never leave you."

She only shook her head and went right on with her argument. "My daughter would count on you to be there and you would be gone. She would suffer because of my bad choices. It's just better not to go there. It's just better to leave things as they are."

He stood over her, burning to get closer, to reach down and take her hand, pull her up into his arms that ached to hold her. But she looked so fragile sitting there, as though his very touch would shatter her.

"I'm so sorry," she whispered on a broken husk of breath. "I'm so sorry but I can't. It's not possible. Not for me."

He didn't know how to answer her. Because words weren't making a damn bit of difference. He could stand here and argue with her all night long.

And where would that get them? What would that fix?

"Just tell me what you're really afraid of." He was actually pleading now. Imagine that. Logan Crawford, whose heart had always been untouchable, pleading with a woman just for a chance. "I can't fix this if I don't know what's broken."

"But that's it," she cried. "It's nothing you can fix. Nothing anyone can fix. I can't let myself count on you—on anyone, not really. I have to look out for my daughter and my heart. I have to be strong, be the mom and the breadwinner, the decision-maker and the pro-tector, too. I don't have the trust in me to let someone else do any of that, not anymore. It doesn't matter how I feel about you, or how much I care. If I can't give my trust, well, it's not going to work."

Trust. There it was. The thing she feared to give. The real problem.

She couldn't—*wouldn't*—allow herself to trust in him.

How the hell was he supposed to break through something like that?

What a spectacular irony. He'd finally found the one woman he wanted to spend a lifetime with. And she couldn't let herself believe in him.

Where did that leave them?

His heart felt so empty, hollowed out. What now?

Should he back off, forget about forever and try to convince her to simply go on as they were?

Really, it was so achingly clear to him now: he'd messed up. Jumped the gun, made his move too soon. He should have kept his damn mouth shut, not crossed this particular line until she'd had more time to see that it was safe to believe in him.

He'd rushed it. He got that.

And it really didn't look like there was any way for him to recover from this disaster.

Shoving his hands in his pockets, he made a last-ditch attempt to salvage some small shred of hope. "So then, I have to know. I want you to tell me. Is it that you need more time?"

She gazed up at him, a desolate look on her unforgettable face. "No." The single word came at him like a knife blade, shining and deadly, flying straight for his heart.

He made himself clarify. "Never. You're saying never."

She nodded and whispered, "I am so sorry."

Well, okay. That was about as clear as it could get. She hadn't hedged. She'd given him zero hope that he could ever change her mind.

And now she was watching his face, reading him. "You're leaving," she said.

Before he could answer, the baby monitor on the dresser erupted with a sharp little cry.

They both froze, waiting for Sophia to fuss a little and then go back to sleep.

Not this time, though. Sophia cried out again. And again. Each cry was more insistent.

Sarah started to rise.

"I'll get her," he said.

"No, really, it's—"

He cut her off. "Let me tell her goodbye. Give me that, at least."

She pressed her lips together and dipped her head in a nod.

He turned for the baby's room.

Sarah watched him go.

Dear Lord, what was the matter with her? She loved him. She did. And he'd never been anything but trustworthy with her, with Sophia.

And yet, she just couldn't do it, couldn't put her future in his hands, couldn't let herself believe that he would never break her heart, never change his mind after she'd given him everything, never turn his back on her and her child.

Sophia's wailing stopped.

Sarah heard Logan's voice, a little muffled from the other room, but crystal clear on the monitor. "Hey there, gorgeous. It's all right. I've got you. I'm right here."

The camera had come on. It used infrared technology so that even in Sophia's darkened room, she could see the tall figure standing by the crib with her baby in his arms.

"Ah, da!" cried Sophia. With a heavy sigh, she laid her head against Logan's chest. "Da…"

"I think we've got a wet diaper here, don't we?"

"Unngh."

The camera tracked him as he carried Sophia to the changing area. Handing her a giraffe teething ring to chew on, he quickly and expertly put on a fresh diaper. "There now. All better."

"Pa. Da." Clutching the ring in one tiny fist, she reached out her arms to him.

He scooped her up against his chest again and carried her to the rocker in the corner. "We'll just sit here and rock a little while, okay?"

"Angh." She stuck the teething ring in her mouth.

He cradled her in both arms and slowly rocked. "I wanted to talk to you, anyway." The baby sighed and stared up at him. "Sophia, I have to go now. I am so sorry, but I won't be back. I want you to know, though, that I would stay if I could. I would be your 'da' forever and ever. I would watch you grow up, teach you how to ride a bike and how to pitch a softball, help you with your homework, chase all the boys away until the right one came along…"

Sarah's eyes blurred with tears. On the monitor, Sophia gazed up at Logan so solemnly, as though she understood every word he said.

He fell silent. For a while, he just cradled her, rocking, looking down at her as she stared up at him. Slowly, her eyes fluttered shut. She let go of the toy. He caught it and set it on the little table beside the rocker.

Several more minutes passed. In her bedroom, Sarah watched on the monitor as Logan bent close to brush the lightest of kisses across her daughter's forehead. He whispered something more, but she couldn't make out the words.

And then, moving slowly so as not to disturb the little girl in his arms, he rose and carried her to the crib. Carefully, he put her back down again, pulling the blanket up to tuck in gently around her. He leaned down for a last light kiss.

A moment later, he came and stood in the open door to Sarah's room. "She's sleeping now. I'm going."

Sarah didn't know what else to do, so she got up and followed him to the front door. He pulled it open. The night air was cool, the dark street deserted.

He stuck his hand in his pocket. She looked down and saw he was holding out the house key she'd given him. She took it. "Goodbye, Sarah."

She wanted to reach for him, grab him close. She wanted to *not* let him go.

But she only stood there, the key clutched tight in her hand. She made herself say it. "Goodbye, Logan."

He turned, went out the door and down the steps to where his crew cab waited.

She couldn't bear to watch him drive away, so she shut the door and kind of fell back against it, her knees suddenly weak and wobbly. Outside, she heard the truck start up, pull away from the curb and head off down the street.

The big, black eye of his fancy TV stared at her disapprovingly. She should have given it back to him. That had been her plan when she allowed him to bring it here—to return it to him when their time together ended.

Sarah shut her eyes. A sound escaped her—something midway between a crazy-woman laugh and a broken sob. As if the TV even mattered. If he wanted it, he would come back and get it.

But she knew he wouldn't. He would want her to have it.

And he wouldn't want to see her or talk to her.

Ever again.

Chapter 12

Somehow, Sarah got through the next day. And the next.

It wasn't easy. She had this horrible hollow feeling—like her heart had gone missing from her chest.

But she knew it had been the right thing to tell him no. To break it off. The longer she had with him, the more painful it would have been to lose him in the end.

She managed to avoid her parents for those first two days, taking all of her appointments away from the office, being too busy to talk when her mom called on Friday.

Friday night was really tough. Sophia was fussier than usual. It wasn't a cold or an ear infection or the pain of teething. Sarah thought the baby seemed sad. And Opal kind of drooped around the house like her little kitty heart was broken.

It couldn't be true that her baby *and* her kitten missed Logan as much as she did. Sophia was too young to even know he'd gone missing—wasn't she? And Opal was a cat, for crying out loud. Cats got attached to their place, their surroundings. Plus, if Opal had a favorite human, it was Sarah, hands down. She'd been Sarah's cat from the first. The kitten sat in her lap while they watched TV and came crying to her when the kibble bowl was empty.

No. Sarah knew what was really going on. She was projecting her own misery and loss onto her baby and Opal. She needed to stop that right now. She'd done the right thing and this aching, endless emptiness inside her would go away.

Eventually.

That night after Sophia finally went to sleep, Sarah sat on the sofa with her phone in her hands and studied the pictures of Logan, Sophia and Petunia that she'd taken that day they had their picnic at the Ambling A. She went through the notebook of Logan's sketches. It hurt so much to look at them. She'd been planning to frame some of them and put them up around the cottage.

But she didn't know if she could ever bear to do that now. Those sketches were a testimony to all she would never have, all she'd made herself say no to.

All she had to learn to let go.

Saturday morning, her mom appeared on her doorstep. "Okay," said Flo. "What is going on with you?"

When Sarah tried to protest that she was fine, her mom kind of pushed her way in the door, shut it behind her, took Sophia right out of her arms and said, "Pour me some coffee. We need to talk."

They sat in the kitchen where the morning sun streamed cheerfully in the window above the sink and the walls were the beautiful, buttery yellow Sarah had chosen herself—and that Logan had made happen. Every wall in her house was now the color she wanted it to be.

Because of Logan. Because he'd kept after her until she finally agreed to the painting party—and then, when she did agree, he'd taken her out to buy the paint and then worked for two days painting and also supervising the volunteer crew.

If not for Logan, she'd still be living in a house with off-white walls and random brushstrokes of color here and there, promising herself that one of these days she would get around to making the place feel more like her home.

Flo put Sophia in her bouncy seat and gave her a set of fat, plastic keys to chew on. Then she sat at the table across from Sarah and took a sip of her coffee. "It's Logan, right?"

"Mom, I don't think we—"

"He's not here and he hasn't been for days."

"How do you know that?"

"Sweetheart, it's Rust Creek Falls. Everybody knows that. No one's seen that fancy pickup of his out in front since Wednesday night."

"Mom, I really don't want to talk about it."

"But you *need* to talk about it. Now, tell me what happened."

"I, um…" Her throat locked up, her nose started running and suddenly there were tears streaming down her cheeks. "Mom, he proposed. He proposed to me and I sent him away."

Flo got up again. She grabbed the box of tissues from over on the counter and set them in Sarah's lap, bending close to hug her right there in her chair. "Mop up, honey. We need to talk." Flo sat down again and sipped her coffee, waiting.

Sarah blew her nose and dried her cheeks.

"Tell me," her mom demanded.

With a big sigh and another sad little sob, Sarah started talking. She told her mom pretty much everything, all about how beautiful and perfect Wednesday night had been—until Logan tried to propose.

Once she started talking, she couldn't stop. She spilled it all, about her disappointments with Tuck and the sheer rat-crappiness of Mercer Smalls, how she just couldn't trust a man anymore and so she knew it was the best thing, to end it with Logan now.

When she finally fell silent, she glanced over and saw that Sophia had fallen asleep in her bouncy chair, her little head drooping to the side, the plastic keys fallen to the floor, where Opal batted at them and then jumped back when they skittered across the tile.

Her mom got up and poured them each more coffee, put the pot back on the warmer and then resumed her seat. "Before we get into everything you've just told me, I have to ask. Are you upset over your dad and me leaving? Is that bothering you? Do you want us to stay?"

Sarah opened her mouth to insist that she didn't, no way, no how.

But before she got the words out, her mom shook her head. "Tell me the truth, honey. Please."

Sarah dabbed at her eyes to mop up the last of her tears. "Okay, it's a factor, that you're going. I will miss you. I mean, all those years growing up, it was like we were strangers sharing a house. And now, it's so different. You and Dad are helpful and fun. You've become the parents I always wished for and it's been so great having you nearby. But no. I don't want you to stay. If you stayed, you wouldn't be getting your dream and I want that, Mom. I want you and Dad to finally live the life you never let yourselves live before."

"But if you need us—"

"You're a phone call away. If I needed you, you would be back in a flash."

"But do you need us to *be* here, day-to-day? Do you need us close by?"

Sarah leaned forward and took her mom's hand between both of hers. "No. You and Dad are going. It's settled. I'm good with it, I promise you."

Her mom pulled her hand free of Sarah's hold, only to reach out and fondly smooth Sarah's hair. "And what about *your* dream, sweetheart?"

"Um. Yeah, well. That's life, you know."

Flo let out a wry laugh. "Honey, you grew up a lonely child in a silent house with unhappy parents. Then you set out to conquer Chicago. You worked so hard, got so far. But sometimes in life, our big plans don't turn out the way we want them to. You had to come home. I know it hasn't been easy for you, with so much on your shoulders. But the past few weeks, you've seemed to thrive. You're really good at running the business. I think you've been happy, especially since you've been with Logan. You've been sprucing up the cottage, settling in beautifully here with a little help from your friends and neighbors. It seems to me you've been having a pretty fine time in your old hometown."

Sarah sat back in her chair and eyed her mother warily. "You've become so upbeat and hopeful. Sometimes it's just exhausting."

Her mother laughed some more. "Well, honey, now think about. Ask yourself, is it maybe just possible that you came home in defeat only to discover that you can have your dream here? Is it possible that taking over the family business is more satisfying work for you than killing yourself at that giant firm in the big city? Is it possible you *like* running your own show, being your own boss? And as for Logan, well, the two of you seem to me like a great match. Didn't he offer you exactly what you've longed for—a good life with the right man, a father for your child?"

"Mom, it didn't work out, okay?"

"But it could." Flo leaned in again. "If you'll just let it."

Sarah glared at her. "Look. You want me to say it?"

Flo sat up straight again and smiled way too sweetly. "I do, yes. I absolutely do."

"Okay, Mom. I'll say it." Sarah sniffed and brushed another random tear away. "I freaked out. That's the truth. He went down on one knee to offer me just what I'd given up on, what I've always wanted most and have learned to accept that I'll never have. And when he pulled out that ring, well, I choked, okay? I just couldn't do it, couldn't reach out and take it." Sarah put her hands to the sides of her head because right at that moment it kind of felt like her brain was about to explode. "I blew it. I really did. I threw away my own dream. I turned away the man I love. I freaked out and now it's too late."

"Oh, sweetheart," said her mother. "As long you're still breathing, it's never too late."

Logan had taken to sleeping out under the stars.

After all, there were a lot of fences to fix on the Ambling A. He was taking care of that—and avoiding any contact with other human beings in the bargain.

The morning after it ended with Sarah, he'd had an argument with his father over nothing in particular. Really, he picked a fight because he blamed Max, at least partly, for the way it had all gone wrong with Sarah.

Then, that same day at breakfast, his brothers were yammering on about some discovery they'd made— an old, locked diary with a jewel-encrusted letter *A* on the front. They'd found it right there in the ranch house under a rotted floorboard and they were all trotting out theories as to who might have hidden it and what might be inside.

Logan could not have cared less about some old, tattered relic that had nothing to do with him or any of them, either. He yelled at them to shut the hell up about it.

Then Wilder made the mistake of asking him what his damn problem was. He'd lit into his youngest brother. They'd almost come to blows.

That did it. Logan realized he would just as soon not have anything to do with his family right now—or with anyone else, for that matter. He'd considered leaving for good, packing up his things and heading back to Seattle.

But the big city didn't thrill him any more than dealing with his family did. Nothing thrilled him. He was fresh out of enthusiasm for anything and everything. Until he could figure out what move to make next, he just wanted to be left alone.

So he'd loaded up his pickup with fence posts and barbwire and headed out across the land. He had a sleeping bag and plenty of canned food. For five full days he worked on the fences, brought in strays, dug out clogged ditches and didn't speak to a single person.

Eventually, he would have to return to the ranch house, have a hot meal, a bath and a shave. But not for a while yet. Not until he could look at his father without wanting to punch his lights out, not until his heart stopped aching.

Come to think of it, it could be a long time before he had a damn shower. Because the ache in his heart showed no signs of abating anytime soon.

On Tuesday, three days after her talk with her mother, Sarah had yet to do anything about how much she missed Logan.

Yeah, she got it. She did. She'd finally had a chance at what she really wanted with a man—and she'd thrown her chance away. It was up to her to go to him, tell him how totally she'd messed up and beg him to give her just one more shot.

But she didn't do it. She felt…immmobilized somehow. She visited clients, cared for her baby, cuddled her cat. Inside, though, she was empty and frozen and so very sad.

Tuesday evening, as Opal jumped around the kitchen floor chasing shadows and Sophia sat chewing her rubber pretzel and giggling dreamily at the mobile of dancing ladybugs hooked to her bouncy seat, Sarah stood at the refrigerator with the door wide open.

She stared inside at food she had no interest in eating and tried to decide what to fix for dinner. Really, she wasn't hungry. There was a half a box of Cheez-Its on the counter. She could eat that—yeah. Perfect. Cheez-Its for dinner, and maybe a glass of wine or ten. Once she put Sophia to bed, she could cry for a while. That would be constructive.

The knock on the front door surprised her. Would it be her mom again or maybe Lily, somebody who loved her coming to tell her to snap out of it?

She almost didn't answer it. Really, she didn't want to talk to anyone right now and she couldn't figure out why anyone would want to give a pep talk to an emotional coward like her, anyway.

But then whoever it was knocked again. She shut the fridge door and went to get it.

"Hello, Sarah," Max Crawford said when she opened the door. He actually had his black hat in his hands. "I wonder if you would give me a few minutes of your time."

Her best option was obvious. She should slam the door in his overbearing, judgmental face.

Instead, she just sneered. "Didn't you get the memo? Logan and I broke up. You got what you wanted. There is absolutely no reason for you to be darkening my door."

"Please," he said, all somber and serious—and way too sincere. "A few minutes, that's all I'm asking for. Just hear me out."

Oh, she wanted to shove that door shut so fast and so hard…

But she didn't. Partly because she was too tired and sad to give him the angry, self-righteous rejection he deserved. And also because she couldn't help but be curious as to what Logan's rapscallion dad had to say now.

She stepped back and gestured him inside. "Have a seat."

He crossed the threshold and sat on the sofa. "Thank you."

She took the easy chair across from him. "Okay. What?"

Carefully, he set his hat on the cushion beside him. "Logan's out on the far reaches of the Ambling A. He took a sleeping bag, a truck-bed full of barbwire and fence posts, a shovel or two and a bunch of canned goods. He hasn't been back to the house since last Thursday."

Alarm had her heart racing and her palms going sweaty. "You're saying he's disappeared?"

"No, he's mending fences and bringing in strays. We been out, me and the boys, checking on him from a distance because he wants nothing to do with any of us. Sarah, you broke my boy's heart."

She saw red. She would have raised her voice good and loud, given him a very large piece of her mind, if it hadn't been for the innocent baby in the other room who would be frightened if her mother started screaming like a crazy woman.

With deadly softness, she reminded him, "Well, I guess you're pretty happy then, since that was what you wanted all along."

"I was wrong," said Max. "I was all wrong."

That set her back a little. She blinked and stared. "What did you say?"

"I just need you to know that I am so sorry, Sarah, for any trouble I have caused between you and Logan. I truly apologize for my behavior. I'm a guilty old man with too many secrets. I see—and I always saw—that you are a fine woman. And my son does love you. He loves you so much. I get it now, I do. Trying to chase you off was wrong. I never should have done that, and that I did it had nothing to do with you. It was a knee-jerk reaction born of my own bad deeds in the past."

Okay, now she was really curious. "Exactly what bad deeds, Max?"

He picked up his hat and tapped it on his knee. "Well, Sarah, at this time, I'm not at liberty to say."

She snort-laughed at that one. "Of course, you're not."

He had the nerve to chuckle. "Sarah, I just want you to know that I am finished trying to come between you and Logan. When you two work it out, I will be there for both of you, supporting you in every way I can."

"*When* we work it out?"

"That's what I said."

"You have no way of knowing that we will work it out."

"My son is long-gone in love with you. His heart

may be broken, but he has not given up on you. He's just licking his wounds for a while, until he's ready to try again." Max rose. "He took his phone with him when he left, so if you were to call in order to put him out of his misery, chances are you would get through." He went to the door.

She followed him—until he stopped suddenly and turned back to face her. For several seconds they just stood there, regarding each other.

Sarah broke the silence. "You know where he is, right? You could take me to him?"

"Yes, ma'am."

"I'll be at the Ambling A ranch house at eight to-morrow morning."

The lines around Max's eyes deepened with his dev-ilish grin. "Now that is what I was hoping you might say."

Sarah decided against Cheez-Its and wine for din-ner—not because she knew she should eat something more substantial, but because she was so nervous about what might happen tomorrow that she couldn't eat at all.

She fed Sophia, gave her a bath and put her down to sleep at a little after eight. Then she sat in the living room with a pencil and a scratch pad trying to organize her thoughts for tomorrow. She wanted to have some-thing really meaningful and persuasive to say when she finally saw Logan again, something to convince him that she truly did love him, that he could trust her with his heart. She needed just the right words, words that would reassure him, make him believe that if he said yes to her, she would not disappoint him ever again.

It was almost nine when she heard the truck pull up out in front.

An odd little shiver went through her and she rose to peer out the window behind the sofa.

It was Logan's crew cab, all covered in dust and dried mud, with a big roll of barbwire sticking up out of the bed.

With a cry, she threw down the scratch pad and ran to the door, flinging it open just as he got out of the truck. She stepped out on the porch and then kind of froze there as his long strides took him around the front of the truck and up the front walk.

He looked so good, in a nice, blue shirt and dark-wash jeans, clean-shaven, his hair still damp. He must have come in from the wild, talked to his dad, had a shower and a shave.

Her heart was going so fast she kind of worried it might beat its way right out of her chest, just go jittering off up Pine Street and vanish forever from her sight.

He stopped at the foot of the steps. "Sarah," he said. That was it. That was everything. Really, how did he do it? He could put a whole world of meaning into just saying her name.

"Yes," she said.

"Sarah." And he came up the steps.

"Yes!" She threw herself into his waiting arms. "All the yeses. All the time. Forever, Logan. I'm sorry I was so scared. I'm sorry I blew it. I choked in the worst kind of way. But I'm over that. I want a life with you. I want our forever. I want it, I do."

His Adam's apple bounced as he gulped. "You mean

that?" His eyes gleamed down at her, full of hope and promise and so much love.

"I do. Oh, yes, I do. I love you, Logan. I've missed you so much. If you give me one more chance now, I will never let you down again."

"Yeah," he said, one side of that fine mouth quirking up in a pleased smile. "That's what I'm talking about." And he kissed her, a long kiss, full of all the glory and wonder and desire she'd been missing so desperately since she sent him away.

She melted into him, happier than she'd ever been in her whole life up till now.

And when he lifted his head he said, "Give me your hand." He pulled the ring from his pocket and slipped it on.

"It's so beautiful." And it was, emerald-cut with smaller diamonds along the gleaming platinum band. "I love it." She cast her gaze up to him again. "I love *you*."

"And I love you. So much. Sarah…" He grabbed her close for another kiss and another after that.

Then someone whistled. They looked out at the street to see one of the neighborhood kids jumping on his bike, speeding off, laughing as he went.

Sarah caught Logan's hand and pulled him inside. He shoved the door shut and grabbed her close again.

She said, "Your dad came to see me today."

"I know. He told me."

"I was coming after you tomorrow."

"He told me that, too. I couldn't wait. So here I am."

She lifted a hand and pressed it to his warm, freshly shaven cheek. "Oh, I am so glad. I want to—"

A cry from the monitor on the coffee table cut her off.

"I'll go get her," said Logan. They shared a long look. He knew the drill, after all. If they just waited, the baby might go back to sleep. "I need to see her," he said. "I need to tell her I'm here now and I'm not going away again."

Sarah blinked back happy tears. "Yeah. Go ahead."

Logan yanked her close and kissed her hard—and then turned for the short hall to the baby's room.

"Reow?" Opal sat beneath the dining room table. Delicately, she lifted a paw and spent a moment grooming it. Then she stretched and strutted over to where Sarah stood by the door.

Sarah scooped her up and kissed her on the crown of her head between her two perfect pink ears. "Logan's home," she whispered.

Opal started purring.

In the baby's room, Logan turned the lamp on low and went to the crib.

Sophia let out the sweetest sound at the sight of him—something midway between a laugh and a cry. She waved her hands wildly. "Ah!" she crowed. "Da!"

"How's my favorite baby girl?" he asked as he gathered her into his arms.

Much later, in bed after a more intimate reunion, Logan and Sarah made plans.

They would live in town—at the cottage for now, and eventually in the larger house where she'd grown up. Before they moved, Logan was going to get that garage-door opener installed and hire some guys to build the breezeway from the garage to the back door. They would keep the cottage for Flo and Mack so they would have their own place in their hometown any time they wanted a break from their adventures in the Gulf.

Neither Logan nor Sarah wanted to wait to get married. Her parents would be leaving soon and Sarah insisted the wedding had to happen before they headed south.

"How about Monday?" she suggested.

He blinked at her in surprise. "Monday as in a week from yesterday?"

"Yep. That's the one. We'll get the license tomorrow and I'll call Viv, explain what I want and see if she can make it happen."

"Sarah, don't most brides take months, even a year, to plan a wedding?"

She laughed and kissed him. "They do, but Viv Dalton is a miracle worker. Just you wait and see."

Epilogue

The following Monday at six in the evening, Mack Turner walked Sarah down the aisle Viv had created within a magical cascade of fairy lights in the center of the dance floor at the Ace in the Hole.

Monday, after all, was relatively quiet at the Ace and that meant the owner had been willing to close for a wedding—but really, since everyone in town was invited and most of them showed up, the Ace wasn't closed at all. The place was packed.

The tables were decked out in yellow-and-white checkered cloths with wildflower centerpieces and candles shimmering in mercury glass holders. Sarah wore a floor-length strapless lace gown that she and Lily had found in a Kalispell wedding boutique. Her white cowboy hat had a long, filmy veil attached to the band. The flouncy, full skirt of her dress was perfect for dancing.

And they did dance. Starting with the first dance. Logan and Sarah held Sophia between them and swayed slowly to Keith Urban's "Making Memories of Us."

They served burgers for dinner and there was plenty of beer and soft drinks for all. Sarah's mom took Sophia home at a little after eight, where a nice girl from up the street was waiting to babysit so that Flo could return to the wedding celebration.

By eleven, a lot of the guests had gone home. But most of the younger men and women were still there when Sarah jumped up on the bar brandishing her wildflower bouquet. Lily caught it with a yelp of pure surprise.

"You're next!" Sarah called to her lifelong friend.

Lily laughed and shook her head. She didn't believe it. But Sarah just *knew*. If she could find the only man for her right here in her hometown, certainly Lily could do the same.

Logan was waiting when Sarah climbed down off the bar. He swept her into his arms and out onto the dance floor. They two-stepped through three numbers and then the music slowed. He pulled her nice and close.

"Why the Ace of all places?" he whispered in her ear.

"You love it."

"I do, yeah—but why did you choose it?"

She gazed up at him, golden-brown eyes gleaming, as they swayed to the music. "I guess because the Ace has always meant romance and possibility to me. I love it here. There's music, people talking and laughing. Everybody's having fun. Truthfully, I can't think of a more perfect setting for us to say 'I do.'"

Right then, Cole and Viv Dalton danced by. Viv and Sarah shared a smile. At the edge of the dance floor, Max was watching, looking way too pleased with himself.

Sarah smoothed the collar of Logan's white dress shirt. "Your dad is such a character. I mean, just look at him, grinning like that. What is he thinking?"

"You really don't know?"

"Not a clue."

Logan nuzzled her silky cheek. "He's thinking, *One down, five to go.*"

Sarah threw back her head and laughed as Logan pulled her closer. "What?" she demanded.

"This." And he claimed her lips in a slow, sweet kiss.

* * * * *

Melissa Senate has written many novels for Harlequin and other publishers, including her debut, *See Jane Date*, which was made into a TV movie. She also wrote seven books for Harlequin Special Edition under the pen name Meg Maxwell. Her novels have been published in over twenty-five countries. Melissa lives on the coast of Maine with her teenage son; their rescue shepherd mix, Flash; and a lap cat named Cleo. For more information, please visit her website, melissasenate.com.

Books by Melissa Senate

Harlequin Special Edition

Dawson Family Ranch

For the Twins' Sake
Wyoming Special Delivery
A Family for a Week
The Long-Awaited Christmas Wish
Wyoming Matchmaker

The Wyoming Multiples

The Baby Switch!
Detective Barelli's Legendary Triplets
Wyoming Christmas Surprise
To Keep Her Baby
A Promise for the Twins
A Wyoming Christmas to Remember

Visit the Author Profile page
at Harlequin.com for more titles.

RUST CREEK FALLS CINDERELLA

Melissa Senate

Dedicated to Marcia Book Adirim and Susan Litman.

Thank you for inviting me to Rust Creek Falls,
one of my favorite places to visit.

Chapter 1

Any minute now, Lily Hunt's first blind date ever—one of the six gorgeous Crawford brothers—was going to walk through the door of the Maverick Manor hotel. Lily waited in a club chair in the lobby's bar area by a massive vase of wildflowers, her gaze going from the window to the door every five seconds. She crossed and uncrossed her legs. Folded and unfolded her hands. Slouched and sat up straight, then slouched again. Tried for a pleasant smile.

She also tried to get the better of her nerves, but she still worried that her date would take one look at her, pretend something suddenly came up, like a family emergency or a bad cough, and hightail it out of there.

Oh, stop it, she ordered herself. Even though she really did fear he might do exactly that. Lily, part-time cook, part-time student, twenty-three-year-old tomboy who lived in jeans and sneakers and had more hoodies than most teenage boys, was not the kind of woman who made a man think, *Ooh, I want to meet her.* That was more her good friend Sarah, who was gorgeous and so nice Lily didn't think it was fair. A month ago, Sarah had been the single mother of an adorable baby girl until she'd found herself falling for one of the Crawfords, ranchers from Texas who'd moved to Rust Creek Falls in July. Now she and Logan were *married.* And happily raising little Sophia together.

The Crawford brother Lily was meeting tonight? Knox. Tall, dark and dreamy like his brothers. She'd met some of the Crawford clan last month when they'd come to the Maverick Manor for dinner. Sarah had introduced Lily, and one brother was so drop-dead gorgeous she couldn't speak, which likely also contributed to why he hadn't glanced twice at her.

Confidence, girl! she pep-talked herself. Sarah had insisted on it earlier when she'd phoned to tell Lily to have a wonderful time and to call her after the date with every detail. And Vivienne Dalton, a wedding planner who'd been the one to fix up Lily with Knox, had also called to make sure she hadn't chickened out. (Yes, Lily had taken some serious convincing to accept the date in the first place.) Lily had assured Viv she was getting dressed and would be right on time at 7:00 p.m., classic date hour at the Maverick Manor. Viv had said, *Honey, I will give you only one piece of advice.* Lily had held her breath, waiting. Viv was gorgeous herself and married to Cole Dalton and ran her own successful business—a walking example of making things happen.

Be yourself, Viv had said.

That old yarn? Being herself hadn't exactly gotten Lily very far. Granted, she had a great job as a cook at the Maverick Manor, the fanciest hotel in town. And people raved about her food, which had done more for her confidence than any appreciative glance from a guy ever could. Lily dreamed about having her own place—a small restaurant or a catering shop. Someday.

Today—tonight—was about her love life.

Two short-term relationships were all she had in that department.

She eyed the door. It was 7:00 p.m. on the nose. Lily had been there for five minutes, unfashionably early. She'd changed for the date in the women's locker room, stashing her work clothes in her locker and putting on her one good dress and one pair of heels and one pair of dangling earrings. She never wore makeup, but Sarah had suggested she try some tonight. So Lily had swiped on Maybelline mascara and sheer pinkish-red lipstick and felt like she was playing dress-up, but she supposed she was. She'd left her long red hair down instead of pulling it into a low ponytail the way she did every day.

Now 7:05 p.m. Knox Crawford was now late. Bad sign? Her stomach gave a little flop. The date clearly wasn't high enough on his priorities for him to be on time. Oh, cripes—now she sounded like her dad! Maybe she was getting antsy too early. *Calm down. Go with the flow. Sip your white wine.*

She took a sip…7:09 p.m.

Seven twelve. Humph.

Lily might not be Ms. Confidence when it came to men, but she would never let anyone treat her disrespectfully, and being almost fifteen minutes late for a date was bordering on rude. Right? Her last date was six months ago (no interest on either side) so she wasn't really up on date etiquette.

Seven fifteen.

"Lily!" came a female voice. "How lovely you look! Job interview here at the Manor? Front desk?"

Trying not to sigh as she smiled up at Maren, a woman she'd gone to high school with, Lily glanced down at her royal blue boat-neck, cap-sleeve shift dress, a cotton cardigan tied around her shoulders, and sandals with two-inch stacked heels. It worked for church and weddings, so she figured it would work for tonight.

"Actually, I have a date," Lily said, taking another sip of wine. *Waiter, bring the bottle!*

Maren eyed her up and down. "Oh. Well, have fun!" she said, tottering on her sexy high heels to the main dining room.

Lily looked around the swanky lobby's bar area at the women sitting with dates or out for drinks and appetizers with girlfriends. Skinny jeans and strappy high-heeled sandals. Form-fitting dresses. Slinky skirts. Everyone looked great and evening-ready. And here she was in her Sunday best.

Oh, Lily, get a clue already!

Seven eighteen. Her stomach flopped again, her heart heading south. She was being stood up. First time she actually "put herself out there," like her mom always told her to do, and whammo: humiliated.

She could be plopped on her couch at home with Dobby and Harry, her adorable dachshunds, eating leftover linguini carbonara and garlic bread, and instead, she was about to burst into tears. Whatever, she told herself. She'd just go home, work on a recipe, watch a movie, play with Dobby and Harry.

Just as her pep talk started making her feel better, her cell phone rang.

She didn't recognize the number but she was sure it was her date—or lack thereof. "Hello?"

"Lily, this is Knox Crawford. I'm so sorry I'm not there." There was some weird background noise as if he was covering the phone with his hand and talking to someone else beside him or something. Double humph. "Look, um, something came up and—"

Oh, did it? *Suuure.*

"And I'm really sorry but I can't make it," Knox said. "I—"

More weird background noise. Weird ocean-roar in the phone as if someone was definitely holding a hand over the speaker. Maybe he had his own female version of Davy Jones there with him. Selena Gomez or Charlize Theron, maybe.

"Hello?" a different male voice said. "Lily? This is Xander Crawford. My brother can't make it tonight, but I happen to be free for dinner and I'll be taking his place. See you in five minutes."

Uh, *what*?

"No, that's okay," she said, hoping her voice didn't sound as clogged to him as it did to her. *I am not a charity case!* The famed ire of the angry redhead? She was about to blow, people! "No worries. Bye!" She clicked End Call and stuffed her phone in her stupid little purse—she hated purses!—stood up, took another long sip of her wine, and stalked back into the kitchen, wondering how a person could feel angry and so sad at the same time.

Xander Crawford. Please. She'd seen him up close and personal and he was too good-looking, too sexy— with a Texas drawl, to boot. She'd clam up and stammer or mumble or ramble, especially because of how weird this all was. And what was she? Someone to pity? The poor stood-up date? No thank you!

She was grateful her fellow cooks and her friend AnnaBeth, a waitress, were all so busy they didn't see her slip back into the break room. She opened her locker, and a photo of her dogs, one of her beautiful mother, and a restaurant review from the *Rust Creek Falls Gazette* that had raved about her filet mignon in mushroom peppercorn sauce with roasted rosemary potatoes and sautéed garlic-buttered asparagus reminded her who she was. Lily Hunt. She was meant to be creating magical recipes and figuring out how to get where she wanted to be in a year or two. Not trying to be something she wasn't: a woman who dated gorgeous, wealthy ranchers the entire town was vying for.

Yes, vying for. There were five Crawford brothers left and, according to Viv, their dad wanted to see them married and settled down, so he'd put the wedding planner on the case to find them the right women. All the single ladies in town had put their names in the hat, and hell, why not Lily, tomboy and all? She was flattered Viv had even asked.

And now some stand-in Crawford was showing up, probably only to save the family name since they were new in town and didn't want their dating reps to be ruined. Yeah, no thanks.

"Well, Mama," Lily said, looking at Naomi Hunt's photo, her red hair all she'd inherited from her sophisticated mother. "I did put myself out there, but it didn't work this time. Maybe next." Not that she'd agree to another date anytime soon.

She changed back into her jeans and sneakers with a relieved *ahhh*, put on her T-shirt and tied her hoodie around her waist. She wiped off the lipstick and put her hair in a low ponytail, closed her locker and headed out the swinging door into the lobby.

Right into the muscular chest of Xander Crawford.

"I'm so sorry," Xander said to the young redhead he'd just barreled into. He'd been in such a hurry to catch Lily Hunt that he hadn't considered that the door into the kitchen might have someone coming through it from the other side. Luckily it hadn't been a waiter with a tray of entrées. "Are you okay?"

"I'm fine," she said, but her eyes were like saucers and her cheeks were flushed.

Maybe it was hot in the kitchen? "I'm looking for Lily Hunt. Do you know her? She works here as a cook. Is she still around?"

The redhead stared at him, and for a moment he swore she was shooting daggers out of those flashing green eyes. "*I'm* Lily Hunt. We met last month in the dining room. I was with my friend Sarah, who's married to your brother Logan."

Oh hell. Awkward.

"I'm bad with faces," he said, which was true. "I've met so many people since we moved to Montana that my head's still spinning."

Not to mention all the women who'd introduced themselves to him over the past month. Everywhere he went there seemed to be a smiling woman, offering her card—some of which smelled like perfume—and letting him know she'd "just love to have coffee or a drink or dinner anytime, hon." At first he'd wondered if women were that friendly in every town in the state of Montana. Until he'd realized *why* women were coming at him in droves. They were coming at all the single Crawfords—thanks to his dad. Maximilian Crawford had made a deal with a local wedding planner to get him them all hitched, and that wedding planner had apparently spoken to every single woman in Rust Creek Falls.

Why was that wedding planner so raring to go? Finding *all* the eligible women in town who might be interested in being set up with a Crawford brother?

Because Max had offered Viv Dalton one million bucks to get them all married.

One. Million. Dollars.

If he and his brother Logan hadn't witnessed the exchange with their own eyes and ears, Xander never would have believed it.

Anyway, Xander had a drawer full of scented cards and had not made a single call. His father shook his head a lot over it.

Still, he was surprised he didn't remember meeting Lily. She had the determined face of a young woman who was going places. He liked it. She had freckles, too. He'd always liked freckles.

He was aware he had a smile plastered on his face. Now she did, too.

"Uh, so," she said, "like I said on the phone, no worries. Let's just forget this ever happened, okay?"

He tilted his head. "What do you mean?"

"Your brother got cold feet about our blind date and canceled. You felt bad for whatever reason and took his place. You know who I don't want to be? The woman sitting across from the guy who gave up his evening to 'do the right thing.'"

"I always try to do the right thing," he said. "But trust me, dinner with a lovely woman is hardly a chore, Lily. I'd love to take you out to dinner if you're up for it."

Her expression changed from wary and pissed to surprised. She lifted her chin. "Well, when you put it like that." She flashed him a smile, a genuine smile that lit up her entire face. For a moment he couldn't pull his gaze off her.

"You're probably wondering why I'm wearing a hoodie and sneakers on a date," she said. "I just changed back into my work clothes. I could put the dress on again if you want to wait a few minutes."

"You look incredibly comfortable," he said, tugging at the collar of his button-down shirt. "Trust me, I'll take jeans and a T-shirt over a button-down and tie any day. Luckily, as a rancher, I'm not often forced into a tie."

She smiled that smile again. "Well, then, guess we're not eating here. Unwritten dress code. And to be honest, though I love the food at the Manor, I have it *all the time*."

"Perk of the job, but I get it," he said. "Casual always works for me. I'm new around here, but I already know Ace in the Hole and Wings to Go pretty well. Either of those sound good?"

"Ooh, I'm craving chicken wings—in extra tangy barbecue sauce."

"Woman after my own heart," he said, gesturing toward the door.

She stared at him for a moment, then rushed outside as if she needed a gulp of air. "Uh, Wings to Go isn't very far." They started walking, Lily stopping to pet a tiny dog with huge amber eyes, then to look at a red bird on a branch. He liked that she noticed her environment—and animals in particular. Xander's mind was always so crammed with this and that he'd walked straight into a fence post the other day. Two of his brothers had a good laugh over that one.

Once inside the small take-out shop, they ordered a heap of wings and four kinds of sauces. Lily got out her wallet, but he told her to put it away, that tonight was on him.

"Well, thank you very much," she said. "I appreciate that."

"My pleasure." He glanced out the window. "Given that it's such a gorgeous night, want to take our dinner to the park? We have a good hour of sunlight left."

"Perfect," she said with a smile. "And good thing my dachshunds aren't with us. Dobby and Harry would clear out the wings before we could unpack them. They'd even eat the celery on the side because it smells like chicken wings."

He laughed at the thought of two dachshunds attacking a piece of celery. He held the door open, and they exited into the breezy night air. She sure was easy to talk to, much more than he expected. Not that he'd expected anything since the only thing he'd known about

Knox's date was her name. "I've always wanted dogs. Maybe one day."

On the way to the park, they chatted about dog breeds and Lily told him a funny story about a Great Dane named Queenie who'd fallen in love with Dobby but ignored Harry, who was jealous. He told her about the two hamsters his dad had finally let him get when he was nine, and how they were so in love with each other they ignored *him*. She cracked up for a good minute and he had to say, she had a great laugh.

Rust Creek Falls Park was just a few blocks away and not crowded, but there were plenty of people walking and biking and enjoying the beautiful night. Since they didn't have a blanket, they chose a picnic table and she sat across from him. For a moment they watched a little kid try to untangle the string of his kite. He looked like he might start bawling, but his mom came over and in moments the green turtle was aloft again. Xander swallowed, the tug of emotion always socking him in the stomach when he saw little kids with their moms. Big kids, too. He was always surprised at how the sight affected him. After all these years.

He turned his attention back to Lily and started opening the bags containing their wings. "My brothers and I love the food at the Maverick Manor. We're there for lunch and dinner pretty often. I'll bet you have something to do with that."

She popped open the containers of sauces. "Well, thanks. I hope so. I love cooking. And I love working at the Manor. I can try all kinds of interesting specials and the executive chef always says yes. Lamb tagine was last night's special and it was such a hit. Nothing makes me feel like a million bucks more than when someone compliments my food."

"I love how passionate you are about your work," he said. "Everyone should be that lucky."

"Are you?" she asked.

He dunked a wing in barbecue sauce. "Yes, ma'am. One hundred percent cowboy. A horse, endless acres, cattle, the workings of a ranch—it's what I was born to do."

She stared at him, her green eyes shining. "That's exactly how I feel—about cooking! That I was born to be in the kitchen, with my ingredients and a stove."

He held out his chicken wing and she clinked hers to his in a toast, and they both laughed.

Huh. Whodathought this night would work out so well? When he'd heard his brother Knox arguing with his dad earlier and then calling his date and canceling, he'd been livid. Not so much at his brother for not just sucking it up and going on the date, but at his father for being such a busybody. Knox might have gone on the blind date if he hadn't learned his dad had been responsible for it in the first place. Xander and Logan had told the other four brothers what their father was up to and to hide behind all large tumbleweeds if they saw Viv Dalton coming with her phone and notebook and clipboard, but Knox had thought the whole thing was a joke. Until Viv had apparently cornered him into going on a blind date with one Lily Hunt. He'd agreed and had apparently meant to cancel, then had put the whole thing out of his mind. Until his dad had said, "Knox, shouldn't you be getting ready for your date tonight?"

Knox's face: priceless. A combination of *Oh crud* and *Now what the hell am I gonna do?*

"What's so terrible about you going on a date?" Maximilian Crawford had said so innocently. "Some dinner, a glass of wine. Maybe a kiss if you like each other." The famous smile slid into place.

Knox had been *fuming*. "I always meant to politely cancel. I've been working so hard on the fence line the last couple days that I totally forgot about calling Viv to say forget it."

"Guess you're going then," Max had said with too much confidence.

Knox had shaken his head. "Every single woman in town is after us. Who wouldn't want to marry into a family with a patriarch who has a million dollars to throw around? No thanks."

"Well, it *is* a numbers game," their dad had said.

Knox had been exasperated. "I don't want to hurt my date's feelings, but I'm not a puppet. I'm canceling. Even at the eleventh hour. She'll just have to understand."

Would she, though? Getting canceled on when she was likely already waiting for Knox to show up?

So Xander had stepped in—surprising himself. He'd avoided Viv Dalton, the wedding planner behind the woman deluge, like the plague whenever he saw her headed toward him in town with that "ooh, there's a Crawford" look on her face. But c'mon. He couldn't just let Knox's date get stood up because his brother was so…stubborn.

And anyway, what was an hour and a half of his life on a date with a stranger? Some conversation, even stilted and awkward, was still always interesting, a study in people, of how things worked. Xander had been try-ing to figure out how people worked for as long as he could remember. So he could apply it to his own family history.

"Best. Wings. Ever!" Lily said, chomping on one liberally slathered in maple-chipotle sauce.

"Mmm, didn't try that sauce yet," he said, dabbing a wing in the little container. He took a bite. "Are we in Texas? These rival the best wings in Dallas."

"That's a mighty compliment. Do you miss home?"

"This is home now," he said, more gruffly than he'd meant. "We bought the Ambling A ranch and are fixing it up. We've done a lot of work already. It's coming along."

"So you and your five brothers moved here, right?" she asked, taking a drink of her lemonade.

"Yup. With our dad. The seven Crawford men. Been that way a long time."

Her eyes darted to his. "My father's a widow, too. I lost my mom when I was eight. God, I miss her."

Oh hell, she'd misunderstood about his mother and he didn't want to get into the correction. "Sorry to hear that."

"I'm sorry about your mom," she said.

Well, now he had to. "Don't be. She's not dead, just gone. She took off on my dad and six little boys—my youngest brother, Wilder, was just a baby. When I let myself think about it, I can hardly believe it. Six young sons. And you just walk away."

He shook his head, then grabbed another wing before his thoughts could steal his appetite. These wings were too good to let that happen.

Change the subject, Xander. "So what else do we have in common?" he asked, swiping a wing in pineapple-teriyaki sauce. "You have five brothers, too?"

She smiled. "Three, actually. All older. So you can guess how they treat me. We all live together in the house I grew up in—the four of us and my dad."

"Protective older brothers. That's nice. Princess for a day for life, am I right?"

She snorted, which he didn't expect. "*Exsqueeze me?* Princess? My brothers treat me like I'm one of them. I don't think they know I'm a girl, actually. I'm like the youngest brother."

He laughed, imagining the four Hunts racing around the woods, playing tag, trying to catch frogs, swinging off ropes into rivers.

"They do appreciate that I cook for them, though," she said. "And I do so because they're hopeless. I told my brother Ryan that I was teaching him to cook and that he should heat up a can of stewed tomatoes, and I swear on the Bible that he put an unopened can of tomatoes in a pot and turned on the burner and asked, 'How long should it cook?'"

Xander cracked up. "That's bad."

"Oh, yeah. He's better now. He can even crack an egg into a bowl without sloshing half on the counter or floor. It's all great practice for me for one day owning my own business—either a restaurant or a catering shop. I'm also studying for a business degree online—just part-time. But I want to learn how to start and run a successful business. I'm covering all the bases."

"Wow, impressive!" he said. "You're what, twenty-two?" She looked young. Very young. Too young for him, certainly.

"Twenty-three."

"I've got seven years on you, kid," he said. "And I'll tell you, following your passion is where it's at. I'm a big believer in that."

She sobered for a moment; he wasn't sure why, but then those green eyes of hers lit up again. "Me, too."

They spent the next twenty minutes talking about everything from the differences between Texas and Montana cattle and terrain, where to get the best coffee in Rust Creek Falls (she was partial to Daisy's Donuts but he loved the strong brew at the Gold Rush Diner), the wonders and pitfalls of having many brothers, and her favorite foods for each meal (omelet, chicken salad sandwich on a very fresh baguette, any kind of pasta with any kind of sauce). They talked about steak for ten minutes and then steak fries, thick and crispy, seasoned just right and dipped in quality ketchup.

The wings were suddenly gone but he could talk to her for hours more. They laughed, traded stories, watched the dog walkers, and she told him funny stories about Dobby and Harry. He loved the way the waning sun lit up her red hair and he felt so close to her that he leaned across the table, about to take both her hands to give them a squeeze. He truly felt as if he'd made a real friend here tonight.

But when he leaned, Lily leaned.

Her face—toward his.

He darted back.

She'd thought he was going to kiss her?

He cleared his throat, glancing at his watch. "It's almost nine? How did *that* happen?" He tried for a good-natured smile, but who the hell knew what his expression really looked like. Xander had never been able to hide how he felt. And how he felt right now was seriously awkward.

He liked Lily. A lot. But did he like her *that way*? He didn't think so. She was a kid! Twenty-three to his thirty. Just starting out. And she was the furthest thing from the women he usually dated. Perfume. Long red nails. Slinky outfits and high heels. Sleek hair. And okay, big breasts and lush hips. He liked a woman with curves. Lily was...cute but not exactly his usual type. Not that he could really tell under her loose jeans and the hoodie around her waist obscuring much of her body.

All he knew was that he liked her. A lot.

As a friend.

"Yikes," she said, that plastered smile from when they first met on her face again. She jumped up. "Dobby and Harry are going to wonder where I am."

He collected their containers and stuffed them back in the bag, his stomach twisting with the knowledge that he'd made things uncomfortable. *Never lean toward a woman*, he reminded himself, *unless you're leaning for a kiss*.

"I live pretty close to the park, so I'll just jog home," she said quickly, tossing him an even more forced smile. "I'm dressed for it," she added. "Thanks for dinner!" she called, and ran off.

I'll drive you, he wanted to call out to her, but she was too fast. He watched her reach the corner, hoping she'd turn back and wave so he could see her freckles and bright eyes again, but she didn't.

Hell if he didn't want to see her again. Soon.

Chapter 2

The Ambling A was a sight for the ole sore eyes. Sore brain, really. Xander had thought about Lily all the way home, half wanting to call her to make sure she'd gotten home all right, half not because she might read into it.

Which made him feel like a jerk again, flattering himself.

But the way she'd leaned in for that kiss…

He would *not* lead her on.

He parked his new silver pickup and got out, the sprawling dark wood ranch house, which literally looked like it was made from Lincoln Logs, making him smile. He loved this place—the house, the land, the hard work to get the ranch the way they wanted. Xander headed in, never knowing who'd be home. Hunter, the second-oldest Crawford (Xander was third born), lived in a cabin on the property. A widower since the birth of his daughter, Hunter and his six-year-old, Wren, needed their own space, but the girl still had five uncles to dote on her. Logan, the eldest, had recently moved to town now that he was married with a baby to raise, but he worked on the ranch, as they all did, so it was almost like he'd never left.

The place sure had changed since the day they'd arrived. They'd mended fences for miles, repaired outbuildings, cleaned out barns, burned ditches and worked on the main house itself when they had the time and energy. A month later, it was looking good but they had a ways to go.

He came through the front door into the big house with its wide front hall and grand staircase leading up to a gallery-style landing on the second floor. He saw his dad and three of his brothers up there, going over blueprints, which meant his dad had proposed a change—again—and his sons were trying to talk him out of it. There was many a midnight argument taking place at the Ambling A. When they heard the door close behind him, they all came downstairs.

"Well, well, if isn't the knight in shining armor," Wilder, the youngest of the brothers, said with a grin.

Xander made a face at Wilder and shook his head, hoping they'd go back to talking blueprints. "Lily is hardly a damsel in distress. She's very focused on what she wants. She can definitely take care of herself." The more he thought about her, about what they'd talked about, her plans, her dreams, the more impressed he was.

Logan smiled. "Sounds like the date switch was a date *match*. Knox's loss."

Knox wasn't around. He probably had left to get away from their matchmaking father.

"So? *Was* it a love match?" Finn asked. "When's your next date?"

Twenty-nine-year-old Finn was the dreamer of the group. He could keep dreaming on this one, because another date wasn't going to happen.

Lily was too young. And Xander was too jaded. She'd barely lived, and he was already cynical about love and guarded.

Xander rolled his eyes. "Get real. She's twenty-three. C'mon. And very nice."

"Ah, he used the kiss-of-death word. *Nice*," Wilder said. "Nothing gonna happen there."

That settled for the Crawford men, they turned their attention back to the blueprints. Xander scowled as they ducked their heads over the plans, gabbing away as if they didn't just dismiss a lovely, smart, determined young woman as "nice."

Oh, wait. He was the one who'd called her that.

But his brothers had stamped her forehead with the word, which meant she wasn't hot or sexy or desirable. All without even laying eyes on her.

They'd written her off.

And so did you. You're the one who put her in the friend zone in the first place.

His dad came in from the kitchen with a beer. "Ah, Xander, you're back from the date! Have you already set up a second one?"

"You don't even know if we had anything in common, Dad," Xander said. "Maybe we weren't attracted to each other."

"I just have a feeling," Max Crawford said with a smile and a tip of his beer at his son. That *feeling* should tell his father otherwise.

"I think we're just meant to be friends, Dad," Xander said.

"Meaning she's not his type," Wilder threw in. "Xander likes his women with big hair, big breasts, big hips and big giggles. All play, no talk."

His brothers cracked up.

Xander supposed he deserved that. He did like curvy blondes who didn't delve too deeply and liked to watch rodeos and have sex without expecting much in return other than a nice night out and a call once in a while. But one of those curvy blondes had managed to get inside him and surprise him, and he'd fallen hard, only to find her in bed with his best friend. The betrayal still stung. All these miles away from Texas.

Max shook his head. "You boys should give 'not your types' a chance. You'd be surprised what your supposed type turns out to be."

Logan raised an eyebrow. "If I remember correctly, Dad—and I do—it was *you* who told me that a single mother of a baby was *not* the woman for me. And she is."

"Told you you'd be surprised what your type is," Max said with a grin.

Logan threw a rolled-up napkin at his dad and shook his head with a laugh. But last month, Xander had caught wind of some of his father's arguments with Logan about dating a single mother. Max had hinted that if the relationship didn't work out, there would be *three* sad hearts—including a child who didn't ask to get dragged into the muck. Xander had known his father had to be thinking of his ex-wife and how she'd abandoned them all. Times like that, he forgave his dad for being such a busybody.

Still, Xander *was* sticking to his type, but this time, there was no way any woman was getting inside. These days, he was only interested in a good time and he always made that clear.

Except that hadn't been clear to Lily Hunt. Oh hell. She'd thought she was going on a date in good faith, that had gotten all messed up, and then he'd stepped in to save the night—and had ended up making it worse. He shook his head at himself. Now he really did want to call her and doubly apologize, but how would *that* sound?

Uh, hi, Lily, sorry for making your night go from bad to worse when you actually thought I was leaning in a for kiss.

Getting stood up by Knox might have been more fun.

He sighed.

But maybe Lily was just out for a good time herself? Could it be? She seemed a little too focused and serious-minded for that, though. Still, with her life so set on track, perhaps she just wanted a nice night out and some laughs. It was possible.

He tried to imagine Lily Hunt, with her freckles and big dreams and flashing green eyes, so full of life, out for a good time, giggling and whispering about what she was going to do to him while raking her nails up his thigh. Frankly, he couldn't. First of all, her nails had been bitten to the quick. And honestly, he didn't want to think of her in any way but as a new friend.

"Well, I need to do some research on the cattle we

want to add to the Ambling A," Xander said. "See y'all in the morning." He took the steps two at the time, wanting to get away from this conversation.

Lily wasn't his type. Plain and simple. And even if she were, he wouldn't be interested in a relationship. Not anymore. Besides, he had the ranch to concentrate on and a new state to discover, not to mention a new hometown to get to know. That was enough.

Just let the night go, he told himself.

Upstairs in his bedroom, he sat at his desk and opened his laptop, fully intending to research local cattle sales. But he found himself going to the website for the Maverick Manor and looking at their lunch menu—just in case he wanted to drop in tomorrow after a hard morning's work.

"French dip au jus on crusty French bread and a side of hand-cut steak fries" was one of tomorrow's lunch specials. He'd just eaten and his mouth was already watering for that meal. Yeah, maybe he'd go to the Manor for lunch and even pop into the kitchen to say hi to Lily.

That was what friends did, right? Popped in? Visited? Said a quick hello? He'd do that and leave. That would make things good between them, get rid of all that awkwardness from tonight. They could truly be friends. Everyone could always use another friend.

But damn if he wasn't sitting there, staring at the list of the Maverick Manor's decadent desserts and thinking about feeding Lily succulent strawberries, watching her mouth take the juicy red fruit.

What the hell? The woman wasn't his type! They were just going to be buddies.

He clicked over to the cattle sale site, forcing his mind onto steers and heifers and far from strawberries and twenty-three-year-old Lily Hunt.

"Ooh, Lily, that hot Crawford cowboy was just seated at table three," whispered AnnaBeth Bellows, a waitress at the Maverick Manor and Lily's good friend. Lily had told AnnaBeth about her date with Xander so Lily knew the hot cowboy had to be him.

She almost gasped yet kept her focus on her broiled shrimp, caramelizing just so in garlic, olive oil and sea salt. She added a hint of cayenne in the last few seconds, and plated it the moment she knew it was done. Sixth sense.

According to Mark, table eight's waiter, the group was from New Orleans originally even though they lived in Kalispell now. Lily always had the waiters find out where her diners were from so she could add a tiny taste of home to their dishes. It was just a little thing Lily did that her diners seemed to appreciate, even if they didn't know why they reacted so strongly, so emotionally to their food. The other cooks thought it was a lot to deal with, but Lily enjoyed the whole process. Food was special. Food was your family. Food was home in a good way, the best way, and could remind people of wonderful memories. Sometimes sad memories, too. But evoking those feelings seemed to have a good impact on her diners and on her. So she continued the tradition.

She placed the gorgeous shrimp, a deep, rich bronze, with its side of seasoned vegetables on the waiter's station and raced to the Out door to the dining room. She peered through the little round window on the door, looking for the sexy cowboy.

Yes, there he was. Sitting by himself, thank God, and not with a date set up by Viv Dalton, which was her immediate fear when AnnaBeth had whispered that he was here.

Of course, he could be waiting on a date.

"Dining alone," AnnaBeth said with a smile.

Lily couldn't help grinning back, her heart flip-flopping. "Could a man *be* more gorgeous?"

"Yes—my boyfriend," AnnaBeth said, "even if Petey-pie has a receding hairline and a bit of a belly. He's hot to me."

Lily laughed. "And Pete's the greatest guy ever, too." Yes, indeed, Lily should aspire to a wonderful guy like AnnaBeth's "Petey-pie." Kind. Loyal. Full of integrity. Brought her little gifts for no reason. Called her Anna-Beauty all the time. Making Lily wistful.

Lily bit her lip. "Okay, why is Xander here after that awkward moment from hell last night on our not-a-date?"

"The *almost* kiss," AnnaBeth suggested, watching for the other two cooks plating, which meant she'd have to rush off to pick up. "I'm telling you, Xander was just caught off guard. He wasn't even expecting to have a date last night, right? But then he did, a wings picnic, and he fell madly in love with you but didn't expect to and now he's here to ask you out again."

Lily laughed. "I love you, AnnaBeth. Seriously. Everyone needs one of you. But life is not a Christmas movie. Even though I wish it were."

"Listen, my friend. You have to make your own magic. Just like you do with your food."

Lily watched Xander close the menu. She wondered what he'd decided on.

"Ah, time to take the cowboy's order," AnnaBeth said. "Back in a flash."

Lily watched them until she noticed her boss, Gwendolyn, eyeing her and then staring at her empty cooking station. She darted to her stove, working on another batch of au jus for today's French dip special.

In a minute, AnnaBeth was back with Xander's order. The special.

She smiled and began working on it and four more for other tables. But to table three's sauce she added just a hint of sweet, smoky barbecue sauce, a flavor that would take Xander Crawford back to Texas where he'd lived his whole life until a month ago.

Could he be here to see her? If he wasn't interested in her—and he sure hadn't seemed to be last night with that not-kiss thing—wouldn't he *avoid* where she worked?

But then she thought of him and the reaction he must get from women, and she was flooded with doubts. There was no way Lily of the hoodie and sneakers would be Xander Crawford's type. When she was young and girls at school would make fun of her for being a tomboy, her mother would always say, *You're exactly as you should be—yourself.* That had always made Lily feel better. And maybe Xander *liked* a down-to-earth woman with flour on her cheek and smelling of onions and caramelized shrimp and peppercorns.

Anything was possible. *That* was the name of the game.

She smiled at the thought, adding a pinch of garam masala to table twelve's sauce since they were honeymooners who'd just returned from India. For table fourteen, visitors from Maine, she added a dash of Bell's Seasoning, a famed New England blend of rosemary, sage, oregano and other spices.

Lily worked on five more entrées, her apron splattered, her mind moving so fast she could barely think about Xander in the dining room, eating her food right now. Was he enjoying it? Did it hit the spot? Did it bring a little bit of Texas to Montana today?

"Five-minute break if you need it," Gwendolyn called out to her. "Your tables are all freshly served so you're clear."

"Ah, great," she said, grabbing her water bottle and taking a big swig, staring out the long, narrow window at the Montana wilderness at the back of the Manor.

"I just had the best French dip sandwich of my life," a deep voice said from behind her, and she almost jumped.

Xander! Standing right there.

"Craziest thing," he said. "I took two bites and started thinking about the ranch I grew up on in Dallas, my dad teaching me and Hunter how to ride a two-wheeler. I was a little mad at my dad earlier, and now I'm full of good memories, so he's back out of the doghouse."

"You can't be in here," she whispered, trying to hide her grin. She shooed him out the back door, the breezy August air so refreshing on her face. "So you loved the French dip?"

"Beyond loved it. It tasted like…home. I know *this* is home now, but that sandwich reminded me of Texas in a good way. And I left behind some things I'd like to forget."

Huh. Like what? she wondered. A bad relationship? His heart?

"It's a little trick my mother taught me when I was young," she said, making herself keep her mind on the conversation. "My maternal grandparents moved to Montana from Louisiana, and my grandmother would add just a dash of creole seasoning to everything she cooked here because it reminded her of the bayou. My mama was a little girl when they left the South, and she never forgot that taste, so she taught me about it. Now I try to add a little taste of home in all my orders. It's easy for the waiters to get a personal tidbit about where they're from or have just been."

He stared at her for a moment, his dark eyes unreadable. What was he thinking? "You're not an everyday person, Lily Hunt."

She wasn't sure how to take that. "Uh, thank you?"

He smiled. "I mean that in the best way possible. I'm not sure I've ever met someone like you. You have a bit of the leprechaun in you."

She narrowed her eyes at him. "Aren't leprechauns supposed to be the worst kind of mischievous?"

"Magical. That's what I meant. You've got a bit of magic in you." His voice held a note of reverence, and she was so startled by it, so overwhelmed, that she couldn't speak.

"I have to have another French dip," he said. "For the road. It was so good I feel like I should get seven to go for my brothers and dad. In fact, can you take that order?"

She grinned. "Absolutely."

"Good. Maybe they'll get off my case about last night's date and stop asking me all kinds of questions. I tried to tell them we're just friends, that it wasn't really a *date* date, since you were fixed up with Knox. But you know how brothers are."

Her heart sank to her stomach, so she wasn't capable of speech at the moment. All she could manage was a deep everlasting sigh of doom.

Why had she let herself believe a nutty fantasy that this man, six foot two, body of Adonis, face of a movie star, a man who could have any woman in this town, would go for the tomboy with red hair who smelled like onions? Why? Was she that delusional?

I love how passionate you are, he'd said more than once in the very short time they'd known each other.

She wasn't delusional. She *was* passionate about life—and love, even if she'd never experienced it. She sure knew what incredible heart-pounding lust felt like, though. Because she felt it right now. With Xander Crawford.

This is what it feels like to fall in love. And it was impossible to stop, like a speeding train, even if the object of her affection just told her "it wasn't a *date* date" and they were "just friends."

Just friends.

Get back to earth, she told herself. *Go make his seven French dips to go.*

"Well, back to work!" she said too brightly, and dashed inside, then realized she'd left him high and dry in the back and he'd have to find his way around to the front of the hotel to return to the dining room.

He'll manage, she thought as she got back to her station to prepare his order. She saw him sneak and dart through the kitchen, her heart leaping at the quick sight of him. Sigh, sigh, sigh.

"Lily, you're amazing," her boss said. "*Seven* French dips to go for table three?" Gwendolyn was beaming at her, so at least she had big love at work if not in her personal life.

Forget Xander Crawford and focus on where you want to be next year: owning your own catering shop or little café, whisking your customers away to home.

Sure. As if she could forget Xander for a second.

Chapter 3

"Am I right?" Xander asked his brothers and father as they sat on the backyard patio of the Ambling A, gobbling up their French dips. "Is this incredibly delicious or what?"

The Crawfords were so busy eating they barely stopped long enough to agree. Knox held up his beer at Xander. Hunter said he wanted two more.

"I'll tell you what *I'm* right about," his father said, taking a huge bite of his sandwich. "That you went to Maverick Manor for lunch just so you could see the pretty chef again. Admit it."

"Yeah, admit it," Finn said with a grin.

What was that old line? No good deed went unpunished? No way would he ever bring these gossips a good lunch again! "I went because I was *hungry.* So how's the roof on the barn coming, Logan?" he asked his eldest brother, hoping the others would shut the hell up.

"Logan, tell Xander instead how wonderful married life is," his dad said. "Someone special to come home to at the end of a long, hard day."

Oh, brother. Literally.

Logan laughed, finishing the rest of his French dip and taking a sip of his beer. "First, that *was* damned good. Compliments to your chef, Xan."

"She is not *my* chef!" Xander shouted.

Six Crawfords laughed. One stewed in his chair.

"Second, Dad is right," Logan said. "Finding Sarah changed my life. Nothing beats coming home to her every night, waking up to her every morning. And raising that cherub Sophia with her? I feel like the luckiest guy in the world."

Huh. Xander eyed his brother. He was dead serious, heart-on-his-sleeve earnest.

"All of you are going to be that lucky, too," the Crawford patriarch said. "You know, I had to be both mother and father to you boys. I didn't always get it right. I guess I want just to see you all settled down and happy. I want you to have everything you deserve. All the happiness."

Logan put a hand on his dad's shoulder.

"To happiness," Finn said, raising his beer. "I'm into it."

"Even Knox can't *not* toast to that," Hunter said.

Xander eyed the always-intense Crawford brother. Knox raised his beer again with a bit of a scowl. Knox had thanked him for going out with Lily in his place, then had grimaced when Max Crawford said, "Now that you're over being stubborn about it, there are a hundred more single beauties out there, Knox, ole boy."

"First of all, I'm still not going out with anyone," Knox had said. "Secondly, there probably aren't a *hundred* people in this town, Dad," he'd added, and had made himself scarce until he smelled the French dips.

Rust Creek Falls was tiny, less than a thousand residents, but nine hundred fifty of those had to be single women. Or at least that was how it had felt ever since Max Crawford had announced—erroneously!—that his six sons were looking for wives.

"Xander, you should probably make a reservation at the Manor for dinner now, just in case," Max said with a grin. "Find out if your chef is working first, though."

Xander got up, tossing his wrappers in the trash can. "I think I hear one of the calves calling for me." He headed for the barn, the too-familiar sound of his brothers' laughter trailing him.

His chef. Hardly!

"Mmm, mmm," he heard his dad say as he rounded the barn. "This roast beef takes me right back to Texas. Coulda ordered it from Joey's Roadhouse, am I right?"

Xander smiled. *Told you.* He'd been taken by surprise as bits and pieces of memories had popped into his mind while eating at the restaurant. Just flickers that he thought he'd forgotten: Logan threatening a bully on his behalf. Knox telling their dad off when he thought their dad was being unfair with Xander about something. The constant runs to the grocery store for milk since six growing boys could finish a gallon after one cold-cereal breakfast. Christmas after Christmas, each boy picking a brother's name from the Santa hat to buy for, the three years in a row that he got Hunter.

His mother in a yellow apron.

Now it was *his* turn to scowl. He didn't often think about his mom. He didn't remember much about her, just maybe the thought of her. There were few pictures of Sheila Crawford in the family photo albums; he had no idea what his dad had done with the rest of them. Max had probably stored them up in the attic, leaving just a few for the boys to have some idea what their mother had looked like. Logan, Xander and Hunter remembered her the most but even they had been too young to hold a picture of her in their minds. Somehow, Xander did remember the yellow apron. And long brown hair.

A calf gave out a mini moo and he shook his head to clear his mind. All this thinking of home and his family's ribbing him about "his chef" nicely contradicted each other. Thinking about his mother reminded him that marriage didn't work out. That even the people you could count on to love you, by birthright, could leave. Just walk away without looking back. Between that and finding his girlfriend and best friend in bed, he gave a big "yeah right" to happily-ever-after.

"Yoo hoo! Anyone home?" a very female, high-pitched voice called out.

Xander came out of the barn to find an attractive, curvy blonde, just his type, he had to admit, smiling at him as she walked over from her car. "Hi, can I help you?"

"I'm so sure you can, honey," she said, her voice lowering an octave. "I'm Vanessa and I was hoping to hire one of you tall, strong, strapping cowboys to teach

me how to ride a horse. I'm a town gal, so no horse or
land of my own."

Xander knew there were plenty of horse farms and
ranches in the area that offered riding lessons. The Ambling A wasn't one of them.

He had a feeling this woman was here for a cowboy
and had zero interest in horses, if her very high heels
and short dress were any indication. But any woman in
the market for a Crawford was looking for a wedding
ring. So despite the fact that Vanessa was his type to a
T, he'd have to sit this one out.

"Ah. We don't offer riding lessons, but perhaps one
of my brothers can give you the rundown on who does."

"I'd be happy to hear it from you," she said, pucker-
ing her glossy red lips a bit.

"I'm not really one of the eligible Crawfords," he said.

She frowned. "I don't see a ring. Unless you're spoken for."

Lily's face flashed into his mind. His chef. That was
weird. "Well, I do seem to be seeing someone, unex-
pectedly," he added, for no godly reason. Then realized
that was why Lily had popped into his brain. She was
his way out!

"For goodness' sake, why didn't you say so and save
me the trouble of flirting?" She fluffed her hair. "Any
of your *eligible* brothers around?"

He smiled and mentally shook his head. A woman
who knew she wanted. Had to give her credit for the
chutzpah. "Let me see if Finn knows about riding lessons. Be right back."

"Finn? I do like that name," she said, peering around.

"Hang on a sec."

He went around the back of the sprawling ranch house to find the Crawfords just finishing up. "Finn, there's a woman here to see you."

Finn perked right up. That was a line he liked. "Say no more," he said before dashing around the house.

Xander smiled. That was easy. He went back into the barn and got down to work, ignoring the giggles coming from Vanessa as Finn flirted.

A flash of freckles and determined green eyes came to mind again. He should let Lily know his family loved the French dip, too, right? She'd probably appreciate hearing that. He could stop by the Manor and say it loud enough for her boss to hear; who couldn't use a gold star at work from a happy customer?

Yeah. He'd stop by and let her know. A good friend would do that, and he had a feeling that was exactly what he and Lily were going to be: good friends. That was it. Sorry, Matchmaking Dad.

The Hunt house was a big white colonial not far from the center of town. Xander glanced up at the second-floor windows, wondering which room was Lily's. He had a vision of himself standing out here at night, tossing pebbles at her window to get her to come out as if they were in high school or something.

Something about this very young woman had him all discombobulated.

He shook his head to clear it and rang the buzzer on the side of the blue door. He liked the color; it was a deep-sea blue that might be interesting for the barns at the Ambling A.

An auburn-haired guy in his midtwenties opened

the door. One of Lily's three brothers, he presumed. He had on a pristine Kalispell Police Academy uniform, including a cap.

"Hey, you're one of those Crawfords," the guy said, his hazel eyes intense on Xander.

"I am. Xander Crawford, specifically. I haven't broken any laws, have I? I haven't been to Kalispell yet."

The guy scrunched up in his face in confusion, then glanced down at his uniform. "Oh, this. I'm on my way to school. Not a cop yet, but I will be in a few months." He eyed Xander, then looked behind him into the house, then turned back. "Got a minute?" he asked. "I was hoping to run into one of you, but I'm rarely in town during the day." He extended his hand. "Andrew Hunt."

Okay, now Xander was confused. "Pleasure to meet you," he said. "So what can I—we—do for you?"

"I'm wondering about your overflow," Andrew said, stepping out onto the porch and shutting the door.

"Overflow?" Xander repeated.

"I heard your father's trying to get his sons married off and offered a wedding planner five million bucks to get the job done. A buddy told me that since then, all the places he goes in town to meet women have dried up. Even at Ace in the Hole, our place to play darts and always meet a few ladies, even if we already know them, there was *no one* there last Saturday night. Just a bunch of guys. Man, it was depressing."

"*One* million," Xander corrected—quite unnecessarily, but still. "And I see the problem."

"So, I was thinking, if you're on one of your dates and it doesn't work out, maybe you could mention that you know a great guy in the police academy and set something up for after six, any night."

Wait, now *Xander* was a matchmaker? Good Lord. "Look, Andrew, I—"

"I know, I know. But listen. I'm about to have my act totally together. I'm ready to settle down. And the playing field has been decimated. Your faults, dude."

Xander had to give him that. "I see your point."

"I'm just saying, if you want to mention my name and availability to any lovely lady you're not interested in, I'd appreciate it."

"I'm not interested in *anyone*," Xander said—quickly. "This is my dad's thing. Not mine."

"Well, just think of me, leaping over walls at the academy and studying for my procedure quiz, a forty-five minute commute each way, all with the intended goal of serving and protecting our communities one day."

Xander sighed. "I'll see what I can do. What's your type?"

"Nice," Andrew said. "I like nice. My last girlfriend? Not so nice. Pretty, but ooh boy."

Xander laughed. "Got it. Nice." He shook his head at that one. "I'll keep this between us."

"Oh, no need," Andrew said. "I've got the family on it, too, but they're no help. You'd think having a sister a couple years younger would mean lots of introductions and dates, but nope. Lily's either in the kitchen here or in the kitchen at the Maverick Manor or hunched over her laptop taking her online class. Thanks, Lily." He smiled.

"Speaking of Lily, I'm actually here to see her."

Andrew tilted his head. "Really? Why?"

Xander stared at him. "We're friends."

"Oh. Yeah, I figured you two couldn't be dating. I mean, she's *super* single, but I can't even imagine her throwing her name into the hat to land some rich cowboy. No offense."

"None taken," Xander said with a smile. He could imagine how Lily had her hands full with this crew if the other three Hunts were anything like Andrew.

"So you're on board?" Andrew asked. "With the overflow?"

"Sure," Xander assured him.

"Awesome." Andrew tipped his Kalispell Police Academy cap at Xander, then threw open the door. "Lily!" he bellowed. "Someone's here to see you!" He headed past Xander to the driveway. "Later, dude," he added amiably, jogging down to his car.

Wondering what he'd just gotten himself into, Xander watched Andrew drive off.

"Be right there!" he heard Lily call from somewhere in the house.

It was crazy, but the sound of that voice? His heart skipped a beat.

How many times had she told Andrew not to scream from one room to another? Lily was in the kitchen, working on a vegan entrée she hoped to introduce as an option at the Manor so that all their guests were covered, and she'd heard Andrew's loud voice as though he were standing right beside her.

She took off her apron and washed her hands, figuring her visitor was Sarah, whom she'd texted to mention that Xander had come in for lunch earlier and had barged right into the kitchen to see her. She'd asked if that could possibly mean he did like her *that way*, even when all signs pointed to a friendship only.

Sarah had said men often didn't know how they felt and figured it out as they went along or sometimes in one fell swoop. If *she* liked Xander *that way*, Sarah had texted, then she should go for it.

But it wasn't Sarah in the hallway. It was Xander.

What on earth was he doing here?

And looking so incredibly gorgeous. She'd never seen him in his cowboy clothes. Dark jeans. Brown boots. A navy T-shirt. And a brown Stetson held against his stomach. *Be still, my idiot heart*, she thought. His slightly long hair curled a bit at the nape of his neck, and his dark brown eyes were on her. The man was too good-looking.

Dobby and Harry were sitting on either side of him, staring up at him. Dobby was sniffing his cowboy boot. Harry was giving him the once-over.

Xander knelt down and gave each dog a pat, earning wagging cinnamon-colored tails. "Well, you must be the famous Dobby and Harry I've heard so much about. And even though you look identical, I bet you're Dobby and you're Harry."

"Name tags give it away every time," Lily said with a grin. "They can never get away with switching places like most twins."

He gave them both another pat and stood up. "I stopped by Maverick Manor to pay compliments to the chef from six other appreciative ranchers, and your friend AnnaBeth said you'd finished your shift, so I thought I'd stop by here and tell you."

Okay, granted, Lily's house was pretty close to Maverick Manor. She could walk there if her very old car broke down. But still, he went out of his way to go see her at the restaurant. Then out of his way again to "stop by" her house?

He liked her. Whether he knew it or not. Her stomach flipped—in a good way—and she had to stop herself from smiling like a lunatic.

Thank God for friends like Sarah who understood men! Crawford men, in particular.

"Something smells amazing," he said, sniffing the air.

Okay, she loved when he complimented her cooking skills. "I'm working on a tofu dish for a vegan option at the Manor."

"In cattle country? Well, if you can make tofu smell that good, I imagine it'll be a hit. I'd pay a million bucks for a Lily Hunt hamburger."

She laughed. "You're going to give me a big head."

"Hey, maybe you could give me a cooking lesson sometime. I'd pay you well for your time." He named a crazy figure.

"Seriously? That much for one lesson?"

"Seriously. But I want to learn to make all my favorites. Teach me how to make that French dip. Teach me how to make fettuccini carbonara, which I crave every other day. Teach me how to make a pizza from scratch without burning the crust."

Teach me how not to fall in love with you, she thought. She was practically a goner.

"Lily, any more of that par-something thingie left?" a male voice shouted from upstairs. Ryan, the brother closest in age to her.

Lily smiled and shook her head. "Parfait!" she called back, even though she'd never stop her brothers from yelling from room to room if she did it, too. "And no, you four attacked it and there was none left for me."

"Sorry!" Ryan shouted back. "If you make more, make like five extra!"

"I see I'm not the only one who can't resist your cooking," Xander said. "Maybe I could observe as you make the tofu dish. Get a handle on the inner workings of a kitchen before we set up a formal lesson."

Xander Crawford wanted to watch her make tofu? "Who cooks for you guys now?" she asked.

"We take turns burning food. Logan's all right on the grill, but he moved out. We order in, pick up and go out *a lot*."

She laughed. "Well, follow me, then." She turned to the dogs. "Dobby and Harry, feel free to go back to snoozing in your sun patch." The dogs waited a beat to see if the newcomer had a treat or rawhide chew for them, and since he didn't pull anything out of his pocket, they lost interest and walked back to their big cushy bed by the window and curled up.

"That's the life," Xander said, smiling as he followed Lily through the living room, past the dining room and into the kitchen.

She'd never been so aware of someone following her into another room before. He was so tall, so built, so *male* that she almost melted into a puddle on the floor. She was very used to being surrounded by testosterone. But this was something entirely different.

Especially so close up. Because the kitchen wasn't

all that big and Xander was right beside her at the stove, his thigh almost touching hers.

Could she handle the heat? That was the question.

Xander was standing so close to Lily he could smell her shampoo—the scent a combination of flowers and suntan lotion. She wore green cargo pants, a white T-shirt covered by a red apron that read Try It, You'll Like It, and weird orange rubber shoes. Her long red hair was in a messy bun on top of her head with what looked like a chopstick securing it.

His awareness of her clobbered him over the head. He used to argue with his brothers over whether a man could be friends with a woman he found sexually attractive, and some said yes and some said no way because the sexual element would always be there and that meant there was more than friendship at work. Xander believed a man could absolutely be friends with a woman.

Since when was he sexually attracted to Lily, anyway? Just because he was noticing every little thing about her? The orange rubber shoes were hard to miss. Right? He was here to learn about tofu, something he knew absolutely nothing about.

And something he had absolutely no interest in, too.

You didn't even know she was making tofu until you were inside the house. You came here on pretense.

This was getting confusing. But an undeniable fact was that he was in this kitchen because he wanted to be around Lily. Listening to her. Talking to her. Looking at her.

He suddenly pictured her naked, coming out of the shower, all that lush red hair wet around her shoulders, water still beaded on her breasts and trailing down her stomach and into her navel. Every nerve ending went haywire and he shivered.

"Caught a chill?" she asked, glancing at him as she browned the little pieces of tofu in a fry pan. "I hate that. This morning I was making pancakes, fifty of them for the bottomless pits I call my brothers and father, and I suddenly got a chill even though I was standing right in front of a gas flame in August. Crazy."

He was hardly chilled. Nope, not at all.

Now she was talking about sesame oil and how to make the tofu crispy for the stir-fry. She was saying something about cornstarch and pepper, but he'd stopped hearing her words and focused instead on her face and body.

Granted, she wasn't curvy. Or big-breasted. Or remotely his usual type. But there was just something about her. He must be losing his mind because he thought it was the freckles. Or the green eyes. Or the wide smile. Or the way she talked so animatedly about the difference between a wok and a sauté pan.

"Going to make tofu stir-fry for your family tonight?" she asked him, holding out a piece of the brown crispy not-meat on a wooden spoon. She brought it up to his mouth, and he looked at her, then slid his lips around it.

She flushed.

He flushed.

He leaned closer.

She…backed away. As if she'd been there, done that, and had lived to tell the tale.

"I, uh, you…have sesame oil on your cheek," he

rushed to say, leaning a bit closer to dab it away. He forced himself not to lick it off his finger.

Saved. He hadn't been about to kiss her. No sir.

He had to get out of this kitchen, this enclosed space, with this woman. She was his buddy, that was all. Even if he *were* attracted to her, she was too young and had big dreams that she should focus on. He was a grumbly, stomped-on, love-sucks guy who wasn't getting over it anytime soon. She needed the male version of herself. A guy as great as she was.

Not that he wanted to think of her with *any* guy.

Oh hell. He needed to go find a Vanessa type and forget about this green-eyed, freckled, curveless chef who had him all discombobulated. Yes. That was what he needed. An airhead who wouldn't make him think, wouldn't challenge him, wouldn't stab a dagger through his chest.

"Appreciate the lesson," he said. "The Crawfords might not be ready for tofu, but I might surprise them one day."

"So how do you want to schedule the cooking lesson?" she asked, stirring the pan.

"Let me check my calendar," he said. "I'm pretty busy right now. In fact, I'd better get going. Later, buddy."

He didn't miss her face falling.

Buddy.

Cripes, Xander. You always go that step too far. Why had he added that unnecessary zinger?

Because now they both knew—for sure. They were friends. That was it.

He smiled awkwardly and then headed out the kitchen door as if the place were on fire.

Chapter 4

Buddy.

Buddy!

Every time she heard that word—in Xander's sexy voice—echoing in her head, she alternated between disappointment and *oh hell no!* She was not going to be buddy-zoned by Xander Crawford when she'd lain awake all night imagining the kiss that might have taken place in her kitchen yesterday.

The kiss that did not happen but could have. He would have swept her up into his arms like in a movie and carried her up to her bedroom—no, scratch that. He would have carried her into his silver pickup, raced her back to the Ambling A and his bedroom, and they'd have spent the afternoon making mad, passionate love and coming up with silly names for their new relationship. Xanlil. Lilxan.

Not exactly flowing off the tongue. Their "celeb" name sounded like a prescription medication.

She smiled, then sighed inwardly as she carried the tray of drinks and treats while Sarah Crawford wheeled her baby stroller over to a table way in the back of Daisy's Donuts. They were going to talk shop—translation: *men*—so they needed to be away from pricked-up ears in the small town. Luckily, there were only a handful of people sitting in the shop, mostly teenagers who couldn't care less about Lily's love life, so she planned to tell Sarah everything.

Not that there was much to tell. But she did need advice. And Sarah was not only way more experienced at relationships, she was married to a Crawford.

Sarah parked the stroller and smiled at her sleeping little Sophia, the seven-month-old beauty so sweet in her pink-and-white-striped pajamas, I Love Daddy in glittery print across the front. The pj's were a gift from Daddy himself, Xander's eldest brother, Logan, who loved Sophie as if she were his own flesh and blood. To him, she clearly was. Lily's faith in everything was always restored whenever she thought about Sarah and Logan's love story.

Two days had passed since their second awkward moment involving leaning toward each other, and Xander Crawford hadn't shown his face in the dining room of Maverick Manor or made arrangements for his pricey cooking lesson. He was clearly avoiding her. Of course, Lily could text him about the lesson, push things a little. But she was not going to chase a man who was making it clear he wasn't interested.

Blast. That was the thing. He did seem interested—

to a point. And then he backed off. She wasn't getting just-friend vibes from the guy. Or maybe she just didn't know enough about men and relationships to understand what was going on here.

Maybe nothing was going on.

Please, Lordy, don't let me be one of those delusional creatures who thinks this and that when there's no there *there!*

Lily took a bite of her lemon-custard donut and sips of the refreshing iced tea, the sugary goodness that was always able to do its own restorative work on her mind and heart. Temporarily for the moment, anyway. As Sarah sipped her iced latte, Lily filled in her friend on all things Xander.

Sarah picked up her frosted cruller. "Yup, I know that advance-and-retreat well. I went through it with a Crawford brother myself. I'm telling you, Lil, it takes men a while sometimes to see what's in front of their gorgeous faces."

Lily eyed Sarah's beautiful wedding ring. "I don't know. I have all kinds of crazy feelings for Xander. *All* kinds. I think he's incredibly hot. So sexy. And he's smart. Funny. Laughs at my jokes. He loves dogs. He's passionate about his work and helping his family restore the Ambling A. Did I mention he's so hot I can barely look at him sometimes?"

"Oh, trust me, I know that well, too. The man is interested, Lily. I wouldn't say it if I didn't think it was true. Sounds to me like maybe he didn't plan on getting involved with someone, though."

"But he has a highly skilled wedding planner setting up dates for him—for all the single Crawfords," Lily pointed out.

"Ugh, that," Sarah said with a grimace. "Has Xander gone on any?"

"I don't know. I hate the thought of him being fixed up with anyone." She took a grumpy bite of her donut, even the delicious sugary confection not making her feel better this time around.

"Well, worry not, my dear. You said he asked you to give him a cooking lesson, right?"

"Right…" Lily prompted, confused by where her friend was going.

"You'll be confined to one room for a few hours, working on a few recipes together—then testing them out. A lot can happen in a few hours." She nodded sagely and took another bite of her cruller, sliding a glance at baby Sophia, who continued to snooze through Lily's man troubles.

Hey, at least she had man troubles. In the past year, she'd had one bad date. That was it.

Why? Because she was shy around men? Because she was a tomboy?

She glanced down at her jeans and blah blue T-shirt with Billy's Bait Shop and an illustration of a worm on a line. Then she looked at Sarah. A new mother. And what was Sarah wearing? A cute sundress and flat metallic sandals. Her friend looked so pretty and pulled together. What was Lily's excuse for dressing like one of her brothers?

Oh God. This shirt *was* her brother's. Ryan's.

You are hopeless, Lily Hunt. This wasn't her or her style. She'd always wanted to tag along with her older brothers and so she dressed like them to play rough like them, and it had just become her look. Huh. Maybe she needed to go shopping. And beg Sarah to come with her and play stylist.

And what? Skinny jeans and a tighter, more feminine top would suddenly make Xander Crawford fall for her? Nope. Didn't work that way. Whatever made Xander so…ambivalent about her had nothing to do with her look. She thought, anyway.

Why was this so confusing?

"Lily, if something is between you two," Sarah added, "it'll happen. Trust me."

Hope bloomed in Lily's heart. She thought about the way they'd almost kissed in her kitchen two days ago. "You are absolutely right."

The thought of something happening between her and Xander—like being in bed with him—almost had her blushing. "I might have to get a little bold." Same with her cooking. Same with working on her business degree. Same with anything she wanted. She had to put herself out there, climb out on a limb and make stuff happen.

Sarah grinned. "Indeed you might. Go for it."

The next time she saw Xander, she *would*.

She needed a new look. She needed new *moxie*. And she felt it roaring up inside her.

Xander decided that if Viv Dalton was going to set him up on dates, he might as well have some control over whom he was fixed up with. Since he'd arrived in Rust Creek Falls, he'd made excuses every time the woman had approached him. He'd see her coming to-

ward him in town, notebook in hand, one hand in a
wave, a determined gleam in her eye, and he'd tap his
watch and turn in the opposite direction. Now he'd actually arranged a meeting with Viv and sat across from
her in her office, watching her big smile fade with every
word he said. Viv was a few years younger than him, tall
and slender with blond hair in a fancy twist. Her eyes
were narrowed on him as though she couldn't quite believe what she was hearing.

He'd been at it for a good five minutes. "She doesn't
need to be very bright," Xander went on. "Chatty is fine,
but let's keep it to small talk."

"Uh, got it," Viv said, barely able to hide the "you've
got to be kidding me" expression on her face as she took
notes. "So let's see if I've got this straight, Xander." She
peered at her notebook. "You're looking for a peroxide
blonde who knows her way around a curling iron, wears
makeup and high heels, and has a 'great giggle'? Great
laugh I've heard before. Great giggle is a new one."

"Look, my dad wants you to set me and my brothers up on dates that might lead to something serious.
So shouldn't I let you know what I'm looking for in a
woman?"

"But you're not actually looking for *anything*, Xander. If I may be so blunt."

Touché. "What I'm not looking for is to get serious,"
he explained. "I think it's important that you know that.
I don't want to hurt anyone, disappoint anyone, lead on
anyone. I'm looking to have a good time—that's it. And
I know what I like."

The way Xander saw it, he could do himself and Andrew Hunt a favor. Anyone Viv set him up with who was

too nice or too interesting or actually had him sharing details of his life the way Lily had within ten minutes would find her name and number passed on to Andrew.

Viv sat back in her chair and clasped her hands in her lap. "I heard that instead of Knox, *you* ended up going out with Lily Hunt. How'd that go? I'm assuming not well, since Lily is the opposite of everything you described as your perfect woman to not be serious about."

Green eyes and freckles and orange rubber shoes came to mind. Tofu. Dachshunds named Dobby and Harry. Suntan lotion and flowery scented hair.

He wondered what kissing Lily would be like. Passionate, he was sure of that. Lily approached everything with zing. Kissing her would be like having all of her. And if kissing her would knock him out, he could only imagine what seeing her naked would do to him. Where else did she have freckles?

"Xander?"

He blinked and realized Viv Dalton was staring at him. Waiting for a response. Oh God. He'd been fantasizing about Lily Hunt. What was happening here exactly?

He cleared his throat and sat up straight. "Lily is a very nice person."

"Ah, nice," she said with a nod.

He frowned. "Well, she *is* nice. She's great. Smart, full of life, passionate about her job, has big goals and dreams, loves her family, dotes on those little sausage dogs. Did I mention she's going to give me a cooking lesson?"

Viv eyed him, scanned her notes and then leaned

forward. "Tell you what, Xander. I'll see who might fit the bill and text you if the right gal comes to mind."

"Perfect," he said, getting up. "No pressure. I like no pressure."

"No pressure," she agreed, standing and shaking his hand. "Good luck with the cooking class."

Was it his imagination or was there a slight gleefulness in her tone?

He wished he'd scheduled that cooking lesson for right now. He wanted to be with Lily, talking to her, looking at her, making a mess in the kitchen with her. But hadn't he met with Viv specifically to set up dates with his type in order to push Lily from his mind? Yes, he'd done exactly that and now he wanted the opposite.

All those things he'd said to Viv about Lily were true. So of course he wanted to be around her. He liked her, plain and simple. Maybe the cooking thing was too much. Too…intimate. Yeah, it kind of was. He could put that off for a while until he understood just what he was feeling for Lily Hunt.

That settled, he decided to go pay her a visit, see if her dogs needed walking since she was so busy with school and her job at the Manor. A friend would absolutely do this.

During the next week, Lily counted five times that Xander Crawford had found a reason to "stop by." *Five* times.

Early in the week, he'd appeared at the back door of the kitchen of the Maverick Manor and offered to take Dobby and Harry for a walk since it was an "incredibly gorgeous summer day" and she was cooped up at work. That sure was thoughtful. His visit had coincided with her fifteen-minute break, so they'd stood outside in the back and chatted about the day's specials, which included homemade spicy onion rings, and how onions did not make him cry like other people, and how he preferred sautéed onions to raw on his burgers. He'd started to go, then had turned back and said he wouldn't able to schedule that cooking lesson for at least a week since he was very busy with work "and stuff" at the Ambling A. Disappointment had lodged so heavily in her chest that she'd been surprised she hadn't tipped over. Then, off he'd gone, her brother Ryan reporting fifteen minutes later that "the tall dude came by and took out the dogs and good thing because I forgot to, sorry."

The next day, Xander had texted her a hello and she'd responded with a frazzled emoji and mentioned she was stuck on a school assignment about business expenditures, and a half hour later, there he was, showing her a few pages of the financials from the Ambling A, and two hours later, everything made sense. Up in her bedroom, he'd spent two hours going over economics and finance—that had to mean *something*. She'd had to force herself to concentrate on the topic and not on the fact that Xander Crawford was sitting on the edge of her bed. She'd done a lot of fantasizing about Xander in that very bed.

The next afternoon, he'd needed a "woman's opinion on which tie he should wear to a rancher's association meeting since he was thinking of running for the board—or maybe not."

Sarah had squealed over that one when Lily texted her about it. The man is crazy about you!

Except he never "leaned" toward her again. Not the next two times he'd dropped in at the Manor—once in the kitchen to rave about the grilled tuna lunch special, or when he'd appeared right before quitting time last night because he thought she might like some company walking home. She certainly did. They'd sat on her porch, watching Dobby and Harry run around the fenced yard. He'd commented on the crescent moon and the Big Dipper, and she'd almost rested her head on his shoulder. That was how natural being with him was. How comfortable she was with him.

That he liked her wasn't in question. But he didn't look at her the way she was sure she looked at him. He looked at her the way she looked at the two male cooks at Maverick Manor. Like friends.

So...what gives?

Being buddies with a man who made you fantasize about taking off his shirt and undoing his belt was a first for Lily. She lost her train of thought midsentence when she was around him or he popped into her mind—which was constantly.

"Lily! I need your help!" came the very loud voice of her brother Andrew from the direction of his bedroom.

She sighed and put down her Economics 101 textbook. She was focusing more on a tall, dark and hot cowboy than on the difference between classical economics and Keynesian economics, anyway.

She headed two doors down to Andrew's room. She coughed as a cloud of men's body spray greeted her. Waving the air in front of her, Lily said, "Wherever you're going tonight, you're gonna need to stand outside for a good twenty minutes to let all that dissipate."

Andrew, who was all dressed up—for him, anyway, since he was either in his police academy uniform or a T-shirt and sweats—eyed his reflection in the bureau mirror as he brushed his short hair. He added a dollop of gel. "No way, sis. According to the bottle, I smell like mountain energy." He took in a deep breath and smiled. "Heidi will love it."

"Who's Heidi?"

"My date for tonight. We're going to the Maverick Manor. You working tonight? Please say yes. I need you to do that thing you do with people's food so that tonight is extra magical."

Lily laughed. "I'm not working tonight, sorry. But I'm sure your date will absolutely love you. Where'd you meet her?"

"I haven't yet. It's a blind date. Thanks to Xander. I owe the guy. He set us up."

Lily gaped at her middle brother. "Xander? How'd that happen? I didn't even know you two knew each other."

Andrew glanced at her in the mirror, then used his fingers to slightly push up the front of his hair. "We met the other day when he came to the house. I asked him if he'd talk me up to any of his dates that didn't work out, and he called me a couple days ago and said he'd met a great young woman and thought we might like each other, so he gave her my number and she called. How awesome is that?"

Yeah, awesome. Xander was going on dates. And passing on the ones who didn't warrant a second date to her brother. She wondered how many Xander *hadn't* passed on.

"Should I wear black shoes or cowboy boots?" he asked.

She glanced at his feet. "Either."

"Oh, big help!" he said. "Thanks."

The thing was, she really didn't know. She wasn't exactly a fashionista. And she hadn't exactly gone on a lot of dates to know what guys wore. Xander had been wearing expensive-looking black shoes on their not-a-date, but his pants were dressier than Andrew's dark gray chinos. "Go for the shoes," she suggested.

He nodded. "I think so, too. The Maverick Manor isn't exactly the Ace in the Hole."

She dropped down on the edge of his bed. "So...what did Xander tell you about Heidi?"

"Just that she was very nice and he thought I'd like her."

"Nice?" she repeated.

"Nice. That was my one request."

Huh. That was a surprise. "I thought guys wanted pretty and hot and fun."

"Some guys, I guess. I'd be happy with all that. But what's the point of hot if she's a royal PITA?"

Lily laughed. "Good point."

Andrew put on his black shoes, glanced at himself one more time in the mirror, said "Wish me luck" and then raced downstairs before she could say another word.

She wondered why the date with nice Heidi hadn't worked out with Xander. Duh, she realized. Because Heidi was nice. And Xander obviously didn't go for nice. A man like Xander Crawford, who could have any woman in town, would want hot. Maybe nice, too, but hot.

Exactly what *she* wasn't.

She groaned.

Whatevs! she screeched at herself. Hot wouldn't get her her own gourmet café or catering shop, now would it? Hard work would. Brains would.

She sighed and trudged back to her room. As she flopped onto her bed next to her econ textbook, her heart sank so low she thought she might crash through the bed onto the floor.

Her phone pinged with a text.

From Xander.

She almost didn't want to read it. How had she gotten his small attentions all week so wrong? She'd really thought there was something brewing between them. But they really and truly were "just friends."

She stayed flopped on her back and read the text.

This might be too short notice, but I'd like to hire you to cook a special dinner for my dad and brothers on Saturday night. We finished repairing a tough line of fence and I'd like to celebrate with a family party. I'm thinking 7:00 p.m. for dinner. We're all pretty much meat-and-potatoes kind of guys, but I'll leave the details up to you.

Saturday night. Two days from now. Hell yeah, she was available. But what was the point? To fall even harder for a man who wasn't remotely interested?

Still, they *were* friends. And he was asking for her help. In fact, he was offering her another paying gig—

and if she wanted to take two courses next semester, she could use the extra money.

I'm in! she texted back ever so breezily when she felt exactly the opposite. And thanks, she added.

Thank YOU, was his response.

If only there was a magic spice or ingredient she could add to the food to make Xander Crawford fall for her.

Okay, she couldn't help it. C'mon, how could she? Of course Lily found an excuse to hustle over to the Maverick Manor to check out this Heidi who was too nice for Xander Crawford. She was sure Heidi would be a plain-Jane type like her. Then she'd know that it wasn't her so much as her look that didn't attract Xander, and maybe she'd feel better.

It's not you, it's me. It's not me, it's you. Who the hell knew?

Big sunhat pulled down low, red hair tucked up under, Lily dashed into the Manor and stood behind the giant vase of wildflowers. She glanced around the lobby for her brother. No sign of him. She was glad there was no sign of Xander, either—on a date with another woman.

She dashed into the kitchen and peered through the Out door into the dining room.

There. Table eleven by the window. Her brother was smiling and chatting. And facing him was... America's Next Top Model.

Or close to it.

What? This was Xander's "it didn't work out but she's nice"? Heidi was tall and busty, Lily noted, wearing a pretty yellow sundress with a flounce near her knees.

She had on high-heeled sandals. And if Lily wasn't mistaken, sparkly baby blue toenails. She also had long honey-brown hair in perfect beachy waves.

Lily watched as Heidi laughed at something her brother said and reached over and touched his arm. Andrew could not look happier.

If this woman wasn't Xander Crawford's type, then who was? Certainly not Lily Hunt.

It was time to give up on him. Cook his family dinner for the celebration, teach him to cook those three favorite dishes, make some money for her future and then move on.

"Lily? Someone called you?" her boss, Gwendolyn, said, rushing over to her. "Great! If you could whip up three filets, subbing the baked for the rice pilaf, that would be great."

Before Lily could say a word, Gwen, wearing her frantic expression, was heading over to Jesse Gold's station, but the cook was nowhere to be found. Gwen flipped a filet mignon and poured béarnaise sauce on it, letting the flames sear it. "Jesse was turning green and almost fell over, so I sent him home. We're booked tonight, so even me pitching in here won't be enough."

"I'm on it," Lily said, whipping off her hat and declaring the filet done and plating it.

This was good, actually. Being so busy would keep her from thinking about Xander and his horde of dates. Beautiful dates.

"Hey, Lily!" AnnaBeth said with a smile as she came in from the dining room. "Your brother's here on a hot date. He's having the filet special, she's having the lemon sole. Oh, and she's from South Dakota, by the way. Gonna work your magic on her fish? Is South Dakota famous for anything?"

Lily immediately thought of chislic, like shish kebabs but without the vegetables. Just delicious little chunks of salted meat on tiny skewers. They hadn't ordered appetizers, but she'd make up a small dish of chislic for them from a filet mignon that Gwen said had ended up searing too long when Jesse had been distracted by not feeling well.

She worked fast and had a little plate ready in no time. "Here," she told AnnaBeth. "You can tell table eleven this is compliments of the chef."

"Ooh, that looks delicious," AnnaBeth said.

Lily smiled and got back to work, starting on Heidi's sole now that her brother's filet was at the rare mark. By the time the sole was done, the steak would be perfectly medium.

"Uh, Lily?" AnnaBeth said, rushing over with the plate of chislic. It was untouched. "Your brother's date took one look at this and said 'Excuse me,' and ran out of the dining room. I think she might be in the restroom."

"Oh no. The dish upset her?"

AnnaBeth bit her lip. "I think so."

Lily plated the entrées and then dashed to the window on the door, AnnaBeth on her heels. Her brother looked worried. He kept glancing toward the arched doorway that led into the lobby.

Oh God. Had she ruined their date? Had "home" brought up bad memories for Heidi?

She had to get back to her station and work on her orders. She had another waitress with four tables that had recently been seated, and she needed to be on point.

They raced back over to Lily's station, AnnaBeth putting the two dishes on the elegant serving tray. "I'll try to find out what's happening."

Lily didn't add her special ingredients to the next three tables of orders she'd received from Holly, the other waitress in Lily's section. Maybe she should mind her own business. She shouldn't even be here at all. Now thanks to her nosy ways, she'd wrecked her brother's date when it had clearly been going very well.

She made two of the special pasta entrées, got three more filets going and two more lemon soles, forcing herself to focus on her work and not her urge to rush back to the little window to see if anyone was still at her brother's table.

AnnaBeth came back into the kitchen with her empty tray.

"Is the food just sitting out on the table getting cold?" Lily asked.

AnnaBeth smiled. "Nope. In fact, come take a look."

Lily's eyes widened and she rushed back over to the window. Her brother and Heidi now sat side by side at the round table instead of across from each other. Heidi was holding up a piece of her lemon sole to her brother's mouth, and he took the bite. Heidi then picked up her napkin and dabbed Andrew's lips, and then they both laughed and held each other's gazes.

She had no idea what had happened, but she was glad it had!

Lily's phone pinged with a text. Probably Xander canceling on hiring her for the party.

She glanced at her phone on the counter. No—the

text was from Andrew. Her brother had practically typed a novel.

Heidi's freshening up in the restroom so just a YEEHA! that you ended up working tonight and made that little SD appetizer for her! Turns out her mom died last year and always used to make chislic every Sunday for family dinner. She got all emotional and excused herself but I found her in the lobby and told her about Mom passing and how Dad still makes her crawdaddy mac and cheese and corn bread every Sunday for us, even though his corn bread is awful, and how we feel her with us. We talked about our moms for a while and then it was like we'd known each other forever. We're going out again tomorrow night! You rock, Lil. Don't know how you do it but I'm glad you do.

Huh. She sent back a heart emoji, her own heart bursting with happiness for him and for herself, since she hadn't ruined his night after all. Au contraire.

At least one Hunt's love life was going in the right direction.

Chapter 5

Xander had exhausted his excuses for checking to see if Lily "needed help" during the past hour that she'd been in Ambling A's kitchen. She'd let him help make the béarnaise sauce for the filet mignon, which had smelled amazing, and also peel potatoes, which he'd found less fun, and then she'd shooed him out to be with his family.

Something was different between them, he thought. She was being kind of…distant. Treating him as if he were a client instead of… Instead of what? Someone she was close to?

A friend?

Why couldn't he seem to get a grip on where he was with Lily? He should be happy she was treating him like a client instead of a crush—if that was what he should call it. In the past week, hadn't he gone out with three women, one set up by Viv Dalton, two who'd asked him out in town, to restore order to his head?

And despite making it clear to Viv that she should set him up with only airheads who giggled, she'd arranged a date with a perfectly nice, intelligent, interesting woman named Heidi whose family had moved to Montana from South Dakota last year. They'd had a lot to talk about, and she'd looked a little surprised when he'd said at the end of the date that he was going to be honest and tell her he wasn't looking for a relationship with anyone and that he knew a great guy who was, if she was interested. Heidi said she trusted his opinion, and voilà, she and Lily Hunt's brother Andrew were on date number three right now, third night in a row.

The other two women he'd gone out with had been more his type. One giggled even when she'd backed her car—she'd insisted on driving since she had a little two-seater she liked zipping around in—into the sheriff's SUV. Then she giggled as the sheriff, who didn't look remotely amused, gave her a Breathalyzer test. They hadn't had an ounce of alcohol to drink at that point, but afterward, Xander could have used a few bottles of whiskey to get through the next hour of dinner. He'd turned down her suggestion of a nightcap in her condo, seen her safely home and then walked back two miles toward town, where luckily his brother Wilder had been passing by in his truck and given him a ride back to the ranch. Man, had Wilder had a good laugh all the way home.

Xander had wanted to cancel the next night's date, but then he remembered how he'd refused to let Lily get canceled on, so he'd forced himself out with Dede, who was the cheerleading coach for the high school and had a bad habit of screaming "Whooooo!" whenever she was excited about something, holding her arms straight up in the air and shaking imaginary pom-poms. She wasn't an airhead at all, it turned out, and luckily, she'd ended the date early, sobbing that she'd only asked him out to make her ex jealous and they'd walked right past the guy in the restaurant she'd known he'd be eating in with his family and he hadn't even blinked.

Dating and relationships sure were hell.

"Go on," Lily said now, making shooing motions with her hands. "I'm fine in here. It's my habitat, remember?"

He nodded and smiled but wanted to stick around. Find out what she'd been up to the past few nights since he hadn't gotten a chance to pop in on her. But her focus was on the heap of steaks and potatoes and asparagus smelling so incredible.

Go, he ordered himself, everything in him resisting leaving the room. "Holler if you get lonesome in here by yourself."

"The kitchen is the one place I never feel lonely," she said, locking eyes with him.

He held her gaze, something—hell if he knew what—spinning up inside him. He couldn't move his feet, couldn't look away.

But then she was shaking the pan with the asparagus, and turning down the burners on the steaks, and he took one last good look at her profile, the freckles on her nose and cheeks, before slipping out, his chest heavy.

The laughter and loud chatter in the living room grabbed his attention as he headed in, the Crawfords all congregated for the party to celebrate another piece of the Ambling A coming together, becoming home.

Hunter sat with his six-year-old daughter, Wren, on his lap, her long blond hair in two of the most crooked braids Xander had ever seen. Hunter had been mother and father to his sweet little girl since Wren was born, and Xander had to hand it to him for doing such a great job. He braided hair and packed day-camp lunches, and stayed up all night when Wren was sick or had bad dreams. The guy had a lot on his shoulders. Sometimes Xander wondered how *he'd* do as a father—not that he had any plans to become one anytime soon.

It was crazy how even when you picked the right woman, as Hunter had done with his late wife, your whole life could go belly-up. It was a sober reminder that Xander was 100 percent correct not to get serious about a woman.

Sharing the big couch with Hunter and Wren were Logan and Sarah, Sarah playing some kind of clapping game with her adored niece. Finn was deep in conversation with Wilder in the two club chairs across from the love seat where Xander sat with Knox, who was deep in thought—as usual. Meanwhile, his father sat in his space-age recliner with features that turned on lights and the television, and massaged his back and neck.

"Well, Crawfords," Max said with a drawn-out shake of his head, "I must say I'm disappointed to see that there's only one lovely woman joining us for dinner tonight. By this point, I expected at least half of you to be seriously involved."

"Can we not alk-tay about this in front of En-Wray,"

Hunter muttered through gritted teeth, nodding his head at his six-year-old daughter.

"I know pig latin, Daddy," Wren said with a grin.

Xander laughed. "And there are *three* lovely women at the table tonight, so there's your quota, Dad. Sarah, baby Sophia and Wren."

His father's gaze moved from Logan's wife and baby to Hunter's little girl, and he grinned. "I stand corrected. But still!"

"Don't you mean *four*?" Sarah asked. "Isn't Lily joining us for dinner?" She glanced around at faces but lingered on Xander's.

"Of course she is," Max said, slapping his knee. "That talented chef did all the hard work—she should get to sit down and relax and enjoy her own masterpiece."

"I agree," Sarah said with a smile. "In fact, I'll go put a place setting out for her. Be right back."

Seat her next to me, Xander wanted to tell Sarah, but of course he couldn't. He watched her dash into the kitchen.

Five long minutes later, Lily came out of the kitchen holding a platter of steaks that smelled so good everyone went silent for a moment. Sarah was right behind her with a tray of big bowls holding roasted potatoes and asparagus. Xander hopped up and asked if he could help bring anything out, but Lily smiled and said this was everything.

Then she glanced around and looked kind of uncomfortable and said, "Sorry that I'm not exactly dressed for a dinner party. I really just expected to be in the kitchen, not joining you."

"What?" Max said, eyeing her. "You look just like the rest of us. One of the boys."

Oh, Dad, Xander thought. *Enough with the asides.*

Lily bit her lip and awkwardly smiled, shifting a glance to Sarah, who was casually dressed but not quite to the degree Lily was. Lily wore a red scoop-neck T-shirt with a white apron over it, loose jeans and blue sneakers, her red hair back in a ponytail.

Luckily everyone else was focused on the aroma and platters and trooped into the huge dining room, Max taking his place at the head of the long farmhouse table. Xander took a seat down at the other end to avoid any marriage-oriented conversation his father might start up. Logan and Sarah sat across from him, baby Sophia sleeping in her carrier on the hutch along the far wall.

Lily took a seat right beside him.

"First, a toast," Max said, raising his wineglass. "To the Ambling A and all the hard work you boys have put into turning this place into a home. I couldn't be prouder of you. I'll include myself in there, since I'm out there busting these old bones every day, too."

They all laughed and raised their glasses, clinking.

"And thank you to Lily, our chef for the evening, for this amazing dinner," Max added.

There was more clinking.

"My pleasure," Lily said. "Well, everyone, bon appétit!"

Platters and bowls were passed around, everyone commenting on how good everything looked.

"Oh, and Lily," Max said, "I have to apologize for my son Knox and all that brouhaha with your date. But it looks like things worked out just fine. I mean, here you are, sitting next to Xander at a family dinner." He winked and loaded his plate with potatoes.

"Really, Dad?" Knox said with a shake of his head. "And no need to do my apologizing for me. I spoke to Lily privately in the kitchen right after she arrived."

Xander had noticed Knox go into the kitchen and come out a couple minutes later. He'd figured his brother was making amends.

Lily's cheeks were as red as her T-shirt. "Xander and I are just friends."

"Just friends," Xander seconded.

"Ah, so we can talk about all the dates you went on this past week," Wilder said. "Any work out?"

"Come on, Xan," his father said. "Tell me you have one *second* date."

Was it his imagination or was Lily pushing her potatoes around on her plate, her expression both grim and forced pleasant?

"Let's leave Xander's private life to himself," Sarah said. "You boys. Seriously!"

"Yeah, let's listen to Sarah," Xander agreed, wanting to hug her.

"Fine, fine," Max said. "Now, Lily, I hear you have three brothers, so you're used to all this testosterone."

Lily laughed. "Definitely."

The conversation thankfully turned to stories about the Hunt brothers and the Crawford brothers, both matched for mischief.

"Oh, Lily," Hunter said. "I'm really sorry but Wren and I won't be able to make your kids' cooking class tomorrow afternoon. I forgot I promised a friend I'd help him move. Wren was really looking forward to it."

"Aww," Wren said, looking pretty sad. "Now I won't know how to make tacos."

"Well, I'll be hosting more kids' classes," Lily assured her. "The next one is for kids a bit older than you, Wren, but I'll have another one for your age group in September. That's just a month away."

Xander recalled Lily mentioning she taught cooking classes at the town rec center, but he hadn't known Hunter and Wren signed up. "Why don't I take my niece to the class?" he said. "I'm free tomorrow afternoon. And then I get to spend some time with my favorite six-year-old."

And Lily, he thought.

"Yay!" Wren said. "I want to learn how to make tacos! I love tacos!"

"Perfect," Hunter said. "Thanks, bro."

Xander nodded back.

Lily sent him an awkward smile. Why was everything like that between them? Awkward and hesitant? Something was up. But what?

"Lily, I don't know where you learned to cook like this," Max said, "but thank God you did. Amazing."

There were murmurs of agreement and the conversation turned to favorite meals, then Lily brought out dessert, which were mini chocolate tarts, and suddenly dinner was over, and Lily was in the kitchen again.

Xander grabbed a few empty platters and took them into the kitchen, hoping no one would do the same. Lily stood at the sink, scraping pans.

"We'll clean up, Lily," he said. "Don't even worry about all this."

She whirled around with a grin. "Really? First the

cook gets invited to dinner and now I don't have to wash pots and load the dishwasher? I'm not usually this lucky."

"Trust me, you especially deserve not to clean up with my dad getting all personal like that. Sorry."

"No worries. I'm well used to dads and brothers ribbing on me." She put the pans in soapy water to soak. "So…sorry the dating isn't working out. Though I guess that's good for my brother. I think Andrew is totally in love."

"Glad to hear it." He wanted to tell her he wasn't dating to find a serious girlfriend, let alone a wife. But was he supposed to blurt out the truth: that he was speed dating to remind him what he was and wasn't looking for?

Not looking for: Real. Serious. Even close to forever.

Looking for: A hot kiss or two. More if the woman was looking for the same and nothing else.

The reality was that Lily Hunt in her T-shirt and ponytail and blue sneakers, with sauce stains on her shoulder, was keeping him up at night by just being *herself.*

Lord. Was he falling for Lily? That was impossible, right? She was seven years his junior and looked like any number of his buddies' kid sisters in her hoodies and jeans.

He wasn't falling for her. He just liked her. That was all. When was the last time he'd met someone and developed a real bond, a real friendship? A long time ago. He just forgot what it felt like, and it was confusing because it had happened with a woman.

Hadn't he said women and men could be friends? Yes, they could.

Case in point: him and Lily.

"Well, we'll see how the dating goes this week," he said. "Viv has three more set up for me and that's just the first half of the week."

Her face fell. Just for a second. But he caught it. She had feelings for him—he knew that. And it was better not to play with her. He was telling the truth about the dates, and she should know so that she wouldn't hang any hopes on him.

If he hurt her, disappointed her, made her think something more could go on when it couldn't…he'd never forgive himself.

She was so young. She had her entire life ahead of her. Practically all her twenties. And big dreams to fuel her. She didn't need some cynical guy already in the next decade of life.

She gave him a tight smile. "Good luck, then." She darted past him into the living room with him trailing her, said good-night and thank you to everyone, and then beelined for the door. Xander almost wished car trouble on her so he could drive her home, but her little silver car started right up.

Leaving him staring out at the red taillights disappearing down the drive.

"Jeez, just admit you've got a thing for her," Logan whispered as he came up behind him.

"What?" he said. "Of course I don't. She's twenty-three, for God's sake. I'm *thirty*." And he was done with caring about a woman, with thinking about the future beyond a couple days. He saw where that had gotten him.

"Whatever you say, bro," Logan said with a smile and a head shake. "In due time. In due time."

"Meaning?"

Logan laughed and looked over toward the living room, where his wife sat on the sofa, lifting their baby up and down and kissing her on the cheek.

"Now you have me married with a baby?" He huffed away to get a beer, Logan's laughter trailing him.

By the time Lily pulled into her driveway, she'd burst into tears three times and had five text messages waiting for her from Sarah.

Told you he has feelings for you! her friend wrote. Taking over for Hunter at the kiddie cooking class? She added a few heart emojis and a chef hat emoji and Lily burst into tears again.

I'll believe it if he ever kisses me, she typed back. Until then, I'm operating under the assumption that he likes me as a friend.

Three dates set up this week. All before Wednesday!

She headed inside the house to find her dad home alone, Dobby and Harry beside him on the couch, a bowl of popcorn on the other side of him. He was watching a *Law & Order* marathon on cable. He took one look at her expression and put the popcorn on the coffee table and patted the space where it had been.

"Come watch, Lil. Did you know identical twins have the same DNA and one could be convicted for the crime his twin actually committed?"

"I don't think I ever thought about it before, Dad," she said, plopping beside him. Dobby came over and settled in her lap, and she stroked his soft ears.

"Everything go okay at the Crawfords'?" he asked.

The food: yes. The company: yes. Her heart: no.

"Yeah," she said, unable to disguise the weariness in her tone.

"You like that tall one with the brown hair, don't you?" her father said.

She stared at her Dad. "They're *all* tall with brown hair. But how'd you know?"

He pointed the remote at the TV and shut it off, then turned to her. "Because you're my baby girl. And trust me, I never forget that. You might think I treat you like one of your brothers, but that's because I've always tried to treat you all the same. But you're the only female in the house, Lil, and you might think you hide your emotions like we try to, but you're bad at it."

Lily laughed, but tears stung her eyes. "I'm falling in love with someone who thinks of me as a friend."

"I wouldn't be too sure," her dad said. "Sometimes it just takes a while for us lugheads to know our own minds. Did I ever tell you how I thought of your mom as just a friend when we first met?"

"What? No way. You always said it was love at first sight."

"More like love at third sight," he said with a smile. "Your mom was so pretty and sparkling I didn't think I had a chance. So I didn't even give her a romantic thought in my mind. But then I got to know her and fell in love whether I liked it or not."

Lily laughed again. "You fell in love against your will?"

"Sort of. I didn't think she'd ever return my feelings. But she did."

Lily always loved hearing about when her mom and

dad met. "Well, I don't think that's going to happen here. I look like a boy with long hair."

"Xander may see much more than that," her father said. "As I always say—don't rule anything out till you know for absolute sure you should."

Dobby licked her hand, which still had the faintest residue of filet mignon no matter how much she'd scrubbed.

"Thanks, Dad," she said, leaning her head on his shoulder.

He gave her shoulder a pat and then put *Law & Order* back on, the identical twin—who hadn't even known he had an identical twin—insisting he was innocent.

She wasn't in the mood for TV right now but she needed something to take her mind off Xander Crawford and her lack of a love life. Plus, it was nice to spend time with her dad. Real time. She'd opened up tonight and she hadn't done that in a long time. Sometimes Lily felt like she was changing every few seconds, new experiences hitting her left and right.

Dobby licked her hand again, and she hugged him to her, the warm little dog like a soothing balm.

After the show, Lily hugged her dad, too, and thanked him for listening—and for the good advice—then headed upstairs. She took a long, hot shower, changed into her comfiest pj's, and then got into bed, tossing and turning for what felt like hours, but when morning came, she felt well rested. Talking to her dad had definitely helped.

Don't rule anything out till you know for absolute sure you should.

Xander had pretty much confirmed she should rule him out when he mentioned his dating schedule. Right?

But he'd also made a point of seeing her later today by taking his niece to her cooking class. *Duh, because you're friends.*

She would never get to the bottom of this at this point.

She stood in front of her bureau, staring at herself in the mirror. On the dresser was a photograph of her mother—beautiful, sophisticated Naomi Hunt. She wore a sleeveless dress, dangling earrings, her hair wavy and loose around her shoulders. She'd lost her mom when she was eight, and her dad and brothers had raised her. She'd wanted to be just like Andrew, Ryan and Bobby, and so she'd never worn dresses or pink or played with dolls. And it had probably been a little easier on her dad not to have to learn to braid her hair or take her clothes shopping or paint her toenails, so he'd let her be.

And now this was what she looked like: one of her brothers. Except even her brothers had more style than she did.

Maybe it was time to change her look—just a little. Wear something besides T-shirts and jeans all the time. Learn to put on mascara without looking like a raccoon. She didn't even own perfume.

She wondered if Xander would be attracted to her if she was a little more girlie. But the problem with that was then it would bother her that artifice had gotten his attention instead of the real her.

She flopped herself down on her bed. How she wished her mama was here to talk with about this stuff.

Not that her father hadn't done a great job last night, she thought with a smile.

She heard one of the dogs scratching at the door and she opened it, and Dobby and Harry jumped on the end of her bed and curled up with their satisfied little sighs.

"We'll see," she told them. "Lots to think about. Maybe I'll even talk it over with you two."

Dobby eyed her, but Harry was already snoring.

Chapter 6

Most Sunday afternoons, Lily taught a cooking class for kids. For the summer, she also offered two workshops for older kids, which met for an hour every week on her three days off. Today was a one-day seminar for five-to eight-year-olds, which a parent or caregiver needed to attend, as well. She adored working with the young cooks.

She scanned the registration list. She had six students—her maximum so that she'd be able to give them all attention—including Wren Crawford. As the kids and their adults arrived in the rec center kitchen, Lily forced herself to stop thinking about Xander and to focus on the class. So far, everyone was here except for the Crawford duo. There were two dads, one with a daughter, one with a son. And three moms, two with daughters and one with a son. Lily checked them all off on her list, kneeling down to say hi to each of her students and handing them their special orange apron that they would take home at the end of class and could decorate with fabric markers.

She couldn't help but notice how nicely dressed two of the three women were. Granted, one was in a T-shirt and jeans like Lily, but the other two looked so polished, one in a flippy cotton skirt and ruffly tank, the other in a blue sundress.

Lily glanced at her jeans and blah sneakers. Granted, she was about to get salsa all over herself, but wasn't that what an apron was for? Ina Garten and Nigella Lawson didn't wear T-shirts to cook in. Why should Lily?

You're not one of the Hunt boys, she told herself. *You're you. Lily. And you've never really figured out what expressing that means—aside from cooking.*

She sure liked Layla Carew's pale blue cotton sundress with the embroidered hem. The woman looked pretty and comfortable and summery. Who said Lily couldn't wear something like that?

No one.

"Is this it?" Layla asked suddenly, looking around. "I thought Hunter Crawford signed up for this class."

"I thought so, too," Monica Natowky added. Monica—wearing the flippy skirt and lots of bangles on her bare, toned arms.

Lily sighed inwardly, her gaze going to their ring fingers. Empty!

Were they here for the kids' class? Or to land a Crawford?

She glanced at the third woman's finger: gold band. And what had Darby Feena come to the kids' cooking class wearing? A T-shirt and jeans. Normal, appropriate wear for the activity!

Still, it would be nice to not always be mistaken for a nanny or a student herself. When Layla had first arrived, she'd gone up to Monica to introduce herself, thinking *Monica* was the teacher.

Ugh. Lily had no time to be thinking about her wardrobe issues. She had a class to get started.

Right then, Xander came in, holding Wren's hand, and Lily wanted to tell him to drop off Wren and leave. Who did he and his brothers think they were? Their single status and gorgeousness were causing a scene all over town, making women act like idiots. Including her. Please!

And boy, did he live up to every bit of that gorgeousness. He wore dark jeans and a green henley shirt, his shoulders so broad and his hips so slim. Lordy, Lily could look at him all day.

"Hi, Hunter," Layla trilled with a toss of her blond curls behind her shoulders. "I'm Layla and this little nugget is Mia."

Lily was about to introduce Xander and Wren to the group when Monica practically knocked her out of the way to rush over to shake his hand.

"Hunter, it's *so* nice to meet you. I'm Monica, and this is my darling nephew, Jasper. Jasper wants to be a rancher someday, too. Don't you, Jasper?"

"Yup," the cute little boy in the Western shirt and cowboy hat said.

Xander looked at both of them as if they were from Mars. "I'm not Hunter. Sorry."

Their gazes went right to *his* ring finger.

"Oh, no apologies necessary!" Monica said. "You must be one of this li'l angel's *uncles*, then."

Oh, brother. Had these two women *really* found out that Hunter Crawford had registered for the course with his daughter and signed up for that reason? Xander gave her a sheepish kind of smile as if he was so innocent. Humph!

Lily broke up this display of ick by announcing it was time to get class started. Monica frowned and darted back to her space. Each student and adult shared one table where Lily had set up bowls of precut veggies. In the first row there was an empty table next to one of the dads; Xander chose that spot instead of the free table beside Monica and in front of Layla. She could practically hear them sigh with disappointment.

"Welcome!" she said in her loud, kid-friendly voice. She stood behind a table full of bowls and her electric hot plates. "I'm Lily Hunt, your cooking teacher for today. Guess what we're making?"

"Tacos!" lots of happy voices shouted.

"That's right. We're making vegetarian tacos. Who knows what vegetarian means?"

A little boy raised his hand, and Lily called on him.

"It means a food that isn't meat!" the boy said.

"Right!" Lily said. "Now, I love beef tacos. And chicken tacos. And salmon tacos. But today we'll make vegetarian tacos with delicious black beans, cheese, salsa, lettuce and tomatoes!"

"Yay!" a few of the more exuberant kids shouted.

"Okay, kids!" Lily began. "I've already cut up the tomatoes because using knives can be really dangerous and only adults should use sharp knives. But I want each of you to come up to my table and point out a tomato from my bowl of whole vegetables. I'll give you a hint what a tomato looks like. It's red. And round."

"I see it!" a girl shouted.

Six pairs of little legs went running over to Lily's table, each pointing at a plump tomato in Lily's big bowl and then taking a small bowl of cut tomatoes.

"Okay, now you can go back to your seats," Lily said. She explained where tomatoes came from, and that they were actually considered a fruit *and* a vegetable. There were lots of animated questions about vines and seeds, and then Lily asked each student to take their big measuring cup and scoop out a half cup of the cut-up tomatoes. Lily demonstrated where to find the markers on the cups, then instructed the adults to show them closer up.

"I love tomatoes!" Wren said, jumping up and down, her blond pigtails flying. "I know how much a half cup is. My daddy lets me help cook!"

"That's awesome, Wren!" Lily said.

Xander shot her a smile, and Lily's knees gave a slight shake.

She headed over to the tables to high-five kids as they measured out the tomatoes, trying not to look at Xander. She kept her attention on the class, sending each student back to her teacher's table to choose a head of lettuce, and after a mini lesson on lettuce, the kids got to shred theirs by hand (after washing up!) and add their half cup of lettuce to their bowls. Lily gave a little talk on cheese next, having the kids taste three different kinds and learning why some cheeses complemented certain foods. Finally it was time to heat the beans, and Lily told them all about where beans came from. For ease of the class, she'd opened up several cans of Goya black beans and the kids gathered around the low table where she had a hot plate, having each kid add a pinch of the various spices. Then the students added diced tomatoes and spices to a bowl for the salsa, some of which ended up on their aprons and in their hair. Finally, it was time to learn about taco shells, and after those were heated up, everyone was excited to build their tacos with their bowl of ingredients.

"Wow," Xander said from the first row. "I had no idea tacos were so educational. I really learned quite a bit."

"Me, too," Monica trilled. "I make the best tacos, don't I, Jasper? We should invite Xander and Wren over to have them this week."

"Wren's a *girl*!" Jasper said very earnestly.

"Boys can be friends with girls, you know!" Wren shouted over her shoulder.

"Well, in any case," Monica said, "we'd love to have you over. Tuesday night?"

Was this woman really asking Xander out right here, in a children's cooking class, in front of everyone? Including his six-year-old niece? Good God.

"I appreciate the invitation," Xander told her, his voice awkward to Lily's ears, "but I'm afraid my schedule is crazy the next few months."

At least he hadn't said yes. But still!

"Ah, well, if you find yourself with a free night, just look me up. Monica Natowsky."

He gave her a tight smile and turned his attention to the taco shell that Wren was filling with her bounty.

"I can't wait to eat this!" Wren said. "Can I take a bite?" she asked Lily.

"Let's wait till everyone's tacos are assembled, because that would be extra polite, right?" Lily said.

"Right!" Wren said, looking around.

"Okay! Looks like everyone is ready. Bite!" Lily said.

The crunching was music to her ears. There was a round of *mmm*s and *this is so good* and a few *I love this class*es.

And then after cleanup and a quick Q&A, Lily dismissed the class, already missing them as the adorable little students left. Monica and Layla were among the last to leave, wistfully looking at Xander, who was deep in conversation with one of the dads.

"Uncle Xander, can I go play in the playground with Molly?" Wren asked.

"I'll watch them," the girl's dad said.

Xander smiled. "Sure, go ahead. I'll be there in a few minutes. I'm just going to say thank you to Ms. Hunt."

Wren wrapped her arms around Lily's hips, surprising her quite happily, then ran out with her friend, Molly's dad right behind them.

And now suddenly it was just Lily and Xander.

"I meant it—I had a blast," he said. "You have a real gift for teaching kids."

"Thanks. That means a lot to me. I really love working with children of all ages."

"Did you know you had a tiny fleck of cheese on your cheek?" he asked, stepping closer and reaching out his hand.

"No, actually," she whispered, her belly tightening. "I did not."

He dusted off the cheese, his brown eyes on hers, serious, intense. And unless she was delusional, which she might be, there was desire in those depths.

He leaned in.

And dammit, even if he'd discovered a black bean in her hair and was leaning close to flick that off, she was leaning in, too.

But this time, he kissed her. His hands were on her face, drawing her closer, his lips firm and soft and tender and passionate all at the same time.

Oh, my.

Yessssss!

Kissing Xander was everything she'd fantasized about—day and night—since their date in Rust Creek Falls Park.

He opened his eyes and stepped back, looking at her, his expression changing. She still saw that unexpected desire, but something else seemed to be shoving its way in. She had the feeling the kiss had taken him by surprise. That he wasn't even sure he'd meant to do it.

Nooo! Desire good. Confusion not good.

"That was some kiss," she whispered, because that was the only voice she had at the moment. "I liked it. A lot."

Sarah would be proud. So would Lily's mother. *State your intent. Stake your claim. Put yourself out there!*

There would be no take-backsies here. Not of that kiss, which she still felt burning her lips.

His smile was warm as he reached out his hand and touched her cheek. The way a man did when he cared about a woman he had just kissed passionately.

Yesss!

"I need to be honest, Lily."

Oh, cripes, she thought, her heart plummeting. *No, don't be!*

"I don't know what the hell I'm doing," he said, taking a step back and leaning against the table. "There seems to be something between us, but as I've said, I'm not looking for a relationship. I'm not looking to start something."

Jeez. Did he have to be *that* honest? Of course she wanted the truth, hard as it was to hear, but couldn't he leave her a little room to hope?

"I got burned bad right before I left Dallas," he said, running a hand through his dark hair. "I went to my girlfriend's condo to surprise her with an engagement ring, to tell her I'd stay in Texas for her instead of moving to Montana with my family. I found her in bed with my best friend—a lifelong buddy I *thought* was my best friend. I told them both to go to hell. A few days later, I left the state with my family, so that helped, but the burn... That followed me, Lily."

She reached out a hand to his arm. "I understand." Her heart ached for him, for how painful that must have been. The shock and betrayal. The loss of two people who'd meant a lot to him. Suddenly, his push-and-pull made sense.

He stared at her for a minute and it seemed like he almost wished she'd been less compassionate. As in maybe he was hoping she'd say: *Well, then don't go around kissing women you don't intend to start something with*, so that he could argue and she could huff away. Giving *him* the out.

She wouldn't ever say that. Granted, she had very little experience when it came to romance and love, but she knew how even a minor rejection had hurt. She could only imagine how hurt Xander had been and the number it had done on his head—and heart. He felt something for her, but he didn't want to *go there*.

"Well," he said, taking another step back. "I'd better go check on Wren."

She wanted him to stay, for them to keep talking— openly and honestly. But she could tell he needed some space, and his niece was waiting for him outside. "Tell her she gets an A-plus for today."

But not you, because you're keeping me at arm's length and you've got long arms.

He hurried out, the door closing behind him.

Lily touched her mouth, the feel of his lips still lingering. Now what? He'd kissed her. A real kiss. Then told her he wasn't interested in more.

Listen when someone tells you something! That would be the wise thing. But her heart was in full control of her right now, and it wanted Xander Crawford.

And Lily Hunt had never been one to *not* go for what she wanted.

After dropping Wren off with Sarah and Logan for the rest of the afternoon, Xander headed to the cattle barn. He needed to do some hard labor, some serious mucking, to get his mind unstuck. Right now, his brain was on a loop about how good it had felt to finally kiss Lily, to do what he'd been thinking about for weeks now. But then his head had come to a hard stop as if it had hit the brakes itself. He didn't know what he thought. Felt. Wanted.

He pulled on plastic gloves and grabbed a rake and

headed into the back stalls. A few minutes in, he knew he was right to take on this chore instead of an afternoon off as had been the plan. His mind was already clearing.

Now all he could think about was how young Lily was. Just starting out in life. And he felt so world-weary and cynical. His trust level was nil. And that diamond ring he'd bought back in Dallas? He'd marched right back to the jeweler, needing that black velvet box out of his hands and life immediately, and thankfully, the shop had taken it back, refunding every pricey cent. That had felt good, at least. But if anyone had ever told Xander that one day he'd fall in love and plan a surprise engagement, only to end up returning the ring the next morning, he would have said they were nuts.

He heard footsteps and the humming of a Frank Sinatra song, which meant it was his dad who'd entered the barn.

Xander poked his head out of the stall to find Max Crawford pulling on a pair of black heavy-duty plastic gloves like Xander had on and then grabbing a rake, too.

"Hey, thought you had the day off," Max said. "I'm on mucking duty today."

"I know, but I could use some hard labor, so here I am."

"Fine with me," Max said. "My least favorite job on the chore chart." He and his rake went into the next stall, the strains of "Fly Me to the Moon" drifting in the air. "Interesting that you need to muck out stalls after taking Lily's cooking class. Almost like that woman has you all topsy-turvy."

He sighed and rested his chin on the top of the rake.

"I guess she does. I didn't move to Montana looking for a relationship, Dad. The opposite, in fact."

"I know you had a bad breakup in Dallas, Xander. But that shouldn't hold you back from finding happiness again."

"You haven't," he said, then wished he could take it back.

But he couldn't; it was out there, hanging over the edges of their side-by-side stalls.

Hell, maybe it was good to finally have this conversation. His dad hadn't remarried, hadn't gotten serious with a woman Xander's entire life.

Because his wife walking out on him, on their family, had been unbearable.

"Sorry," Xander said, feeling like a heel. "That's your business and I have no right—"

"Yes, you do," Max said. "You have every right. If I'm going to push a determined wedding planner on you and your brothers, you have a right to know why I don't practice what I preach."

Xander came out of the stall and stood in the doorway of his dad's. His father was tall and imposing but somehow looked so…vulnerable.

"I just want you boys to be happy. To have what I didn't. I might have given up on happiness for myself but hell if I'm gonna stand by and watch what that taught you boys. You need love. Partners. Family. That's what makes the world go round, Xan. Bitterness just makes it come to a screeching halt."

Xander nodded, and then walked into the stall and embraced his dad, Max stiffening with clear surprise at first, and then hugging him back. "I know. Believe me."

He headed back into his stall and started mucking away. And for the next couple of hours, he and his dad worked in silence, Xander's mind clearer but no answers on the horizon.

Chapter 7

Communication from Xander Crawford following The Kiss:

Sunday night, a text: Thanks again for the fun and informative cooking class today. Wren had a great time.

Response: My pleasure.

Monday morning: I woke up craving lobster rolls for some reason. On the specials menu at MM?

Response: No, sorry.

Monday night: Lobster rolls tomorrow?

Response: No, sorry.

Later Monday night: Jeez, I thought I had an in with the chef.

No response.

Tuesday morning: Just checking in.

Response: Smiley face emoji. Super busy—have a great day!

The old Lily might have raced over to Kalispell Monday morning to buy lobster and all the fixings for lobster rolls. Eager to please. Like a puppy. The old Lily might also have kept the text conversation going on Tuesday by asking open-ended questions.

But a new Lily had taken root inside her—every day, with every satisfied diner at the Maverick Manor, every "great job, Lily" from her boss, every decent grade on her schoolwork, every time she understood a difficult business concept. Add to it these new feelings for a man—the first time she'd truly fallen in love—and Lily felt different in her bones. Like a woman instead of a kid.

On Wednesday afternoon, Lily bit into her cruller at Daisy's Donuts, Sarah Crawford sipping her iced latte while baby Sophia napped in her stroller at their table by the window. She filled in Sarah on the big kiss and the conversation that followed—not the details of what Xander had shared about his ex, but just the gist that he had a big closed sign over his heart.

Sarah's eyes lit up. "This kiss says everything!"

"I want to hope so. But he told me he's not looking to start anything. *That* actually says everything."

"He's a cowboy who's been kicked in the head by unexpected love," Sarah said. "He needs time to reclaim his own mind. And when he does, watch out, Lily."

Lily laughed. "I love your optimism. But I won't hold my breath." She bit her lip, thinking about that kiss. Sometimes she could still feel the imprint of his lips. "You know what? I'm not even going to think about it. Xander needs to figure out how he feels, right? I think

I should just take a step back. Kind of like I was doing with my responses to his texts."

Sarah took a bite of her chocolate cider donut. "I have to say that the way you responded to those messages sure kept them coming. I love the 'Just checking in.'" She laughed. "Poor guy."

Lily smiled. "I like this newer, wiser me. I'm not sitting around endlessly thinking about him and his deal. I'm focusing on work, school and my future. Which I hope includes him, of course," she admitted.

"I have faith," Sarah said with a big nod.

Lily sipped her own iced latte and couldn't help but notice again how nice Sarah looked—for just coffee out with a friend. Sarah wore pale pink capri pants, a white tank top with a ruffled hem around the V-neck, and adorable multicolored leather sandals that wrapped around her ankles three times. She was the sleep-deprived mother of a baby and yet she wore a little makeup and earrings and she smelled like a hint of perfume— not baby spit-up. She looked this way because she wanted to. It truly had to be that simple.

"I want a makeover," Lily said.

Sarah's eyes lit up. "Ooh!"

"I want to look like *me*—the me I've never explored because I was too busy wanting to fit in with my brothers and be accepted by them. I want my outside to match all the changes I've made on the inside. I'm going for my dreams."

"Including the six-foot-two-inch one?" her friend asked.

Lily smiled, then bit her lip. "Crazy thing is, Sarah— he likes me *this* way. Salsa on my cheek, onion-scented hands, loose jeans, no makeup, no style. He likes me as I am." The truth of it practically knocked the breath out of her. The way he looked at her—even on that first nondate in the park—was proof. The kiss was proof.

Xander Crawford likes me, she thought, a rush of happiness swelling in her belly. *He's attracted to* me.

"Okay, now I'm going to cry," Sarah said, tearing up. "I know exactly what you mean."

"But wanting this makeover is for *me*. About *me*. I want to find out who I am if I let myself really go for it. So will you help me?"

"Is right now too soon?" Sarah asked with a grin. "I wish I didn't have my dentist appointment in fifteen minutes or we could take off for Kalispell now and hit the shops and salon."

"Need me to babysit?" Lily asked.

"Actually, I have a sitter all lined up who should arrive any minute now."

"Oh, well next time, call me," Lily said. "I love taking care of Sophia." She looked at the beautiful sleeping baby, her bow lips quirking.

One day, I want a Sophia of my own, she thought—for the first time. She sucked in a breath as a sense of absolute wonder overtook her. She'd never really thought about getting married or having children; she'd always figured she would, but the notion had always seemed a few years down the road. Several years.

Lily bit her lip again as she wondered if falling in love with Xander Crawford had anything to do with her sudden baby fever.

"How about tomorrow morning for the makeover?"

Sarah asked. "Ooh, Lily—you can debut your new look at the dance Saturday night!"

"I wasn't planning on going," she said, thinking about the Rust Creek Falls Summer Sunset Dance, held every year in a different location. The whole town always turned up, apparently—well, except her, and no one had ever asked her to the dance, not that she couldn't have gone with a girlfriend. Dances had never been her thing. Starting with semiformals in middle school and working up to the senior prom, which she hadn't gone to, either.

"I know for a fact Xander will be there," Sarah said, wriggling her eyebrows. "All the Crawfords are going."

"Oh, great," Lily said. "I can watch Xander dance with every single beauty in town. Wonderful way to pass the time."

"Want to know a secret?" Sarah asked. "But you can't tell Xander I told you."

Lily leaned closer. "Scout's honor." She held up three fingers.

"Logan confided in me that Xander actually told Viv Dalton to only set him up with women he'd have nothing in common with. Viv reported him to Max, their dad, who was asking for a status report and why Xander wasn't engaged yet." Sarah laughed. "That man. Seriously."

"Nothing in common with?" Lily repeated. "Why bother, then?"

"Want to know Logan's theory?"

Lily leaned closer again.

"Logan thinks his brother is trying to just get his dad off his back—by dating at all—and only agreeing to dates with women he won't fall for because he's already fallen for someone and can't deal."

Lily's eyes widened. "That's some theory."

"With a lot of truth to it. Doesn't that sound about right?"

"I'm hardly used to flattering myself, Sarah. The man kissed me. Once. That doesn't mean anything."

"We'll see," Sarah said with a devious grin. "So tomorrow—girlie day in Kalispell?"

"I have to be at work at four. Otherwise I'm free."

Sarah actually clapped with excitement. "Can't wait."

Huh. The *new* new Lily at the Summer Sunset Dance. With Xander in attendance. Could be very interesting.

"There's my adorable niece," came a very familiar masculine voice.

"Did I mention my sitter is Xander and that I asked him to meet me here?" Sarah asked with yet another devilish grin as she stood up. "How nice that both of you are in the same place at the same time and will have to communicate in person. You might even ask him to the dance Saturday night," she whispered.

Ooh, Sarah was good—Lily had to hand it to her. Even if she wanted to bop her friend over the head with the rest of her cruller.

Sarah then leaned over the stroller to give Sophia a kiss on the forehead. "Be good for Uncle Xander and Auntie Lily," she whispered.

Lily's eyes widened. Auntie Lily. Uncle Xander.

Technically, Lily had always been Auntie Lily, before Sarah had even married into the Crawford family.

"Xander, thank you so much for babysitting!" Sarah said. "Lucky for me I ran into you at the Ambling A this morning just when I was fretting over needing care at the last minute. Turns out I could have asked Lily since she has the afternoon off."

Yup, Sarah was *good*.

He smiled, giving Lily a nod but keeping his attention on Sarah. "My pleasure, really. Least I can do since you'll be stuck in a dentist's chair." He turned to Lily. "Nice to see you," he said awkwardly.

"You, too," she said.

Sarah gave her a quick hug, gave Xander a quick rundown on what to expect—which was Sophia sleeping for the next hour—thanked him again and then dashed out.

"So you're free right now?" Xander said. "Want to help me babysit? I'd do anything for my sister-in-law, but if Sophia wakes up, I have no idea what to do. Logan gave me a few lessons over the past few months in how to hold her, but I'm not even good at *that*."

Lily laughed. "Consider me at your service."

He blushed slightly, and maybe she shouldn't have said that. Of course, she hadn't meant anything flirty by it, but hell, she was the new her and maybe she *had*.

Xander tried not to stare at Lily, but he could barely drag his eyes off her. The past few days he'd thought of little else besides that incredible kiss in the rec center kitchen. And he needed to concentrate when he was working at the Ambling A. Yesterday he'd almost knocked himself out by stepping on a rake he hadn't noticed lying across the barn floor. This morning, his brother Finn had apparently said "Earth to Xander" three times before he realized someone was asking him something out by a pasture fence.

So when he'd run into Sarah, who'd looked frantic about a dentist appointment and needing someone to watch Sophia, he'd volunteered. Babies slept a lot, right? He figured he'd park his keister in Daisy's for the hour and a half, drink three or four caffeinated beverages, give the stroller a gentle rock if Sophia got fussy, and have a little time to himself to get his head clear.

He was having to do that a lot lately.

And here, right in front of him, was the woman keeping his head in the clouds.

A little wail came from the stroller, a tiny fist jutting out in complaint.

"Someone woke up on the wrong side of the stroller this afternoon," Xander said with a smile. He unbuckled the harness and carefully scooped out Sophia, holding her the way Logan had taught him and rubbing her back. Hey, this was as easy as he thought it would be.

Until Sophia started screeching.

"Thought I was getting the knack of this," Xander said, frowning. "Guess not."

Sophia's cheeks were red and she started waving her tiny fists.

"It's me. Uncle Xan," he said, rocking her side to side and bouncing her in his arms. "Peekaboo!"

"Waaah!" Sophia screamed.

"What am I doing wrong?" Xander asked.

"Sometimes a baby just gets fussy and needs a new face," Lily said. "Want me to try?"

"Waah!"

"Please," he said, handing Sophia over.

Lily took the baby, rubbing her back and cooing to her. Sophia seemed to like that. She was still flailing her arms but her cheeks were less red. "There, there," she whispered, rubbing her back some more.

Sophia stopped crying.

"Lucky you were here. Or Eva would have kicked me and Sophia out," he said, sending a rueful smile over to the donut shop manager behind the counter.

"How'd you get so good with babies?" Xander asked. "You're the baby of your family."

"I've always babysat. Since I was twelve. And before I started offering cooking classes to supplement my income, I worked part-time at a day care in the infant room."

"I've done group-brother babysitting so that Logan and Sarah could get some time to themselves, and among the five of us, we did pretty well, thanks to Hunter, who knows what he's doing. I thought I had this."

Lily laughed. "I can just picture you Crawford brothers hovering around a tiny baby, trying to figure her out."

"We're pretty clueless, but hey, we do love our niece."

"She's one lucky little girl to have such doting uncles." She gazed at Sophia, giving her another bounce and letting her stretch her legs. The baby seemed much happier. "Well, I've got the next couple hours free, so I'm happy to help. Why don't we head to my house and change her and give her a bottle if she's hungry, then take her for a walk?"

He liked the idea on two counts. He'd have a pro with him just in case and he'd get to spend time with Lily. "Sounds good. And thanks."

Sophia did not want to go back in the stroller, so

Lily held her while Xander wheeled the stroller out of Daisy's Donuts.

"Hi, Xander!" trilled a feminine voice.

Lily glanced up to see a pretty woman with long dark hair and an amazing body smiling at Xander as she approached the shop. The brunette gave Lily a quick assessing glance, seemingly decided she was no competition and turned her megawatt smile back to the hot rancher.

Xander nodded politely and kept walking, the woman's sexy smile turning into a sulky frown.

"Get that a lot, huh?" she asked as they headed up North Broomtail Road.

Who'd think it would be such a drag to have attractive women throwing themselves at you? But it was.

"Thanks to my dad, yes," he said. "First there are the women who are looking to meet Mr. Right, and my dad created his own dating service with six men. Now five. Then there are the women who heard a rumor that my dad promised Viv Dalton a million bucks to get us all married, and they figure there's big money in the family. So, double whammy."

Lily smiled. "Don't forget the women who simply like the idea of going on a date with an interesting cowboy newcomer. That was me, you know. When Viv asked if I wanted to be set up with Knox, I wasn't thinking about marriage or a million dollars. I was just thinking it sounded like fun. A rancher from Texas? With five brothers? I'd bet we'd have a lot to talk about."

"Touché," he said. "But women like you are few and far between."

"I don't know about that, Xander. I think women and men—everyone—just want what their heart desires."

"That's a nice way of putting it," he said.

"People are just people, Xander. Not everyone is for everyone—that's the thing to know. Everything else is none of our business."

"Meaning?"

"Let's use your family as an example. Knox clearly wasn't the guy for me. If he was, he'd have gone on the date. But he didn't so we didn't get the opportunity to see if there was something there. You stepped in, and we hit it off. Knox and his reasons for canceling are not my concern or my business. What matters is who I *do* connect with. Not who I don't and the reasons why."

"You learned this in Economics 101?" he asked.

Lily laughed. "I've been doing a lot of thinking lately about what draws people together and pulls them apart. Why some people work and some don't. Half is chemistry and half is timing."

"I'll buy that. And if the timing is wrong?"

"Then that chemistry goes to waste. All that connection, interest, fun, desire, sharing, talking, laughing—buh-bye."

He glanced at her. "That seems like a shame."

"Yup, sure does."

For a twenty-three-year-old newbie at life, she sure was smart about human interaction, he thought. Maybe too smart.

They arrived at Lily's house, Sophia still content and surveying the world—or Rust Creek Falls—from Lily's arms. As they headed in, Xander hoped he'd run into Andrew so he could find out how things were going with Heidi. The two had gone out a bunch of times already. And they were a good example of what Lily was talking about. Xander hadn't been the guy for Heidi, but one suggestion of Andrew Hunt and voilà—they were practically engaged.

Chemistry and timing. If you had both, you had everything.

He and Lily had chemistry, but the timing? Not so good.

The Hunt house turned out be empty. Everyone was still at work, so Lily suggested they hang out in the living room and let Sophia crawl around the big soft rug. But first, Lily took her in the bathroom to change her, and strange as it was, he missed the two of them when they were gone, even for the two minutes it took Lily to return with a smiling Sophia in her arms.

They both lay down on opposite sides of the rug to create a pen of sorts for Sophia, making peekaboo faces to get her to crawl to them. Sophia shrieked with delight every time Xander revealed his face. He laughed, having too good a time playing house with Lily and Sophia.

Way too good a time.

As Sophia crawled all over Lily, the beautiful redhead making exaggerated faces at the baby and blowing raspberries on her belly, he was completely transfixed.

He could see himself coming home to Lily and their baby.

Whoa, he thought, bolting upright. Where had *that* come from?

"So how many kids do you want?" Lily asked. "Someday, I mean."

"Honestly, I've never really thought about that. I like

the idea of a big family like I had, older siblings, younger siblings. Always someone around."

"I don't know about the younger siblings, but I liked growing up in a big family, too. I always envisioned four kids at least."

"Four little redheads," he said with a grin. "And freckles across their noses."

She touched a hand to her nose. "These were the bane of my existence when I was a teenager. I've gotten used to them."

"I like freckles." *I like* your *freckles. I like everything about you.*

The smile that lit up her face almost did him in. He watched her lift Sophia into her arms and hoist her high in the air. *Focus on the baby, not the woman. You're babysitting. That's all that's going on here.*

His father had set some crazy roller coaster on high speed and so, Xander had met Lily Hunt in the first place. Otherwise, he wouldn't know her. He'd be working the Ambling A, focusing on renovating the ranch, his new family home—his new life. Falling for a woman who could destroy him with a snap of her fingers? No, thank you. Not again. He might have feelings for Lily, but hell if he'd let them go deeper than he already had.

To reinforce that, he let himself think about something he'd forced from his mind six weeks ago.

Britney in bed with Chase. The woman he'd been about to propose to. And his lifelong best friend.

We're so sorry. We didn't mean for it to happen. We're in love, Xander. This isn't just some affair.

Yeah, that made it better.

He felt himself tightening up, the walls closing in.

Good. Because he felt like himself again. Like the man he'd been the past six weeks. Keeping to himself. Working hard.

Ping.

The sound shook him out of his bad memories, and he leaned his head back, sucking in a breath.

Lily had received a text, and as Sophia crawled over to him, Lily grabbed her phone. "Sarah's all done." Lily texted something back. "She'll be by to pick up Sophia in a few minutes."

Good. He needed to get out of here. Breathe some open air.

Relief flooded him when Sarah arrived. Lily settled the baby back in her stroller, and there it was again, that tug of his heart as he watched her. He was barely aware of the small talk he made about what a good baby Sophia was, how Lily had saved the day with her mad baby skills. The door closed behind Sarah, and then it was just the two of them.

Leave. Head to the door. Go.

But he was rooted to the floor. He wanted out. He wanted to stay. He didn't know what the hell he wanted.

"Thanks for helping out," he said. Awkwardly, with his hands in his pockets. "I guess I'll go now."

"Any time," she said.

And still he didn't move.

They stared at each other for a moment, both just… standing there.

"You know, you never did get your cooking lesson, Xander. If you have time now, I could show you how to make a delicious bacon and cheese omelet, which is exactly what I'm craving this second."

You should leave. This woman has mystical, magical powers over you.

Which was clearly why he *couldn't* leave. And besides, he was hungry.

"That does sound really good." He followed her into the kitchen, dying to pull her into his arms and kiss her again.

But she now had a carton of eggs in her hands, and had instructed him to crack five in a bowl. He was so focused on her face, her freckles, her lips that he hadn't heard half of what she'd said in the past few minutes.

He took the carton and got busy cracking, getting only two little bits of shell in, which Lily scooped out with a spoon.

"Anyone home?" a male voice shouted from the front door.

Good thing, too. Because he'd been about to lean in again. Close. Despite everything he'd been feeling just ten minutes ago.

"Sounds like Andrew," Lily said. "In the kitchen," she called back.

"What else is new?" Andrew said as he came sauntering in with Heidi right behind him. He smiled. "Ah, *this* is new," he said at the sight of Xander. "Or is it?" he asked with a grin.

"Xander and I are friends," Lily said, cutting her flashing green eyes at her brother.

"Got it," Andrew repeated with a little too much mirth in his voice. "You're just friends."

"Xander," Heidi said with a warm smile, "did I ever thank you for fixing me up with Andrew? I've meant to."

"I'm glad it worked out," Xander said.

"It's worked out and then some," Andrew said, dipping Heidi and giving her a dramatic kiss.

Heidi laughed and swatted him. "I'll tell ya," she said to Xander and Lily, "over the past few months I must have gone on thirty dates. I thought maybe I was just too picky or that I'd never find my guy. And then out of nowhere, a date very strangely fixes me up with another date—and he's the one. You just never know. Life is crazy."

"I love that," Lily said. "And I agree. You just never know. Being open, saying yes—that's how you find what you really need."

"Exactly," Heidi said.

Again, he thought about what Lily had said about chemistry and timing. Heidi could have so easily told him no way, that she didn't need a blah date setting her up with her next blah date. But she'd been open to possibilities, and now it looked like she and Andrew were headed somewhere serious.

Possibilities. Exactly what he didn't want to explore. For damned good reasons.

"So I'm giving Xander a cooking lesson on the art of omelets," Lily told her brother and Heidi. "Bacon and cheese. If you guys are hungry, stick around and you could join us."

"I love bacon," Andrew said. "So I guess this is our first double date, Lily."

"Just *friends*, remember?" Lily said.

Did "just friends" want to kiss her the way he'd imagined doing so a second ago? No.

"I'm going to try not to burn the bacon," Xander said

to change the subject. He grabbed the package from the counter and used a knife to slit open the side.

"Well, we'll be in the living room," Andrew said. "Sorry in advance about all the PDA you might be forced to witness."

He got another swat from Heidi for that, and then Xander was once again alone with Lily in the kitchen.

"They're very sweet," Lily said. "I'm so happy for my brother. His life is really coming together. Now if you could just get Bobby and Ryan hooked up, they'll be out of my hair, too."

He laughed. "Sorry, but I told Viv I'm done with the fix-ups. So I won't have any referrals to make."

She stared at him. "Oh?"

He nodded, using the tongs to lay the bacon in the big square fry pan. *I thought I could stop thinking about you by dating women I'd never really be interested in. But nothing makes me stop thinking about you.*

Silencing that inner voice, he barked at himself, *Get your mind back on the cooking lesson. Get control of your own head, man.*

"So you were saying I can pan-fry bacon or bake it in the oven?" he asked. "I think my dad bakes it. Half the time it's burned."

"That might be a temperature issue. And keeping it in too long. With bacon, you have to keep a steady eye. I like frying because the smell fills the air faster and I like how the oil jumps in the pan. I know, I'm crazy."

He smiled. "It's fun getting your wrist singed by splatters of burning oil?"

She laughed. "I've been through it all, cooking wise. I can take a little heat."

Can you? You're twenty-three. So young. So inno-cent. So...idealistic.

Her idealism was one of the reasons he admired her so much.

God, he wanted to kiss her.

She started talking about cooking temperatures, but he missed everything she said. Her long red hair, despite being pulled back into a ponytail, made him want to run his hands through it. He wanted to kiss every freckle dotting her nose and cheeks.

"Smells good!" Andrew called from the living room.

Xander had barely been aware the bacon was frying. He made himself pay attention as she showed him how to scramble the eggs, which of course he knew, how to let the omelet set and cook at the same time, when to add the cheese and bacon and when to fold it. They had two pans going, two omelets in each, and suddenly they were ready and smelled amazing. The ones he was responsible for looked a little lopsided, but still delicious.

"We'll eat these," he said. "My first diners can have yours."

She laughed, and again he wanted to pull her against him and just hug her, hold her.

He didn't know how long he was going to be able to contain his feelings for her. If he even should at this point. Maybe they could just see what was between them. Maybe it wouldn't last, they could get each other out of their system, and he could go back to being Not Getting Involved Xander.

"Going to the dance at Sunshine Farm on Saturday night?" he asked as she showed him how to slide the omelet onto a plate.

He suddenly imagined them pressed chest to chest, her arms draped around his neck, his around her waist as they swayed to a slow country ballad. The warm, breezy summer air blowing back her long red hair…

She added a handful of grapes to each plate. "I was just talking to Sarah about it today. The Rust Creek Falls Summer Sunset Dance. Sounds fun. Will you be there?"

"I think all the Crawfords are going, so yes. I'll show my face but I don't know how long I'll stay."

"Well, I'll definitely see you there, then. You'll save me a dance before you rush off into the night?"

"I will," he said, dragging his eyes off her and onto the plates.

It was almost like a date. But not quite. He'd see how it felt, dancing with Lily. Thinking of her as his. A slow ease into giving in to his feelings for her.

It was a start, right?

Chapter 8

Kalispell was the nearest big town to Rust Creek Falls, a forty-five minute drive but worth it for the access to shops where Lily could look through clothing racks and jewelry displays, and maybe even get her makeup done at a beauty counter. She'd been going to Bee's Beauty Parlor, which was right next door to two of her favorite places—Daisy's Donuts and Wings to Go—ever since her dad realized her hair would need trimming every few months and that his attempts were woefully uneven. Lily had even called Bee's to make an appointment for a real haircut, but they were booked solid because of the dance. Luckily Sarah had gotten recommendations for salons in Kalispell and now Lily was sitting in a huge swivel chair in Hair Genie, a trendy-looking salon in the center of town, Sarah standing beside her.

"So what do you have in mind?" her stylist, Ember

(Lily had no idea if that was her real name or not), a chic young woman all in black, asked as she assessed Lily's hair, running her fingers through it, picking up strands and examining the ends. "Very healthy. You can do anything with this thick, straight, silky texture."

Lily looked at Ember's gorgeous mane, which was exactly what she wanted hers to look like. "I love *your* hairstyle. Would that work on me?"

Ember smiled and nodded. "Absolutely. I just have some simple long layers. Keeps it easy for me to pin up so it doesn't get in my way when I'm working, but the layers give the thick, straight texture a lot of oomph and swing."

"That's perfect for you, Lily," Sarah said, standing on the other side of her and looking at her reflection. "Lily's a chef," she told Ember.

"Then it's vital to keep the front layers very long so they don't fall in your face," Ember said. "Plus, you can dress up the cut or keep it casual—just like with fashion. Let it air-dry or a quick blow-dry for a casual look. Use a heated styling brush or curling iron and you can do amazing beachy waves."

"Perfect. I put myself in your hands," she told Ember. Then she grinned at Sarah. "I'm so excited!"

"Me, too," Sarah said. "Okay, I'm gonna go read magazines—something I never get to do."

Lily looked at the shiny silver scissors in Ember's hand and felt like this moment marked the culmination of everything she'd worked so hard for the past year. Working toward her degree in business. Quitting the Gold Rush Diner for a swanky restaurant like the Maverick Manor and getting promoted to line cook (she had been a prep cook her first six months, but the few times she'd filled in for a cook had caught her boss's attention). Making plans, even if they were just in her head at this point, for having her own place someday, whether a small restaurant or her own catering shop or even both. Her look would now catch up with the woman she'd become on the inside.

She closed her eyes, wanting her haircut to be a surprise.

Twenty-five minutes later, Ember announced she was all done and that it was time to unveil the new Lily Hunt. Sarah came running over and Lily heard her gasp.

She opened her eyes.

Wow. "I love it!" Lily shrieked. Her hair was still long, the layers starting at her shoulders and flipping back a bit to blend in with the rest of her hair. Ember had her move her head from side to side like she was in a shampoo commercial.

"You look amazing!" Sarah said. "It's gorgeous! Chic and stylish but still casual at the same time. It's perfect!"

Lily shot out of her chair and threw her arms around Ember.

The stylist laughed. "I love getting that reaction. See you in six weeks for a trim. Or since you live a bit of a distance, you can just have a local salon keep up the trims, and come to me if you want to make another change. I am your hair genie," she added with a grin and bow.

"Squee!" Lily shouted as she and Sarah left the salon. She couldn't stop touching her hair and shaking it. "I'm going to make you sick after a while, Sarah."

"I completely get your excitement," her friend said.

"Ooh, let's check out that clothing shop." She pointed across the street at On Trend, a boutique. "Look at that pretty dress in the window."

Lily was already staring at it. It was a knee-length sundress, a pale pink with spaghetti straps. Sexy and playful. And perfect for the dance.

They linked arms and dashed across the street and into the shop.

Lily found the dress in her size and slung it over her arm, then Sarah directed her to the racks of jeans, wagging her finger when Lily looked at a pair of her usual type of jeans.

"Try these," Sarah said, picking up a pair of dark-wash skinny jeans. "And these. And these."

A saleswoman gathered what they'd chosen so far and hung the items in a dressing room. Sarah came over with armloads of tops and sweaters and pants. Lily had an armful of her own.

Ten minutes later, Lily was in the dressing room. She started with the pale pink dress.

She took off her T-shirt and shorts and slid the dress over her head, the soft fabric lovely against her skin. It fit perfectly, neither tight nor loose. She stood back and looked at herself, tears poking her eyes.

Yes. Yes, yes, yes. This is me.

She stepped out of the dressing room and Sarah literally clapped.

"It's beautiful! It fits you so well! Oh, Lily!"

Lily stared at herself in the floor mirror. "I always shied away from pinks because of my hair, but something about the light pink works. Have I ever worn spaghetti straps? I don't think so."

"You look amazing," Sarah said.

"Want to try these cute shoes with it?" the sales-clerk asked, holding out a pair of silver ballet flats with a pointy toe.

The shoes looked great with the dress and were shockingly comfortable for not being sneakers or the clogs Lily usually wore to work.

A half hour later, Lily brought her "yes" pile to the counter, her gaze drawn to the intimates section. "Maybe a couple of sexy bras and matching undies would round out the plain white cotton and little purple flowers on my current collection."

"Definitely," Sarah said with a grin.

Two lace bras, one a blush color, one black, and two matching pairs of underwear joined the stack on the counter. She was getting the dress, two pairs of skinny jeans, two pairs of slim capris, one black pencil skirt, three tops with cute details and two pretty cardigans. Plus three pairs of shoes—the silver ballet flats, a pair of charcoal leather heels that she could actually walk in and strappy sandals. All the pieces worked together so that she'd have outfits. She couldn't wait to move her current wardrobe of loose, boring jeans and T-shirts to the back of her closet.

Next they stopped in a cosmetics shop, a saleswoman giving her a tutorial on a natural and an evening look. When the woman capped the pink-red lipstick and Lily looked in the mirror at her makeover, she gasped again.

"Whoa. I've never worn this much makeup. But it doesn't look like I'm playing dress-up. It just looks like an enhanced me."

"Exactly," the woman said. "You look very elegant."

"Me, elegant," Lily repeated. "First time anyone's ever called me that!"

Sarah grinned. "Welcome, Enhanced Lily!"

Lily laughed, peering at herself in the mirror, still unable to believe she could look like this if she wanted. "I wonder if Xander will even notice."

Sarah's eyes probably popped. "What? Are you serious?"

Lily sighed. "I don't think what I look like is the issue."

"Well, if the T-shirt and jeans Lily has that man all wrung inside out," Sarah said, "imagine what the sexy Lily is gonna do to him!"

Huh. She hadn't thought of it like that before.

Lily grinned.

"Yes, you're going," Max Crawford bellowed at Knox in the family room at the Ambling A on Saturday afternoon. "And you're going," he said, pointing at Hunter. "And you're going." This was directed at Finn. "The kvetching around here—over a casual summer dance. Give me a break! You're all going and that's that!"

"Well, I guess we're going," Wilder said on a chuckle.

"No one wondered if *you* were going," Knox said to Wilder, a guy who'd always lived up his name. "Of course you're going."

"Damned straight I am," Wilder confirmed. "At least thirty women asked me to save them a dance."

Little did those women know that Wilder was about as interested in marriage as Xander was.

"Ditto," Finn said.

Now *there* was the single women of Rust Creek

Falls's best chance of Viv Dalton's "dating service" ending with a walk down the aisle. The dreamer of the family, Finn was always falling in love. Out of love just as fast and hard, but then back in love—with the same enthusiasm. Xander didn't get it.

"Just thirty?" Hunter asked. "Try at least a hundred here."

"Once again," Knox said, "I doubt there are a hundred single women in this town."

"Feels like it, thanks to dear old Dad," Hunter pointed out.

Knox gave a firm nod. "That's the truth."

Logan rolled his eyes. "Oh, you poor, poor guys. Going to a social event where you'll dance with women and have some good food and meet new people."

"Oh, shut up," Xander said. "Once you settled down with Sarah, you were able to walk along the streets of this town in peace again. You have no idea what we go through." He grinned and held up a palm for a high five from Wilder, sitting next to him on the sofa.

Logan threw a pillow at him, and Xander's gaze caught on his brother's wedding ring. Xander sure hadn't seen that coming—the marriage—but Logan had surprised them all. Not only had he fallen crazy in love but with a single mother of a baby. Watching his older brother become a father to little Sophia sometimes stopped Xander in his tracks, stole his breath. Because it was so unexpected? Because it made Xander wonder about himself and whether he'd have a family of his own someday? A wife, a baby? Despite all his head-shaking to the contrary, the thought of a wife and child had been creeping into Xander's head lately.

Like at Lily's house. When they were babysitting Sophia. When he was watching Lily with his niece. All sorts of insane ideas flew through his mind.

Eh, he thought. One Crawford brother out of six did not mean they were all headed in the direction Logan had gone. He glanced at his brother, who always looked happy these days. Content. Purposeful.

Logan had the lightest hair of the six Crawfords—that *had* to have something to do with it. The darker-haired brothers would remain single the way they were supposed to.

While Finn and Wilder got in an arm-wrestling match, Knox and Logan betting on the winner, and Hunter confirming with his sitter what time she'd be over to watch Wren, Xander took the opportunity to slip away unnoticed. He headed up to his bedroom and shut the door on the voices and laughter in the family room.

Two hours until the dance. Xander moved over to the window overlooking the front of the house, the pastures and fields, the cattle just standing there calming him down. He had no idea what he was so revved up about, anyway.

Because he thought of tonight as a date of sorts? It wouldn't be, not really. It was just a casual dance, being held outdoors at Sunshine Farm, which Eva and Luke Stockton had turned into a guest ranch last year. Sure, he'd dance with Lily once, maybe twice. He'd probably stay for a half hour and then leave.

He'd lost track of how many women asked *him* to save them a dance. Except for one. The only one that mattered. Lily. Which meant maybe he should dance with a lot of women. He might have Lily Hunt on the brain but he didn't want to.

You followed your heart once before, and you got slammed in the gut with a sharp right hook. Punched in the head, too. Knocked out. That was how it still felt.

Britney and Chase were married now. Just like that. They'd flown to Vegas, figuring their families and friends would stop giving them a hard time about their sudden union and how they'd betrayed "that poor Xander" if they proved they were the real deal. So they'd taken a road trip and married in a chapel in some fancy hotel.

Xander knew this because Chase had written him; how he got his address in Montana, Xander had no clue. But Chase had sent a letter, a real letter, not an email, again saying he was sorry about what happened, that he'd mourn the end of their friendship for the rest of his life, but that he found the right woman, the only woman, and though it killed him that she was his best friend's woman, Britney was his life.

The letter had arrived a couple weeks after Xander had moved to Montana with his family. At the time, he'd quickly read it and almost ripped it up, but then shoved it back in the envelope and stashed it in his top dresser drawer under a pile of socks, where things went to die. Like the one photo he had of his mother. Like a photo of him, Britney and Chase at a carnival photo booth.

Xander went to his dresser and stuck his hand under a bunch of rolled socks until he found the photo. Britney, long blond hair everywhere, Chase with his military-short cut and Xander, with his long dark hair. In one of the four little black-and-white photos, Britney was laughing uproariously at something Chase said while Xander laughed, too. Now that he thought about it, their romance had probably started that day.

Interesting that Xander had held on to the photo. He had no idea why he had—and didn't want to think about it right now. Back under the socks it went, the dresser door shoved shut.

He moved over to his bed and dropped down on it, his gaze landing on his bedside table, on the old diary lying there. Xander had almost forgotten about the diary entirely. He and his brothers had been replacing the rotted floorboards in this room, which Xander had wanted because it faced the front yard and he always liked to face forward, when they found something buried. A jewel-encrusted diary with the letter *A* on the front. *A* for the Ambling A? The ranch had come with the name, and they'd all liked it, liked the unknown history that was behind it, so they'd kept it. Plus, they were ambling men themselves, weren't they?

The diary was worn with time and age—and locked. Someone had buried this diary under the floorboard and had either forgotten about it or passed away. The Ambling A had been a vacant mess for decades until the Crawfords bought the property and started renovating, so who knew how long the diary had been buried under the floor. Or why. Xander had thought about trying to pick the lock, to see if there was anything interesting in the diary about the Ambling A, ranch secrets or a clue to whose diary it was, but a simple attempt to get the lock open hadn't worked and then he just lost interest in the old journal. He wasn't one to write down his thoughts and feelings, though maybe it would help.

Dear Diary,

I found the woman I was about to propose to in bed with my best friend. People suck. Love sucks. Forget the whole damned thing.

Yup, that was how his diary would start. Then maybe he'd get to something like this:

Dear Diary,

There's a redhead named Lily who has me all bewitched. She's not my type. At all. Except for the fact that I can't stop thinking about her or imagining myself in bed with her. So does that make her my type? I guess it does.

Xander gave a rueful chuckle and stood up. He was losing his mind.

While he was pulling out a shirt, he envisioned himself dancing with Lily under the stars, in the moonlight, his woman in his arms.

His woman? He was *definitely* losing his mind.

Chapter 9

"What?" Andrew Hunt said on a croak.

Lily, halfway down the stairs of her house, almost took her phone out of her new little beaded cross-body purse so that she could snap a photo of her brother's face and his priceless expression. *Surprised* didn't begin to capture it as he stood in the foyer.

Or Bobby's. Or Ryan's. Or her father's.

"What?" Andrew repeated, his mouth still dropped open, jaw to the floor.

"Lily?" Ryan asked, peering closer at her as he came out of the kitchen with a beer.

"That's not Lily," Bobby, right behind Ryan, said with a firm shake of his head. "Who are you and what have you done with our baby sister?"

"Oh, my God, that is definitely Lily," her father said, one hand over his mouth, another over his heart.

Oh, brother—literally. She sucked in a breath and finished walking down the stairs, the four Hunts staring at her, mouths still agape.

"I mean, Lily, I've seen you in a dress a time or two," Andrew said, "but this isn't just you in a dress. This is…"

"Lily as a nominee at the Academy Awards," Bobby said. "Wow," he added.

"Fairy Godmother up in your room or something?" Ryan asked, the Hunt green eyes completely confused.

"Can't a girl doll up a little for a dance?" she asked innocently, moving over to the large mirror above a console table in the hallway. She checked her appearance for a stray bit of mascara or something in her teeth.

But nope—she was camera ready.

She'd gone with the pale pink sundress with the spaghetti straps, the hem ending in a swish just above her knees. She wore the pretty earrings she'd bought in Kalispell, silver filigree hoops, and three delicate silver bangles on her left arm. The ballet slippers, which kept the outfit casual and simple, were perfect for an outdoor dance at Sunshine Farm. Makeup, including the famous "smoky" eye Sarah had taught her to do, a sweep of mascara, pink-red lipstick, her layered hair all shiny, bouncy and loose, and a spritz of a perfume sample she'd gotten in the boutique—and she was all ready to go.

Oh, and the blush-colored lace bra and panties underneath it all.

She took a final glance at herself in the mirror, gave her hair a fluff and turned toward the Hunts, who were still all staring at her.

"Uh, *what*?" Andrew asked again.

Lily laughed and faux-bopped him on the arm. "You guys know I've been making a lot of positive changes lately. Working on my business degree, upping my game with my recipes and cooking techniques at the Maverick Manor, really thinking about my future plans, saying yes to experiences I normally wouldn't." She didn't add that those yeses included one to Viv Dalton when she'd asked if Lily wanted to throw her name into the Crawford brothers dating pool. But it was a great example of how she'd gone from *Nah, but thanks* to *Why not?* "So I wanted a new look to reflect who I feel like on the inside. I'm not the scrappy tomboy chasing after you guys in the woods with an insect net anymore."

"Well, you'll always be that girl," her dad said. "But you're this woman, too."

Aww, her father had tears in his eyes. Now he was going to make Lily cry and she would mess up her mascara. She'd practiced applying it four times last night until she got it right, somewhere between natural and enhanced.

"You look flipping amazing, Lil," Andrew said.

"Beautiful," Bobby agreed with a bow.

"You know I like to rib you," Ryan added, "but I have to agree. Wow."

She grinned, thrilled with the response. "Thanks, guys. That means a lot. I'm all dressed up with somewhere to go." *Yes, I am! And look out, Xander.* She couldn't wait for his reaction.

Andrew glanced at his watch. "Speaking of the dance, I need to go pick up Heidi. See you all there."

"Want a ride, Lil?" Ryan asked. "I didn't even think

you were going or I would have asked earlier. Bobby and I are picking up a couple friends, then heading over."

"I'll take my car," she said. "But thanks." The Hunt brothers headed out, and Lily breathed a sigh of relief, glad to not be under the microscope any longer.

"Should *I* go?" her father asked. "Dances aren't usually my thing, but…"

Lily felt her eyes widen. "You should!"

"Well, if you're going and look like a princess, I could certainly put on a nice shirt and comb this rat's nest on my head and sway to a country tune or two. Say hello to some people."

Lily's heart leaped. "Go change," she said with a smile. "Maybe your blue shirt with the Western yoke and the gray pants? Or even a pair of dark jeans?"

His eyes lit up. "Back in a jiff," he said, taking the stairs at a dash.

Lots of changes happening in the Hunt household, she thought with a smile. Her. Andrew in a serious relationship with Heidi. Bobby and Ryan in business together with their auto-mechanic shop. And now her dad, who'd dated here and there over the years but never let anything serious develop, was going to a town dance when he never had before.

Five minutes later, her dad was back downstairs, in the Western shirt and jeans Lily had suggested, and his good cowboy boots. He'd combed his hair and even added a little bit of his aftershave.

"You look great, Dad," she whispered, trying to avoid crying.

He nodded, dusting off imaginary lint from his shirt.

"*We* look like a million bucks. Shall we?" he said, holding out his arm.

Lily grinned and wrapped her arm around her father's, her heart about to burst.

Xander saw her hair first. And just a swath of it because she was surrounded by people. He'd been on the lookout for Lily since he'd arrived at the dance about fifteen minutes ago, but there had been no sign of her. Now he'd caught a glimpse of that unmistakable red hair, those lush fiery tresses. There was something different about it, the bit he could see. Sleek and…sexy.

He moved closer, craning his neck around Henry Peterman, who was six foot four, built like a linebacker and blocking his vision. He went around Henry, and stopped dead in his tracks.

Whoa.

It was Lily—he was sure of it. But she looked nothing like the Lily he'd known for the past few weeks.

Damn, she cleaned up well.

Henry was saying something to her, and he saw Lily smile politely and respond, then step back. Another guy took Henry's place. Then another.

"Sorry, but I promised my first dance to someone," he heard Lily say.

That was his cue. He sure as hell *hoped* so, anyway.

"Lily?" he said strangely in the form of a question. Whoa, whoa, whoa. "You look beyond beautiful."

She smiled, those gorgeous green eyes all lit up. "Thanks. I needed a change."

"This is some change," he said. "Stunning." He stared at her, completely tongue-tied all of a sudden and unable to think of another thing to say. "Uh, I could go get us some punch. Nice night," he added. *Smooth, Xander. You're great at conversation.*

"I'd rather dance," she said, holding out her hand.

Her soft, pretty hand. She wore sparkly blue nail polish, silver bracelets jangling on her arm. He took her hand and led her over to the dance area, which was pretty crowded. The band was playing an old Shania Twain song he'd always loved, a slow one.

He barely heard the whispers around them as she slid her arms around his neck. *Is that Lily Hunt? Oh, my God, that's Lily. Holy buffalo, did you see Lily Hunt?*

"Guess I'll be getting that a lot tonight," she said, her eyes only on him.

They were practically chest to chest. So close he could see every individual freckle across her nose.

His hands were on her waist, on the soft, silky fabric of her dress. "Pretty in pink," he said. "Isn't that a movie?"

She smiled. "I've seen it at least ten times," she said, tightening her arms around his neck. She glanced around, then looked back at him. "It really is such a gorgeous night. I've heard that this dance is the town's way of saying goodbye to summer every year. I'm definitely not ready to see summer go."

"Me, either." He'd associated Lily with summer since he'd met her at the beginning of August, their first date, if it could really be called that, on a wings-and-sauce picnic in the park.

"And I love all the white lights strung in the trees," she said, staring up at the lights. "So festive and pretty."

"Like you," he said. He hoped to God he wasn't blushing because his cheeks sure were burning.

She laughed. "You're not used to seeing me like this."

"No. I could get used to it, though. I think. You looked great the way I met you. And you look great now."

She stopped swaying and stared at him, her expression...wistful. "That means a lot to me. Thank you."

They continued dancing, his throat going so dry at being this close to her, holding her, breathing in the delicious, sexy scent she wore, that he needed some punch or he'd pass out.

"How about that punch now?" he asked.

"I've love some."

He headed past throngs of people, most of whom he recognized now from town and the rancher association meeting he and his family had attended. Logan and Sarah were slow dancing at the edge of the dance area, Andrew and Heidi making out as they swayed not too far away.

Xander said hello to Luke and Eva Stockton, who owned Sunshine Farm and had turned it into this gorgeous guest ranch with a welcoming main house and cabins dotting the property. He saw a couple of his brothers talking to Nate Crawford, who owned the Maverick Manor, and his family, distant relatives of Xander's clan. A bunch of attractive women crossed his path with smiles and "save me a dance, will you, cowboy?" Yes, two had actually said exactly that. He finally made it to the punch and downed a cup, then poured two more and headed back over to where he'd left Lily.

Except she wasn't there.

He should have known better than to leave her alone! Of course she'd been surrounded by men the minute he'd left and was probably now dancing with someone.

The thought turned his stomach.

His gaze ran over the dance area. He saw Wilder with his arms around a pretty brunette. Finn was talking more than he was dancing with a blonde. Max Crawford was chatting up two women who looked to be his age by the buffet table. The Jones brothers—millionaire cowboys who'd moved to town over the past couple of years from Tulsa, Oklahoma—were dancing with their wives, and Xander made a note to meet one or two of them tonight since they'd also come to Montana from out of state.

Finally, he caught a swish of the red hair. He craned his neck around two women who were looking longingly at Hunter as he was deep in conversation with their nearest ranch neighbor, and yes, there Lily was. Dancing.

With Knox.

What?

It wasn't a slow song, so his brother didn't have his arms around her. And Lily's arms were up in the air at the moment as she laughed at something Sarah, dancing next to her with Logan, said.

Now Knox was whispering something in her ear. Lily laughed and touched Knox's arm.

A red-hot burst of anger swelled in his gut. Knox had had his chance to date Lily and had opted out. *So move along, buddy.*

He marched over with the two cups of punch, someone's elbow almost knocking them out of his hands.

"Hey, Lily," he said with a fast glare at his brother. "I have our punch."

"Oh, great!" Lily said. "I'm so thirsty! All this dancing."

"None for me?" Knox asked with too much amusement.

Xander narrowed his eyes at his brother.

Knox chuckled at what had to be the murderous expression on Xander's face. "I was just apologizing again to Lily for how I acted a few weeks ago. The date that wasn't. I was telling her all about Dad's master plan to get us all hitched and how the whole idea made me nuts after I'd already agreed on a date."

"I completely understand," Lily said. "And besides, I got to meet Xander," she added, those beautiful green eyes looking straight into his.

"I'll go say hi to Nate," Knox said. "Thanks for the dance, Lily." He smiled and walked away, sending an infuriating wink at Xander.

Lily took one of the cups of punch and held it up. "A toast."

He raised his, as well. "To?"

"To change," she said, holding his gaze.

Dammit. She had him there. Change, progress, forward movement made the world go around. Stagnancy was a slow death. Case in point: Xander moving to Montana. He might have stayed back in Dallas, stewing in his bitterness. Instead, he'd opted for an entirely new state, a new life, and he'd met Lily. A woman he couldn't stop thinking about.

"Change is good," he agreed.

They clinked cups and he watched her drink, tossing back her head, her long, creamy neck so kissable-looking.

"Thanks for this," she said. They put the cups down on a tray of empties on a table, then headed toward the buffet, where there were light appetizers and tiny sandwiches.

"Must be hard to eat anyone else's food but yours when you're the best cook in town," he said, popping a mini quiche in his mouth.

She laughed. "That is some serious high praise. Thank you. But I'm hardly the best. All the cooks at the Manor are amazing. And Sarah and I had lunch in Kalispell that blew me away. I had no idea vegetable soup could be that good."

"Maybe we could go check out one of the restaurants in Kalispell sometime," he said. "I'd love some Thai food. Or really good Italian."

"Are you asking me on a date, Xander Crawford?" she asked. "Or are we just friends?"

He felt his cheeks burn. "I… We're…" He gnawed the inside of his cheek. "I'll go get us more punch. Be right back."

The minute he left he realized that by the time he got back, she'd likely be dancing with someone else. *That is what you get, idiot*, he chastised himself. *"I… We're." Stammer, stammer, stammer. Jeez. What the hell was that?*

But he had no idea what he meant it as. Date. Friends. He just knew he wanted her to himself.

He hurried over the five feet to the punch bowl, filled two cups and yup, when he got back, Lily was dancing with some guy in a straw cowboy hat. He had a good inch on Xander, too, which bugged him.

At least it wasn't a slow dance.

The song ended and he saw Lily smile at her partner and dash away—right toward him.

"Why do I keep leaving you by your lonesome?" he asked.

"Because you have to torture yourself before you accept that there is something going on between us, Xander Crawford."

"Say how you really feel," he said with a smile.

"Hey, this is the new me. The real me. We're at a dance on a beautiful summer night. I'm in this pretty pink dress. You have on that gorgeous brown Stetson. My favorite Dierks Bentley song is playing right now. Seems like just the place to see what's what."

He handed her the punch, feeling like he'd been socked in the stomach. She was 100 percent right. They downed the drinks, tossed the cups and hit the dance floor.

The moment her hands slid around his neck, he knew he wasn't letting her go again, wasn't letting her out of his sight.

"So what's this about an old diary you and your brothers found buried in your bedroom?" she asked, looking up at him. "I overheard Logan and Sarah talking about it. You guys found it under the floorboards?"

"Funny, I was just thinking about the diary earlier tonight. It's on my bedside table—locked. I tried to get it open with a letter opener, but I need something smaller. Plus, should I really be opening it? I don't know."

"Whose is it?" she asked, her hands both hot and cool on his neck.

He shrugged. "No idea. Someone must have hidden it under the floorboard to keep it from prying eyes and either forgot it when they moved or wanted it buried forever. I really don't know. There's a letter *A* on the cover of it. It's jewel-encrusted and was probably all fancy and expensive when it was new."

"An old jewel-encrusted locked diary!" Lily said. "Something so romantic about that! I wonder whose it could be."

"Don't mean to eavesdrop," Nate Crawford said from behind Lily. A tall, good-looking man around forty, Nate was dancing with his wife, Callie. "If it looks really old and has an A on the cover, it probably belongs to someone in the Abernathy family—that's where the Ambling A ranch originally got its name. The Abernathys left town a generation ago, though."

"Wow," Lily said after Nate and Callie excused themselves to the buffet table. "It would be great if you could get it back to an Abernathy. Imagine the family stories written in the diary."

"Or family secrets," Xander said.

"Those, too. Still would be so wonderful to return it."

He nodded. "I'll ask around about the Abernathys."

The song changed, a slow one this time, and Xander found himself pulling Lily a bit closer.

"If that's okay," he whispered.

"Oh, it's more than okay."

He breathed in the flowery scent of her hair. He could stand here holding her forever.

"Cutting in," said Henry, the huge linebacker of a

cowboy. He practically knocked Xander out of the way to get to Lily.

"Her dance card is full, sorry," Xander snapped.

Lily stared at Xander, crossing her arms over her chest.

"Say what now?" Henry asked, looking confused.

"Lily promised all her dances to *me*," Xander explained.

Now Lily's stare turned into a glare—at Xander.

Henry shrugged. "Oh. You two are a couple? I didn't know. Sorry." He left, walking up to a pretty blonde standing at the edge of the dance area.

Yeah, that's right.

"I didn't get a chance to tell Henry that he misunderstood," Lily said, raising an eyebrow.

"Misunderstood what?" he asked, not liking where this was headed.

"That we're a couple. We're just *friends*. Isn't that what you keep saying? Of course that means I can't promise *all* my dances to a buddy, Xander. You understand, right?"

Grrr. "I… We…"

Now there was merriment in those flashing green eyes. "That didn't work out too well for you before."

She was right. It didn't. And he was done with all that.

Lily. His Lily.

He tipped up her chin and kissed her. Hard and soft. Passionately. One hand stayed at her waist as the other went into those lush red strands.

And dammit, there was that parade clanging in his

head again. Cymbals. Marching band. Someone singing hallelujah.

They were *a lot* more than just friends.

"Well, I guess he wasn't mistaken," Lily whispered.

Chapter 10

Ooh la la, Lily thought, wrapped in Xander's arms, his soft, warm lips on hers. *Make this kiss last forever.*

"Can a guy cut in?"

She peeled open one eye to see Xander glaring at a cowboy in a white cowboy boots. "Sorry, but we're kissing here," Xander said.

"Yeah, I know," the guy said, wriggling his eyebrows.

"Ew?" Lily said, grimacing at the creep.

Xander made a fist. "Want to know *this*?"

"Possessive dudes are out," the guy said, shaking his head as he walked away.

A beautiful breeze swept through Lily's hair just then, and the creep was forgotten. All she saw was Xander's handsome face and his dark eyes. All she felt were stirrings she'd never experienced before. All she wanted was to be alone with him.

"Maybe we should go kiss somewhere more private," she whispered.

"In total agreement," he whispered back.

He took her hand and led her along the edges of the crowd, craning his neck for a good spot where they could be alone. But everywhere they looked, people or couples had taken over, even on the far side of the barn, where a pair of teenagers was making out, both of them giggling as she and Xander popped their heads around and said, "Sorry."

"There's always the Ambling A," Lily said. Boldly. Very boldly.

Those dark eyes of his locked on hers. He knew exactly what she meant.

And she did mean that. She wanted to be alone with Xander Crawford. In his bedroom. In his bed.

"It's closer than my house," she rushed to add. "And who knows when my dad might head home. Your father looks like he's having too good a time to leave anytime soon." She nodded her head over to the buffet table, where Max Crawford held court with four women.

"Nice to see him getting out and enjoying himself," Xander said. He seemed almost grateful for the reprieve in their conversation. The change of subject.

Because they both knew if they made love tonight, there would be no turning back.

"My dad, too," she said. Peter Hunt was pouring a cup of punch for a woman Lily recognized from the circulation desk at the library. *Good for you, Dad*, she thought with a smile.

Oh, wait, she thought. She'd given her dad a ride here so she needed to tell him she was leaving for a bit. He had a key to her car so could just drive himself home if need be.

For a bit? Hopefully they'd be gone for hours.

She pulled out her phone and sent her dad at text: Going for a ride with Xander. He'll drop me home so feel free to take my car home.

He sent back a kiss and heart emoji, then a smiley face. Have fun. And yes—too much fun.

Oh, Dad, she thought with a smile as she put her phone away. Always so supportive.

"So," Xander said. "The Ambling A."

She nodded. Twice.

He took her hand and led her to where a zillion cars and pickups were parked. "I wisely parked in a place where I could get out easily," he said as he opened the door of his silver truck for her. "I thought I'd be leaving in a half hour. Alone."

"Surprises are great, aren't they?"

"This one sure is," he whispered so low that she wasn't entirely sure he'd said that, but thought he had.

They headed out toward the ranch, the radio playing low, the windows halfway open to let in the warm and breezy summer night air. In ten minutes they were at the Ambling A, not a car in sight.

"It's our lucky night, for sure," he said. "No prying eyes." He helped her out of the truck and took her hand, leading her into the house.

She'd been here recently, cooked in the kitchen, eaten at the dining room table, talked and laughed with all the Crawfords, and now the house felt comfortable and familiar and dear. He gestured toward the stairs, and up they went.

Oh God, oh God, oh God. Suddenly a dream she'd had for three weeks was about to come true and she could hardly believe it.

The overhead light was off in Xander's bedroom, just the table lamp casting a soft glow over the bed with its blue-and-white quilt and four pillows.

Xander closed the door behind him—and locked it. "Finally. A little privacy. A lot of privacy, I amend."

She smiled. "I'm not used to all that attention. I'm not sure if I liked it or not, to be honest." Debuting her new look at the dance was half fun, half the opposite of fun. At first, the reaction had been welcome. But when guys started buzzing around her just because she suddenly looked "hot," to use the word one cowboy had whispered in her ear as he'd walked past, Lily had had enough.

"I didn't have this 'Cinderella' night so that I could dance with fifty guys or have more dates than all you Crawfords combined," Lily said. "I just wanted my outside to reflect my inside."

"I think I know what you mean. I've always seen you, Lily Hunt. No matter what clothes you're wearing or if you smell like flowers or garlic, I see you. And I've always admired that person."

She stepped toward him until she had him backed against the door, her arms snaking around his neck. "I know. Even when things got awkward on that first date, I *knew*. I caught you by surprise, Xander Crawford."

He grinned. "You sure as hell did. Kapow!" he added, faux-punching himself in the jaw with his right hand, which he then slid around her waist.

She leaned up on her tiptoes to lift her face toward his and he met her in a kiss that almost had her knees wobbling. Good thing he picked her up in his arms, never breaking that kiss, and carried her to the bed.

She was on Xander's bed. Oh God. Oh God. Oh God. Yesssss!

A thousand butterflies let loose in her stomach just then.

Lily wasn't a virgin—but her two short-term relationships, where both guys had been as fumbling as she was, hadn't exactly taught her the art of sex. When she was nineteen and had decided to finally lose her virginity to her first real boyfriend, she'd summoned the courage to ask a close girlfriend how you knew what to do. Her friend had told her she wouldn't have to think about it at all, that desire would lead the way, and she could respond in any way that felt right and natural. Lily had thought that was good advice and it had actually made her feel more equipped. Her first time, she'd felt more anticipation than desire and the experience hadn't exactly been all that comfortable. With the second relationship, the guy was so shy that she had to lead the way. So nothing remotely like TV or movie sex had ever happened in her life.

She had a good feeling that Xander knew what he was doing.

He lay beside her on the bed, on his side, his hands caressing her hair, her face, her back. And then he was kissing her again, and she closed her eyes, almost unable to process all the emotions swirling inside her. She moved closer against him, kissing him with equal passion. There was too much clothing between them, she thought, her hands in his thick, wavy dark hair.

"A little help with the zipper?" she asked as she sat up, glancing at him.

The grin he gave her made her laugh. "My pleasure," he said, kneeling behind her.

He unzipped. Then he slowly moved the spaghetti straps off her shoulders. He kissed the sides of her neck, her collarbone, and she shimmied out of the dress, never so grateful for having bought new undergarments.

"Ooh, that's sexy," he said, taking in the blush-colored lace demi bra and matching bikini panties. "You're sexy."

Lily Hunt, sexy. No one had ever said *that* before.

She went for his belt buckle, and again, the happy surprise on his gorgeous face emboldened her even more.

"I've always said, you're a woman who knows what she wants and goes for it," he said as he kicked off his jeans and she unbuttoned his shirt.

And kissed her way down his chest.

Who *was* this woman?

One of the best parts of tonight was that she knew it wasn't the makeover giving her confidence. It was the way Xander Crawford made her *feel*. The real Lily had truly come out of her shell, every last bit of her.

In less than a minute, they were both naked. Lily felt his gaze on her, and she didn't feel exposed or shy or awkward. She only felt desire. And desirable.

Xander reached into his bedside table drawer and out came a little square foil packet.

And then he was kissing her again, his hands everywhere, his lips everywhere. The moment they became one, Lily gasped and lost all ability to think beyond how incredibly good she felt, how happy she was.

How in love.

Lily's eyes fluttered open, and she almost pulled the quilt over her head to go back to sleep when she remembered: this wasn't her bed. And she wasn't alone.

A smile spread across her face as she turned her head slightly to the right to see if she'd dreamed the whole thing.

Because it had been a dream. Wow.

But nope, Xander Crawford was right there, fast asleep. He didn't snore, either.

She watched his chest rise and fall, rise and fall, mesmerized by his pecs and the dark swirls of hair. She wished she could stay in this bed all day—all the days of her life—but she had to sneak out before a whole bunch of Crawfords woke up and caught her creeping down the stairs.

She gave Xander one last look, drank in every gorgeous bit of him, then picked up her pink dress and slipped it on, put on her shoes, found her little beaded purse and slung that over her torso. She wanted to kiss Xander goodbye but didn't want to wake him, so she tiptoed to the door and pulled it open as gently as she could.

Lily peered out left and right. The coast was clear. She dashed down the stairs and was almost at the bottom when she realized she'd ridden here with Xander.

Which meant she was going back upstairs. Very quietly. She'd have to wake Xander, after all.

Which she was now looking forward to.

Unless things would be weird? Awkward? The morning after with its bright light? She turned around and took the first step back up, suddenly not wanting to move too quickly.

What if Xander regretted their night together?

She was barely on the fourth step up when the front door to the Ambling A opened and Lily froze, her back to it. She had no idea who it was who'd come in.

Someone who'd also had a good time at the dance, clearly.

"That red hair can mean only one woman," the male voice said. "Hey, Lily. How are ya?"

She tried to force the embarrassed grimace off her face and turned around. It was Wilder, Xander's youngest brother. He looked a bit rumpled but otherwise as handsome as all the Crawfords were with his slightly long brown hair and the piercing dark eyes.

"I'm well," she said, then rolled her eyes at herself. Could she sound more stiff? "I'm doing just great. How are *you*? Have a good time at the dance?" The questions rushed out of her mouth to put the focus back on him.

"Oh, yeah," he drawled. "Almost too good a time." He took off his cowboy boots and left them by the door. "So you're in the same clothes you were in last night, but you're just getting here?" he asked.

Thank you, Lord! Because she was on her way up the stairs, Wilder must have thought she'd just gotten here.

"Long story," she said, figuring Wilder Crawford was not really interested in her love life.

"Let me guess. You had too much of the spiked version of the punch, fell asleep under a tree, woke up with leaves in your hair, then remembered you promised your buddy Xander you'd give him a cooking lesson and so here you are."

Um, no. She wanted to tell him she wasn't the kind of person who passed out under trees at parties, but she wanted to run with the idea that she hadn't just tried to sneak out of the house after spending the most amazing night of her life here.

"Well, I see I made you blush, and honestly, Lily? Don't worry about it. If you knew *half* the crazy times my brothers and I have had, then you'd really have something to blush about. And I'm not even talking about the women coming and going. Ask Xander to tell you the story of the time he had three dates in one night. People say I'm the wild Crawford who lives up to my name? Xander has us all beat for notches on the bedpost. Including here in Rust Creek Falls. He's not even the tallest of us. Personally, I don't get it…"

Her stomach dropped.

What?

As Wilder went on about how much each Crawford could bench-press, Lily tuned him out, suddenly wishing she hadn't given him the impression that she and Xander were "just friends."

Now instead of being embarrassed at getting caught, she wanted to run away. Maybe bawl.

"Well, I'll go wake Xander. Bye!" she croaked out and dashed up the stairs.

"If you're making pancakes, make at least ten for me!" he called up.

Oh God. Did everyone hear that? Had Wilder woken up the whole house?

She raced into Xander's room, shutting and locking

the door behind her, her heart beating so loud she was sure it was what woke Xander.

"You've got too many clothes on," he said, propping up in bed. "You've *got* clothes on."

Calm down, Lily. Don't go all just-how-many-women-have-been-in-this-bed *on him. Everything that happened before last night was the past.* Last night was a new beginning for them both.

Right?

She could feel the exact spot her heart was bruised. Dead center. Was she another "notch on the bedpost" as Wilder had unwittingly put it?

Back in high school, the guys had had a brief sickening game they'd dubbed "least likely." Whoever got the most girls they were least likely to kiss to kiss them, won. Won what, Lily didn't know. Unearned respect from the idiots, she guessed.

That week, ten guys, most from the football team, had asked Lily if she wanted to take a walk—with a gleam in their eyes. The first time, she'd been so bewildered that one of the hottest, most popular guys in school had sort of asked her out that she'd said yes, without any idea if she actually liked him or not. Turns out they had nothing much to say on their ten-minute walk, but all he'd been after was a kiss on the lips. Once he got it, he'd said, *Booya!* And run back toward the school. The next morning, Lily had heard a group of cheerleaders talking about the bet and how skater dudes were suddenly asking them out—as if.

Lily had said no to the next nine guys who'd "asked her out."

And had had a hard time trusting in a man being attracted to her *for* her ever since.

But with Xander, she knew he was. She knew it and believed it the way she knew her own name.

So forget the past. Everything is about now. Now, now, now.

Never mind that *now*, she felt very unsure of herself. No. Not of herself. Of *them*.

"Wait," Xander said, frowning. "Were you about to leave?"

"I actually did leave but got halfway downstairs when I remembered I didn't drive here. So I'm stranded."

He grinned. "Guess that means you'll have to come back to bed." He held up the side of the quilt.

"I ran into Wilder on the stairs," she said, arms across her chest. "At first I thought he caught me doing the famous walk of shame, but turns out he thinks we're just friends, so he gave me an earful about the women who've come and gone from this very room since you've been in Rust Creek Falls."

"Wilder talks too much," he said, shaking his head.

"You were supposed to say 'fake news.'"

His expression softened as he realized he'd confirmed her worst fears.

"I won't lie to you, Lily. I've had a couple of very short-term…experiences. Just the first couple weeks after I moved here and felt really overwhelmed by everything."

Her arms fell to her sides and felt like they weighed a hundred pounds each. Like her heart right now.

"I was so upset about what happened back in Dallas," he continued, reaching for his pants. "I wanted to forget and so I went out a lot those first couple weeks. Not even here in town, but in the surrounding towns to be more anonymous."

"You're my third lover," she blurted out. Then immediately wished she could take it back. She dropped down on the edge of the bed, facing away from him. "The first guy? There was no second time. I think we both just wanted to get our virginities over with and it wasn't exactly a spiritual experience." She sighed. "The second guy and I lasted a few weeks but we didn't have any chemistry except when it came to discussing pastry—we met in a baking class." She stood up, then dropped back down. "My point is that I don't have much experience in any of this. And you clearly do."

"Well, I've got seven years on you," he said, getting up and pulling on his jeans. "I'm thirty years old. Friends of mine have been long married with two kids by my age."

She turned to face him, stunned silent for a moment by the sight of the morning light hitting the muscled planes of his chest. Just hours ago, her hands had explored every millimeter of that chest. His entire body.

And now…everything was wrong.

And everything hurt.

He walked around his bed to his dresser and pulled a blue T-shirt out of a drawer. "One of the reasons why I was so hesitant about us," he said, putting on the shirt, "was because I know what getting emotionally involved leads to."

Dammit. Was he going to do this? Had she actually set this conversation in motion? Oh God.

No. Wait one minute. She was not about to blame herself for talking about reality. The truth. If he wanted to revert back to the guy who hid from life—and love—well, that wasn't her fault.

It just happened to hurt like hell.

Crud.

Had she really thought her night with Xander was going somewhere? That he'd suddenly be over his past and trust in the world again?

Yes, she had thought so.

Maybe because she was as young and experienced at life as he'd said she was.

"I thought there was more between us," she said. "Was I wrong?"

He held her gaze for a second, then turned away, his attention out the window. "You weren't wrong, Lily. But I guess this conversation just brought up all the reminders that—"

He stopped and sat down on the edge of the bed, running a hand through his hair.

"Reminders that…?" she prompted.

"That I'm jaded and bitter. And you're young and hopeful and idealistic and have your whole beautiful life ahead of you."

"That's total bunk, Xander Crawford. You're just scared spitless that you feel more for me than you intended. And so you're pushing me away."

"Lily—"

But again, he stopped talking.

"When you find someone truly special, you don't let them go, Xander. Do you realize how rare it is?"

"Is it?" he asked.

"Oh, so I'm just a dime a dozen?" She glared at him,

grateful the anger was edging out the hurt. No, wait. There the hurt was. Punching back for control.

At least the anger was keeping her from crying. That she'd do in private.

"This wasn't how I envisioned the morning going," he said, standing up. "Not at all. I thought we'd make love three more times, then I'd sneak you into the shower with me, and then whisk you off to the Gold Rush for scrambled eggs and home fries and bacon and a lot of coffee and then we'd go back to my place for a repeat. That's what I thought this morning would be."

Now she did feel like crying. "I wanted that morning, too, Xander. I still want it."

"But you want a lot more than that, don't you?" he said gently.

"Hell yeah."

"I'm sorry, Lily. I messed up by kissing you in the first place because I just couldn't resist you. And now I've made this huge mess of things. I'm very sorry."

"You're sorry for sleeping with me?" she said, her voice sounding more like a screech. This time, the anger had knocked out the hurt with a solid left jab. "How dare you!"

"Lily, no, I—"

"I need a ride home. And I'd like that ride to be *silent.*"

He let out a harsh sigh and headed for the door.

Tears pricked the backs of her eyes.

Lily raced down the stairs, dimly aware of laughter coming from the direction of the kitchen. She could hear a couple of voices. She had to get out of there before anyone saw her—especially now that this really was just another notch on Xander's bedpost.

She tried hard to keep the tears from falling, but down they came. Lily flung open the door and ran out, zooming for Xander's truck. She got in, wiping away her tears. *Take a deep breath. Do. Not. Let. Him. See. You. Cry.*

By the time he got in the driver's seat, she was composed.

Do not think about last night. How you kissed at the dance. How you two drove to the Ambling A with all those feelings, romance in the air, love in the air, all your hopes coming true...

She wanted to blame it on herself for falling for Xander when he told her by his actions alone on their first date that he was going to smash her heart to smithereens.

She wanted to blame it on that blasted Wilder Crawford—and her unfortunate timing of running into him—for telling her stuff she had no business knowing. Or wanting to know.

But the blame for her feeling like she'd just been kicked and Xander's probably feeling like hell? That was on Xander himself—and his stubbornness.

But as he started the truck and pulled out, something occurred to Lily. Something the old Lily would have thought of immediately. The new Lily had too much confidence, though, so the news flash hadn't seeped into her consciousness until now.

Maybe it had nothing to do with Xander living in the past and being stubborn.

Maybe he just didn't love her back.

Chapter 11

Xander pulled up in front of Lily's house, Dobby and Harry sitting outside on the porch, Harry on his back on the mat, taking in the brilliant sunshine of late August. Xander wanted to run up and rub that furry little belly, feel Harry's soft-as-silk floppy ears, talk to her dad, ask her brothers how things were going at the auto mechanic business, where they'd fixed his brother Finn's brake issue the other day. He even wanted to hang out with Andrew and hear how things were with Heidi. Xander's first fix-up.

At least he brought love to someone. Two someones.

Please don't rush out of the truck until I get to say something, he thought, but couldn't make himself speak the words. He didn't know *what* he wanted to say.

I'm sorry didn't cut it. There was so much more to say but he couldn't put words to it.

He turned off the ignition and turned to face her. "Lily."

But nothing else came out of his mouth.

She waited. She tilted her head. Waited some more. Then she said, "Everything between us led to last night, Xander. And last night was something beautiful. Personally, I think you're crazy for turning your back on it. But if that's your choice, I guess I have to respect that." She cleared her throat and reached for the door.

"Last night *was* beautiful," he said.

"And?" she prompted.

"And…maybe it's better we cool it now rather than someone gets run over by a Mack truck down the road."

"You're the only one driving that truck, Xander," she said—between gritted teeth. Then she got out of the car and stalked to the door in her pink dress, the dogs jumping up to greet her.

He watched her pet both of them and bury her face in their fur, then hurry inside, the dogs behind her.

The door closed and he felt so bereft.

He felt *something* for her, that was not in doubt.

He started the truck and drove toward the Ambling A. A hard day's work would help set his mind at ease by taking his brain off Lily completely. But by the time he got to the ranch, his mind was a jumble. Memories of last night, of what it was like to make love to Lily, to be one with her, how complete he'd felt, kept jabbing at him.

He didn't want to feel complete, though. That was the damn problem. He'd felt complete in Dallas with Britney to the point that he was going to propose.

And wham. Knocked upside the head and left for dead.

A little dramatic, but that was how it felt.

He needed a walk, and the now overcast morning suited his mood. He'd survey the miles of fence line out past the barn, see if any part of it needed repair. He wrapped a tool kit around his hips, then headed out on foot to the fence, a good mile away. As he neared it, he could see his brother Knox with his tools, working on a long gap in the wiring.

"Guess we had the same idea for this morning," Xander said.

Knox glanced up. "Glad you're here. I could use a hand." Knox used a tool to stretch the wire, and Xander wrapped the wire around and around the next section to secure it. "I was riding fence when I noticed it." He glanced for Xander's horse. "You walked all the way out here?"

"A lot on my mind," Xander said.

"Yeah, ditto. But after working so hard there's no way I'd want to hoof it back, so I brought the trusty steed." He nodded up at the beautiful brown mare.

"Still mad at me for dancing with your chef?" Knox asked. But Xander could tell his brother wasn't kidding.

"Yes, actually. Dammit." He sighed and ran a hand through his hair. "Not dammit that you danced with her. Dammit that she *is* 'my chef' and I'm screwing it up. I really care about Lily. I more than care about her. I just don't *want* to. If that makes any sense."

"Unfortunately, it does. All part of our legacy."

Their legacy. The six of them rarely talked about

their upbringing, and he figured that was what Knox was referring to.

"With our family past, who the hell wouldn't be wary of love and marriage and all that stuff?" Knox asked, not looking up.

Xander didn't know all that much about their mother, but she'd been considerably younger than their father, jumping into the marriage not long after they'd started dating. And he knew that Sheila Crawford had left Max and their six young children for another man—and never looked back.

If his mother had been able to do that, anyone could. Britney sure had.

So why wouldn't Lily? When she had her whole life ahead of her at just twenty-three?

She was probably right when she'd said, in so many words, that the past was running his life, that it had too tight a grip on him. But right now, that grip was stronger than hers.

"You'll figure it out," Knox said, shaking him out of his thoughts.

"Meaning?"

Knox tightened the final piece of wire. "Either Lily will win out or the family legacy will. Logan got lucky. Maybe you will, too."

Huh. He hadn't really thought of it that way before. But he knew luck had nothing to do with Logan settling down with Sarah and baby Sophia. *Love* had won out.

For some crazy reason, he felt a little better than he had when he'd first walked out here. Maybe because he forgot that love *could* win.

* * *

Lily was glad she'd had to work today. One of today's specials was the Aegean pizza she'd introduced to the menu, an immediate hit, and she'd made at least thirty of them since the Manor had opened for lunch. She had her eye on the six in her oven as she sliced chicken and chopped garlic and green peppers for the next batch, trying to not pop all the delicious feta cheese in her mouth before she ran out. Her waiters had reported on where her diners were from, but she couldn't exactly add barbecue sauce or cayenne pepper or roasted chestnut shavings to the Aegean pizza without ruining it, so she kept her special additions to the other entrées. She'd made several big pots of minestrone soup, adding a bit of this and that to it to bring her diners a bit of home. Five tables had ordered servings of the soup to go, so that had brought a smile.

And she wasn't feeling much like smiling today.

When she left for the day and arrived home, she didn't even bother going upstairs to relax or take a bath to soothe her weary muscles and mind. She hit the kitchen. She had a few clients around town who loved her cooking at the Manor and hired her to make special-occasion meals or texted her that they were ill and could she drop off what they were craving. This evening, she was making split pea soup with carrots and tiny bits of ham for Monty Parster, her seventy-five-year-old widowed client who had a cold. Monty was usually robust and volunteered in the library, putting away books that had been returned, and Lily adored him. She'd make him a pot of his favorite feel-better soup on the house.

"And this is the living room," she heard her dad suddenly say, along with two sets of footsteps. One with a definite heel.

"Why do I smell something amazing?" a woman's voice asked.

Oooh, did her dad have a date over?

"That must be my daughter, Lily. She's a chef at the Maverick Manor. Best cook in the county, maybe even the state. Or the country!"

"Well, whatever she's making certainly smells like it," the woman said.

Lily liked her already.

"Lil?" Peter Hunt asked as he poked his head inside the kitchen.

"Hi, Dad," she said with a smile, stirring the pea soup as it simmered. It *did* smell good.

He pushed open the door, and behind him was an attractive woman around his age with shoulder-length dark hair and warm hazel eyes. "Lil, this Charlotte McKown. We met at the dance last night."

Lily extended her hand. "It's so nice to meet you. The dance was wonderful. I must have eaten ten of those little ham-and-cheese quiches."

"Me, too," Charlotte said. "And a little too many of the mini raspberry cheesecakes."

Lily laughed. "Yup, same here."

As her dad escorted Charlotte to the powder room so she could freshen up before their dinner at the Manor, Lily gave the soup a taste and declared it done and perfect. She shut off the burner just as her dad came back into the kitchen, a big smile on his face.

"Our first date was breakfast at the Gold Rush

Diner," he whispered. "We were so full of French toast and pancakes and bacon that we skipped lunch."

"So this is an all-day date?" Lily asked with a grin. "Dad, I'm thrilled."

"We have a lot to talk about. She's widowed, too. And has four grown kids just like me. She takes Pilates and does yoga and volunteers in the clinic. She's a great person."

"Sure sounds like it," Lily said.

They could hear the powder room door opening, so her dad kissed her on the cheek and dashed out.

Lily laughed. Her dad sure seemed to be falling in love.

Next would be Ryan and Bobby. They'd probably each met someone at the dance, too.

Oh well, she thought. At least most of the Hunts were happy. She carefully poured the soup into a big container, put a lid on it, grabbed some crackers and sourdough bread and then headed out to her car.

A few minutes later, she was in Mr. Parster's little Cape Cod–style house. He sat in a recliner with a crocheted throw over him, a box of tissues beside him. Lily prepared a tray with the soup, which was still piping hot, and the crackers and bread, and a glass of lemon water, and brought it out to him, placing it on a table that wheeled right over his lap.

"Ah, my favorite split pea," he said. "Did I ever tell you that you make it just like my wife did?"

She smiled. "You gave me her recipe. It's my favorite version, too. I make it for the Manor, too, and it's always a hit."

He took a spoonful. "Ahhh," he said. "So good.

And trust me, it's you, not the recipe. My second-oldest daughter made this for me the last time I was sick, and I tell you, it was terrible! Something was just missing. Not that I told her that!"

Lily smiled. She adored Mr. Parster.

He took another spoonful, then nibbled on a piece of the sourdough bread, which Lily had made herself as well yesterday. "I'm sure that hoity-toity Maverick Manor pays you a fortune, but you could be making a killing by going into business for yourself as a personal chef. I'd hire you to make every meal for me. Good thing I actually like to cook myself or I'd go bankrupt. Oh, speaking of, will you be teaching another cooking class for seniors? I'm interested in Asian cooking."

"Wait," she said. "You think I could make a living as a personal chef? Here in Rust Creek Falls?"

"Are you kidding? You'd rake it in. Those who are sick. Single parents. Working parents. Dolt bachelors who never learned to crack an egg. Special occasions. Parties. Work events. Trust me, everyone knows when Lily Hunt is working at the Manor and they go those days."

"Really?" she asked. Mr. Parster was a bit of a busybody who was on at least five town boards, so it was possible he was in the know.

"I don't go around blowing smoke," he said. "Anyway, just an idea." He ate two more spoonfuls. "Heavenly. How do you get these carrots so soft and delicious?"

She laughed. "I'm very happy you love the soup. And thank you for the compliment. Well, the rest of the soup is in the fridge with reheating instructions. Want me to stick around? Make you some tea?"

"Nah," he said. "My other daughter is coming with a German chocolate cake. She's a much better cook than Karly. Don't tell her I said that."

Lily laughed. "Sworn to secrecy."

As she headed out to her car, she couldn't stop thinking about what he'd said. Personal chef? She'd thought about having her own restaurant one day, something small to start, to learn the business and grow as a chef. Or her own catering shop for events. But being a personal chef hadn't really occurred to her. Made-to-order dishes for individuals and families? And businesses and events, too? Hmm. A more personal touch.

She could have her own business doing what she loved.

She could even turn her little gift for reminding people of their best memories and home into her work.

Lily's Home Cookin'.

Her heart leaped and pulse sped up. Yes! She would start her own home-based food business as a personal chef. She could offer meal-prep kits and ready-made dishes and make herself available for parties and events. She could be all things to all stomachs!

Lily's Home Cookin'.

This time, when tears pricked her eyes it was because she was overcome with joy. Her mother would be proud of her. She knew it.

She drove home, thinking about the business plan she'd need to create. Using what she'd learned in school, doing some more research online and really homing in on what she envisioned for her business, Lily could even approach the bank about a small business loan. She wouldn't need incredible overhead to start, but she'd need decent padding for the ingredients she'd need, cookware, containers and labels, advertising, an accountant and her own space.

Yes. It was time to find her own home, a condo or small house with a good-sized, modern kitchen. Her dad would understand and he'd also be proud of her.

All that settled in her mind, she turned on the radio, planning to sing along at the top of her lungs to her favorite station, but there was a commercial on. Of course.

"Northwest Montana's Best Chef Contest this weekend in Kalispell," the radio host was saying. "Deadline to enter is tonight at midnight. See details online at NW Montana's Best Chef Contest dot com. Good luck, local cooks! Ten thousand big ones would even get me to enter—if I could cook a burger without charring it to death."

One of her favorite songs came on, but Lily snapped off the radio. *Ten thousand dollars?*

Ten. Thousand. Dollars.

More than enough money to get her business off the ground, pay first and last month's rent on her own place and have some cushion for emergencies.

She had to enter that contest. She had to *win* that contest!

Lily pulled into the driveway and rushed inside, dashing upstairs to her desk and opening her laptop. She typed the name of the contest into the search engine, and there it was. According to the site, the first round was an elimination event on Friday night—all hopefuls would make the same dish, based on the same recipe and the same ingredients. The top ten entrants would move on to round two. Three finalists would be chosen to move on and after the next round, one winner would be named. And awarded ten grand and the right to call herself Northwest Montana's Best Chef. *Note*, she read. *All entrants must bring an assistant who will aid only with prep, help fetch ingredients, cookware, utensils and plates during the competition, and help with time management.*

Wait—*what?*

An assistant?

She raced out of her room into Andrew's. Not home. Neither were Bobby or Ryan. She texted all three.

Busy this weekend? I need an assistant for a cooking contest in Kalispell.

Within fifteen minutes, she had a "no can do" from them all. Andrew had a special orientation at the academy. Bobby and Ryan were booked solid at the auto-mechanic shop. And she already knew her dad had two special dates planned with Charlotte because he'd texted her so while she'd been in the powder room during their dinner out.

Sarah had a baby—no way could Lily, or would Lily, even ask her. Two other very busy girlfriends were also not likely to be available.

There *was* one other person she could ask. He might be free. And willing.

But if he said yes, could she really bear spending the weekend with him? Her heart would break a tiny bit more every time she looked at him.

She *had* to enter the contest—and win.

Which meant picking up the phone and calling Xander Crawford.

Chapter 12

Lily grabbed her phone, sucking in a deep breath. She punched in his number and brought the phone to her ear, her heart beating a mile a minute.

"Lily?" he asked. "Everything okay?"

"Everything's fine. I just need a favor. A big favor."

"My answer is yes," he said.

She flopped down on her bed, eyebrow raised. "You don't even know what the favor is."

"Don't need to, Lil. I'd do anything for you."

Tears stung her eyes. This time, not from joy. But from the bittersweet poke at knowing how much he cared about her—and how she'd never have him the way she wanted.

I'd do anything for you—except be in love with you or lie to you about it.

The cooking contest, she reminded herself. She had

to think only of that. "Does 'anything' include being my assistant for the weekend at the Northwest Montana's Best Chef Contest? We'd leave Friday night and return Saturday night. I know you probably can't do it—it's last minute and practically all weekend and—"

"How many aprons should I pack?" he asked. "Do I own an apron? Do I get to wear a chef's hat?"

She almost burst into tears. She had to cover her mouth with her hand and squeeze her eyes shut. That was how touched she was that he was going to help her.

"I'll bring the aprons," she managed to say. "And yes on the chef hat."

"Count me in, then," he said.

She could barely catch her breath. "Thank you, Xander. You have no idea how much this means to me to enter the contest." She told him all about her business plan, the idea for Lily's Home Cookin' and how the ten thousand would get her started and then some.

"I always said you'd run the world someday, Lil. I'm happy to help you. And honestly, any time you need something, I'm here for you. I'd do anything for you," he repeated.

Except be in love with me. Except be with me. Except commit to me.

At least she had her weekend assistant. And she knew she could trust him to work hard and fast. The time they'd spent in the kitchen at the kids' cooking class and his few cooking lessons gave him a good familiarity.

Now she'd just have to get through the weekend with total focus on the three dishes they would make instead of on the man she loved.

She could do that. She *would* do that.

"Are you free now to discuss what I'll be doing?" he asked. "I could be over in fifteen minutes."

Wait—he wanted to come over?

"You could explain to me what you'll be cooking and what I'll need to do to help, how the contest works. I don't want to be the one who ruins the whole thing for you by chopping something in the wrong dimensions."

Lily smiled. "Well, there's a website with a ton of information. But sure, why don't you come over, and we'll go over it, and work out a plan based on what I know. The actual dishes I'll be making are a surprise."

"Oh, *that's* always helpful in a competition," he said.

"Right?"

"Be right over, Lil," he said.

She held the phone on her heart for the next few minutes, unable to get up, unable to think.

She could barely get through knowing the man she loved was coming over to talk about the contest. How in the heck would she get through a weekend that promised to be incredibly high stress as it was?

She just would. You *want it*, you *make it happen*. Wasn't that her motto? Sure, sometimes it *didn't* happen, à la Xander Crawford.

But it had to this weekend with the ten thousand bucks. It just had to.

A weekend away with Lily? Yes.

Helping Lily with something very important to her? Yes.

She'd get her assistant and he'd get his friend back. Win-win.

He drove over to her house, greeted by Dobby and

Harry, who ran out for their vigorous pet-downs, Lily standing in the doorway.

She wasn't in the pink dress but she still didn't look like the Lily he'd always known.

She wore very sexy jeans that molded to her body. A V-neck tank top that showed her curves. And sandals that revealed sparkly green toenails. Her gorgeous red hair was sleek and shiny and loose around her shoulders.

She looked too hot.

And man, he thought she'd looked hot before this change.

With the dogs at his shins, he headed in, trying not to stare at Lily.

"I can't thank you enough, Xander," she said. "I know we left things kind of awkward, so…just thank you."

He nodded. "Happy to help." He followed her up to her room, and she shut the door behind them. He sat down at her desk chair; she grabbed her laptop and sat cross-legged on the bed.

The bed, of course, brought back memories of the last time he saw her on a bed. In bed. Under his covers.

"So what's my role?" he asked. *Stop looking at her legs. Stop looking at her hair. Stop looking at her.*

She told him what the site said about the assistant's role. "So, you can chop veggies, gather ingredients, get me a sauté pan, and you can say, 'Lily, you have a half hour left.' But you can't do any actual cooking."

"Well, that's good because I'm pretty bad at it."

"I recall you making excellent omelets," she said. "Even Andrew remarked on how good it was."

"Nice try, Lil. But *we* took the ones that I made. They had the good ones *you* made. Remember?"

"You did a great job turning the bacon with the tongs and getting the cheese out of the fridge," she said with a grin. "And that's pretty much your role at the competition."

He raised an eyebrow. "Except I don't know a sauté pan from a colander."

"Good point. Let's hit the kitchen and I'll give you a tutorial. You can even take notes."

He actually pulled a tiny notebook with a little pen in the spiral from his back pocket. "Of course I'll take notes. I've gotta help you win."

She got up from the bed, her gaze on him, and it took everything in him not to reach for her, to say he was sorry, that he had no idea what he was doing.

But she'd already opened the door and was waiting for him.

In the kitchen, she knelt down in front of a cabinet and pulled out a bunch of pots and pans. She put them all on the counter. "Which do you think is a sauté pan? You'd cook fish in it or chicken or make an omelet."

"Probably this one," he said, pointing at one with shallow sides. "I think."

"Correct!"

"Soup or chili or spaghetti pot?" she asked.

"I'd think it would have to be pretty high to be a spaghetti pot, and I know when my dad makes chili, it's always in some huge pot." He pointed to the pot he thought would be right.

"Correct again!" she said. "A-plus so far."

They went through all the pots and pans, then moved on to the cooking utensils, covering everything from spatulas to colanders to food processors.

"Catch!" she said, tossing a green pepper at him. "Get ready to slice, dice and chop."

He caught it after it bounced against his chest. "Catch!" he said, tossing it back.

She got it in one hand. "Catch!" she said, turning around and tossing it behind her.

"Ha, got it!" He laughed, tossing it up in the air and catching it with his left hand. "Who knew you could have so much fun with food?"

She grinned. "I did."

"You're going to win the contest. I know it."

She smiled, then sobered fast. "You really believe in me."

"Sure do. I've had your French dip. That's all I need to know."

Lily laughed and he realized how much he'd missed that beautiful sound. He wished he could always make her happy. "Well," she said, clearing her throat. "Time for the cutting lessons."

For the next hour, she showed him how to slice thin and thick, how to dice, how to peel and separate garlic cloves.

They'd been in the kitchen for three hours when she let out a giant yawn.

"Someone needs to get her cooking contest rest," he said. "What time are we leaving tomorrow?"

"I need to be there no later than six."

"I'll drive. Pick you up at four forty-five just to be safe. Better to be a half hour early than a few minutes late."

She wrapped her arms around him and kissed his

cheek, and again he wanted to pull her against him and never let her go.

"Thank you so much, Xander. You are a true friend."

Friend. Buddy. Nice. Just friends. The words echoed in his head.

They were going away for the weekend. Together. Staying—he assumed—in the same room. Or was he just hoping they were?

"I guess I should book a room for myself?" he asked as he washed his hands in the sink.

"I already did. We have two single rooms but the guy taking the reservations said they were among the last rooms available. So phew."

His heart sank.

You can't have it both ways, man, he reminded himself.

Late that night, after a practice dinner on her family that they all raved about, and another half hour lying on her bed staring up at the ceiling, and another half hour going over the contest website for every detail, Lily decided to start packing. She set her suitcase on her bed and opened it, wondering what to take—for the competition *and* a weekend away with the man she was madly in love with.

For the competition, she'd wear her new jeans and tank tops and bring two light cardigans, plus her trusty lucky clogs, which were comfortable and nonslip and made her feel grounded.

For the weekend away with Xander, she'd bring the sexy underwear (because why not? Even if he never saw it, she'd know it was there) and the sleeveless little black dress and strappy sandals.

Hell yeah. You never knew.

She grabbed her phone and texted Sarah: Entering a weekend-cooking competition in Kalispell. Guess who my assistant is?

OMG. No way.

As friends. But hopeful.

Me too! Wow! Good luck on both fronts!

Just after she sent back a smiley face emoji, someone knocked on her door. At her "come in!" her brother Andrew poked his head in.

"Got a minute?" he asked.

"Sure."

He came in and sat down on her desk chair. "I just wanted to say thanks, Lil. Everything is because of you."

She put down her phone and stared at Andrew. "What's because of me?"

"Me being really happy. Having Heidi in my life. Dad dating for the first time in forever. I think he's in love."

Lily smiled. "Dad does seem really happy. I met Charlotte. She seems great. But how is either relationship my doing? I didn't introduce you to Heidi or Dad to Charlotte."

"Still it's *because* of you. When I watched you enroll in school for business administration, it spurred me to really think about what I wanted for my future—and I enrolled in the police academy. Then you made pals with a Crawford, and I got the cojones to ask him if he'd pass my name and number to any date he thought would work out. And I met Heidi. You said you were going to the annual dance that you never went to and Dad goes and falls in love. It's all thanks to you. You made really positive changes in your life and now we're doing that, too."

Her heart pinged. "Andrew, you're gonna make me cry."

"Mark my words—Ryan and Bobby will be engaged by Christmas."

Lily wondered if either of them had met someone special at the dance. Both were a little more private than Andrew, who'd always worn his heart right on the ole sleeve. She had seen her other two brothers talking to a couple different women through the night, so maybe they had. The dance seemed to be magical for all the Hunts.

She recalled watching Andrew dip Heidi during a slow song and kiss her. She'd even snapped a photo, which she'd surprise him with one day. "And what about you?" she asked, wiggling her eyebrows.

She could see his cheeks flush and a big dopey smile light his face. "I've already been looking at rings. Maybe you could help me pick one out? I want to propose on her birthday in October."

"Awww! Andrew! I'm happy for you! And of course I'll help you ring shop!" She gave him a big hug.

Now all she had to do was get her own love life in order. And she had a whole weekend to work on it.

Chapter 13

The Northwest Montana's Best Chef Contest was being held in the Kalispell Luxury Lodge, which was a bit on the outskirts of town. The sprawling one-story guest ranch had an enormous hunter-green peaked roof with the name of the hotel across it. It wasn't as luxe as the Maverick Manor, but there were wide planked floors covered with gorgeous rugs, leather love seats and armchairs in sitting areas, and pots of flowers everywhere. On the other side of the hotel reception desk, two women sat at a registration table for the contest. There were at least thirty people in line, mostly in rows of two. The chefs and their assistants.

"Yikes, I hope being in line by the deadline counts," Lily said to Xander. It was only five thirty so she was sure they'd make it to the table by six.

The guy in front of her, wearing a bright purple apron, turned around and said, "It does—I asked!"

"Phew," Lily said. "Thanks."

Xander slung his arm around her, and she felt instantly cheered. They'd chatted nonstop on the way to Kalispell, a forty-five-minute drive, and she wondered if both of them were filling in any potential silences before they could happen. Maybe he'd figured she'd use the time to talk about what had happened between the night of the dance and the next morning. But she was not going to bring that up.

This weekend would speak for itself.

She just had to let it.

He seemed to sense she was a little nervous about what to expect from tonight's elimination round, so while they waited in line he stayed mostly silent, though his arm was a constant comfort around her shoulder.

The line moved quickly, since there were two people handling the check-ins. Finally, Lily was up.

"Hi, I'm Lily Hunt for the competition," she said to the blonde on the left.

As the woman handed her a form to sign, a name tag to fill out and instructions to report to the Sagebrush Ballroom down the hall, someone tapped her on the shoulder.

"Lily!" a male voice said with faux cheer.

She knew that voice.

She turned around. Ugh. It was him. The bane of her existence at the Gold Rush Diner in Rust Creek Falls, where she'd worked for a year as a short-order cook before daring to apply for a line cook job at the Manor. Kyle Kendrick. What a jerk. Luckily, his reputation preceded him because when he tried to get a job at Maverick Manor, her boss, Gwen, had apparently said: "You should watch who you insult while walking down the street. My husband and I were coming toward you and you told him to stop hogging the sidewalk with his 'beer gut.' I almost punched you out myself, but he stopped me."

Kyle was slightly built and not very tall and had a fake-angelic look because of his wavy, light blond hair and blue eyes, which probably saved him from getting beat up as often as he might have. Though she had seen him come to work with a few bruised cheeks.

He was still at the Gold Rush. The only reason he'd lasted there so long was because he was good at his job. Not only good, but fast. She wondered if anyone from the Manor was here for the competition. She hadn't seen any of them, but they might have checked in earlier.

"I plan to win this thing, Hunt," Kyle said, a pretty blonde woman checking her phone beside him. "I want to open a bar and grill focusing on my signature steak-burger. People at the Gold Rush tell me they prefer mine to yours at the Maverick Manor. And for less than a third of the price."

Well whoop-de-do. "I wish you luck," she said. "See you inside." She took Xander's arm, and they headed to the Sagebrush Ballroom. *Please let me be stationed far away from him*, she said in a little prayer.

"My brothers and I had steakburgers the other day at the Gold Rush," Xander said. "And I happened to hear a waitress yelling at someone named Kyle to watch his language, so I know he was there. The steakburger didn't come *close* to yours."

"I knew I liked you," she said with a grin.

She'd almost said *I knew I loved you.* Almost. Thank the universe she'd caught herself.

They entered the Sagebrush Ballroom and got on another line, this one much shorter. There were hundreds of chairs, most full, set up at a good distance from several rows of tables where ten people stood making something on what looked like hot plates. Three more people with clipboards were walking among the tables, taking bites of something, then jotting something down on their clipboards.

Oh gosh. This had to be the elimination round. Hot-plate cooking? And what were they making? From the smell of it, could be grilled cheese.

She watched a different man with a clipboard and headphones hand the woman in front of her a number, then direct her to take a seat. Then it was Lily's turn.

"You're number two hundred forty-six," the man said to Lily. He wore a name tag that read Hal. "You can take a seat and wait for the grouping with your number to be called."

Lily's eyes practically bugged out. "Did you say two hundred forty-six? That's a lot of entrants."

"Tell me about it," he said. "Our judges' stomachs are getting seriously full. But the deadline to register here at the hotel just passed, so there shouldn't be too many more of you. Good luck," he added before gesturing for her and Xander to take seats.

"Suddenly I'm not as sure of myself," Lily whispered to Xander. "There could be three hundred people entering, who all think they have what it takes to win."

"Yes, but only you truly do," Xander said, slinging that strong, comforting arm over her shoulder again.

She smiled and shook her head. "I'm glad you're here," she whispered.

"You've got this."

Lately, Lily felt like she could do anything. But when Xander was by her side, she *knew* she could.

"Numbers two forty through two fifty, please appear in a line at the first table. Chefs only—no assistants."

"Gulp. I'm on my own," she said, standing up.

"Like I said, you've got this." He kissed her hand and she almost gasped. "For good luck," he added.

She wouldn't mind a *real* good-luck kiss—on the lips—but she'd settle for the hand. *For now*, she thought with a devilish smile.

She hurried up to the table with the nine others on their way. Ugh again! Kyle Kendrick was right in front of her. Of all the times to arrive, she had to pick the same time he had?

"Hope your grilled cheese doesn't burn," he said, barely turning around.

"Oh, yours, too," she said, rolling her eyes.

Interestingly, while the line formed, staff were scrubbing at the hot plates to get rid of any former cooking residue. At least she wouldn't be dealing with a burned-on mess from her predecessor.

The ten of them were directed to enter the rows of tables and to stand behind the hot plate with their number beside it. Kyle was two forty and the first in his row. Lily was first in her row at the table adjacent.

The man with the clipboard appeared. "Welcome to the elimination round! I'm Hal and your emcee for the competition. Because we have so many entrants, this seemed the best way to narrow down the field to the top ten chefs. Good luck to all of you!"

Lily eyed Xander, who had moved to the front row, close to where she stood. She smiled at him, and he flashed her a thumbs-up.

"You will each make the perfect grilled cheese with the simplest of ingredients," Hal continued. "White bread. American cheese and half a cup of butter. A staffer will now hand out your ingredients."

Next to the hot plate was a butter knife, a plastic spatula and a salad-type plate. A young woman handed Lily a small tray containing two slices of bread, the butter and two slices of yellow American cheese.

Once the ten hopefuls had their ingredients, the man with the clipboard continued. "You have fifteen minutes to make the perfect grilled cheese, which will then be voted on by our three judges. Ready, set, turn on your hot plates!"

Lily pressed the little red on button. She could feel the hot plate warming up.

Hal looked at his watch. "Three, two, one, and begin!"

Lily dropped some butter on the hot plate, then slathered both sides of the bread, every speck, with the remaining butter. Because she couldn't control the temperature of the hot plate the way she could a burner at home, she decided to put one slice of cheese on each piece of bread and start that way. Once the cheese started melting, she flipped one onto the other, gave a gentle press with the spatula, then flipped, then flipped again. When the outside of the bread was golden brown and the cheese looking perfectly gooey, she turned off the hot plate and slid the grilled cheese onto the plate.

"One minute remaining!" the man with the clipboard said.

Lily flipped the sandwich over on the plate, then cut it, hoping she'd timed it right and the cheese was sufficiently gooey in the center. Yes—looked like it was!

She glanced over at Xander, who was at nodding at her with a smile. *Looks Lily Hunt good*, he mouthed, and she grinned.

A judge began on each section of the table. A blonde woman cut a piece of Lily's sandwich, her expression giving nothing away. She took another bite, then jotted down something on her clipboard. The two other judges did the same.

Their group was then dismissed.

Lily rushed over to Xander. "I have no idea how I did. Hot plate grilled cheese isn't exactly my specialty."

"Probably why they chose that method—because the best chefs will know how to make an incredible grilled cheese with very limited resources. And I'm sure yours will be among the top ten."

She dropped down on the chair beside him, watching the next group go. The smell of burning cheese soon filled the air, but the good AC system and fans took care of it. The poor chef responsible started to cry, then shut off her hot plate and stormed off.

"Well, that's one less cook to worry about," Xander whispered. "And who knows how many others stalked off before the results were announced."

Lily fidgeted in her seat for the next half hour, till it

was over and Hal announced that the judges would have their results within minutes.

"Gulp," Lily said, grabbing Xander's hand and squeezing it.

He kissed her cheek and she felt so comforted that she just leaned her head against his shoulder.

"Okay, entrants!" Hal called out. "Thank you all for coming and making your grilled cheese for us! We know that all of you are great chefs, but alas, only ten can move on to the next round. And so, in no particular order, here are the names of our final ten contestants!"

Lily squeezed Xander's hand harder.

Hal had named eight chefs so far—five women and three men, including that horrid Kyle Kendrick, who'd let out a "Yeah, baby!"

Please, please, please, she prayed silently. *Pleeeeeze!*

"Our ninth contestant is Lily Hunt."

Lily's mouth dropped open just as Xander pulled her into a hug.

"You did it!" he said, kissing the top of her head. "You rock!"

She barely heard the name of the tenth contestant. All she knew was that Xander's arms were around her and she'd made it into the next round.

Right now, life couldn't get better.

"I'm sorry, but I only see a reservation for Lily Hunt," the woman at the hotel reception desk said. "A single. There's no reservation for Xander Crawford—and we're booked for the competition. There's a hotel two miles away you could try."

Two miles away from Lily? No, Xander thought.

"Surely you have *one* extra room somewhere in the hotel for a hardworking rancher assisting the best chef in Montana," Xander said, turning on the charm. He *could* when it was necessary.

"Northwest, but thank you," Lily said.

Xander put his arm around her shoulder. "All of Montana. The country, probably."

The woman behind the reception desk had an "aww" look on her face, but it didn't seem to help the cause. "Sorry. As I said, we're booked solid. There's just one reservation for your party."

Lily frowned. "But I was told we'd have two single rooms. Adjoining."

"I'm sorry, miss. There's nothing I can do."

"I can check into the other hotel," Xander told Lily. "No biggie."

Lily shook her head. "No way. We'll bunk together."

"You sure?" he asked. Innocently. As if he hadn't been hoping she'd say exactly that. Sharing a room with Lily tonight? Just what he wanted.

Sometimes a guy needed time to think while the object of his confusion was right there.

"Of course." She leaned toward the woman behind the desk. "Please tell me the bed is at least a full size and not a twin?"

"It's a full," she assured her with a smile.

Xander nodded at Lily. "Well, there you go. Room for us both." Except Xander was six foot two and a hundred eighty pounds. He hadn't slept in a full-size bed since middle school.

Once they were registered—and Xander insisted on handing over his credit card—they went to the elevator.

Lily was quiet on the ride up, probably a little uncomfortable about sharing a room after all that had happened between them—and not happened—so he held both their bags and let her have her thoughts.

"You're sure you're okay with sharing a room?" he asked as he led the way to a door marked 521. "I can be back and forth in a flash. Two miles is nothing."

The truth? Two miles was forever when it came to being near Lily. He could barely stand being away from her back home.

"It's fine," she said. "We're…whatever we are. I can handle one night. You'll just stay far on your side of the bed."

"Scout's honor," he said, holding up the three-fingered symbol.

Unless neither of them would be able to resist the other and a twin bed would have suited just fine, he thought.

The room was tiny. Barely enough space for the bed, which sure looked small, a dresser with a TV over it, a desk and chair in the corner, and a small bathroom but a jetted tub. He'd definitely take advantage of that.

While Lily unpacked her bag, he opened up the curtains. They did have a view of the mountains. Way off in the distance, but they were majestic and beautiful. He could stare at mountain peaks all day.

"So, what should we do tonight?" she asked. "There's a restaurant in the hotel or we could go explore Kalispell. There are some great restaurants."

"Let's explore," he said.

She smiled. "Just give me five minutes to change."

He was wearing a button-down shirt and his nice

jeans, so thought he'd just stay in that. He went over to the full-length mirror on the wall by the bathroom and gave his hair a tousle, smoothed his shirt and then went back over to the window to look at the mountains of Glacier National Park.

"All ready," Lily said, coming out of the bathroom.

He turned toward her and gaped. Holy cannoli.

Humina, humina, humina.

She wore a sleeveless black minidress with a V-neck, a delicate gold necklace dangling in just the hint of cleavage. *Sexy* did not begin to describe how she looked. Her gorgeous red hair was sleek past her shoulders, and her slightly shimmery red lips beckoned him close.

All of a sudden he realized he was standing a foot in front of her. Staring.

"You surprise me constantly," he whispered. "There are so many facets to you and I love them all."

"Do you?" she whispered back.

He'd tripped a bit on the word *love* once it had left his mouth. But he'd meant it and nodded. "You're amazing, Lily Hunt."

She smiled and now it was her eyes that were shimmering. "You always know what to say. It's what I love about *you*."

"Well, I don't say what I don't mean."

She squeezed his hand and then headed for the door as if she needed to escape this conversation, and he understood why. He was confusing. He was confusing her. And he hated that about himself. His words, his actions very clearly said something about how he felt about Lily. But he seemed to be ruled by a very stubborn brain that had called a halt to letting him really feel all that she engendered in him.

They left the hotel and drove to downtown Kalispell, a very different town than Rust Creek Falls. Home barely had five hundred residents. Kalispell around twenty thousand. The streets were bustling with tourists and residents, heading into the many shops and restaurants.

Xander parked in a public lot, and they started toward the main drag. "Thai?" he suggested, pointing across the street. "Italian? Japanese?"

"You know what I'm dying for? Barbecue. Or chili. Something that sticks to your ribs."

"Say no more. My brother Hunter told me about a new American place that has both. Montana Hots, it's called." He did a search on his phone. "Just four blocks up."

She smiled and wrapped her arm around his. "Gorgeous night. It's fun getting out of Rust Creek Falls, though I love it there. All these people and the different shops and eateries. Sure is exciting."

"I agree," he said, opening the door to Montana Hots. The place was pretty big so there wasn't a wait. They decided on a table outside with huge planters of flowers creating a barrier to the next restaurant.

Lily ordered Grandma Cheyenne's Blue-Ribbon Chili. Xander went for the ribs, which came with way too many sides, but he never passed up garlic mashed potatoes and coleslaw.

"I wonder if one day I'll have a place like this," she said once the waitress left. "I always thought I'd have a restaurant of my own. But I'll tell ya, when my client, Mr. Parster, said I should be cooking for the town as a personal chef, something just lit up inside me like a firecracker. I instantly knew that's what I want to do right now. Have my own business, cook to order, develop a clientele. Maybe five years down the road, I'll seriously think about a restaurant."

The waitress returned with their drinks, two spiked lemonades.

"You can definitely count on seven hungry Crawfords being on that client list," he said. "So if I want a rib eye steak and roast potatoes delivered to my home, all I have to do is text you?"

"Yup. I'll do meals on call, but I'm also planning a meal kit business. I provide the ingredients, all wrapped up, and cooking instructions, so there's no shopping or measuring necessary. An easy-to-make meal for two or four or six. I'll have a rotating menu. I'll also have a menu for all dietary plans. Gluten free, vegan, vegetarian, low-carb, you name it. Lily's Home Cookin'. That's what I'm naming my business."

"Lily's Home Cookin'. I could have that every day. And most likely will."

She held up her lemonade with a smile, and he clinked their glasses.

Suddenly he pictured himself sitting at a table in a house, their house, about to gobble up whatever incredible dish his Best Chef in Montana had dreamed up.

Their house.

Sometimes, when he thought of him and Lily that way, in a fantasy way, he didn't get all tied up in knots over the reality. Sometimes, it just felt right.

Their entrées were served, his ribs incredible and

Lily's chili, which she held up to his mouth in a big spoonful, equally delicious. They talked about their own grandmas' chili, though in Xander's case, it was Grandpa's chili that everyone in the family lined up for when they got together. They talked about her hopes for Lily's Home Cookin', and then Lily said something that had him practically choking on his garlic mashed potatoes.

"I think in about six months, once my business is in a good groove, I'll be able to focus on my personal life. I've really ignored it for far too long."

He paused, his fork hovering in midair. "Your personal life? What do you mean?"

"Well, my love life. I might be young, Xander, but I'm an old soul. I think, anyway. I'm ready to settle down. Find my guy. The man I'm meant to be with forever."

He swallowed, the dry lump going down hard.

"I may even ask Viv Dalton to set me up." She smiled and took a spoonful of her chili, then tore off some corn bread.

How could she eat at a time like this?

When she was talking about finding a husband. Another man. Not him.

He was not ready to let her go.

But he wasn't ready for anything else, either.

Cripes.

Luckily, she changed the subject to corn bread and how her dad always made it on Sundays. "Even when we all realized I was a really good cook, he still insisted on making the Sunday corn bread the way my mom used to. I love that."

"Is it any good?" Xander asked, then finished off the last rib.

"I love my dad like crazy, but no. It's terrible! I'm not even quite sure what he keeps forgetting. Maybe a different ingredient every time."

He smiled. "Corn bread is like French fries and pizza. Even bad, it's good."

Lily laughed, that sound he loved. And the thought of some other guy hearing that melodic, happy laugh for the rest of his life was like a punch to his gut.

Dinner over, they decided on dessert somewhere else, and found a make-your-own frozen yogurt shop full of customers. Xander made a bizarre pistachio, mocha-chip concoction, with a zillion toppings, while Lily went for the strawberry shortcake fro-yo with multicolored sprinkles. They walked and ate, people watching, window-shopping, oohing and ahhing over cute dogs of all sizes in a pet store display.

And then they were done with their desserts and it was getting late, so they headed back to the hotel since they needed to be in the hotel kitchen at 7:00 a.m. Apparently, the Luxury Lodge had three kitchens, and for the weekend, the competition would be using the small one designed specifically for room service.

Lily was quiet in the elevator up to the fifth floor. Because she was thinking about tomorrow?

Or tonight?

Probably both. He slid the card key into the slot on the door, and they headed inside, his gaze landing on the small bed. They would be sharing that tonight.

"Well, I'll just go change into my pj's," Lily said.

He swallowed. Would her pj's be as sexy as her little black dress?

She dashed into the bathroom with some garments

in her hand and her tote bag. A few minutes later she emerged in navy blue gym shorts and a fitted white T-shirt.

Yes, her pj's were as sexy as her black dress.

Her hair was in a topknot, and he could barely take his eyes off her long neck. There were freckles on her neck.

"Your turn," she said, slipping into bed, sliding to the very edge. He was surprised she didn't fall between the bed and the wall.

He grabbed a pair of basketball shorts and a T-shirt, changed in the bathroom and came out to find Lily with the blanket pulled up to her chin. He slid beside her, trying to not brush against her, but the bed was pretty small. Lying next to her without touching her was going to make for a hell of a long, sleepless night.

"Good night," she whispered.

He turned to face her. "Good night. Good luck tomorrow."

She smiled, the slight illumination from the moonlight that spilled in through the filmy section of curtains lighting her beautiful face, the freckles he loved so much. "You're my good-luck charm."

"Glad to be," he said.

She closed her eyes and then turned to face the wall, so he turned to face the windows, knowing he'd get zero sleep.

Chapter 14

Lily must have been so tired and stressed about the competition and about sharing a room with Xander that she'd fallen right asleep. How she'd managed that, she had no idea. But the next time her eyes opened, it was morning, her cell phone alarm buzzing at 5:45 a.m.

Xander was on the floor, bare-chested, doing crunches. Of course he was.

"Morning, sleepyhead," he said. "You're gonna knock 'em dead this morning."

"God, please don't let me poison a judge," she said, her eyes widened.

He smiled. "Lil, it's an expression."

Deep breath, girl, she told herself. "I'm just so nervous. I have to win. I have to."

"You will. Believe it and it shall be so."

She laughed. "Who said that?"

"I forget. Yul Brynner in some movie?"

She cracked up and shook her head. "Last one in the shower is a rotten egg!"

"Are you inviting me to shower with you?" he asked, standing up. All six foot two of him. Bare-chested.

"Absolutely not." Though she'd love it. But no way. She was not letting anything about their not-romance get in the way of making it into the next round.

He grinned. "Go ahead. Ladies first."

She grabbed some stuff from the closet and her tote bag and shut the bathroom door behind her. The hot shower did her worlds of good, soothing her muscles, cramped from trying not to brush up against Hottie when he'd first slid in bed beside her last night.

She got dressed in her new skinny jeans, her lucky red T-shirt with the Daisy's Donuts logo on it, and her trusty clogs, and then took three deep breaths. She dried her hair with the weak blow-dryer on the wall, then emerged to find Xander doing push-ups.

Hot. Hot. Hot. He got up and headed in the bathroom with his clothes, and was out within ten minutes, dressed casually and looking gorgeous.

The lobby offered a continental breakfast for guests, and though Lily could barely eat right now, they stopped there. With a strong cup of hazelnut caffeine in her and half a blueberry muffin, she was good to go when they hit the kitchen at six fifty.

As she and Xander entered the kitchen where the contest would be held all day, there were murmurs that it would be like *The Great British Baking Show*, where they'd be given the ingredients and a recipe, and would have to make the same thing.

"You're all going down," Kyle Kendrick said with a toss of his blond bangs.

"In your dreams, blondie," a woman with very long dark hair said.

Hal, the emcee with the ever-present clipboard, came in. "Okay, contestants and assistants. Each of you was given a number when you entered the kitchen. Please stand at the station that has your number on the cupboard."

Lily was number five—which had always been one of her favorite numbers. Her birthday was on the fifteenth. And she'd been hired at the Maverick Manor on May 25 of the previous year. Lots of good fives in her life.

She'd met Xander on August 6, but it was close.

The kitchen had ten stations, each with its own four-burner stove, oven, stainless steel counter space, mini fridge, sink and cupboards. She and Xander stood at the counter, which faced the front of the kitchen, where Hal stood with his clipboard and headset.

"This morning, you will make a perfect Western omelet. Seven of you will be eliminated. Three of you will move on to the final round this afternoon. In the drawer of your counter you will find a recipe for the omelet. You will find all the ingredients and utensils you need in your station, along with a full spice rack. You will have twenty minutes to make your perfect Western omelet. Oh—and I will answer your burning question: yes, you may alter the recipe to suit yourself. Of course, that may get you in trouble or it may put you in the lead. Who knows?" he added with a devilish grin. "Assistants, you may take one minute to familiarize yourself with the cupboards while the cooks peruse the recipe. Ready, set, go!"

While Lily pulled open the drawer and took out the recipe, Xander opened the cupboards and the mini fridge. The recipe was basic. She'd definitely enhance it. This was about being the best—not being safe.

This morning at the continental breakfast buffet, she happened to overhear two of the contestants talking about the judges. Two were married and from New Orleans originally; they'd gotten married there on a Mississippi riverboat cruise, which made her think they probably had good associations with their hometown. Perhaps a little taste of home in her Western omelet would give her a slight edge with them, and be just delicious enough to sway the third judge. Lily had no idea where he was from.

"Contestants! You have twenty minutes. Starting in... three, two, one, cook!"

"Okay, what do you need?" Xander asked her.

"I need a medium sauté pan and a spatula. I'll grab the ingredients."

In moments, the right pan and the perfect spatula were on the counter. Lily got the burner to the right level, added butter to the pan and began beating five eggs. She added a small amount of milk, then beat the mixture some more.

"Xander, I need you to finely dice one onion, one green pepper and one yellow pepper. Put all your love for beautiful vegetables into your work. Meanwhile, I'll dice the ham."

"Got it!" Xander said, rushing to the pantry. "All my love for onion and peppers coming up." He pulled out the ingredients, got out a chopping board and began dicing away. "Love you, onion that I'm cutting with a really sharp knife. Chop, chop, chop."

"Um, could you keep it down over there?" snapped the guy at the station to their left. He was in his forties and wore a neon-green apron that said I Can Explain It to You but I Can't Understand It for You. How nice. "I'm trying to concentrate."

"I can talk *and* concentrate," Xander told him. "But I'll try to lower my voice."

"Gee, thanks," the guy said.

Lily smiled at Xander and rolled her eyes, then continued dicing the ham. She added it to the pan, giving it a stir.

"Done," Xander said, bringing over his chopping board.

He slid the very nicely diced vegetables in the pan, and Lily sautéed them in the butter, waiting until they softened. Hmm, the onions and peppers and ham smelled heavenly. Of course, the entire kitchen smelled amazing.

"You stupid buffoon!" the woman at the station to the right of Lily screamed. At her assistant—who was red in the face. "How could you drop the eggs? We only had five!" The woman turned to Hal with the clipboard. "Hal, I can get more eggs, right? My idiot sister dropped ours and they're all over the floor."

"Sorry," Hal said. "No more eggs in your fridge, no omelet, so that disqualifies you. Please pack up and leave the kitchen. You are *not* Northwest Montana's Best Chef."

The woman was seething. "And this is not *Top Chef*!" she yelled, then stalked off, her poor sister trailing.

"Sorry," the sister said meekly, and ran off after the former contestant.

"Ooh, that's too bad," Xander said. "Thanksgiving sure won't be fun for them this year."

"Right?" Lily said, shaking her head.

"And then there were nine!" Kyle Kendrick called out.

Jerk.

"Ten minutes, Lil," Xander said.

She nodded and flashed him a thumbs-up, then Lily added the eggs to the pan, debating whether to add a little cheese. There were four kinds in the fridge, but a true Western omelet, a purist one, didn't have cheese. She'd skip it.

"Four minutes, Lily," Xander said.

"Four minutes left!" the assistant behind their station bellowed.

"Oh hell!" someone shouted. "The omelet's stuck to the pan!"

"I am so gonna win," said Kyle Kendrick. "No one makes an omelet like I do. No to the one!"

"Yes, chef!" his assistant said. She happened to be the pretty blonde Lily had seen draped over Kyle last night in the lobby as she and Xander returned from Kalispell.

Lily rolled her eyes so hard that Xander cracked up.

"Find that funny, do you?" Kyle said, glaring at him. "You'll see."

Now it was Xander's turn to roll his eyes.

"Eyes on your own paper, kids," Xander whispered.

Lily laughed and high-fived him.

"Two minutes, chef!" Kyle's blonde said.

"Two minutes, Lil," Xander said, getting a glare from Kyle.

She loved that he was having a good time. Competitions could seriously stress out some people, but Xander rolled with it, doing a very careful and good job.

Just before she flipped the omelet she added a hint of tabasco sauce and a dash of cayenne pepper across the omelet to bring that little taste of New Orleans. The omelet looked absolutely divine, if she did say so herself.

"Can I eat that?" Xander asked.

"If there's any left over," she said, giving her shoulders a shimmy. She waited until the bottom of the omelet was the perfect shade, then flipped the sides onto each other.

Done.

She plated, added a sprinkle of kosher salt and a little pepper—and waited.

"Time!" Hal called. "The judges will now begin their rounds. Please provide three forks."

Xander handed Lily three forks, which she placed on three folded napkins next to the plates.

The female judge came over and studied the omelet and then made some notations. She took a bite, then another, looked at Lily, and made a notation, then moved on.

When her husband, one of the two male judges, took a bite, Lily swore he closed his eyes with a tiny sigh, but that might have been her fantasy. He made his notes. The third judge took three bites, always a good sign, and jotted his comments.

"My goodness!" said the female judge to a contestant two rows behind Lily. "How much salt did you add?"

Lily heard crying. She felt so sorry for whichever contestant it was that she didn't even turn around. Xander didn't, either. He just squeezed her hand.

"That's two down!" Kyle announced. "Eight of us left."

"Jerk," Xander whispered.

After conferring with the three judges, Hal stepped forward. "And the three contestants moving into round two are..."

Lily held her breath.

Xander tried to remember the last time he'd prayed. When he was a kid, around four or five. He'd wait at the window for his mother to come back, but she never did. So he started praying every night, since someone at school had told him that was how you got stuff you wanted.

His mother had never come back.

He prayed now—to the universe, to nature, to the big man upstairs. *Let Lily's name be called, please!*

"Kyle Kendrick!" Hal announced.

Crud, Xander thought.

"Boo-yah!" Kyle said, fist-pumping his way up and down the aisle. "Where do the winners stand?" he asked.

"You can stay at your station for now," Hal said. With the teensiest note of disdain, unless that was wishful thinking. Probably was.

"Kerry Atalini!" Hal called next.

There were six contestants left. Xander took Lily's

hand and held it, and he wondered if she could feel him praying beside her. He was thinking that hard.

She closed her eyes, too.

"And our third and final contestant moving on to the final round—Lily Hunt!"

Her eyes popped open. Xander picked her up and whirled her around, then kissed her solidly on the mouth.

"You did it!" Xander whispered in her ear. "And this afternoon, you will beat both other contestants and win the ten grand!"

She threw her arms around him and hugged him and he held her tight. He was so proud of her. So proud *for* her.

"Contestants, we will reconvene at noon on the dot in this kitchen for the final round. Only one of you will be named Northwest Montana's Best Chef!"

"Sorry, Lily, but it's going to be *me*," Kyle said, sauntering by her with his assistant trailing him on her high heels. How she puttered around the station in those three-inch things was beyond him.

Xander ignored him. "Any idea what the final-round meal is?" he asked Lily as they left the kitchen and headed for the elevator.

"No clue. But I feel ready for anything. Thank you so much for being a great assistant, Xander."

"You taught me everything I know," he said, batting his eyes.

She gave him a playful sock on the arm. "Seriously. Thank you."

"You are very welcome."

The moment they got into the room, Lily said she wanted to take another shower and get the smell of peppers and onions out of her hair and skin. When he heard the water turn on, he wished he was in that shower stall with her. Washing her beautiful body. Lathering up her hair. Making soapy love to her.

He parked himself on the desk chair, his attention on the bathroom door. On the water running. He had Lily on the brain. Every part of him craved her, wanted her.

The water stopped. The bathroom door opened. Lily came out, her hair damp, her body wrapped in a small white towel.

She stared at him as she walked over, then straddled him on the chair.

Ooh boy.

Hadn't he said she was full of surprises?

"One of us has too many clothes on," she whispered.

"Yeah, *you.*" He slowly undid the towel, reveling in every gorgeous naked bit of her.

She undid his belt buckle. Then the snap of his jeans. The zipper came down. He picked her up in his arms and carried her to the bed, grabbing a condom from his wallet—he always kept one in there, but he'd brought five for this weekend. Wishful thinking. And good thing he had.

Then they were under the covers, a tangle of arms and legs and hungry lips.

Once again, she rocked his world. That was no longer a surprise.

"I love you," she whispered as she climaxed, and Xander froze. Just for a second.

But Lily must have felt it because she pulled back a bit, looking at him. "I shouldn't have said that. I didn't mean to say it—it just burst out of my mouth."

"Lily, I…"

"Oh, that again," she said, the look of disappointment so pronounced that he tried to force the words but they still wouldn't come.

Did he love her? All signs pointed to yes, but then why couldn't he say so? Why couldn't he even say so to himself?

He heard her sigh. "I should really be focusing on the next round," she said. "I'd better get dressed and go in search of some strong coffee. I don't know what came over me, why I jumped your bones. Let's forget the whole thing. I'm just running on competition adrenaline. This. Never. Happened." He'd come to know her so well that he could see she was hiding her misery behind a plastered-on fake smile.

"Lily, I—"

But she'd grabbed some clothes from the closet and shut herself in the bathroom.

When she emerged, he was dressed, too, and hoping they could talk, but again, he was tongue-tied. Stuck, really. That was how he felt: stuck. In what, by what, he wasn't sure.

"I'll see you at eleven fifty in the kitchen," she said, grabbed her tote bag and rushed out of the room.

Xander might not know if he loved her, but he sure felt like he hated himself at that moment.

Lily sat in the lobby, sipping her second excellent cappuccino, trying not to think of the humiliation she'd just endured.

I love you.

I…don't. Sorry.

Fine, he hadn't said that. But the "Lily, I…" followed by nothing said as much.

She knew this already. Why had she jumped his bones? Why had she blurted out the true depth of her feelings for him?

Because you love him. And you're not hiding anymore. This is me. I'm a passionate person who loves hard and if I feel it, I'm gonna express it.

Tears stung her eyes and she blinked them back.

She'd tried to be so tough last night, telling him she was looking forward to finding her guy and settling down soon. She'd been hoping to make him realize she wasn't going to be around forever, that some other man would snap her right up.

But he hadn't even reacted. And so she'd changed the subject and tried to move on from thinking about romance to just focusing on the contest.

But the high of making it to the final round was so profound that she'd felt like Wonder Woman for a while there, floating up to their room in a haze of happiness and pride. She'd been named a finalist with Xander beside her, Xander helping her. That made it all the more sweet.

And in the shower, all she could think of was how badly she wanted him in there with her. She'd planned her little daylight seduction right then and there. And she went for it.

So had he.

Until she'd come out with the *I love you*.

Cripes.

"Hi, Lily!" said a female voice.

It was Kerry, the other contestant besides Kyle in

the final round. Kerry was in her late twenties or early thirties with dark pixie-cut hair and black framed eyeglasses. She had a tattoo of a pink cupcake on her shoulder. Lily recalled that her assistant was a woman who looked a lot like her, her sister probably. "How amazing is this?" Kerry said. "Almost three hundred entrants, and it's down to three of us. I can't even believe it."

"I know. I can't, either. I came here hoping and praying but not expecting."

Kerry smiled. "Ditto. Although I think what's-his-name expects to win."

"Ugh," Lily said. "He's from my hometown. He's good but he's not exactly the nicest guy."

"Well, then I hope it's one of us. Ladies unite!" she said with a grin. "What do you plan to do with the money if you win?"

Lily explained about Lily's Home Cookin' and hoping to get that business off the ground without having to take out a loan.

"What a great idea!" Kerry said. "I love it. I live an hour from here in the opposite direction or I'd definitely order me some Lily's Home Cookin'."

Lily grinned. Kerry was a sweetheart. "So how about you? What are your plans?"

"I really want to open a small casual café where moms can bring their kids and the little ones can run around. I'll have a train set on a table, and dolls and trucks and Legos and blocks. A reading nook. I love to cook but my real love is baking, so I'll have amazing pastries and maybe offer some light kid fare, like grilled cheese. I know I do that really well."

Lily laughed, recalling their elimination round entrée. "Right? Do you have a child?"

"Samantha," Kerry said, a wistful look coming over her face. "She's two and a half and the love of my life. Her dad took off on me, but left me with the best part of himself, so hey, I'm happy. My mom's watching her for me while I'm here."

"Aww, that's really great. My assistant is the love of my life but he just thinks of me as a friend."

Kerry gave Lily a "you're crazy" expression. "Uh, I saw with my own eyes how that incredibly hot guy looks at you, talks to you and acts around you. He's a man in love. Trust me."

Sarah seemed to think so, too. Why was Xander the only one who didn't see it? "Well, he doesn't want to be, unfortunately."

"Ah, good thing is that you can't stop progress. He'll come around." She glanced at her watch. "It's eleven thirty. I'm gonna go freshen up for the big moment."

Can't stop progress. Hadn't Lily herself said that recently?

"See you soon," Lily said. "Thank you, Kerry. And good luck."

"To you, too, sweetie," Kerry said.

Lily finished her cappuccino, staring out the window, wondering if it could be true, that you really *couldn't* stop progress. Thing was, *was* there progress with Xander when he kept taking a giant step backward?

Sigh.

The final round was a chili cook-off.

Lily seemed really excited about that, all signs of her

earlier distress gone. She had a smile on her face and fierce concentration in her eyes, and Xander knew she was full speed ahead on winning this thing.

That was just one of the things he loved about her. Her determination. Her drive. She might be hurting, but she was going to be named Northwest Montana's Best Chef.

"You've got this," he said, squeezing her hand at their station. He wanted to ask if she was okay, if they were good, but this wasn't the time to talk about them. They had to concentrate on the contest.

"Let's do it!" she said, those beautiful green eyes flashing with spirit.

I love you, too, he thought. And almost said it right there.

I love you, Lily Hunt. I flipping love you!

Holy hell. He loved her!

Minutes later, he had to table that incredible revelation to focus on being Lily's assistant. He chopped and diced, he handed over the packages of meat and beans, he found the right pots and pans and utensils.

Kyle Kendrick boasted up a storm at the station in the middle, snapping at his assistant, who Xander hoped would tell him to shove it and walk out on him. But unfortunately, she kept taking his unnecessary criticism. Hopefully, she'd get sick of it soon enough.

"Ow!" shrieked the woman on the far right station. Kerry, her name was. "Burned myself a bit."

"You okay, Ker?" Lily called over.

"I'll live!" Kerry called back.

"Can I concentrate here? Jeez," Kyle complained.

"Oh, shut it, Kyle," Kerry announced with glee. Her

assistant, also with short dark hair, clapped. Xander almost clapped, too. Kerry's assistant wrapped the burn in a Band-Aid, and Kerry was on the move again, dashing between stirring pots and pans.

Finally, time was up. Lily's chili smelled amazing. Looked amazing. Tasted amazing. She had to win this. She *had* to.

The three judges took their bites. Made their notations.

Hal appeared again in the front of the stations, the three judges beside him, ready to announce the results. "In third place, Kyle Kendrick!" Hal announced.

Kyle's mouth dropped open. "There has to be a mistake. *Third?* No."

"Third," Hal said, consulting his clipboard. Kyle glared at him and stared at the judges. They each nodded.

"This blows. I'm outta here," Kyle said. He stalked off, leaving his assistant just standing there.

"You deserve better," Xander said to her.

The blonde shrugged and sighed and went racing after Kyle.

"In second place…" Hal began.

Xander held his breath. He grabbed Lily's hand and squeezed, hoping he wasn't cutting off her circulation.

"Lily Hunt!" Hal continued.

What? There has to be some mistake. Second? No.

Jeez. Now he knew how Kyle felt.

He looked at Lily, who attempted a smile. "Hey, I tried, right? Second out of almost three hundred is pretty darn good, right?"

"And our winner, Northwest Montana's Best Chef, is… Kerry Atalini!" Hal said.

The judges began clapping. So did Lily. In fact, she ran over to Kerry and gave her a big hug.

"Congrats, Kerry. I can't wait to visit your café and eat an amazing chocolate croissant while I watch the little ones play trains," Lily said.

Kerry hugged her back. "Thank you, Lily. Can we keep in touch?" They exchanged email addresses and cell phone numbers, and then Lily was back over at their station.

Kerry was presented with her check for ten thousand, and Xander could feel the absolute wistfulness coming off Lily.

"I wish you'd won," he said. "You're the best chef in the world."

Lily squeezed his hand. "At least Kyle didn't win."

"True."

"Let's go home," she said. "I need home."

He nodded, and they thanked Hal and the judges, then left the kitchen and headed to the elevator.

When the door of their room shut behind them, Xander planned to grab Lily in his arms and tell her he loved her, that he'd been bursting with it ever since the start of the chili cook-off. But as she packed her things, the words wouldn't come again. They were stuck behind something.

What the hell? he wondered. *Tell her. Say it!*

If he said *Lily, I...* and couldn't get anything out beyond that, she'd have every right to punch him in the stomach.

"Ready?" she asked, overnight bag slung over her shoulder.

"You okay?"

She nodded. "I really am. I'll apply for a loan on Monday morning. There's a chance I'll get it. Of course, the bank may say I'm too young and untried and don't have enough work history under my belt. But I have a solid business plan. So we'll see."

"I'll front you the money, Lily. I believe in you and I'd be honored to invest in your business. You can pay me back in French dips, filet mignon in garlic butter and cooking lessons."

Her mouth dropped open. "You're going to just give me ten thousand dollars?"

"Yes. I am. For the reasons I just stated."

And because I love you.

But again, the words wouldn't come.

"That's incredibly generous of you," she said. "*Beyond* generous. That you believe in me means the world to me, Xander. But I can't—and won't—take your money. I might be the Rust Creek Falls Cinderella with my makeover, and I definitely believe in Prince Charming, but I'm no princess and I plan to rescue myself. Know what I mean?"

He stared at her, speechless for the moment, but not surprised.

This is why I love you.

So why couldn't he say it?

Chapter 15

On Tuesday afternoon, Xander was in the barn, doing his favorite chore—cleaning out the stalls—when his mind was full of its own muck. He hadn't spoken to Lily since Saturday night, when they'd returned from Kalispell. The ride home had been on the quiet side; Lily had been clearly tired, and they hadn't talked about *them*. Or the most memorable experience he'd ever had in a chair.

He closed his eyes, remembering. Lily in that tiny white towel. Straddling him.

I'm no princess and I plan to rescue myself...

"Hey, Xander," a male voice said.

His brother Knox. "Ran into Lily in town coming out of the bank this morning. I don't think I've ever actually seen someone kick up their heels, but she truly did. I asked her if she won the lottery and just deposited it or something, but apparently she applied for a business loan yesterday and was approved today."

He grinned. Go, Lily. Yeah!

"She's starting her own personal chef and home-cooking kit business," Xander said. "Was I that focused at twenty-three?" He shook his head, full of admiration for Lily.

"Your plan at twenty-three was to date as many pretty women as possible," Knox reminded him. "So no. You were not."

Xander laughed. "Yeah, I guess so. I kept underestimating Lily because of her age. Do you know that because she didn't win the ten grand in the cooking contest, I offered her the money myself and she turned it down? Said she'd rather get a loan and take care of herself."

"She's awesome. No way around it."

Xander nodded, leaning on the rake. "I kept thinking she was too young for me. But maybe I was just using it as an excuse."

Knox rolled his eyes. "Duh. Of course you were. You got burned in Dallas and understandably wanted nothing to do with falling in love again. I get it. But then you *did* fall in love again. And you can't handle it so you're costing yourself the best thing that will ever happen to you. The woman you *love.*"

Xander stared at his brother. Knox was always on the intense side, but he was talking straight from the heart right now. "I do love her. I really do."

"So go get her. *If* she'll have you."

You can't live in the past, she'd said.

I plan to rescue myself, she'd said.

What she'd done was rescue him. From *himself.*

He loved her. With all his stupid, guarded heart, which now felt stretched open wide. He tried to think about Britney and Chase, smiling their fool faces off at the carnival. But all he pictured in his mind was a pair of flashing green eyes, those freckles and that glorious red hair. He tried to picture his mother in her yellow apron and himself waiting by the window. Again, all he saw was Lily, stirring that pot of chili, adding the green chilies and the extra cayenne pepper to infuse the food with home.

To him, Lily meant home. She *was* home.

Knox grabbed the rake out of his hand. "Almighty Lord, Xander. Go. Run."

"I have a stop to make first," he said, heading out of the barn. At the door, he turned back. "Knox?"

"No more excuses. Go!"

"No more excuses," Xander said. "I just wanted to say…thank you."

The ever-serious Knox Crawford nodded, then broke into a smile.

Cloud nine would be a lot better if Xander were up here with her, but she was so dang happy she found herself skipping from room to room of her house.

I got the loan, I got the loan, I got the loan! Lily's Home Cookin' is coming your way, Rust Creek Falls, so watch out! Or better yet, get yer bellies ready!

She turned on the radio on the kitchen counter, swaying to her favorite country station while putting together her very first Lily's Home Cookin' kit. She'd run into Viv Dalton in Daisy's Donuts when she'd taken herself

for a celebratory iced mocha latte and had told her all
about the loan and her new business. Viv had been so
excited for her and said she'd put in an order right then.
A home kit for beef bourguignon. Viv's husband loved
the intensive, time-consuming dish, but they were both
so busy right now, and if they could make the meal together without having to shop and prep for it, that would
be ideal.

Exactly what Lily hoped many, many, many residents
of Rust Creek Falls would think about her service. Lily
had almost walked right into Xander's brother Knox
on her way out of the bank this morning, and he said
he and his family would keep her in business for years.

Which made her wonder. How was she going to see
Xander every day, maybe—very likely, actually—as a
customer, and not go crazy?

Stop thinking about him! she yelled at herself. Focus
on the beef bourguignon. She had her little containers all ready to go—the chunks of succulent beef, the
bacon, the chopped, sliced and diced vegetables, even
the flour and oil. As she snapped the lid on the last container, the tomato paste, she couldn't wait to sketch de-
signs for her own labels.

She packed up her cooler bag, included the red wine
necessary to make the beef bourguignon, and added a
bottle of champagne that Lily had gotten as a gift from
one of her clients so that Viv and her husband could
celebrate with their meal. She thought about what Viv
had said earlier, that she shouldn't really be ordering
something so fancy when business was so— But then
she'd stopped talking and looked distracted and uncomfortable, and Lily realized that Viv's wedding planning

business, which she operated with her friend Caroline Clifton, might be in financial trouble or having some setbacks.

Huh. Maybe that was why Viv had been so quick to agree to a million-dollar payout from Max Crawford if she married off all six Crawford brothers! Not that anyone wouldn't take that deal, but Viv had sure run with it and now the whirlwind of dates made total sense. Viv needed that money.

If this Rust Creek Falls Cinderella had a fairy godmother, the closest to it would be Vivienne Dalton herself. After all, it was Viv who'd suggested Lily throw herself into the dating pool for a Crawford. Viv who'd arranged the date with Knox. Which led to her date with Xander in the park.

Tears stung her eyes even though she was smiling at how Viv had believed in her ability to hook a gorgeous Crawford when she'd been a tomboy with tomato sauce on her shirt and flour-stained baggy jeans.

I owe you, Viv, she thought, reaching into her wallet for Viv's check and ripping it up. Lily grabbed her phone and sent Viv a text.

I'm dropping off your beef bourguignon kit in ten minutes, as discussed. Oh, and I ripped up your check— this special meal from Lily's Home Cookin' is on me. You're my first official client!

Wow, really? Thanks! Viv texted back.

No, thank you, Viv, Lily thought with a smile. *I might not have ended up with love, but thanks to you, I found it.*

With ten minutes to kill, Lily eyed the *Rust Creek Falls Gazette* on the kitchen table and sat down to poke through it. Ooh, she could check apartment listings! She turned to the Apartment and Condos for Rent section, glancing through a few possibilities. But there was a small house for rent, zoned for business and residential use, right in the center of town off North Broomtail Road.

It was a little out of her price range, but she could cut back in other areas. She'd hang out her shingle, and have her customers come to her for meal kits or to place catering orders. With her loan, she could renovate the kitchen to her specifications, but considering she wouldn't have four hungry Hunts constantly in the kitchen and eating up her good ingredients and leftovers, she might not even need such a huge work space. She circled the ad for the house, then grabbed her phone, pressing in the telephone number for the real estate agent.

But the doorbell rang then, so she put the phone down and got up to answer it.

Xander. In a suit and tie and a Stetson.

He took off the hat and held it against his chest. "Lily, I have so much to say to you."

She tilted her head and waited. "I'm listening."

"I didn't come to Rust Creek Falls expecting to fall for anyone. You know I've been burned before."

Please don't be here to apologize for not loving me. I couldn't take that.

"But then out of nowhere," he continued, his dark eyes intense on hers, "a smart, focused, talented, passionate, honest, funny, dachshund-loving, hoodie-wearing gorgeous redhead with sparkling green eyes captured my heart before I even knew she had it in her possession."

Lily gasped and her knees wobbled. She could barely breathe—or speak.

"I didn't think anything scared me, Lily. But all this time, I've been so damned afraid of how I feel about you. And you know what?"

"What?" she managed to whisper.

"You taught me a lot about courage. And let's face it, I just love you too much to let you go."

He loved her!

"Lily, I want to start over with you. Can we?"

She couldn't speak. She couldn't move.

Finally she found her voice. "Nope, we can't start over. But we can pick up where we left off," she added with a grin. "So where were we?"

"On a chair. Naked. In a Kalispell hotel room."

"Maybe we can go back this weekend," she said. "And re-create that moment—changing what happens next."

"Done," he said. "I do want to change what happens next. But now. Not a minute later." He got down on one knee, opening up a black velvet box. A beautiful diamond ring glittered. "Lily Hunt, will you make me the happiest guy alive by becoming my wife?"

"Yes!" she screamed at the top of her lungs.

He stood up and slid the ring on her finger, then picked her up and whirled her around, smothering her with kisses.

"Yes," he repeated. "Forever."

"Forever," she said.

* * *

They delivered Viv's beef bourguignon—and the big news that Viv was two down, four to go on the Crawford bachelors. Lily held up her left hand, the emerald-cut diamond, surrounded by diamond baguettes on a gold band, twinkling.

Viv yelled so loudly her husband came running. The four of them cracked open the champagne Lily had brought, then she and Xander left them to make their romantic meal for two. With leftovers, of course.

Then Xander suggested they book a room at the Maverick Manor for a little privacy, so after surprising the heck out of their families with their big news—Knox wasn't the least bit surprised—he booked the honeymoon suite at the Manor.

More champagne. Chocolate-covered strawberries.

And the love of her life, her fiancé, her soon-to-be husband, beside her in the enormous four-poster bed.

Xander held up a chocolate-covered strawberry and dangled it in front of her mouth. "Want to know a secret? The first night I met you, I went home and thought of feeding you strawberries. Now here I am doing it."

"Ha! I knew you liked me from that first not-a-date." She accepted half the strawberry while he ate the other half, then their lips met in a kiss.

"We'll live happily—and hungrily—ever after," she said.

He kissed her again, wrapping her in his arms. "You know that little house you mentioned you saw in the paper?" he asked. "What do you think of us buying our own ranch close to town and I'll build you your own cooking studio and make you the Lily's Home Cookin' sign for it? State-of-the-art kitchen, display cases, reception counter, waiting area—the works."

"Told you I believed in Prince Charming. Here he is," she said with a smile, then burst into tears.

"I hope those are happy tears," he said.

"My cup runneth over, Xander. Thank you. Yes, yes, yes, a million times yes. Maybe while you're at it, you can build a doghouse for Dobby and Harry."

"Definitely," he said. "I love those furry little beasts."

"And I love you."

He kissed her, and they lay together for a moment. "Oh, I just remembered I brought something with me I wanted to show you." He reached into his overnight bag and pulled out an old jewel-encrusted book.

"It's that diary you and your brothers found in your bedroom!" she said, sitting up.

"Yup. I jimmied it open with a screwdriver. I figure it's the only way to find out who it belongs to so that I can try to get it back to its owner."

"Any clues?"

He opened it up to a middle page, and Lily leaned closer to glance at the yellowed pages. "I read through some of it and whoever kept this diary was seriously in love. He or she was involved in a passionate love affair with someone referred to as only 'W.'"

"Ooh, that looks like a love poem," she said, pointing to the right-hand page.

"'My fair W,'" Xander read, "'I cannot stop thinking of you, dreaming of you, wishing we were together. Soon, I hope. Forever yours.'"

"Aww," Lily said. "So romantic!"

He smiled. "I'll go through it and see if I can find

some names. It's probably someone from the Abernathy family, so if I come across a first name, maybe someone with history here in town will recognize it."

"Are you going to write me a love poem?" she asked, kissing the side of his neck.

"I'm not much of a writer, but I promise to cherish you just as much as our surprise diary writer cherished the fair W."

"Me, too," she said, and they snuggled in to start the diary from the beginning.

Epilogue

A week later, Lily, in a white satin wedding gown she'd found in a Kalispell bridal boutique and had altered in record time, walked down a red carpet aisle in the Rust Creek Falls Community Center on the arm of her father, who was crying the entire way. She and Xander had chosen this venue over the swanky Maverick Manor because the center could hold the entire town—and the entire town had been invited to their wedding. Between the Hunts going back generations in Rust Creek Falls, and the Crawfords becoming famous for the million-dollar wager on their bachelorhood, everyone wanted to come. The more, the merrier.

Lily now stood with her gorgeous tuxedo-clad groom in front of the minister, so happy she thought she might burst. Xander's brothers were his groomsmen, and his father his best man. Lily's matron of honor was Sarah, and five of her dear friends who'd scattered after high school had come back for the wedding, even on short notice, all managing to find a pale pink dress and silver shoes.

She thought of herself in that pale pink dress and silver ballet flats at the Summer Sunset Dance the night she and Xander had made love for the first time. To her, that color scheme would always represent new beginnings. So she'd chosen it for her bridal party.

In a rush of words and with shimmering eyes, they were pronounced husband and wife, and Xander kissed her so passionately that there wolf whistles, and she even heard Dobby and Harry, guests of course, giving two short barks each.

The reception was held outside under a beautiful open-air tent. Lily had called for a potluck, and everyone had brought something. Food equaled love, and Lily wanted everyone's love at the wedding.

After the first dance, Max Crawford asked to give a toast, and spoke for quite a while about how love kept surprising him. First, Logan had found it with Sarah. Then Xander with Lily. "Watch out, Knox, Hunter, Finn and Wilder. It's gonna come at you hard when you least expect it, with the woman you least expect it with." He winked at Viv, who smiled back, then they all raised their glasses and drank to true love. Surprising love.

Lily smiled at Viv, too. If her wedding planning business was in trouble, at least Lily had helped by taking down one more Crawford brother—and hiring Viv to plan this shindig.

Everyone was crowding around the buffet tables, where champagne and heaps of food waited for the guests. Lily had decided to make her own chili—not the recipe that hadn't won her the cooking contest, but her mother's recipe, a chili to die for. She'd added a little of everything under the sun so that as many people as possible would be reminded of home.

"Brings me back to Texas," Xander said after taking a bite. "There go those crazy memories again. Hunter putting a frog down my shirt. Me beating Logan for the first time in a race." A look of surprise crossed his face. "Hey—strangest thing," he said. "The next memory that flashed at me was you in your T-shirt and jeans, a hoodie wrapped around your waist in the doorway of the Maverick Manor kitchen."

Lily gasped. "That was here. In Montana. The night you showed up as my date."

"Because *this* is home now. Home is always going to be where you are, Lily Crawford."

There were clinks on glasses, which meant the new husband had to kiss his new bride. Under the Big Sky Country's brilliant late-August sun, Xander dipped Lily for the kiss of all kisses, and Lily knew they had indeed found home in each other forever.

* * * * *

WE HOPE YOU ENJOYED
THIS BOOK FROM

HARLEQUIN
SPECIAL
EDITION

Believe in love. Overcome obstacles. Find happiness.

Relate to finding comfort and strength in the
support of loved ones and enjoy the journey
no matter what life throws your way.

6 NEW BOOKS AVAILABLE EVERY MONTH!

SPECIAL EXCERPT FROM

⊕ HARLEQUIN
SPECIAL EDITION

*When a cheating scandal rocks Shanna Jacobs's
school, she's put under the supervision of her ex,
Lynx Harrington—who wants the same superintendent
job she does. Maybe their fledgling partnership will
make the grade after all?*

Read on for a sneak peek at
Rivals at Love Creek,
*the first book in the brand-new
Seven Brides for Seven Brothers miniseries
and Michelle Lindo-Rice's debut with
Harlequin Special Edition!*

"Now, I know the circumstances aren't ideal, but I'm looking forward to working with you."

She appeared to struggle, like she was thinking how to formulate her words. "I wish I was working with you by choice and not circumstance. Not that I would choose to," she said with a chuckle.

"I hear you. If it weren't for this situation, we would still be throwing daggers at each other during leadership meetings."

"Put yourself in my shoes. If you were going through this, how would you feel?" she asked, rubbing her toe into the carpet. "Honest answer."

"I'm not as brave as you are, and I have more pride than common sense."

She blushed and averted her eyes. "I would have resigned if I didn't have a mother and sister to consider. Pride is secondary to priority."

He felt ashamed and got to his feet. He went over to her. "You're right. I'm thinking like a single man. If I were married or had other responsibilities, I'd do what I'd have to and keep my job. I was hoping that Irene—" He stopped, unsure of the etiquette of bringing another woman into the conversation.

"No need to stop on my account. I know you had— have—a life."

Lynx wasn't about to talk about Irene, no matter how cool Shanna claimed she was with it. "I'm ready to fall in love, get married and install the white picket fence."

"How do you know you're ready?" she asked.

He rubbed his chin. "I'm at the brink of where I want to be professionally. I want someone to share my success with me."

"I get it," she said, doing that half-bite thing with her lip again.

Don't miss
Rivals at Love Creek
by Michelle Lindo-Rice,
available July 2022 wherever
Harlequin Special Edition books and ebooks are sold.

Harlequin.com

Love Harlequin romance?

DISCOVER.

Be the first to find out about promotions, news and exclusive content!

Facebook.com/HarlequinBooks

Twitter.com/HarlequinBooks

Instagram.com/HarlequinBooks

Pinterest.com/HarlequinBooks

YouTube.com/HarlequinBooks

ReaderService.com

EXPLORE.

Sign up for the Harlequin e-newsletter and download a free book from any series at **TryHarlequin.com**

CONNECT.

Join our Harlequin community to share your thoughts and connect with other romance readers!
Facebook.com/groups/HarlequinConnection